The Mystery of the Missing Book

ALSO BY JUDITH CUTLER

ANTIQUE SHOP MYSTERIES
Book 1: The Mystery of the Missing Book

FRAN HARMAN MYSTERIES
Book 1: Come to Harm
Book 2: Do No Harm
Book 3: In Harm's Way
Book 4: No Harm Done
Book 5: No Harm, No Foul
Book 6: Road to Harm

KATE POWER MYSTERIES
Book 1: Murder the Boys
Book 2: Murder by the Canal
Book 3: Murder by Arson
Book 4: Murder by Fraud
Book 5: Murder in Devon
Book 6: Murder on the Job

THE MYSTERY OF THE MISSING BOOK

Judith Cutler

JOFFE BOOKS

Revised edition 2025
Joffe Books, London
www.joffebooks.com

First published by Allison & Busby in Great Britain in 2004
as *Drawing the Line*

This paperback edition was first published in Great Britain in 2025

Cover art by Cherie Chapman

ISBN: 978-1-80573-384-3

For Terry Robert:
thank you for your constant kindness and expertise

CHAPTER ONE

Quality Antiques Fair

They didn't intend you to miss it, did they? It was AA-signposted for miles. The trouble was, once you'd got off the road, you had to drive all the way round what seemed like an entire farm just to reach the car park. Detling. The windiest exhibition site in the world, according to Griff. It's really Kent's county agricultural showground, which might explain why they expect hardier souls than antiques dealers.

'Go and don your thermals, Lina, ducky,' Griff had said that morning as we sat at the breakfast table. 'It may be almost May but put plenty on. Layers, that's what you need at Detling. Layers, and plenty of them. None of your crop-tops showing your belly button.' He waved a pudgy finger. 'Or you'll get a spare tyre, you know you will! Did I ever tell you . . .'

I knew it was rubbish, of course, Griff's theory that if you exposed flesh to the cold you'd grow a layer of fat to keep yourself warm. Blubber, he called it. All the same, I'd pick out a couple of sweaters and a body warmer. Better blubber you could take off at will than blubber that you couldn't. And I really couldn't risk cold hands, not when I was handling china all day. I'd rather have looked beautifully svelte for Marcus but the chances were he wouldn't have noticed anyway: he'd be too busy keeping his eyes open for customers.

'My dear child,' Griff interrupted himself suddenly, placing his teacup with an emphatic little tap on a saucer that was equally fine china but from a different century, 'milk in Earl Grey! Didn't your mother teach you anything?' Before I could say anything, he got up, going bright red and wringing his hands. 'Silly me! No, worse than silly! I'm so sorry.'

I got up too, to give him a hug. 'You've been better than any mother,' I declared, quite truthfully. 'Any of mine, anyway. Apart from Iris, maybe — and the best thing she ever did was introduce me to you.'

How many mothers had I had? Not 'real' ones, of course. Foster-mothers. Iris had been the last in the line. Halfway through my stay with her they'd decided she was really too old to be fostering, but she'd kicked up such a stink when they suggested I should move for the eighth or ninth time that they let me stay. She had hated the idea of casting me off alone at sixteen, when social services decided people in care were officially ready to tackle the world, so I'd stayed, paying what little rent I could afford from my earnings in a number of jobs that Griff described as sweated labour. When I was eighteen and we both reluctantly agreed it really was time for me to move on, she'd somehow persuaded Griff to take me on as his live-in assistant. They'd been friends ever since she'd been his landlady when, as he put it, he'd trodden the boards. If she was anything like she'd been to me, she'd have been the softest touch around, so kind that you really didn't want to take advantage of her and felt awful if you did. The deal was that Griff would teach me all he knew about antiques, which was a great deal, and I would do the housework, which in a cottage like this was very little. Although the scales were balanced heavily in my favour, the deal suited us both very well. What memories

I had of less happy arrangements were polished over, if not quite wiped out, like the scratch marks on this table.

But there was one memory I did wish I could bring back. Occasionally a tantalising snippet of a visit I must have paid with my birth mother slipped into my mind, but it would slide out as quickly as it had come. I had a little box of treasures some kind social worker had preserved: a few photos of people I didn't recognise, a handful of books Mother must have read to me, a couple of strings of beads that made Griff shake his head and tut, and what I suppose must have been her engagement ring. The stone was so tiny and of such poor quality it spoke of a young man — my father? — with more hopes than money. When Mother'd died — no, there was no drama about it, much as I'd dreamed there might be in my early teens — in a bus crash, there were no aunts or grandparents to take on her toddler. If the giver of the ring had still been around, he didn't offer either.

'Iris is a dear soul,' Griff agreed. 'But her ways with tea and coffee are truly deplorable.' He produced half a lemon from the fridge. He slipped the merest sliver into another china cup — this one Victorian Spode — and returned the lemon to the fridge. The knife went straight on to the washing-up pile. No dishwasher for Griff. No point, really: all our meals at home were served on finest china, absolutely not guaranteed to be dishwasher-proof. The only difference between our china and the sort you see in museums or stately homes was that theirs matched. Nothing in our kitchen matched anything. Nothing in the cottage matched anything else, come to that. Perhaps that was why it was so cosy and homely. Griff always referred to himself as a snapper up of unconsidered trifles — 'but at least you'll never find my hand in a placket,' he'd giggle. '*A Winter's Tale*, dear heart, and *King Lear*, both plays you say you'll get round to reading one of these days. Whatever are our schools coming to if they don't encourage you young things to read the Bard?'

'Not the schools' fault,' I sighed. 'I wasn't at any of them very long.'

'If you'd spent a lifetime at the best, I don't suppose you'd have read enough Shakespeare. Certainly not Chaucer in the original. Now that's what I call a cup of tea.'

He came back to the table, helping himself to toast from a silver Christopher Dresser rack I'd picked up for him last Christmas. As always, he turned it so I could see a different facet. 'Details, dear heart. Look at those details. Not that you haven't an eye for them. But occasionally you let your mind wander. Now, for instance. We have to leave the house in fifteen minutes and you haven't even started your coffee, child!'

It was a very twenty-first-century cafetière, but the coffee it produced ended up in an eighteenth-century Derby can. No, nothing to do with tins of peas. It's the term for tiny handleless cups. Griff had been right to wean me from crock mugs: the coffee really did taste better. Honestly.

If I'd been on my own and in a hurry like we were now, I'd have scraped marg out of a tub and with the same knife scooped jam from the jar. But Griff held that if one got sloppy in little things, one could get sloppy in big ones. So despite our haste, I passed him butter in a Shelley dish and marmalade in a glass saucer of unknown provenance. The marmalade's provenance was immaculate. It came from our own kitchen, made from genuine Seville oranges cooked in Griff's own jam kettle. I didn't know how it compared with other people's marmalade, but supermarket stuff wasn't in the same league.

* * *

We might have been on the road a minute or two later than scheduled, because you can't just dump old china in the sink and leave it to soak. The village was still asleep, however, as I pulled the van on to the main street. Bredeham might be a cosy village, but Griff still made sure we locked the van up in the garage every night; the six-foot high garden gates were electronically controlled. Like the shop — a retired lady called Mrs Hatch was looking after that today — the white Kent boarded cottage and its tiny garden had the latest in security systems. As Griff pointed out, it wasn't that we had much worth stealing, it was the damage criminals could do while they were hunting, or, worse, their revenge when they'd realised that there was nothing worth stealing.

Griff double-checked every lock behind me, pithering around until I was ready to scream with frustration. It wasn't as if I was driving a nippy little sports car and could make up for delays by putting my foot down once we'd picked up the motorway.

If I was anxious, Griff didn't seem to give a damn. He sat in the passenger seat waving his hands in the sort of gestures he probably used to make on the stage. He'd point at the countryside, admittedly very pretty at this time of year, and come up with snippets of poetry to do with cherry trees and others heavy with blossom. Being Griff, he didn't observe that after a day bent under wind like this the trees would shed all their lovely petals, littering roads and fields alike with confetti.

'I told you our late start wouldn't matter,' Griff observed complacently. 'The gods have blessed us with virtually empty roads.'

They had, and I wasn't about to argue. The roads in the South East have got stuck in some time warp, narrow and twisty, like in some fifties movie. Don't ask me why major towns should be joined by winding lanes, not decent dual carriageways. But then, don't ask me why once-flourishing towns like Dover and Hastings should have become so out at elbows that no sensible holiday-maker would want to stop off there when they're within spitting distance of France. Perhaps that was why they'd built the M20 and the M2 — to make it easier for people to spend all their money in Europe, not at home. At least the M20 was a boon to two of Kent's residents, Griff and me. Though we didn't go to every antiques fair, not by any means, we set up our stall at enough to need motorway access to major sites all over the country. Did the M25 help or hinder our progress? That was a matter of frequent, if not deep debate. OK, bickering.

Detling was only on our doorstep — spitting distance, as Iris would have said. Our stall there — it was really Griff's but in business just like at home he treated me more like a partner than an employee — was at least indoors. It was in one of the couple of big halls, a couple of hundred yards apart. Ours was no better than a barn really, matting covering uneven bare earth. Whenever anyone moaned, someone would point out that floorboards would be much less convenient for the usual occupants, sheep or cattle.

Outdoors, even in this arctic blast, were dozens of poor saps of stallholders who couldn't rake up the indoor pitch fee. They smiled and waved cheerily as we lugged our boxes and they lugged theirs. But we knew they'd keep at least as anxious an eye on the weather as they did for punters: if you're selling rugs or upholstery the odd April shower can be a pain, a downpour a disaster. Most of them were much lower in the food chain, however, selling all sorts of 'collectables' that Griff despised — especially when people bought them instead of the proper stuff we had on sale.

Our beady eyes wouldn't be on punters yet. There's always a couple of hours for dealers only — or Joe Public rich enough not to worry about the hiked-up admission charges designed to keep him out. First we set up. When you watched Griff it was obvious why he'd needed a young, fit assistant: maybe Iris really had been thinking of him as much as of me. He was getting very stiff about the knees, and he always found some excuse to let me handle the most delicate stuff. He wouldn't admit it, but one or two of his knuckles looked shinier than the others, and if he thought no one was looking he'd rub a finger as I would if I'd shut one in the door. His stage photos suggested he must be nearer eighty than seventy. I made sure I tackled not just the expensive china but also any heavy lifting. I might be only five foot two and fool people into thinking I'm delicate, but I'm whippy with it and can lift weight for weight with most of the dealers here.

As soon as we could, we started prowling around, buying here, selling there. Yes, to other dealers. Sometimes a stallholder specialising in, say, eighteenth-century glassware would have picked up a Victorian first edition, or an Art Deco person wanted to shift some Derby. So swaps or little deals were taking place wherever you looked. My brief was to look out for Victorian china, and some early twentieth-century pottery called Ruskin, which a collector down in Devon was after and was willing to pay silly prices for next time we were at West Point. It was silly prices that kept Griff and me in marmalade.

Not as silly as the labels put on that row of teddy bears. If they'd been Stieff or Merrythought, they would have been good-quality toys in the first place. These might have been lucky to claim their origins in Woolworths: why didn't people realise that tat was tat, whatever its age? I wouldn't have paid in bottle tops what these people were asking for in pounds.

Griff caught my eye.

I blushed.

'Dear heart, it's no shame to be searching for your heritage. I know what you're looking for — that teddy in the little photograph. But I fear you'll have to settle for your old Griff buying you one for your next birthday. But not,' he added, flaring his left nostril, 'one from this stall.'

I nodded. It wasn't just the system's fault that I had hardly any possessions. It was partly mine. You get so used to throwing things away — McDonald's containers, plastic bottles — that you don't always value better things. At least, I didn't, not even the little I'd got. It was only thanks to Iris that the social worker's cache remained — I'd had a quarrel with myself one night and thrown the lot in the bin.

'Harrods, perhaps,' Griff added grandly. 'Next time I'm in Town.'

As if there were just the one.

I shook my head. 'You know I wouldn't want anything posh.'

He looked pained. 'How many times have I told you one should always buy the best one can afford?'

'You couldn't cuddle a posh bear,' I argued. 'You'd be too worried about wearing its fur out.'

'Dear heart, you shall have one to cuddle. But ere long you'll have a young man in your bed to cuddle.' He suppressed a sigh.

As well he might. Last time I'd flirted with someone — a guy we met in a bar in Stafford — blow me if Griff wasn't flirting with him too.

He nudged me. 'I believe that Person wishes to speak to you.' In an undertone he added, 'A young man by all means. But not from this stall. You know, if they allow stuff like this — and have you seen all that plastic rubbish over there? — I can't see us coming here again.' He drifted off before I could stick my tongue out at him.

"Allo, gorgeous! Lina! 'Ow are you, darlin'?'

I turned, not bothering to smile. It was Ralph Harper, not one of my favourite dealers. He sold furniture, but mostly wrong 'uns. Oh, all the wood might be old, but he'd attach legs from one table to a top from another and had the brass neck to pretend the resulting mish-mash wasn't a fake. Chests of drawers, dressing tables, chiffoniers: nothing escaped his help. The trouble was he could undercut proper furniture dealers, many of whom no longer did this or other fairs he patronised.

'And how are you enjoying this delightful weather?' Ralph asked in the sort of nudge-nudge, wink-wink way he might have asked about last night's sex.

'Fine,' I said. 'Thanks.'

'Looking for young Marcus, are you?'

'Not specially,' I lied. Perhaps these extra layers — not one too many! — would make me look attractively curvy, in a sort of Marilyn Monroe-ish sort of way. Michelin-woman, more like.

'Well, he was looking for you. Something about a ginger jar. High-fired.'

That meant the most expensive type of Ruskin. I shrugged. If I started leaping up and down with enthusiasm Ralph was the sort to beetle over and buy it himself and then try to sell it on to me at a grossly inflated price. Given what the jar should fetch, if perfect, grossly inflated would mean sky high. All the same, once I'd mooched gently away, peering at any trays of junk that might just produce a Worcester loving cup or a Regency spectacle case for another regular client in Birmingham, I made a beeline for Marcus. I wouldn't do anything indecent like demand to see the Ruskin. No, I'd talk about this and that and ask him about Larry Copeland, his cousin, and maybe drop a hint about a disco I'd seen advertised at a local pub. Marcus would be staying in their trailer's caravan overnight and might welcome a different sound from his cousin's snores. He might even welcome a bit of company. Mine. So long as I drove Griff back to Bredeham and promised to be sufficiently awake on Sunday morning to get him back to Detling bright and early he'd be happy to lend me the van.

Marcus' cousin's stall specialised in prints, tarted up for punters and beautifully framed. Mostly they came from tatty old books he'd picked up for peanuts at country house sales. The reasoning was that since the books were falling apart anyway it didn't do any harm to slice out and indeed rescue the odd page. That's what decent, legitimate dealers did. Others cannibalised books that could — should — have been saved. Both types framed the pages, delicately repairing any damage to any original colour they might have. Opinions differed about how to deal with uncoloured etchings. Some folk left them as they were, plain black and white. Others coloured them, tinting them carefully by hand. That was what Marcus was doing now. Each prettifying brush-stroke would make the finished product more saleable and thus more valuable. Except in another sense it took away all the value. I didn't interrupt. Actually it was quite pleasant simply standing and watching. Marcus had lovely hands, with long thin fingers usually rolling a spliff he was happy to share and the sort of profile that reminded you of those aristocratic young men poncing round in fifteenth-century Florentine portraits. But he was so engrossed I moved away, looking at some of the other stuff already laid out. There was no sign of the Ruskin jar. To my right was a bin full of eighteenth-century maps of all of the South East: Essex; Sussex; Middlesex; Surrey; Kent. Then there were some bird prints, and, Copeland's speciality, sporting prints. There was also a big sheet, half covered in tissue. I blew the tissue back. Seventeenth, possibly even sixteenth century. A folio sized frontispiece. From a book I knew.

* * *

'Griff, I've just found this book I know! A page, anyway. Very old. All these strange plant-things curling round the outside of the title page,' I gabbled. 'Then in the middle, just where you'd expect it in fact, the title. I reckon it's in Latin.'

Griff passed me coffee in the Thermos lid, pretending to be calm. 'Something else they fail to teach in schools these days, alas. Have you any idea what it might have said? Or must I drift over with feigned casualness myself?'

'Nature something or other.' Why had I never worked harder at school? OK, why had I hardly ever gone to school?

'Nature *exactly*?' he pressed. He sounded very interested.

'*Naturam*?' I hazarded.

'Or *Natura*?' There was no mistaking his excitement.

If I wasn't careful I'd say it was, just to please him. But it sounded right. 'It could have been. Then there was another word. It couldn't be *Rerum*, could it?'

He clasped his pudgy little hands across his chest. '*Natura Rerum! The nature of things*. Nothing to do with flora and fauna as such — more a philosophical treatise.'

'What about all the plants and things?' My fingers described them in the air.

'Well, more to do with what makes a plant a plant as opposed to an animal. I suppose you didn't notice a date?'

'Come on, Griff — all those Xs and Ms! You know I can never work them out!'

'Author?'

'A Gentleman.'

Feeling carefully behind him, Griff sat down on the edge of a packing case.

'Actually,' I said, trying to think straight, 'it wasn't Roman numerals. No, it was ordinary numbers. It said — would 1589 make sense?'

'*Natura Rerum*. A Gentleman. 1589. Lina, dear heart — do you know what you've found?'

'A book I know,' I insisted.

'More than that!'

'All right,' I said, knowing I had to humour him before he'd humour me, 'tell me.'

'Lina — unless I'm very much mistaken — you've hit the jackpot!'

CHAPTER TWO

'*Natura Rerum* is one of the rarest books there is! In the whole world, Lina. Only two or three extant,' he continued. His voice had risen to a squeak.

'You mean — only two or three still in existence? Out of how many?' Funny how my head was working. Half of it wanted to think about the book as precious and important in its own right, the other kept on hammering away about its value to me.

'No one knows for sure. But who in their right mind would cannibalise one? It'd be worth infinitely more whole.'

'No one who knew what it was,' I said slowly. 'Copeland's a print dealer, not an expert in old books.'

'Marcus?'

I shrugged — absolute negative. 'He's got some sort of art qualification. When he's not doing that water-colouring stuff he sculpts embarrassing nudes for the export market.'

Griff looked at me sideways. 'Dear heart, are you sure, absolutely sure?' He didn't mean about Marcus.

'Sure as I'm standing here,' I said. But standing still was very difficult when I wanted to go and snatch it and bring it safely here. Or just dance on the spot.

'I know you've got a nose — sometimes you sniff out such unpromising items from such unlikely places I wonder if you're got a bit of a divvy in you — but for you to recognise it when Copeland doesn't—'

'I told you,' I said, grabbing his hands and shaking them from side to side, 'the thing is that I've actually seen the book itself. The whole book. When I was very young,' I continued. 'It's part of my very earliest memory. It was somewhere my mother took me. It certainly wasn't her family. So it had to be—'

'Your father's side.'

I took a breath. 'So you see, if I can trace that book—'

'Maybe you can trace your father,' Griff finished for me, sighing. He looked at me from under his eyebrows. 'My child, I've said this before, and I daresay I'll say it again: this may not be wise. Looking to the future is, in my humble experience, far better than looking back. Far less dangerous. Leave it. I beg you: go and flirt with another young man or two.'

'Flirt! I never flirt!' I pouted.

'My cherished one, you never stop.'

'In any case, shouldn't we be after that book? It'd make our fortune!'

There was a long pause as if ideas were coming that he should have had five minutes ago. 'Believe me, if — and it has to be said it's an enormously big "if" — if that frontispiece is genuine and comes from a genuine copy of *Natura Rerum*, then the bibliophile world and his wife will be looking for it. And not for sentimental reasons, believe me.'

'"A big if"! You're not saying it's a forgery!'

He nodded sadly. 'Ralph Harper's not the only one who tampers with things.'

I couldn't speak. Giving me something between a hug and a shake, Griff said in his everyday voice, 'Be that as it may, I noticed a pretty little Worcester posy bowl over on Josie's stall — ever such an ugly repair. Now Josie said she was interested in that Majolica plate you've been working on. If she won't offer you enough, try that new lad down by the exit to the loos: he looks pretty damp behind the ears. And there's a darling little Art Deco oil and vinegar set on someone else's stall — I would have thought that it would repay your ministrations threefold.'

That was Griff's way of reminding me that I was at Detling to work. Although I was fizzing with a mixture of excitement and anxiety, there was no point in arguing. And, now I needed money desperately — whatever Griff said, I had to buy that page — work made the best sense.

The idea was that each time I bought damaged ware cheap and restored it to a saleable state I would plough the profit into more and more items, thus bringing in bigger and bigger returns to my part of the business. I'd agreed with Griff that I should keep back a small proportion to keep me in clothes and what he called gewgaws. Actually, most of the jewellery I bought was from fairs like this, since I was into retro-chic in a big way. Plus if I didn't like something I could always sell it again, usually at a profit. This was my very own money, not something to contribute to the stall. Today I was wearing a big pair of Lalique glass ear-clips, lovely to be seen wearing but murder on the earlobes. I had an original — but not *the* original — mounting card tucked into my box of tricks. You never knew when such odds and ends might come in handy. I transferred it to my bag. I could always take off the clips — which would be a relief all round — and, attaching them to the mounting card, flog them this morning. Though it cost a month's gewgaws, a year's, *Natura Rerum* would be mine. Well, a small part, at least.

Josie was an elf of a woman, probably never more than five foot tall and now shrunk into a wizened question mark. Griff said she'd got something that hunched spines called osteoporosis. She might have been any age between sixty and ninety. She looked with grudging approval at the Majolica plate I showed her. I'd spent hours soaking off disgusting old glue, which left a thick, ugly scar where some ham-fisted idiot had tried to repair a nice clean break, and replacing it with slow-setting, practically invisible epoxy-resin. The plate was now almost as good as new. Or old. It wasn't really valuable anyway, not a sixteenth-century piece a dealer would have given his teeth for. Nineteenth-century manufacturers had twigged that naïve tourists to Italy would give a mint for what they thought were mediaeval plates. I suppose you could call what they produced either forgeries or tributes. This particular plate yelled it was nineteenth century. The young woman in the centre — a damsel, Griff called her — sat there like some drapery-hung sack of potatoes. Queen Victoria on a bad day. I'd been tempted to paint in a double chin, for spite.

The price Josie offered, I wished I had. I didn't like offending Josie, because apart from being an old mate of Griff's she'd let me loose on odds and ends when I was still at the kindergarten stage. But I wanted at least fifty per cent more. Mumbling that I'd think about it, which meant leaving the posy bowl where it was, I drifted to the exit Griff had told me about, in search of the new lad. The only male stallholder around was about sixty. Still, Griff always did like a spot of poetic licence, so I dawdled to a halt. A rather prissy floral sign at the back of his stall announced, *Arthur Habgood, Devon Cottage Antiques.*

He seized the plate like a starving man grabbing his dinner. '*Istoriato* Rafaelle ware!' he crowed.

I pointed out the join. I'd rather not have done, but I had my reputation — and Griff's — to think of. Never, ever, he'd said, should one ever try to pass off damaged goods as the perfect article. Not if one wanted to stay in the trade. I'd seen plenty of people flourishing in the trade like dandelions while ignoring his dictum — maybe even *because* they ignored it — but felt better, if poorer, being straight.

Habgood favoured me with a rundown of the genre, full of detail, mostly wrong. I smiled and nodded, not daring to offend a potential buyer by a look at my watch or even a glance back at Marcus. But if he didn't stop waffling soon, all the profit in the world might be in vain, and that frontispiece in someone else's hands.

'And how much did you want for this?' he asked at last.

'I'd really keep it on our own stall,' I lied, 'but it's not really our period.' Not true either: wherever possible, Griff preferred perfect goods. 'I suppose my best would be—' I gave a price a hundred per cent more than it was worth.

New to the business he might be, but he hadn't come down in the last shower of rain. The look he cast under his ill-kempt eyebrows was shrewder than I'd expected. Don't tell me he'd been playing me at my own game, boring the socks off me so I'd ask for less.

He offered what Josie had offered. But when I picked up the plate, shaking my head emphatically — if anyone was going to get a bargain it would be someone I owed a favour — he shuffled his hand into his back pocket and fished out a few scruffy tenners. When he fanned them out I counted forty more than Josie's price.

Wrinkling my nose, I made as if to walk away. But we both knew I'd turn back. 'Throw in that cracked Staffordshire figure — you know you can't sell it as it is — and it's a deal. And I'll let you have first refusal when I've restored it.'

He shook his head, removing a note from the wad. 'That's my best if you want the figure.'

I picked it up. With a little help from me it would fetch a great deal more than a tenner. 'Deal,' I nodded. As money changed hands, I said, 'You're new on the circuit, aren't you?'

'On the circuit, yes. But I've had a shop in Totnes for years. Then there was foot-and-mouth and September eleventh and the Americans stopped coming over and flashing their lovely greenbacks.'

'So you took to the road?'

'They said this was supposed to be a quality international fair,' he said gloomily. 'I didn't quite expect the NEC but I did expect indoor loos.'

'There are some indoor ones right opposite the other hall. New ones.'

'They aren't here, are they?'

I couldn't argue. What I needed was some sort of exit cue. 'So where's your next gig?' That wasn't very good. 'So I can prioritise this.' Which might sound as if I were about to dash off and do it straightaway.

'Stafford. Another agricultural ground.' He made it sound like a slaughterhouse.

'Don't worry, it's a couple of notches up on this. Not just the ground, but the quality of goods on sale. Look, I've got to go and see a man about a dog.'

'OK. Nice doing business with you, er—?' His smile showed off more filling than I'd have wanted the general public to see.

'Lina.'

He came out with a joke I'd come to dread. 'Lena as in Horne, I suppose.' The smile broadened. What teeth weren't filled looked like crowns. Like every other old geezer, he added, in case I'd never heard of her, 'Lena Horne the singer. More my generation than yours, of course.'

Very true. 'Lina as in Evelina. Evelina Townend.'

I could practically see his tonsils his grin was so broad. 'Not every day I meet a character from Fanny Burney.'

Not every day I got chatted up by a man old enough to be my grandfather. I gave what Griff called my winsome smile and slipped away.

Trying to look cool and serene I hotfooted it to Marcus' stall. To my relief he was still prettifying maps, and my frontispiece was still unsullied, just as I wanted it. A memory in black and white was worth half a dozen blurred by watercolour.

It was priced in letters and numbers, but neither Marcus nor Copeland would have been much use deciphering the Enigma codes, so it took me about five seconds to realise that my bounty wouldn't buy more than about half of it — and that was before they popped it into a gold-leaf frame.

The only thing to do was lay my cards on the table. Some of them, at least.

At twenty-four or five, Marcus wasn't much older than me but while I still appeared in my mirror as something like an overgrown schoolgirl — until I'd popped on what Griff called my slap, at least — Marcus had shed anything that smacked of his teens. He cultivated what some of the women I'd met called his Mr Darcy look. I thought he looked more like the Duke of Wellington, in those portraits when he was still plain Arthur Wellesley. Not all that plain, come to think of it. Calculating eyes and a nose to sneer down. But sexy with it. Marcus rarely calculated, except when dealing with punters with more money than taste, and never sneered — not, at least, until he'd stowed their cash in his back pocket. He always greeted older women with a courtly kiss on both cheeks. Since he and I were eyeing each other up as possible dates, he simply flapped a hand as I approached his stall. Maybe I'd suggest that drink for tonight.

Or maybe I wouldn't. When I brought the conversation round to the frontispiece, he did rather peer down that nose.

'Out of your league, Lina, I'd have thought. Or has someone commissioned you to get it on the cheap? In which case, add another hundred and we'll split it.'

'No, not a commission. And I want it as seen — not tarted up or framed, thanks. So you can give me the real price, not the wish one.'

'What on earth do you want it for? It's not your Victorian pretty-pretty china. Not branching out, are you?'

'I want it for a friend,' I said, touching the side of my nose.

'Since when have you had the sort of friend to give something that pricey?'

No, I wouldn't be suggesting that drink after work. Not unless he stopped being a pain in the bum and named a sensible price. I said nothing and waited.

To be fair, what he asked wasn't outrageous, not when you considered how rare Griff had said the original book was. All the same, I haggled a bit — not the best move, since I'd be asking for credit, whatever the price. And yes, even if he'd asked double, I'd have had to raise the cash somehow. No, I wouldn't consider the possibility that it was a fake.

At last he came down another twenty pounds. 'Strictly cash, mind. And don't tell Copeland.'

'You may have to tell him, though. I want to pay in instalments. Here you are. A hundred on account.'

His Wellington eyebrows shot up. Had I met my Waterloo? I almost expected him to send for some pantalooned aide-de-camp to sling me out of his tent. I played the pathos card. 'Look, it's for Griff's birthday. A big birthday.' Well, all birthdays were big when you were that age. 'And I don't want him to know.'

'So when do you plan to pay the rest?'

'Soon as I sell my gewgaws and some more china.'

'Like, today?'

'More like next fair,' I said, wishing I hadn't inherited this truth gene from wherever. 'Unless you know someone who'd like three old Worcester cups and saucers and a pair of Lalique earrings?'

He stroked his long chin, graced with just enough stubble to be sexy. 'I couldn't say — no, hang on! There's a woman with one of the outside stalls. She'd got a load of costume jewellery.'

I pulled a face. An outside stall implied she needed to keep her overheads really low. My Lalique wasn't Christmas cracker tat: it was quality glass. But I could try.

As I turned, it was Marcus' turn to tap his nose. 'No need to say anything about this to Copeland,' he muttered.

I hadn't intended to. How such a dish as Marcus came to have such a ferrety-faced cousin I'd never know.

'What about when he tells you to start painting it?'

He shrugged. 'Better get the rest of that cash quick,' he said.

I nodded and at the sight of Copeland melted away. I'd ask about the Ruskin later.

* * *

Clouds, which when we'd set out had been white, fluffy pompoms emphasising the blue of the sky, were now congregating in ominous black banks. My heart bled for the poor dealers trying to work out whether to cover all their gear to protect it or to leave it where it was in hopes of a quicker sale. One look at the jewellery stall Marcus had mentioned told me I was wasting my time: it wasn't even good paste, but cheap brightly coloured glass in fancy absolutely-not-gold settings, the sort of thing Iris said she wore with taffeta dresses and seamed nylons when she went to dances she called hops when she was a teenager. I was drifting sadly away when I remembered the other display hall, a couple of hundred yards from ours. No. Don't ask. That's just how it is. Mostly this one held furniture, some of it good quality, but there was sometimes a stall specialising in glass. It was there today, the owners rather belatedly setting up, unwrapping early twentieth-century glass from France and Germany. It might be an acquired taste — Griff loathed it — but I loved the iridescence and the weird colours, which needed clever lighting to show them at their best. I'd have murdered for that bluey-purple Loetz vase . . . And what were they unpacking now but some Lalique. A couple of birds, which I really liked, though I'd have said they were 1930s, no earlier, and a nymph: lovely, opalescent things. Under their professional lights my earrings probably looked just as good. I knew that they were really from the sixties, and not this stall's period at all, but couldn't resist a try. And managed it. I never mentioned a date, honestly, and they were so sure they were on to a bargain, they practically tore them off my ears. Who was I to argue? I left the backing card in my bag: it'd come in useful another day, maybe. Meanwhile, I pondered which was worse: the pain of the clips or the pain of the circulation coming back.

No, I didn't feel particularly proud of myself for conning them, but from day one Griff had dinned into me that I should always do my homework. If I didn't, and I got my fingers burnt, I'd only got myself to blame. The same rule, he'd added softly, also applied to other people.

So now I had an extra hundred or so in my hand, when I should have had sixty at the most. Marcus was clearly impressed when I pressed most of it into his hand. Most but not all: some sensible bit of my head refused to let me sell my seed-corn. With just a bit of cash, I might do another couple of deals. 'Say,' he began, 'I was wondering—'

But at that point Copeland hove into view. He seemed to have the knack of materialising when he was least wanted. I put on my most innocent smile. 'Ralph was saying something about a Ruskin ginger jar. High-fired,' I prompted.

'Ralph Harper? That bastard spends so much time on his fakes he wouldn't know the truth if it poked him in the eye,' he snarled. He softened. 'Come on, Lina, it's not our line at all.'

Behind him, Marcus was waving his arms and pulling faces. He might have been practising for a gurning competition.

I took the hint and looked at my watch. 'Hell. I didn't realise it was this time. They'll be opening the gates to the punters any minute.'

'Tell Griff there's a nice big queue already,' Copeland said, meaning I was to shove off and stop cluttering up the place.

I shoved. I needed punters too.

CHAPTER THREE

There are days when punters positively leak money. It oozes straight from their hands into yours. OK, so you give them something back — often something that's worth half what you've put on the price label, knowing you'll be haggled down. But on days like that they don't even ask for discount for cash.

There are other days when visitors treat a fair like their own personal *Antiques Roadshow*, bringing their own stuff, 'just for you to have a look at.' Yes, they want a free valuation. Other times they'll simply finger things, observing that they've got better at home, and spending nothing at all.

It looked as if today might have attracted the second sort of punter.

'They come, they touch, they disparage,' Griff sighed, sipping afternoon tea, his face wrinkled as if he was in great pain. Even I thought the tea tasted nasty, but he'd insisted on having some simply, he said, to pass the time. 'And then they go.'

He was right. They had gone. And none had come in to replace them. Of any sort.

'There's always tomorrow,' I said, catching crumbs from a slice of treacle tart, no more homemade, despite its quaintly printed label, than the Greenwich Dome. I hoped I sounded more optimistic than I felt. I needed quick sales to get my hands on the frontispiece.

Today's empty hours had given me rather too long to consider Griff's theory that it was probably a forgery. I'd sneaked back for another look when I'd seen Copeland sidle off with his outdoors jacket on leaving Marcus in charge. He wasn't keen on showing it to me again, but as I pointed out, I now owned at least the ink, if not the paper. The paper felt and smelt right, and the ink was the sort of colour that old ink goes. There was even one very neatly cut side, as if someone had sliced it from a book using a razor or craft-knife. I'd casually asked Marcus if he knew anything about its provenance, a word I'd never even heard of before I joined Griff. But now I knew a provenance was essential, for expensive pieces in general and pictures in particular. Even for butter dishes and marmalade. If the seller could tell you where something came from, and, better still, could show you paperwork to back his claims, then the less likely it was to be a piece meddled with by someone like Ralph Harper. The downside was that it was likely to be very much more expensive if it had spent its days in some gentleman's residence, as Griff put it, than if it turned up dirty and unloved having done time at boot sales. Marcus had sworn he knew nothing about the page's provenance. And I'd been inclined to believe him.

All the same, I had to bring it home soon. 'What do they say on the film, about tomorrow being another day?'

Griff loved his old films. Pouring the remains of his tea into the aspidistra we kept handy, supposedly to dress the stall but really, I was sure, for Griff's slops, he managed a smile. 'They do indeed. Which is why you mustn't even think of marking down those Worcester cups and saucers,' he added in a stronger voice. 'Now, you did a lovely job on that Rockingham plate, but it's still a tad battered. You could drop that by twenty pounds for a quick sale.'

'I might if there were any customers to sell to. Where is everyone?'

'Some football match, I daresay.'

And even if I sold the pretty plate, I still wouldn't have enough to take home my treasure, not without leaving myself quite skint. I didn't doubt that Marcus would keep his word, but I wouldn't put it past Copeland to hand me back my cash with a smirk telling me he'd simply had to accept a much higher offer.

'Go and do another circuit, child. Anyone happening to drift this way would think we were about to witness a public hanging. Weren't you talking about having an evening out with that hirsute young man? Or has the financial deal compromised your relationship?'

'You tell me.' Despite myself, I must have sounded very short.

Griff rearranged a couple of items and returned to his seat, hitching a tartan travelling rug round his knees and reaching for *Sanditon*. 'I know it's not Austen's greatest, but I try to read all her *oeuvre* at least once a year. You should read her yourself, dear heart. Even though I can't guarantee scenes where young men who should know better plunge into ornamental lakes.' He paused for me to laugh at our memories of the TV *Pride and Prejudice* he'd shown me on video. To please him I did. Now why couldn't I have a Colin Firth come dripping into my life? Because he was old enough to be my father, that was why. 'Start with *Northanger Abbey* — that's all about a young woman from a humble background becoming a heroine.'

'Hmm. I'll try it this evening.' Yes, I'd be sitting cosily at home listening to the radio with Griff when I'd rather be out in a loud bar with Marcus. Fed up as I was, however, I wouldn't bite back at Griff. Anyone prepared to become mother, father, teacher and employer all rolled into one to a complete stranger was entitled to a bit of respect. And a lot of love. I knew he was worried about me, so I tried not to sulk. I adjusted a couple of our spotlights, tweaked our sign, and, waving what I hoped looked like a cheery hand, set off.

If I was gloomy, some of our mates looked downright miserable. Hardly surprising: if they didn't sell — preferably at a profit — stuff they'd paid good money for, they wouldn't be able to pay their bills.

Despite the morning clouds, it hadn't rained. That wasn't much comfort to the hardy outside brigade, whose faces had frozen into the sort of smile Griff called a facial rictus, with which they'd no doubt welcome any passing punters. There were a couple of stalls selling what they claimed were 'collectables'. I gave them a miss, but felt this pull to the jewellery stall I'd sneered at earlier. Where was it? There was something hidden amidst all that glitter that was calling me so strongly I almost whispered to it to stay where it was.

Chokers. Bracelets. Rings the size of knuckle-dusters. Yes. There in the tray of rings, so small it was almost invisible, was a white gold ring. Someone had thought it was silver. And the emerald, not much to write home about, was set in purple enamel. A few tiny diamonds completed it. I'd no idea why, but I knew the little trinket was important. Thank goodness I'd known not to clear myself out. Perhaps I did have a bit of the diviner's gift, as Griff always swore I did — antiques, not water, you understand.

I waved it under the dealer's nose.

'Twenty pounds?' She was uncertain, hopeful. And therefore vulnerable.

I pulled a face. 'Come on. Trade. I'm with Griff. Griff Tripp.' Kind Griff, honest Griff. Griff who might or might not approve of what I was doing.

'So you are. Well, say fifteen. And that's only a couple of quid more than I paid. Pretty, isn't it?'

* * *

Griff popped a jeweller's glass into his eye and peered. 'I knew you were a divvy!' he crowed. 'Its intrinsic value isn't much more than you paid, though the band and setting are, as you realised, white gold. Tiny emerald. Diamonds no more than chippings. Enamel. Oh, I'd say a little more than a hundred, so you're still in profit.'

'There's a but coming up. I can feel it. What's the but, Griff?'

'A nice but.'

I grinned.

'I know a lady who collects this sort of thing. Women's Social and Political Union — Suffragettes, to you and me. These were their colours. There's a story behind this ring. And it's that story that may bring you in some hard cash. That's the good news. The bad news is that the lady in question lives in America.'

'So I may have to wait.' I could feel my face fall.

'"One auspicious and one dropping eye"! Poor Lina. Would you like me to make you a tiny advance on your undoubted profit? Enough to buy that damned page?'

The whole hall probably heard that I would. Thank goodness my dear Griff was the sort of gay who liked being hugged by women. Removing his shoe, he pulled out a warm and slightly damp wad of twenty-pound notes. 'How many?' Without waiting for a reply, he peeled off five. I was home and dry.

And, of course, frustrated. Completely frustrated. Now I had the frontispiece, how did I find that vital thing, its provenance? It was clear that Marcus neither knew nor cared, and Copeland was in a foul mood over what he declared a completely wasted day. He was no worse off than the rest of us, and possibly better: several people had gone off with his distinctive carrier bags. Admittedly they were small or middle-sized bags but a sale is a sale. Copeland's presence seemed to quench any desires Marcus might have had for a drink or any other designs he might have had on me. Meek as a lamb he helped pack the more valuable prints and put away his paints.

Not to be outdone I withdrew to Griff's stall, packing with what I hoped looked like terrifying efficiency.

Griff blinked, and said mildly, 'So the miserable churl doesn't deserve your tenderness. But I must tell you that that bit of Coalport does. Gently does it, dear heart. Now, what do you say to treating ourselves at the pub on the way home? It's been a long day and I fancy we have quite a lot to celebrate.' He glanced at Marcus, scurrying after Copeland like a whipped puppy. 'All the same, quite a lot.' He patted the carrier bag holding my page and a bulge in his pocket, caused by a box holding the WSPU ring.

Yes, I was frustrated in every sense of the word. But Griff was making a real sacrifice in offering to eat out. He hated the noise and smoke of a pub, even when we tucked ourselves into the smoke-free zone, swatting rather pettishly at any stray wisps he fancied might be coming our way. The expression on his face if he had to move a leftover ashtray would make you think he was handling raw sewage.

'What'd be even nicer,' I lied, 'would be to stop off at that big Sainsbury's in Ashford and pick up some bits and pieces for you to cook. And maybe a bottle of bubbly to go with it.'

It was worth the wait I'd let myself in for while he flitted happily round, making up his mind which vegetables would go with which meat, just to see his face light up.

'Do you really mean it? Or, dear heart, I saw this wonderful recipe in a magazine at the doctor's the other day!' Which meant he'd torn it out and stuffed it in an overfull carrier bag hanging behind the kitchen door.

'Of course I mean it.' And I'd buy a small item on my own account from the stationery section while he pottered round the chill cabinets.

* * *

'A loose-leaf folder!' Griff picked it up off the kitchen table. 'For me? Lina, it's lovely of you to give me a present—' He held it as if were no more use than a slice of old bread. He might have asked out loud, 'But what do I use it for?'

I mustn't be disappointed. 'You see these polythene wallets? They're open at the top. You can slide pieces of paper inside. There. Schoolchildren sometimes use them for projects or essays.'

'So you're expecting me to—?' His face was still screwed into doubt.

'*You* don't have to do anything. While you cook the dinner, I shall sit down at this end of the table with a pair of scissors and your recipe bag and I shall trim all the jagged tears and pop the recipes in the wallets. So if you like them, you'll know where to find them, and if you don't like them all you have to do is fish them out and throw them away.'

He'd put on his glasses to look at the folder. Now he took them off again and polished them furiously. 'That will be very useful. More than useful. And all the kinder since I know all you want to do is pore over that page.'

He nodded at it: he'd put it flat on the piano he never played but couldn't persuade himself to sell. He said it would be a sign of giving in — what to he never specified.

'You think it's all right?'

'It's got all the signs of being authentic,' he said cautiously, wandering over to peer at it again. 'But I'd like to have it — very quietly — authenticated. UV lights, ink samples, paper samples.'

'That'd cost more than a week's gewgaw money,' I reminded him.

'But there's more than one way, in the vulgar parlance, to skin a cat. We could show it to Titus.'

'Titus Oates! That revolting man!' He was worse than Ralph Harper, with nasty freckled convolvulus hands.

'Some may say he's merely a master forger. Others may say you should set a thief to catch a thief. Titus knows every trick in the book. And every rival in the marketplace. If that's not kosher he'll know. And he'll know who forged it.'

'Wouldn't Copeland?'

He looked me straight in the eye. 'Would you fancy asking him?'

'I suppose I could always ask Marcus—'

'Not, I'd have thought, if you still harbour any carnal thoughts of him.'

'Carnal?'

'Look it up, cherished one. The dictionary is in its usual place. I, meanwhile, will go and put the van away and lock the garage.'

He always did that, if he was embarrassed about anything, sex, usually. Well, only sex, come to think of it, and heterosexual sex at that. So I didn't need to look anything up. Instead, I swung the keys from his hand and headed for the van. Even as I checked the electronic locks were doing their job, I could hear in my head what I knew Griff would ask at bedtime: 'It's all right and tight? You're quite sure?' I'd only just managed to persuade him not to go out in all weathers to double-check. So yes, I was sure, quite sure.

* * *

I could have slipped down after supper to the Hop Pocket for a game of darts with the lads, and Griff wouldn't have complained. He rarely complained. The only time he came near it was when I was planning to embark on some body piercings and told him enthusiastically about where I was going to have them. He let me rabbit on for ages, not saying a word. At last he reached across the table I was working at and picked up a fruit bowl I was trying to rescue. It had been mended years ago, ugly staples reinforcing the blackened glue.

'What do you feel when you look at those?' he asked quietly.

I shuddered. 'They're — they're just awful. It'll take me ages to soak out the plaster of Paris holding them, and I'll never really be able to get rid of the scars.'

'Quite. An insult . . . a violation . . .' He looked at me under his eyebrows.

Neither of us had said anything more. And no, I didn't have any piercings. When I briefly contemplated a butterfly tattoo on my shoulder I thought of how pained he'd looked before and dropped the idea stone dead.

So I didn't go down to the pub. Not after Griff had gone to the trouble of cooking a wonderful Chinese meal, complete with bits and bobs. Griff did things properly. And he was teaching me about wine, too — or rather, trying to. I could tell the difference between red and white, but that was about all. Oh, and rosé, of course. Too much lager when I was too young, he said, and seemed to think that if I drank lots of water I might clear my palate. Whether my palate improved I couldn't say, but my skin did: I was becoming quite presentable.

Tuning the radio, he found some music he liked, though I wasn't sure I'd ever get the hang of string quartets, and dozed while I finished the recipe clippings and thought about working on one of my stash of chipped and otherwise damaged china. But the sort of delicate brushwork I'd be doing needed the very bright light of the workroom, and I didn't want to disturb Griff by getting up to leave the room. So I found *Northanger Abbey*, which he'd casually left on a Chinoiserie occasional table, and made a start. Not exactly your *Bridget Jones's Diary*. In fact — put it down to the big meal, the wine, the warmth of the room or those toiling violins — I did what Griff had done. Without the snores, I hope.

Until the burglar alarm went off. Very loudly.

* * *

'Swine, aren't they?' PC Baker sighed.

No, the Kent Constabulary hadn't officially dashed out to our aid. No way. Seems there's a policy about what constitutes urgent and what doesn't. And breaking into an old man's cottage doesn't.

We owed our police presence to the fact that one of our neighbours was in the police. Tony Baker was not much older than me, with a motorbike he called a classic, which he only rode on special occasions. Bikes didn't do much for either Griff or me, but as Griff said, it was nice in these blasé days to see anyone getting enthusiastic about something. Tony had heard the alarm — who this side of the Channel hadn't? — and had seen me belting down the road yelling. So he'd come to join the party.

'But you had your CCTV working?' Tony continued, trying to sound official despite the fact he was wearing nothing but slippers and a towelling bathrobe in a rather nice shade of dark blue.

'Indeed we did. And the video was loaded and working. So we should have footage of the perpetrator,' Griff said, remarkably alert after his nap. 'Thank goodness we've got all that electronic gadgetry. The camera's activated as soon as the outer doors are locked.'

'That's the house doors?'

'The gates, actually, since there is valuable stuff in the van. There's a separate system for the house, which we keep on all the time.'

'Even if you're inside?'

'We can isolate different areas. Yes, we lock ourselves in. It's the work of seconds to unlock and get out in the unlikely event of a fire,' he added crisply, before Tony could so much as raise an eyebrow.

'Shall we have a look at the video?' Tony suggested.

Griff toddled off to find it, leaving me to make coffee. Tony looked as though he'd like to be macho and slosh down a double espresso, but accepted my offer of milky decaf, our preferred tipple at this time of night. It would have been more chic to call it latte, of course, but Tony didn't seem to mind, especially when it came with some of Griff's biscuits. I'd have preferred him not to take the last two shortbread fingers, but cheered myself with the thought that a cop with that discernment ought to be a bright cop.

We all thought he was until we were watching the video. And the alarm went off again.

This time there were two of us to give chase. Griff tried to make it three but Tony pushed him back, yelling to him to lock up behind us. I forgave him the shortbread. I'd have forgiven him almost anything for the sight of him vaulting the gates — not easy or elegant in a robe and birthday suit — in pursuit of our burglars. I followed more slowly; oh, yes, I'd learned more at school about scaling fences than I ever had about the Norman Conquest. Or any of the books and plays Griff was always wanting me to try.

If I saw nothing, it seemed Tony didn't do much better. If our village had run to street-lighting we might at least have had some idea of what make of car was involved. We chased after something that might have been a new style Fiesta but had to give up. We were still looking up and down the street when we heard a yell and a thump. And our burglar alarm started up again. Griff. It had to be Griff!

If we'd moved fast before, we flew now.

'It's all right. It's all right. No damage done!' he called cheerily, hauling himself to his feet.

A couple of front doors opened, light spilling into the street. No, no one had seen anything, as Tony was quick to establish. Or heard anything, though I found that harder to believe. Griff dusted himself down.

'I thought I heard footsteps coming back this way,' he said. 'So I popped my head out of the door. I know. I'm sorry,' he added, squeezing my hand. 'He took a swing at me as if he was going to push past me, so I pressed the panic button.'

I slipped past. Better switch it off now, while we still had one or two neighbours on speaking terms with us.

* * *

So none of us had seen anything worth seeing, unless you count unlit cars and a person in a black hoodie: Griff couldn't say whether it was a man or a woman. 'That's one of the prices you pay for freedom from light pollution,' he sighed.

'That bloody parish councillor and his obsession with amateur astronomy,' Tony nodded, brightening when Griff produced a bottle of whisky and some glasses.

I shook my head at the whisky. I never knew how those people in films could gulp a tumbler wholesale. Just a sip burned my throat, and since I didn't have to be one of the men, I could be girly and fish out an alcopop, avoiding Griff's eye. Tony didn't seem to have a problem, though he did blink at the colour. Maybe wine would be more sophisticated.

'So what's on the movies tonight?' he asked, waving the video.

If we hadn't predicted what we'd see it would have been quite an anticlimax. We picked out black-clad figures — again, they could have been either sex — lit only by our security lights, the ones our councillor had tried to have banned on the ground of unnatural interference with his telescope. There'd been a terrible rift in the village, but after a spate of shed burglaries — yes, that's right, garden sheds — a lot of people had succumbed and bought lights. Our councillor had subsided but was now waging war on drying washing and mowing lawns on Sundays.

Tony shrugged but didn't seem inclined to make a move, even though Griff topped up his glass with just a miserly minimum. It was well past Griff's bedtime so I wasn't surprised when, after a couple of yawns he didn't trouble to smother, he asked, 'Are we able to hope, Tony, that you'll be able to act in some official capacity on this evening's events?'

'I can put in a report, of course. But on the basis of this—' he waved at the video '—I can't see us getting very far. Can you?'

'Not unless you have other criminals using a similar *modus operandi*,' Griff agreed. 'They create a disturbance. And then — they must know that The Law is sitting here looking at their video — they try again. And when they've lured him satisfactorily into the street, they make yet another attempt. Reminds me of my apple-scrumping days,' he added, smiling back at the past.

Tony didn't look as if he bought Griff's theory of cunning thieves with a plan. He gathered himself up with whatever dignity he could — not a lot, given his outfit — and made for the door. 'One last question, Griff: you wouldn't have anything especially valuable on the premises tonight? Something someone might have seen in your shop today?'

'Nothing at all,' Griff said blithely.

CHAPTER FOUR

I didn't bother asking Griff why he'd lied to Tony. He'd always said that unless you absolutely had to you should never volunteer information to anyone. Presumably his dictum included the police, even in the friendly form of Tony. The other reason was that I felt guilty, very guilty. On that deathly quiet afternoon at Detling, my little display of glee — OK, my very big display of glee — had probably caught the attention of every single person in our hall. Many antiques dealers pride themselves on their detection skills, hunting down provenances, for example. Had someone taken it into their head to find out why I was so happy? They could have found two reasons, couldn't they? One of which, the frontispiece, spent the night under Griff's half-tester bed, the other coming into my bed on my finger.

So what should we do with them the following morning? There was the shop's safe for the ring, of course, but maybe that was too obvious. As for the frontispiece, if it were the genuine article, there was no way we could fold it and stow it in the safe too. Not that we had any time to waste discussing the problem: our late night had left Griff very slow and any attempts to speed him into the van were met with a grumpy snarl. So both items would stay where they were. Just as I'd herded Griff upstairs to clean his teeth, the phone rang. It was Mrs Hatch, who had looked after the shop yesterday.

'Might one speak to Mr Tripp?' Until I'd dropped into Griff's world, I'd only heard voices like hers on old newsreels of Royalty: she certainly had more plums in her mouth than our Queen.

'I'm sorry: Griff can't talk just now.' I didn't spell out how literally true that was, though I was sure Griff would enjoy it when I told him later.

'Is he not well?'

'Bathroom,' I confessed.

'Oh, dear. Men's troubles?' she enunciated sympathetically.

I didn't know much about men's troubles, except that they presumably involved sex, and it was more likely he was having difficulty with his Dentufix, or whatever held his plate in place. So I just said, 'Hmm.'

'Poor dear man. I was reading about this wonderful herbal cure — solves the problem without the need for an operation, they say. Or has it got too serious for that?'

I pinched my nose hard. I knew it was really a cure for nosebleeds, but it might work for the giggles. 'He doesn't tell me the details,' I managed.

'Of course not. No, indeed. I'd quite forgotten you weren't his real granddaughter. Now, the reason I rang was that there were a couple of very unsavoury-looking characters hanging round the village yesterday. Two men. They spent hours in the shop. I thought you should know. My finger was poised over the panic button. Absolutely poised.'

'What were they looking for?'

'You never know with these types, do you?'

What types? 'What did they look like?'

She dropped her voice as if she was going to say something rude. 'Foreign, my dear. It wouldn't surprise me if they were bogus asylum seekers.'

I tried not to bristle. Having come unpleasantly close to being down and out myself, if I'd had a spare coat I'd have gone and given it to someone really homeless. It wouldn't have mattered a jot if they were foreign or English — after all, the English system hadn't done me too many favours. So I took a deep breath.

'What did they pick up and look at? Or ask to see?' Tony would have been proud of me.

'They didn't touch, Lina. You know how I feel about people touching. But they hung around and peered.' She got about three separate sounds out of 'peered', one of them definitely 'ah'.

'What at?' Heavens! I should have said, 'At what?'

'My dear, at everything!'

Really helpful, that. No wonder cops faked evidence, if they had witnesses like Mrs Hatch.

I ploughed on. 'When did they come in?'

'Oh, let me think. About midday. And then they drove off in a little car. Filthy dirty.'

No, she didn't know what colour or have a clue about a registration number. Forget about its make: I doubt if she'd be able to identify anything smaller than a Rolls Royce.

She promised to be on her guard all day and rang off, sending her best wishes to Griff in a voice that sounded as if he were on his deathbed with this mysterious, unmentionable problem.

'Silly old bat,' Griff dismissed her when I told him.

This time I didn't wince at his double-checking of locks and alarms. I helped him.

'She's always carried a torch for me, poor creature,' he continued, as I drove down the village street. 'Thank goodness times have changed, Lina. Fifty years ago a man like me might have been grateful to a woman like that as a beard.'

'A beard?' Mrs Hatch didn't have a problem with facial hair.

'Camouflage.'

A hand gripped my stomach. I swallowed hard.

'But don't for a moment, dear heart, think that that's why I invited you into my life! Please, please believe me! I asked you because I could see that *au fond* — that's French for *at bottom*, another phrase for you to remember — you were a sweet child and because Iris had this absurd idea that I needed looking after as much as you did. And you do look after me, beautifully.'

I shook my head miserably. What was the difference between being a beard and being a carer?

He turned towards me, tugging against the seatbelt. 'More than that — I do wish you'd stop this confounded van and look at me, Lina — you've become my friend.'

I pulled over. Usually I park well. This time I didn't.

Griff put a paw on mine. 'Lina, you are my best friend and I'm honoured by your friendship. I'm proud of you. I wish you were my blood daughter — or granddaughter or whatever. But no matter how closely we were related, I couldn't love you more than I do.'

I squeezed his hand. He flourished his handkerchief, pressing it into my spare hand.

'I don't know why Iris thinks I look after you,' I muttered. 'The cooking, the washing and ironing — you do everything.'

'That's only because I have someone to do it for,' he said. 'You wouldn't have wanted me to turn into a disgusting old man with stubble, and stains on his trousers?'

I shook my head, my face still buried in his handkerchief. It was beautifully ironed and smelt of lavender. I'd made and stuffed the little sachets myself as a stocking-filler present last Christmas. I hope he heard what I said: 'I wish you were my real dad. Or grand-dad. Because—' But the words stopped coming. I never could say the words 'I love you'. And I knew I wouldn't stop looking for my real father, however much I loved Griff. Couldn't stop.

Griff fished for another hanky, which he used himself. 'Dear me; all this emotion before half the village is even awake! Come, Lina, start this transport of delight and drive us to our destiny!'

I did. It was a good job I could talk about Mrs Hatch's suspicious characters as I drove along. 'The trouble is, her description's useless, and they don't seem to have had any particular target.'

'If they were pro's they wouldn't let her see if they had.' He put on a middle-European accent. '"Take me to your silver! Show me your diamonds!"'

'But a pro wouldn't turn up on a day he'd know all the best stock would be with us in Detling.'

'Unanswerable.'

'And if they turned up at midday, they wouldn't have known about either the ring or my frontispiece,' I mumbled.

'Is that what you're worried about?'

'I wasn't exactly poker-faced when you lent me the cash,' I said.

It took a moment or two to reply, as if he was arranging things before he said them. 'It did cross my mind, after all that performance last night. And I think we should keep an open mind. And be very careful. But young Tony promised to check the police records — and I wager he'll come up with a gang who work that way regularly.'

'Their *modus operandi*?' I hazarded.

'Well done.' He patted the hand I'd left on the gear lever. 'I do rather think you've inherited my love of words, my love.'

* * *

It was easy to laugh with Griff, and he embarked on a long series of risqué stories, including one about a male nude sunbathing beach described by one of Griff's gay friends as his asparagus patch, which kept us in giggles as far as Detling. It was only the sight of several police cars in the trade car park that switched off our smiles.

''Allo, 'allo, 'allo,' Griff said, going into old-fashioned village-bobby voice. 'Wot 'ave we 'ere?'

They'd heard about my ring! The stallholder had accused me of sharp practice! If it hadn't been for Griff's kind hand on my shoulder, I'd have done a runner. But it seemed the very pressure brought me to my senses. In the antiques trade, it isn't just *caveat emptor* (perhaps Griff was right about inheriting those words), but *caveat* seller, or whatever the proper Latin should be — *vendor*? That sounded more Latin. I'd have to ask Griff. Even thinking about him made me go sane. The police wouldn't have come mob-handed for one woman. Something must have happened overnight.

Gossip: we'd soon pick up the details from the other dealers. And we did. Several versions. They ranged from a huge robbery from all our stalls to a clever heist involving international art thieves and Old Masters. Since I couldn't recall seeing a single painting worth nicking during the whole of my wanderings I discounted that. Pity. I hated it when little people like us were hurt, either physically or in our pockets. The big guys, now — I might have held them down while the Inland Revenue and the Fraud Squad did their worst.

In fact neither theory was right. It looked as if there might have been an attempted break-in, foiled by the security staff before it amounted to much more than vandalism. Just to make sure nothing had been taken, the police sent us to our stalls to check; there was to be no wheeling and dealing till they'd ticked us off their list. No Joe Public either, of course. Although outside there'd seemed to be hordes of officers, inside they were spread very thinly and took forever to speak to each dealer. Imagine my surprise then, when Griff suddenly piped up about our incident at home.

'What time was this, sir?' The WPC, who didn't seem to be much older than me, seemed really interested.

Griff gave a brief account, mentioning the heroism of Tony and the uselessness of our video evidence.

'Do you still have the tape?'

'Constable Baker took it with him — to see if he could get the images enhanced. Admittedly it was less in hope of finding our potential burglars, than of catching someone else's actual thieves.' He smiled, as if enjoying the balance of his sentence. He didn't mention Mrs Hatch's unsavoury customers until I prompted him.

'They were sniffing round as if casing the joint,' he concluded, a roguish smile creasing his face. He loved stealing someone else's trade lingo and using it himself.

The constable didn't see anything to smile at. Instead she confirmed a couple of details, adding, 'I wonder if your Mrs Hatch could identify the men from photographs. That would be very useful.'

Somehow I stopped myself leaping up and down and yelling that the two men were the innocent victims of prejudice. After all, they might just be a pair of local crooks — there were enough down in Kent, goodness knows — and justice ought to be done. Preferably before they nicked my precious page or the valuable, if less precious, ring. Oh, yes — and well before they'd laid their hands on Griff's miniatures or Regency silhouettes or anything else he loved too much ever to sell.

* * *

It would have been nice if the police had had to hold back huge queues while they were conducting their enquiries, but the day was a repeat of the previous one. Another football match? I drifted over to ask Marcus. He was engrossed in his painting, looking like — Drat it, Griff would have told me who he looked like. That flash pianist whose music he said was out of fashion these days, the one who started the fashion for pianists to sit side on to the audience when they played. Whoever. Anyway, there he was, with a couple of women practically touching him up and a thin, middle-aged man wearing more cosmetics than me ogling him. I'd always meant to ask why he didn't do his painting at home. You wouldn't catch me mending my china in full view. And now I realised why. Copeland was obviously using the gorgeous Marcus to attract customers, not just to see the work being done but to be allured by the young god who was doing it. Men and women. Oh, no! Did this mean the reason Marcus wasn't specially interested in me was because he was gay too? Surely not. Unless he was using me as — what had Griff called it? — a beard. Sweat trickled down my back, like it did when I'd bought a wrong 'un. I'd have to ask Griff: he'd know.

Copeland was hovering discreetly in the background, ready to relieve Marcus' fans of their money.

Trying to be polite, while I worked out what I was feeling, I flapped a hand. 'Looks like another quiet day,' I said.

'It's the play-offs for promotion to the premier league, of course,' Copeland snapped, as if my presence might put people off. 'Don't you and that old queer ever read the papers?'

'Not those pages, no,' I said, prickly on Griff's behalf. 'I believe if you read the other pages you'd find the correct term was "gay".'

'It's certainly queer that you're living with him.'

'We're housemates, that's what. Nothing queer about that.'

'What do you when he brings his boyfriends home? That can't be a very edifying sight, not for a kid your age.'

If only I knew what *edifying* meant. I didn't, so I simply snapped, 'His sex life is no more your business than mine is.' I wasn't going to tell this brute about Griff's occasional and very discreet away-days with friends. And certainly not about his long-term friend Aidan.

I turned pointedly away from Copeland, and drifted over to Marcus. I know: I was off my head. But I'll swear the words came out of their own accord. 'That drink we didn't have last night — why not make it tonight?'

'Because,' came Copeland's voice, 'he'll be packing up here, that's why. Not making sheep's eyes at a cunning little tart like you who he lets sweet talk him into selling my property at a crazy price. Just piss off, will you?'

The punters abandoned Marcus for much better entertainment. He flushed and looked everywhere except at me.

Cunning little tart, was I?

I looked Copeland in the eye. 'I'd have thought you'd be grateful to me, paying though the nose for something with no provenance at all. Come off it, Copeland — have you been taking lessons from Titus Oates?'

And then I beat it. Fast.

CHAPTER FIVE

If anyone kept a list of things in history better not said, that would have gone down as one of them, wouldn't it? I didn't dare tell Griff, because he'd know I'd only lost my cool because Copeland had been snide about him and our relationship. And by losing my cool, I'd lost any chance of wheedling out of Copeland — and possibly Marcus — where the frontispiece had come from.

Sh— No, Griff didn't like me to swear. Poo, then or even Pooh, as in Bear! I wished I'd never seen the thing.

No, I didn't. I was glad I had and I was desperate to know all about it.

Which meant that somehow or other I'd have to catch Marcus on his own and be extra nice to him so that he'd raid Copeland's files. Otherwise I'd simply no idea how to find out anything about the frontispiece's origin. Correction — provenance.

During the course of the day several people were extremely nice to me, far nicer than usual; others cut me dead. It didn't take me long to work out that all this was because everyone had heard about my spat with Copeland. Two lovely old friends of Griff's, who might not have been flattered by his private description of them as 'absolute darlings but the ugliest dykes in the Western world', insisted on buying me an ice cream, which I hadn't the heart to refuse, though I'd just had a burger and chips. Fortunately

Titus Oates himself wasn't gracing this fair, but I knew the grapevine would carry the news swiftly and unerringly to him, and he might just want to sue me for slander, with which he'd been known to threaten customers who queried some of his absolutely genuine Shakespeare letters.

A sudden late afternoon rush just at the time we should have been packing up meant Griff was too busy to ask any embarrassing questions. He sold in very rapid succession some highly gilded and therefore very pricey Royal Doulton plates, and some nice early Wedgwood, so there was much less to pack and the promise of plenty of good food and drink for the rest of the month. The Rockingham plate Griff had suggested yesterday I might have to reduce went for its asking price, so I was happy to do a deal with a nice American on some Worcester, the profits being shared equally between my gewgaw fund and repaying Griff's loan.

All the same, in the van I felt as I used to when confronted by an irate school attendance officer. OK, anything Griff would say would be more in sorrow than in anger, to borrow one of his quotations, but I'd still feel guilty. Sure enough, he coughed with embarrassment, but just as I was braced for a real wigging, he said mildly, 'Mrs Hatch would have been proud of you, dear heart. She tells me she likes gals with courage — the sort of gal who made the Empire great.'

'So long as she doesn't want me for peace-keeping duties! Oh, Griff, it wasn't very bright of me. To make two enemies in one day. Well, quite a lot more, since people will take sides.'

'But some of them will take sides with you. Old Titus included, I daresay. He's always told me he likes people with guts. You might just get away with it, so long as you greet him with a cheery grin and don't look hangdog like you do now. On the other hand — well, let's wait before we cross any bridges. Now, let me see: there's a house sale tomorrow. We should pick up some useful stuff there . . .'

* * *

Some silly old lady had decided she was going to live forever, and didn't need to make a will. The result was that a firm of Eastbourne solicitors was no doubt rubbing its collective hands together in glee, just like Griff when he saw a heap of unloved china, at all the money they were going to make from selling up the estate. A meagre knot of relatives stood round looking glummer and glummer as good stuff went for poor prices. Ralph Harper was there, sneering at some lovely Edwardian Regency-style mahogany bedroom furniture by Waring and Gillow. Even without the name, you could see that though the wood hadn't seen wax polish for a few years, it was high-quality stuff. He was next to a sleek-looking man wearing a leather jacket to die for, who muttered occasionally. Did I spot a little ring, dealers promising to keep prices down and then haggle between themselves? I was afraid so, and almost jumped for joy when a young couple forced the price up, just because the suite would look good in their bedroom. We got a complete 1903 Royal Worcester tea service embarrassingly cheaply. The current fashion was for much more highly decorated ware, but as Griff pointed out, at that price we could afford to keep it in the attic till tastes changed and prices went up accordingly. There was some nice Gaudy Welsh, but another dealer snaffled the lot. Since he had to pay well above the odds, Griff didn't so much as sigh.

We went home with a lot of odds and ends, too, the usual mixture of 'best' and everyday items, with the everyday ones often worth a lot more than those the owner had thought were treasures. I hadn't spotted that the old dear's cats had eaten off Coalport plates, but Griff had. For penance, I'd clean off whatever yucky gunge was encrusting them. So we had a week's work at home ahead of us, a quiet time unless one of Griff's fellow Thespians popped in for a cup of tea and regaled us with what Griff called the latest *on dits*. You might have thought the prospect was pretty tedious, but I really enjoyed restoration work, from appraising what could and what should be done to putting the final glaze on a piece. Most of my skills I'd learned from Griff himself, but not all. He had friends in the business all over the country, and I'd spent a week with two of them, an elderly brother and sister up in Wolverhampton, picking their brains. They could manage such fine work that people called on them from museums and stately homes; Griff's hands were now too shaky for all but the most everyday jobs; I was somewhere in between. One day, if I ever allowed myself to think ahead, maybe I could give up what Griff called the peripatetic life and settle down in the cottage next to Griff's with roses round the door, a couple of kids I'd bring up beautifully and a little part-time job I could do while they were at school. Not the usual sort of part-time job where employers screw the last drop from their underpaid staff, but one that paid really well. People were actually prepared to fork out more than a vase or figurine was worth to someone who'd make it look right after a disaster with a duster or a family pet. And that someone would be me. So these days if I found a job fiddly or tedious, I'd mark it down as part of my apprenticeship — we didn't call it that, but that was what it was.

Today's job was repairing a Worcester figurine using plastic modelling clay. I was shaping a tiny hand — you get the proportions right by studying your own hand. Once you've done that, you can use a pair of callipers to make sure the new one matches the intact one. If they've both broken off — poor Venus de Milo isn't the only woman with problems — then you have to remember that a hand is a little shorter from finger to wrist than the face from brow to chin. And it takes two hands to cover the whole face. Easy. OK, it's easier on crude Staffordshire figures, but not so satisfying.

I'd almost finished rubbing down any roughness between the fingers when Griff came in, popping a cup of tea on my worktable.

'Another nice day,' he declared. 'And the forecast's good. I think we'll go to Oxford for this Thursday's fair.'

'But it's mainly a craft fair. And you don't like craft fairs.' I found them useful because they often included a stall selling specialist paint brushes — I like best quality sable 00's for this type of work — but our sales never really justified the trip.

'All the same,' he said, picking up my tea and drinking it before drifting away. At least he took the cup, too. Cup, not mug. Cup complete with saucer. Typical 1920s, nothing special, but pretty.

* * *

There was no question of my arguing or letting Griff go off on his own on the grounds that I'd be more useful either in the shop or at home working on china. I'd seen his driving, and I'd seen Oxford traffic. For better or worse I had to go. It would have made him very unhappy if he'd known I'd turned down a drink with a lad from the village to go with him so I said nothing. To be honest, I was quite glad of the excuse. What would a girl like me have to say to a bloke who was well on the way to being a psychologist? Not a lot, except as a subject for his research or as a guinea pig. And I didn't think I wanted to be either. At least the Marcuses of this world took me at face value. Took me, or to be more accurate, left me. On what Griff was desperate not to call the shelf.

We went up on Wednesday evening, staying overnight with more of Griff's friends. Not being very tall I was happy to fetch up on the sofa, where I was joined by a cat like a feline teddy bear, the sort of bear that pushes its bedmate on to the floor, not the other way round. So I was a mite grumpy and surprisingly stiff when we set out, the cat smiling graciously and waving a Queen-like paw in farewell. We were heading for Gloucester Green, just by the coach station, so at least I could follow signposts and didn't have to rely on Griff's map reading.

It didn't take long to set up.

'There,' he said, standing back to admire our handiwork, 'we may be nearer the bric-a-brac end of the range than I like, but horses for courses, Lina. Always remember that: horses for courses.'

I nodded at his sage advice. OK, I'd heard it a hundred times before, but it would upset him if I told him I had. And he had enough to upset him. It was another slow day. Very slow. And because it was focused on crafts, not many of our mates were there to talk to. I drifted off to do some shopping, but it didn't take me long to buy the brushes and gold leaf I needed.

'Now,' Griff said, handing me the Thermos as I returned, 'there's no point in both of us hanging round like spare dinners. Off you go to the Bodleian.'

'The Bodleian?' I repeated, sounding stupid even to my own ears.

'The Bodleian Library. They have a copy of *Natura Rerum*.'

'How do you know?'

Looking horribly smug and patronising, he touched the side of his nose.

Think anger management. I breathed out hard and remembered I really needed the answer to something else. 'You mean you can just go in and ask for it?' That was better.

But it wasn't — I'd somehow upset Griff. He flushed and looked at his feet. 'I should imagine they won't just point to a shelf and tell you to take a look. Oh, there'll be some sort of system, dear heart, but don't ask me what it is. We poor Thespians had little need of scholarship in my day: you didn't need to study the *Folios* to act in weekly rep.'

So he'd never been in the place. And if the thought made him feel nervous, you can imagine how I felt.

'Go on. It's only five minutes away. Straight down George Street and into Broad Street. Can't miss it. Go on. Before we have a rush!' He gestured grandly at the empty aisles.

I nearly wet myself with anxiety. 'But—'

'But me no buts! Away!'

I didn't know what it was with me and Oxford and Cambridge. I'd done fairs at posh hotels and at provincial universities, and no one had treated me as a sub-human. But these grand buildings, honey-coloured in the May sunlight, both terrified me and filled me with resentment. They said that they were for clever, witty people who knew about things I could never hope to imagine, let alone understand. They said that they were for people who spoke with no trace of accent, who could be relied on to use the correct cutlery (didn't they say grace in Latin, for goodness' sake?) and who would go on to hold the top jobs as if by right. Their sort of people could buy and sell my sort of person and not notice the small change.

But I was resentful too. Why didn't the schools I attended send pupils here? Why should they be denied because they only had one parent and mostly didn't eat breakfast or any other proper food and went to schools with rowdy kids and frightened teachers and leaking roofs?

I was well into my political speech — in my head, you understand — when I was nearly run over by an old trout on a bike. Actually, she wasn't that old. But she was dressed like a bag-woman, hair in a bun that hadn't been fashionable for forty years, if then, clothes such unpleasant greens and tans you couldn't imagine anyone dyeing fabric those colours, let alone making them into complete garments and selling them in shops.

Oh, dear. I sounded more like Griff every day. And I'd got so worked up I'd walked straight past the entrance to the Bodleian. It felt like an omen. But I couldn't walk back to Griff and say

I'd chickened out. Straightening my shoulders, I strode in as if I owned the place.

It didn't last, of course, the courage. It melted away like ice in the microwave as my strides dwindled to a halt by the enquiry desk.

I was spoken to — not greeted — by a clone of the woman on the bike, except this one wore immaculate black and white. 'Yes?'

'I wish to see *Natura Rerum*. By a Gentleman. 1589.' I was gabbling so fast by the time I gave the date I doubt if she understood me. I started again, trying to breathe. 'It's a rare book. I understand you've got a copy. I'd like to see it.'

'On what grounds?'

'Sorry?'

'On what grounds?' she repeated, mouthing as if I was deaf.

At last I worked out that I had to have a reason. 'I just want to see it.'

'On what *academic* grounds?'

I wasn't going to tell her that I wanted to see if its frontispiece matched mine. 'Pure interest,' I ventured.

'This is a research library. We cater for scholars only. *Bona fide* scholars only,' she enunciated again, but with a little smile that said that I wouldn't know what *bona fide* meant.

'I may not be a *bona fide* academic,' I said, producing one of our business cards, 'but I am a genuine antiques dealer and would like to see the book.'

'Volume,' she corrected me. 'Anyone wishing to use the premises or any of our volumes has to present a written application, supported by academic references. Unless, of course, you are a student of the University.' She flipped the card on to the counter. I'd already proved I didn't qualify, hadn't I?

By now there was a little knot of interested spectators. Some were no doubt simply going to pay an entrance fee and gawp, like I'd done at the *Book of Kells* when Griff had taken me to Dublin for his birthday. That was in another posh university library, oozing pride in itself. Others were fidgeting files and looking at their watches: *bona fide* students, no doubt. They looked young and vulnerable, just like I felt, perhaps because they were swotting for exams or something. I'd better not hold them up. Flashing them a vague smile they could interpret as apologetic or wistful, I turned on my heel and walked away. I should have said something sarcastic to the woman on the desk, maybe, but I was afraid if I said another word I'd disgrace myself by bursting into tears. Either that or I'd shower her with some of the words I had learned at school — mostly in the playground.

The last person in the queue touched my arm. It was a girl with a jumper identical to mine. 'Don't take any notice of her. There's a quite a decent guy on duty after lunch — you might try talking to him.' She had a nice Bradford accent. Perhaps those buildings had misled me.

But a glance over my shoulder told me they hadn't. Impervious to the anxious students, the librarian was peering at me, following my progress out of her domain.

'I really feel I should apologise on behalf of the University,' said another soft voice. This was male, and belonged to a man of about forty, wearing jeans, a Next sweatshirt and non-designer trainers. 'There must be a way round your problem,' he added, running his hand across an almost bald head, what was left of his unattractively greasy hair curling over his collar. 'Have you got time for a coffee? There's quite a good place round the corner. Not too noisy.'

He didn't look like a white slave trader and I needed a double espresso. I only hoped I wouldn't slop any of the precious liquid, my hands were shaking so much.

He smiled reassuringly as he set the two cups down and sat opposite me. 'Perhaps I'd better introduce myself,' he said. 'Dan Freeman. I teach . . . Er, at Keble.'

CHAPTER SIX

It seemed that Keble wasn't a place but a college, and not just any college but one of those making up Oxford University. But Dan didn't seem to think any the worse of me for not knowing.

'The trouble is, if you've lived all your adult life in a place, you assume everyone knows it as well as you do. And that everyone knows the rules as well as you do. Though it must be said that some of them are pretty arcane. Er, that's to say, weird,' he added, in case I didn't understand the word.

'Such as?' I prompted. I wouldn't have known it if Griff hadn't taken me in hand.

'Well, take the Bodleian. Originally it was called Duke Humphrey's Library, by the way, because it was he who was a major influence on it. Humphrey, Duke of Gloucester, was the brother of Henry VI. The part he built is still there — it dates from 1426. But the whole thing became known as the Bodleian when it was refounded in 1602 by one Thomas Bodley, who was a very rare bird, a wealthy scholar.'

'So what's arcane about its rules?'

'Two things, I suppose. One is that every single book published in the UK has to be deposited there.'

'They must have lot of storage space,' I said dryly. I wasn't too sure about this potted guidebook history. Worse, I didn't know why I wasn't sure. Perhaps it was so pat; perhaps it was because I didn't really like his voice, which, compared with Griff's orotund delivery (yes, his words, not mine), was thin and papery.

Dan looked nonplussed, continuing, 'The second thing is that the guy in charge is forbidden to marry.'

I'm not sure what response he expected, but whatever it was, it wasn't the one I gave, which was a snort of laughter. 'From what you read in the papers, some dons here wouldn't find that rule hard to observe!'

'It depends what papers,' he said coldly. 'The gutter press has always had it in for Oxford.'

Before my eyes he was changing into a clone of the librarian, his skin drying into wrinkles, his greyish eyes hiding behind bifocals. It was if someone had rubbed him out, and forgotten to colour him in again.

Apologise or press on? In the best imitation I could manage of Griff's superior tone, I said, 'Foreign powers' espionage networks have never found it hard to recruit gay dons from Oxbridge to spy for them.'

I loved his double take. While he was recovering, I asked, 'So whereabouts is Keble? Have I passed it this morning? I came from the coach station,' I added innocently. Well, the market was only what Iris called a good sneeze away.

'No. It's out by the Parks,' he said, as if that was miles away. It wasn't. Last time we'd been up, Griff and I had walked there to look at the dodo in some Victorian-built museum with lovely cast-iron pillars supporting the roof. Griff didn't walk anywhere if it took longer than half an hour there and back, and since he wasn't exactly a marathon runner that meant not far.

By now I was wondering what Dan's game was. At first, I'd thought he really was embarrassed by the way the librarian had treated me. Now I wasn't so sure. I'd sunk the coffee and would have died for some food, but I didn't have enough cash on me to treat him and I certainly didn't want to ask him for anything else.

'What was it you wanted to see in the library?' he asked, and took a sip from what I was sure was an empty cup, as if he wanted the question to sound casual.

'Just some old book I read about on the Internet,' I said. Griff was always checking out dealers' and other websites, so that sounded a reasonable explanation.

'You seemed quite upset when she wouldn't let you see it.'

'I don't like snobs,' I said roundly. Funnily enough, it was the thought of Mrs Hatch that made me add, 'Social or intellectual snobs.' I felt her pat me firmly on the back. I might build an empire yet.

'Will you make another attempt?'

'My motto's always been, *Nil illegitimi carborundum*,' I said, blithely quoting one of Griff's mates, a man who made Julian Clary look shy and retiring. *Don't let the bastards grind you down* was his rough translation of what Griff assured me was even rougher Latin.

Dan's eyebrows flew upwards.

'But I clearly need some form of ID,' I added, getting back to the matter in hand.

'Maybe I could help there,' he said.

Why should he offer? When gift horses turned up as easily as this, I wanted to have a good peer round their mouths. On the other hand, what did I have to lose? 'How?'

'I could write a letter of support on college headed notepaper, telling them you were a scholar from — say — America researching—'

I shook my head. 'Not America. There are copies of — the book I want to see in libraries over there. And I'm not too hot at the accent. Australia?'

'Why not? Any particular university?' There was an edge to his voice I couldn't place.

I produced the innocent beam I use on punters who are dithering between two items. 'You choose. Preferably an obscure one.'

'I don't know any,' he bleated.

'Internet,' I said crisply. 'I bet they're all listed there. With course details.' But why did he want to help me if he was going to baulk at the first difficulty? I had to sit on my hands to stop scratching my head. He didn't give the impression he wanted to get off with me, and if he suddenly tried, I'd deal with him like I'd dealt with propositions from no-hopers in bus-shelters or sleazy bastards like Ralph Harper.

What if that meant I didn't get to see my book?

He flicked a glance at his watch, the sort of black plastic affair usually worn by spotty, skateboarding youths. 'Why don't I go and invent a CV for you and meet you here — say, three-ish? If we leave it that late that old trout will be off duty and her replacement is certainly more approachable.'

Since the girl who'd been nice to me had said the same, I nodded happily. 'But I'm putting you to a lot of trouble. Why don't I just come along with you? There's no need for you to make a double journey.'

'Another arcane rule — no women in our rooms,' he said.

Which struck me as odd, all the things I'd heard about student life considered. However, if I'd never even heard of his college, I could scarcely argue. Not if I wanted his magic Open Sesame letter.

* * *

'So we're meeting up after lunch,' I told Griff, passing him a sandwich.

'This sounds like love at first sight. Though that's more commonly supposed to be mutual.'

I shook my head emphatically. I wasn't exactly head over heels with the gorgeous Marcus, and this guy wasn't in the same league. Not even in the same game.

'Why's he being so chivalrous?' he asked, narrowing his eyes.

'I've been wondering about that myself. Yes, I even asked him point blank.'

Griff nodded his approval.

'When I pressed him he said it was because he liked bugging the system. He'd been in the Socialist Workers when he was young and still hated authority even though he was authority himself, now.'

Griff weighed the idea. 'Not entirely implausible. And you've got your mobile phone in case he misbehaves. But you're not happy, are you, dear heart?'

'Not a hundred per cent,' I admitted. 'But there's no way I can see *Natura Rerum* without special pleading, and his is as special as I'm likely to get. Come on, Griff: remember what Iris always says? *Faint heart—*'

'*—never won fair lady*,' he concluded. 'But you have to look convincing too — more like a *Clerke at Oxenford*, if I remember my Chaucer right.'

I gaped. 'You don't mean I have to wear a gown!'

'I think they only wear them on special occasions or for lectures. And if you're claiming to come from the Antipodes, then you're scarcely likely to have tucked one into your backpack. No, I meant things like a file and writing implements — though I'm sure these will be taken from you if you penetrate the *sancta sanctorum*. Oh, the most sacred place of all — where they keep rare books!' he explained pettishly. 'The magnifying glass presents no problems, at least.' He produced the one we always keep handy. 'And although I could be accused of over-egging the pudding, a pair of spectacles.'

'Dan'll know I wasn't wearing specs this morning.'

'Well, tell him your contact lenses started to hurt — or even that you didn't want anyone to recognise you after this morning's debacle. The truth's often useful. Now, before you bleat you can't afford glasses, look what I came upon this morning, in the midst of what I can only refer to as debris.' He dug in his jacket pocket and came out with a spectacle case. 'Nothing special, I know, but I got it for peanuts.'

It was a slender case, black-japanned papier mâché and mother-of-pearl. I crowed, 'We can sell that for thirty pounds at least! It's just right for that woman from Birmingham — I don't think she's got that particular design'

'In that case you'll be able to mark it up a little more. Say thirty-seven. But look inside!'

I flipped the end. What would add even more to a devoted collector was that the original specs were still there. It always gave me a funny feeling, sad that someone had died and that even their most intimate possessions had been sold, and yet pleased to be handling something that connected me closely to them. Griff, who needed reading glasses himself, often found he could wear pairs a hundred, even two hundred years old. I'd never managed to myself, because, though I say it as shouldn't, as Iris would say, my sight's perfect. All the same, I couldn't resist doing what I always did — I tried them on. And could see, if in a rather foggy way. If I perched them on the end of my nose, as Griff always did with his reading glasses, so he could look over them, there wasn't a problem anyway.

'Excellent,' I confirmed. 'What do I look like?'

'A bit like a female Harry Potter. You really will have to get that mop of yours trimmed, dear heart. Preferably by someone other than that village damsel who seems to regard a pudding basin as an adjunct to coiffeur. Next time you make a big sale—'

'I shall pay back every penny you lent me. OK? And then I'll think about my hair.'

'So long as you can still see under the fringe well enough to know whether it's night or day — not to mention to do your restoration work. At least we should be hearing from my WSPU contact soon. It's name-your-price time — lovely!' He rubbed his paws in glee. 'And then I think a celebratory visit to an expert cutter is called for. A trendy chain in Maidstone or Ashford, perhaps — unless you want to go wild and pay Tenterden prices?'

In your dreams, Griff. But he had Aidan, his special friend, over there, and I always tried to find some excuse to leave them alone a few hours. We'd see. Meanwhile he was right, of course — the fringe was a nuisance when I was doing close work. I'd toyed with the idea of simply taking the scissors to it myself, but that would have upset him even more.

I was half expecting Dan Freeman not to be there when I presented myself outside the Bodleian at three. But he was already waiting, pacing as anxiously as if he were expecting his best girl. As I lurked, once more wondering about his motives, he even checked that horrible watch a couple of times in two minutes. When I sauntered up, I'm surprised his sigh of relief didn't blow the place down. Don't tell me he really had fallen for me. No. I'd been too inconsistent for anyone to relate to: if I'd been even thinking about chatting up someone like me, I'd have backed away sharply.

His smile nearly split his face. Why didn't he treat himself to some nice manly moisturiser? It wasn't as though it wasn't advertised almost as widely as women's. And if he was a teacher, surely he could afford it. Unless he spent all his money on books.

Books!

At this point an alarm bell went off in my head. I switched it off. For a start, I hadn't told him what book I wanted to see. Secondly, even if he knew and even if he managed to wangle a look too, he still wouldn't have a clue why I wanted to see it. I'd better make sure it stayed that way. Or had I? I was so desperate I wasn't making sense of anything. But I'd better have some reason to offer if — more likely when — he got round to asking me again.

He passed me an envelope — used. Instead of simply crossing through the address, he'd torn off an address label. So while I couldn't confirm who he was, it looked as if he wasn't a specially trusting guy either. The envelope contained the new Evelina Townend. Although I was British born, with nine GCSEs and four A Levels (at this point I had to hold my mouth to stop laughing aloud), I'd taken a gap year in Australia, where I'd decided to remain to take a degree in English at the University of — wait for it! — Wollongong. Well, that sounded Australian enough to me. I was now a post-graduate student of bibliography, with a special interest in late sixteenth-century non-textual embellishment. Was I, indeed? Dan's letter heading said so — he'd invented a Wollongong one rather than using Keble's. The reception staff seemed to think both the letter and my CV were OK, so after a series of questions that almost included my shoe size and my blood group I was shown to a small waiting area. But Dan wasn't. It seemed even a university lecturer needed more than a passing interest to have a gawp at such rare tomes. At last I was ushered into a dimly lit room and provided with a pair of cotton gloves. The leather binding rang no bells, as the librarian, also gloved, opened the book, supporting the front cover on a block. But then she opened it to the frontispiece. That rang a whole peal of bells in all sorts of complicated changes. Oh, yes. That was my frontispiece. I bent to smell it.

Suddenly I was standing in a patch of sunlight. It was warm, warm enough to feel in a room that was otherwise chilly. There was a small fire. The grate it hid in was very large, whitish-grey marble, with a set of firedogs that screamed for some polish. There was a big desk, covered with papers and newspapers and dirty plates. On all the chairs — and there were a lot of them — was more rubbish.

I scanned it now. Gardening gloves. More newspapers. Piles of old orange-and-white and green-and-white Penguins. Bottles. Where were the people in all this? I could hear but not see them. They were having a row, no doubt about that. I was supposed to be looking at the big book, to keep my mind off them.

Someone was coughing. But that was now, in this tiny, underlit room.

The young woman who'd admitted me.

I looked up and lost the other room and the sunlight. 'Yes?'

'Are you all right?'

'Fine.' I thought that was what she might want me to say. 'It's overwhelming, isn't it, touching a book this old. So very rare . . .' I shifted the fixed magnifying glass they'd provided: yes, I'd had to surrender everything else, as Griff had predicted.

'I'm afraid I can only allow you another couple of minutes. With books this rare even low levels of light are hazardous.'

'Please — this is my dream.' I held up my hand for silence, as if in the presence of something sacred. But even though my heart was almost overwhelmed with emotion, I must use my eyes. Must. Was my frontispiece the same as this? Exactly the same?

'Don't you wish to see the rest of the volume?'

I supposed I'd better. But it was she who opened it, not me, supporting it tenderly with her free hand.

'It's really the frontispiece that's most relevant,' I managed, grasping at words I never usually used. It was as if Griff's hand was holding me up. 'I don't suppose it was ever transferred to computer?' Maybe not the right lingo, but she'd surely know what I meant.

'I think maybe Harvard have photographed theirs. It's certainly not in our system. Look, you really have had more than your ration, you know.' She closed the book firmly. 'You must leave now. You can collect your belongings . . .'

* * *

Unfortunately while I was good at dissembling, I didn't cope well with direct questions. And I was so spooked when I emerged into the bright sun of Oxford that I'd probably have confessed to being a serial killer if asked nicely. That's my excuse for being so unguarded when Dan shook me by the arm and asked if I was all right. 'You look as if you've seen a ghost,' he added.

'I ha— could use another coffee,' I gasped, hoping he wouldn't notice the hesitation. Griff had slipped me a few pound coins so at least I could add, 'My shout this time.'

He didn't argue, and we walked in silence to the place we'd been that morning.

'Well?' Dan prompted, as I carried the cups back to our table.

'Well, thanks to your letter, I managed to get in and I saw the volume I wanted,' I said, glad to hear that my voice was returning to normal.

'Good,' he said. 'I'm glad to have been of use.' He cocked his head to one side, obviously asking a question.

I'd better try to buy time till the caffeine had pulled my head was completely back together. 'Such a palaver. Do you have to go through that every time you want to use books?'

'Members of the university are allowed more freedom,' he said, as cagey as me. 'But we all had to be vetted before we were allowed to borrow or use the reading rooms.'

I nodded. I couldn't think of anything I particularly wanted to say. But emotion always makes me hungry, so, on my feet again, I offered to get him some cake. Perhaps some Death by Chocolate would restore my brain a bit. Maybe I wouldn't care if it didn't.

We ploughed through our enormous portions — we ought to have shared one, but that seemed altogether too friendly too fast — without saying much. In fact, I had a distinct feeling that he wanted to get away from me as much as I wanted to get away from him. So that we didn't sit in complete silence, I asked him about his teaching and whether university students were as hard work as schoolchildren were supposed to be — and were, if my experience was anything to go by. He talked a bit about under-funding, which was something I was an expert on, in personal terms at least. At last, without a single direct question, he looked at his watch, made a token offer to pay, and got to his feet. I was so amazed I nearly blurted out the whole lot to him. Instead, I simply thanked him very much for his help, and hoped he hadn't been put to too much trouble. Then, since Griff had told me that the gesture never came amiss, I stood up and kissed him lightly on the cheek. Amiss it might not have been, but it wasn't welcome. Perhaps he was deeply committed to a relationship or the sort of gay who didn't like female contact. It would have been good to have Griff with me to check him out. At any rate, he swallowed a couple of times, muttering things about hoping to see me again someday but making no effort to make it happen, and bolted.

I had a fair idea that Griff wouldn't be overwhelmed with customers, so I started with the next move in my search for my father. I needed a bookshop. There had to be bookshops in Oxford! Yes, I'd seen a big one, opposite the Bodleian. Blackwell's. They wouldn't have the hang-ups of the library about letting in a non-student. But they'd probably have preferred me to buy books than prop up a shelf looking at them, especially as they were big, glossy ones. The fireplace I'd remembered earlier that afternoon was too big for an ordinary house, the furniture on too grand a scale. And in any case your ordinary semi wouldn't run to a copy of *Natura Rerum* on its shelves. So I leafed through as many guide-books, including one to Oxford itself, and coffee table books as I could, desperate for a clue.

I was so engrossed I didn't realise it was my mobile that was ringing until an irritable assistant nudged me. Griff, of course: was I all right?

'Fine. Still doing a spot of research,' I said.

'So long as you're all right. But remember the Oxford rush hour,' he said, ringing off.

Once driven, never forgotten. So I replaced my last book and was on my way. Only to see Dan Freeman just across the street. I was about to yell and wave — he had been uncommonly generous, after all, giving his time and asking no questions — when I saw him turn and wave to someone else. No, he hadn't needed to ask me anything. He was waving to the young woman now running towards him. The young woman who'd shown me *Natura Rerum*.

CHAPTER SEVEN

'All that this Dan character and the rule-bound librarian know, dear heart, is that you were interested in *Natura Rerum*. They couldn't have known why. And for the life of me I can't see how that knowledge will benefit them. Can you?'

I stared at the brake lights of the car in front. I'd been staring at them for five minutes. Why hadn't the driver slipped into neutral and used his handbrake? Better still, cut the engine? It was my generation and the next one that would be picking up the tab for all these thoughtless emissions. Why didn't I get out and sock him? Or stuff something up his nasty polluting exhaust pipe?

At least he'd given me a reason to feel angry. I hadn't had one before, but I was seething all the same. And I didn't know why. Or perhaps it wasn't anger. One of my various social workers had pointed out to me that I wasn't very good at identifying and labelling my feelings — as if that would have made them easier to deal with.

'No,' I replied eventually. 'But that doesn't mean it won't. People don't do what he did without a reason. Not unless they're exceptionally warm, kind people and he never gave that impression. Oh, sugar!' I smacked both hands down on the wheel. Then I realised it was well after six, after all, so I could have sworn all I wanted.

Griff coughed. 'Jane Austen would have despatched her protagonists — that's the literary term for hero or heroine, dear heart, and as such should be committed to memory — to their bedchamber for a period of solitude and quiet reflection. Much as I would suggest you needed the same, I'm afraid your bedchamber is many hours away.'

I nodded. The M25 had done its worst, and we were trapped in the middle lane, knowing, thanks to the overhead gantry, that there was an accident at the next junction. That was six miles away. After that we had another fifty before we reached Bredeham.

Griff switched on the radio, not to Classic FM, which I was getting used to and even enjoying sometimes, but to Radio Three. In a way it made sense, because BBC local radio traffic reports cut into whatever it was playing at the time. Actually it made it worse to have no fewer than four successive cheery voices from different stations telling us we were well and truly stuck — which we knew already.

Griff did what I knew he'd do. He folded his arms, dropped his chin on his chest and fell asleep. When Radio Three started to talk full time, I flipped back to Classic FM, so he'd stay nicely soothed. One of us needed to be calm and refreshed.

I ought to be over the moon. I wasn't. For a start, I was still puzzled. Why should a man who seemed to be some bigwig in the University — even a lowlife like me had heard of fellows and professors — bother with me? Only seemed to be a bigwig, of course. Freeman had never actually come out and said what he was. Perhaps he wasn't a lecturer at all. All that stuff about the Bodleian — it was all in that guidebook I'd flicked through in Blackwell's. Anyone could have mugged it up and spun it out as their own knowledge. He'd never said anything about himself I could check up on and had made sure I hadn't seen where he said he was based. Why hadn't I used the sense I was born with and followed him? Answer: I hadn't been born with very much.

Going back over the day didn't help much. The snotty librarian had snubbed me so loudly that one of the girls in the queue had overheard enough to speak kindly to me. But she hadn't repeated the name of the book I was after — had she? If she had, with her penetrating tones, every last person in Oxford would have known what I wanted.

Freeman hadn't mentioned the name of the book at any time. No, not all day. Not even after I'd seen it. Yet I'd been visibly shaken. It would have been the most natural thing in the world to ask which book had upset me. Not to mention why. Griff would have said it was stupid, thick-skinned men from Mars stuff, and that there was nothing sinister. But having seen him with the librarian who'd escorted me — no, I wasn't buying innocent explanations. Why, if he'd known such a responsible person, hadn't he simply barged in at the outset, towing me along behind him, and said, 'This woman's harmless: why not show her the book'? Or phoned her or whatever.

Even Classic FM was talking about the M25 crash now in the seven o'clock bulletin. Seven was the time Griff poured our first official drink of the day and sat us both down to relax. Not today. Not that Griff wasn't relaxed. He was still asleep, snoring so hard that from time to time he'd wake himself up and shuffle in the seat to make himself more comfortable. Then off he'd drift once more.

I found some mints and chomped.

The young woman who'd shown me *Natura Rerum* had seemed pukka enough. She'd had an ID clipped to her jumper. But she'd not asked the questions I'd have asked, just in an ice-breaking sort of way. 'What are you researching on now? What are you going to do when you've finished?'

No. I wouldn't count that against her. She must see hundreds of researchers a month, proper researchers who'd pour out the story of their student loans and top-up fees and debts and how they'd need to get a top-earning job to pay everything off. That's if they were anything like the odd students who dropped into our shop to see if we'd got any part-time work to offer. Earlier in the year one optimist had offered to catalogue all our books, which Griff sometimes got lumbered with at house sales. The old fox had insisted they were already categorised: 'Those we can sell, darling, and those we take to the Oxfam shop.'

We'd had other students telling us in great detail about their theses. So perhaps the Ice Maiden had been sensible not to engage in conversation.

But they had known each other, she and Dan Freeman. They had known each other. And deep inside, just as I'd always known when I was simply being passed from pillar to post as a child, I knew I was being taken for a mug. I was being used. And I was very angry. And something else too. Was I afraid?

I was certainly confused. After all my lip chewing and head-scratching, all I could come up with was a very feeble theory. There were always rumours floating round the antiques world about what was coming on to the market and what mustn't be touched because it was hot. Had the academic world a similar grapevine? Was there a rumour that there was another copy of *Natura Rerum* around and everyone was trying to find it? That might make sense. After all, academics went to antiques fairs and might have seen my frontispiece. If, of course, my copy was a fake, they might have seen other frontispieces.

And they knew I was a dealer. At least the snotty librarian did. I'd only been and given her my business card. It was a good job Griff was asleep — he wouldn't have liked the words I said not entirely under my breath.

Yes, I was definitely afraid. And even more angry.

Thank goodness the traffic was almost stationary: in a paddy like this I could have been lethal at sixty miles an hour.

Calm down, Lina. Just breathe — though God knows what's in the stuff that passes for air in a jam like this — and listen to the radio.

It began to work. I could think of a plus side, just about.

Yes, I reminded myself, as at long last the car in front inched forward, I had seen *Natura Rerum*. Seen it; touched it, even if that was through cotton gloves; knew it was real. And I'd still got my own page and the memories it had conjured up. I'd cling to them. Maybe I'd get some more. Griff had always worried about my very poor memory, but one of his medical friends had suggested it might be because I had more to shut out than welcome in. Now Griff tried to give me what he called mental press-ups, little exercises in remembering, like learning new words like 'protagonist', and I was getting better. Slowly. The rate I was going I was sometimes afraid that by the time I'd got proper recall I'd be old enough to be losing my marbles anyway. But I'd never told Griff that. Protagonist. There. I'd remembered it.

Way along the motorway, someone pulled out a giant plug. We started to move, first at five miles an hour, then at ten. And it wasn't all that long before we were doing a merry forty, and the lither cars sixty and more.

I didn't want to wake Griff but I needed a loo, and Clacket Lane services called.

What with one thing and another I was almost staggering I was so tired. I floated the idea of a cup of tea while we had the chance.

'Tea? The muck they serve in places like this? My dear Lina, what have I done to deserve that?'

'Coffee then?'

'Even fouler. Think what awaits us at home!'

I stomped in silence back to the van.

Catching up with me, Griff coughed. 'If you'd rather I drove—'

Griff insisted that his driving had flair. His afternoon tea had involved a fair drop of gin or whisky with some of our colleagues, so goodness knows how creative that would have made his attitude to other road users. I shook my head firmly.

'The thing is,' I continued, waiting for a gap in the traffic to slide into, 'that at least I've got a bit more memory back.' The break had perked me up, after all. 'Maybe if we go through some books together I shall recognise the type of window I saw, perhaps even the fireplace. And you'll know what period they are and be able to point me in the direction of some houses.'

'Point you in the direction! What do you propose to do then? March up to the front door and ask to see the study?'

'Yes. Well, no. Not exactly. There's loads of stately homes open to the public, aren't there? So I shall tour round and see if anything else strikes a chord.'

He was silent for a bit, as I pulled out into the middle lane. The M25 would shortly be splitting in two: we needed the right-hand fork for the M26. 'We'll be able to rule some of them out,' he said, once the manoeuvre was complete. 'You need to start with those that have the original family still living there — tucked away out of Joe Public's sight, of course, but still there. There's no point in trying those that no longer have families living in them—'

'We can leave them till last,' I agreed. 'When all else has failed. After all, there's no knowing my dad'll still be living where I saw him.' Or still be alive. But I didn't even want to think about that possibility. 'He might have had to sell up. But there'd still be some sort of record.'

Even to my own ears I sounded hopeful rather than sure. To Griff's — well, who could tell? He pulled his cap over his eyes and pretended to be asleep again, a sign he knew he couldn't win an argument.

* * *

It wasn't me who finally won it, but my WSPU ring. Griff's contact was so pleased with it she forked out fifteen hundred pounds without blinking. You always wish you'd asked for more, of course, but while it was fair — indeed, vital — to be greedy with strangers, Griff said, you should be more charitable with friends. In any case, wasn't the mark-up good enough? Fifteen to fifteen hundred?

I won't say Griff took me by the hand and led me to the bank to stow it all safely, but he would have been so upset if I'd blown the lot that I had to be sensible. First I repaid him; but since he insisted on opening a new account for what he called our joint venture capital, it was hardly repaying. Then I had my hair cut, ending up as today or even tomorrow as Mastercutters of Tenterden could make me, even though Griff might have preferred yesterday or even three weeks ago.

Then Griff took me shopping. 'You never know,' he said darkly, 'when you'll need to look the part.' He never specified what part. So we spent a morning at a big shopping mall near Ashford called the Outlet. Griff might make all the sewage jokes he liked — he always called it the Cloaca, for instance — but it did good deals on a lot of things. It didn't need Griff to tell me that the trouser suit I found looked good, but it was he who picked out a shirt that really set it off and rooted round till he'd come up with a lovely pair of boots.

Lastly I bought what I considered a real investment: a year's National Trust membership. If I was going to tool round all these historic piles, I was going to do it on the cheap. And even if I didn't find my father, I'd at least have had what Griff called a good visual education.

I also joined the mobile library. It'd certainly be cheaper to borrow all those books of photographs than to try to buy them, and the driver/librarian was so helpful I knew it was my duty to keep the service on the road: if it weren't used regularly some bright spark on the council — maybe our no streetlights, no washing on the line on Sundays man — would axe it in the interests of economy.

I fretted. I wanted to be out there straight away, that instant, dashing from place to place. But I couldn't, and didn't even mention it because we had a little trouble at the shop. Nothing serious. No reappearance of Mrs Hatch's bogus asylum seekers, whom Tony's colleagues had, they claimed, checked out and found no sign of. This was a dear little old lady popping in and putting her bag down in a very obvious place while she picked over stock. Next thing she's accusing Mrs Hatch of lifting her purse. Outraged, Mrs Hatch calls the police, only to have the little old lady in tears because she's now found the purse and isn't she silly? Not so silly she hasn't managed to stow in her clothes half a dozen Georgian silver spoons and a couple of other small but expensive items. That's how silly. By the time Mrs Hatch discovers all this, the police have actually run the old dear home. Except it isn't her home, as the police, who, rather red about the face, discover when they go back.

Tony Baker was as glum as if it was all his fault when he called round to return our videotape.

'Sorry it's taken so long,' he said, sitting on the floor and stretching his legs in front of him. They were extremely long, and, as I knew from our gate vaulting, nicely shaped, as was his bum. 'The bloke who's a real expert on these things was off sick, and there was a huge backlog of public order tapes he had to work through before he got to yours. You know how it is: kids drunk out of their skulls picking fights with lampposts.'

'And what did this bloke find?' Griff asked, topping up — or, as he put it, refreshing — their whiskies.

I sipped my wine. If Tony thought bright-red alcopops uncool, then I'd aim for a bit more sophisticated. I'd rather this hadn't been a rather girlie pink, but Griff had promised me that rosé was coming back into fashion as a summer evening drink.

'Absolutely nothing. Just these people in black with their hoods up. One might have been a woman, but there's no saying. Have to wait till they try again, won't we?' he added, winking at me.

We managed hollow laughs. Mrs Hatch was now so rattled that she was threatening to leave.

'Nothing as coarse as handing in her notice, you understand, Tony,' Griff laughed. 'Mrs Hatch isn't an assistant, darling. She helps out.'

'Tax? National Insurance?' Tony looked as if he ought to sit up and make notes.

'Dear me, no, darling. Nothing so vulgar!'

Was it being called darling or a real sniff of wrong-doing that had got Tony almost upright?

'She slips items into the shop and sells them, having fallen into what I suppose you'd call genteel poverty. I value them at a vastly inflated price and because they're in a reputable shop and beautifully presented she makes a few pounds. Far more than if she took them to auction or asked a dealer to sell them. She gets to chat with some nice people—'

'Usually,' I put in.

'And she can save on heating bills. All the time she's providing a very respectable presence in my little emporium, and if anyone wants to buy any of my stock, takes their money. A wonderfully symbiotic relationship.' Without looking at me he leaned across to the bookshelves and passed me the dictionary. 'Hence no tax or NI. And hence problems for me if she goes. We'd have to pay someone at the going rate or close the shop on days we're away doing fairs. We're off to Harrogate for the weekend,' he added, 'so do, dear boy, keep an eye open for any burglars who may or may not be hermaphrodite.'

I'd returned the dictionary but now he passed it to me again. Symbiotic — that sounded like Griff and me. Hermaphrodite? Ah, a bit male and a bit female.

'I'll make sure there are regular patrols in the village—'

'You mean once a month instead of once a year. Darling, what a comfort.'

Tony muttered something about resources and manpower. But he added, chin up, 'And of course I'll pop round at the start and end of my shifts. Usually I change into and out of uniform at the station, but if you thought—'

'I'm positive a spot of blue serge about the place is just what the doctor ordered. The doctor and Mrs Hatch. Take my advice and tread warily — she's a very predatory lady.'

CHAPTER EIGHT

Next on our calendar was a big, three-day event at yet another agricultural showground — Harrogate. Like many of our colleagues, we'd spend the nights in caravans we'd towed up behind our vans. When it wasn't in use, ours lived on a farm on the outskirts of the village, Griff having views on the parking of caravans in front of people's houses as strong as our councillor's on Sunday Observance.

With great reluctance Griff had agreed to give me some time off if things got quiet: I'd logged two National Trust properties to check out, Beningbrough Hall and East Riddlesden Hall. I'd have liked a peep at Castle Howard, but though Griff thought all my dreams were pretty wild, even in the wildest ones I didn't imagine I'd come from there. In any case, I'd looked up the present owners on the Internet and there was no family resemblance between us at all.

Apart from rubbernecking at tourist sites, I had another plan. Copeland would almost certainly be there, his maps of the South East replaced by ones of Yorkshire. Marcus would be painting away at his end of the stand, but even Marcus couldn't paint all evening as well as all day. He'd need a break and it was the least I could do to see he got one. The day's work over for us all, Griff would be seeking out old cronies who owed him a drink. I'd be left either watching the titchy little black-and-white TV that was all the caravan ran to, or, of course, reading. A drink, better still a meal, with Marcus would be much nicer. I'd seize a moment when Copeland had his back turned and suggest just that. I might imply a lot more than just that, even though I wasn't so keen on snogging him these days. Griff wouldn't like the idea of my using him, I knew that, but where I'd sprung from it was use or be used. I was pretty sure that it was Marcus' philosophy too, even though he had much less excuse than I did.

It wasn't Marcus who goosed me, though, just when I had my hands full of a Victorian Royal Worcester vase, heavily ornamented and laden with gilding. It was worth about eight hundred pounds — goodness knew why Griff had got hold of it, because he certainly hadn't been able to sell it. Every time he saw it he gave an exaggerated wince, saying it was too vulgar to piss in. Highly impractical too, at least for a woman. Not like those mini chamber pots eighteenth-century fashionable ladies used to resort to during extra-long sermons and so on. They looked like gravy boats without the pouring lip. In fact, I'd seen half a dozen in my time being sold as gravy boats. I'd also seen chamber pots sold as planters, which only goes to show.

I placed the vase very carefully on its display stand, even adjusting its spotlight, before I turned. Maybe waiting for a reaction would faze the assailant a bit. No, it wouldn't faze Titus Oates, showing awful teeth in a smelly leer. I'd have slapped the smarmy face grinning down at me if I'd been one for physical violence. No, it wasn't any particular moral objection. It was practicality. Strong I may be for my size, but some of the men I worked amongst were strong for their size too — which was a great deal bigger than mine. No doubt Titus had come to talk about my comment to Copeland. Even though I suppose I owed him an apology for slander, it would have been really satisfying to knee him in the groin and bloody his nose as it came down. But then, he was a good foot taller than me, with hands like hams, despite the delicacy of the work they produced. And it was his hands I was interested in at the moment.

And there they were, gone. They soon reappeared, clawing the air as he tried to scrabble upright. But Marcus was leaning over him, in the sort of pose that would have told the most casual observer that it was in Titus' interests to stay put. He reinforced the message by plonking a trainer-shod foot on Titus' chest.

'You don't do that to my woman. OK?' He shot his forefinger to within an inch of Titus' nose, straightened, and strode off.

'What a marvellous exit line,' Griff cooed. 'But does this mean you have something to tell me, Lina?'

'Not till we're alone,' I said out of the corner of my mouth.

'It was a very definitive statement. And gesture.' He held out a hand to help Titus to his feet. But he grunted that he could manage, which he did, stalking off with a stride that was intended to tell anyone interested that he could easily have had the better of the argument.

So should I be pleased that Marcus had done something so dramatic? It certainly seemed to settle in whose company I'd be spending the evening.

'Even given this new-found relationship with you, it was very brave of the young man,' Griff observed. 'It isn't just Titus he's offended, it's Copeland, too. Little cousin's supposed to do what the big boss man says, not strike off — literally — on his own.'

I nodded, but I'd rather have dealt with Titus myself, not least because Griff had probably been right to suggest I show him my frontispiece. It would take one master forger to know another, and a quick word from him might save me all these stately house explorations. Not that I wasn't looking forward to them — but I knew they were long shots. If I'd grovelled, not that I was keen to, especially after the goosing, I might have got instant information. Now it might have to be the sort of mega-grovel I wouldn't be at all keen on.

The neat figure of a security guard was strolling towards us. 'Bit of trouble, was there, miss?'

Griff didn't need to press my arm in warning.

I smiled, shaking my head. 'A bit of a lad thing. That's all.'

'Yes, dear boy — it's all done and dusted. But thank you so much for your interest — indeed your very presence makes us feel so beautifully protected.' From a girl, the eyelash fluttering would have been OTT. From Griff it made you want to giggle or spew, depending on your mood. It was the guard's battle-dress top that did it. Griff never could resist a man in the sort of uniform that showed a bum to perfection, especially when the uniform was bottle green.

The guy took no obvious notice, but walked slowly away with that sort of legs apart macho roll that's supposed to tell you that what's between the legs is irresistibly massive. The question was, who was he supposed to be attracting? Whoops: whom.

Griff gave his departing back a twiddle-fingered wave and then, as if nothing had happened, he returned to completing the set-up of the stall. A glance at my watch told me he was quite right. It was almost seven and the first batch of punters would be let in at eight, if they were prepared to pay a ten-pound premium for the privilege. Only an hour for horse-trading! I grabbed some of the house-sale items I'd cleaned up and set off on my rounds.

* * *

I was waiting in line for hot breakfast rolls — I'd made enough in half an hour to treat Griff and me — when Marcus came and stood beside me. Normally I'd have teased him about queue-jumping, but there were obviously more important things to talk about than how soon we'd all get served.

'Since when have I been your woman?' I asked. No point in beating about the bush.

'Since you asked me out for that drink and Copeland shoved his oar in. I felt really bad about that, Lina. I'm sorry. Look, how about tonight? A drink and a bite to eat? Go on.'

'I don't like leaving Griff on his own,' I said not quite truthfully. Fat chance of Griff being without a drinking crony or two, but I didn't want Marcus to think I was too eager.

'There's this really good pub I found last time I was here. Just down the road. There's a disco on tonight. Go on — why not?'

Griff called it playing *agent provocateur*. Or was it Devil's advocate? 'Copeland won't like it.'

'Copeland knows what he can do. You can tell him yourself if he starts moaning.'

I produced the sort of girlish giggle Griff would have been proud of. 'No, thanks!' I said. It wasn't as if I was proposing to end up in the sack with Marcus, though if Copeland was on the town too, I'd certainly suggest we went back to their caravan. No, no matter how much I might sometimes fancy Marcus — and just at the moment I wasn't at all sure I did — I had a quite different agenda from his. Sex wasn't on mine. Just a look through Copeland's filing system.

* * *

That afternoon there were far too many people milling round for me even to think about leaving Griff without help. We'd marked all the prices very clearly, but we also had a bottom-line price for people who haggled. This was marked both in code on a sticker and in a little exercise book, the sort you can get in Woolworths. So it should have been impossible to sell something for less than you paid. But occasionally, if Griff didn't eat enough lunch to blot up his gins, he might be too fuddled to remember what the letters stood for. That was when I stepped in. Today might just have been a liquid lunch day. So I sat him down with a sandwich and large cup of coffee and smiled sweetly and made money. A lot. If I looked across at Copeland's stall I saw far more of Marcus than usual, because he'd been roped in to sell and wrap. All around money was changing hands, at least if the full carrier bags were anything to go by. Were we still in the same country as the Detling fair, only a couple of weeks ago?

* * *

'That was a really good day, wasn't it?' Marcus remarked, digging into one of the White Lion's huge steaks as evidence. 'All those punters descending like locusts. We made a mint. How about you?'

I nodded, trying to work out where to start on my steak. I'd hesitated a minute before choosing it, because I reasoned I ought to go Dutch and steak never comes cheap. This one certainly didn't, but since it came with all the trimmings, plus a bowl of salad, I reasoned I'd be able to pass on the pudding and save a bit of cash that way. 'Good enough.' Griff hated me to talk about takings, or actually about money at all. There'd always be people richer than us and people poorer than us, and it was no one's business except the bank manager's. That's what he said. And to be honest, it wasn't one of my favourite topics because I still had a niggle of envy when I saw how much money people had to throw around. Even if it was sometimes in my direction. But I didn't want to snub Marcus. We'd had a bit of a snog on the walk over here — apart from his designer bristles he was a very good snog — and I wouldn't mind another later. So I'd better find something to say. 'What about your hand, though?' I pointed with my knife at his bruised and scuffed knuckles. Then I remembered you should never point with a knife. Or presumably a fork. I must ask Mrs Hatch. 'Didn't that trouble you?'

'Actually, you've no idea how I enjoyed flooring Oates. Bullying bastard.'

'But very good with his pen. A master.'

'A man does that to you and you call him a master!'

I thought for a minute he was going to push away from the table and leave me and the steak. But he didn't. Instead he jabbed at the chips as if they were Oates' eyes. 'He's a cheat and a liar and a — a sexual predator. And he ought to be in jail. And you let him put his hand—'

'I didn't let him!'

'You didn't stop him.'

'I was holding eight hundred quid's worth of vase!'

'But—'

'I suppose I could have sloshed him with it. It'd have to take a bit of explaining to the insurance people, though.' I risked a grin. Mistake.

He thrust his lower lip out, like a cross little boy. 'But you didn't do anything. Anything at all.'

I said more sharply than I meant, 'That didn't mean I wasn't going to.' It was the first time anyone had ever jumped in like that to my rescue, and though half of me was rather flattered, or I wouldn't be sitting opposite Marcus now, half of me would still have rather fought my own battles. Even battles with Titus Oates. I'm not sure how. I'd gone over and over it in my head. There was no doubt I'd been in the wrong to refer to him as I had done. If I'd seen him first, I'd have apologised, preferably in front of other people, to stop him trying to raise the stakes.

'Sorry.' He hung his head. 'I should have realised.'

I knew things were going badly wrong but I wasn't sure how or why. I did what Griff would have done, reached for his undamaged hand and gave it an encouraging squeeze, but that didn't seem right either. And when I rubbed his leg with my foot, he drew it sharply away. What was it with this man who could match the Duke of Wellington's disdainful stare? He'd made a public declaration, after all: why not a bit of private action? I was certainly dressed for it, in a tank top and short skirt that left little to the imagination, despite Griff's clucks that that was precisely where things like body parts should be left.

Maybe I could free him up at the disco. Otherwise, I didn't see myself getting my hands on Copeland's records.

* * *

It wasn't like it was supposed to be in any of the teen mags I'd read when I was young. You were supposed to fall on each other, tearing off each other's clothes, pausing long enough to grab a condom, of course. The wretched things had been the subject of the only lecture on sex Griff had ever given, with a packet of them in an embarrassed hand: 'Pregnancy at your age would be bad enough, dear heart, but believe me chlamydia or the clap could be even worse.'

Tonight there was no falling, no tearing, and definitely no need for a condom. If it hadn't been for the chill that had fallen during the meal, not thawed by a couple of hours at the disco, I'd have said it was the fact that we were in the caravan Marcus shared with Copeland. It was bigger than ours, with their territories carefully marked out. Copeland had the lion's share. And I suppose we were rather sitting in the lion's den, waiting for the roars that would announce his return. OK, he was supposed to be spending the night with a regular squeeze, but you never knew. I'd have thought the danger might have added a *frisson*, but while I might have been *fissioning* madly away, Marcus was most definitely not.

He had his back to me, making coffee in the tiny kitchenette.

I had to say something. 'Are you sure Copeland won't be back?'

'I'd be surprised.'

'Well, in that case, can I ask you something? And will you give me a straight answer?'

'It depends,' he mumbled, extra busy with mugs and spoons.

I didn't ask why he wasn't interested in me. I asked about something far more important. 'That frontispiece. Where did he get it from? I really need to know.'

'What difference does it make? You got an absolute bargain. Can't you leave it at that?'

So that was part of the trouble, at least. Copeland thought Marcus had let it go too cheaply and was no doubt taking his anger out on him. 'How much more did he want for it?' If it would make things better between Marcus and me, I could use some of today's earnings.

'Another fifty.'

I got to my feet. 'Let's go back to my caravan and I'll settle up now.'

'It's all right. He's stopped it out of my wages.'

'That's not all right at all.' I dug in my bag. There wasn't much cash there after the meal, but there were two tens tucked deep in the lining for emergencies. 'I'll go and get the rest now.'

'No. It's all right, I tell you.'

He sounded so ratty it clearly wasn't.

I'd try my original tack. 'Where did he get if from?'

He shrugged. 'Where does my coz get anything from?'

'I don't need to know that. But I do need to know where that one, single, particular, individual page came from. Where does he keep his records?'

'Records?' He looked blankly round the caravan.

'I'm not talking about his CD collection, Marcus. His business records. Lists of who he buys from, who he sells to. I don't need state secrets or stuff he doesn't want the taxman to know. Just the provenance of one single sheet of paper.'

'You'll just have to go on wanting, won't you?' came a voice from the open door.

Copeland had come home. And I wouldn't say he was pleased to have a visitor.

CHAPTER NINE

Marcus crumpled, almost visibly. I wasn't the crumpling sort. Not even when man like Copeland ran his eyes up and down me in an appraising way that reminded me horribly of Titus Oates. There was a lot on show to appraise, of course, and the indication was that even if Marcus hadn't found it exciting, his cousin might.

I looked from one to the other. It wouldn't do my cause any good at all if Marcus thought his cousin was violating my maidenly modesty and dealt with him as he'd dealt with Oates. Tact and a lot of diplomacy were called for, so loudly I could almost hear Griff saying the words in my ears.

'I'd best skip the coffee, Marcus, thanks all the same. It's time I was getting back to Griff.'

'Make sure you knock,' Copeland suggested, slinging my jacket from the sofa where I'd left it. I caught it and slipped it on. 'Don't want to disturb the old goat.'

I pulled myself up straight. There was that headmistress who always gave me a rollicking when I'd really messed something up by starting, 'I thought we'd agreed—'

I tried it myself. 'I thought we'd agreed not to insult my guardian when he's not here to defend himself. That was a great evening, Marcus,' I lied. 'We should do it again sometime soon,' I added in what I like to think is a sexy voice. 'Very soon.'

Copeland got the message all right. His coz and I had had a carnal relationship: that was the word, wasn't it? Marcus preened himself.

'Tasty bit of totty, is she?' Copeland asked.

'I think you should discuss that when I've gone,' I said pertly, adding a bit of a flaunt for good measure. 'Could you pass me my bag, please?'

Copeland obliged. 'Isn't lover-boy going to walk you home?'

'No need,' I said, at exactly the same moment as Marcus announced he was. So I gave way gracefully. I was quite glad of a bit of company, although we only had a hundred yards to go. I wouldn't have minded another snog, just in the abstract, as Griff might have said. Maybe we'd have had one if someone hadn't quietly emerged from the shadows near our caravan. As snogging's not a spectator sport, I squeezed Marcus' hand — the good one — and, giving the twiddle-fingered wave that Griff favours, blew him a kiss. Just for good measure, I called a soft, 'Goodnight,' as I fished for my keys.

I think he took a step towards me as if to say something. 'Yes?' I prompted.

But the figure rushed past us and disappeared. Then Marcus disappeared too. It could have been in pursuit, but I rather think it was back to his caravan to avoid more cousinly scorn. Wonderful. OK, early night for Lina. I'd make Griff and me a cocoa — his bedroom light was on — and have an earlyish night. As early as it can be when it's past midnight.

Against all our rules, the caravan door was unlocked.

I stepped inside. 'Griff? Griff?'

I mustn't panic. Perhaps he'd been too drunk to lock up behind him.

Even when he was legless, Griff was never too drunk to lock up.

A groan. From his bedroom. No, not that sort of groan.

It was only a step to the bedroom door. I was so afraid of what I might find I could hardly open it. But if he was groaning, he must be alive. Speed might be important.

He was lying on his stomach, face to one side. He groaned again. Was this just a too-much-booze, sore-head groan? Or was he ill?

'Griff? Griff?' I shook his shoulder. The bones were horribly near the surface compared with Marcus'.

'Hello?' But this shout came from the caravan door, which in my panic I'd forgotten to close, let alone lock.

I turned quickly. A security guard? Yes, the guy Griff had so shamelessly wooed this morning.

'What—?'

He stepped inside. 'Is the old guy all right?'

For nearly twenty years I'd known never to give straight answers. 'Why shouldn't he be?'

'Because someone's socked him, that's why. I've just been to get my first aid kit here.' He waved a green plastic box.

Thank goodness for expert help! I stood back to let him in.

By now Griff had turned on his back; his snores rumbled round the whole caravan. Some nights we'd had in the caravan I'd had to get up (I slept on a sofa that pulled down out of the wall to make a narrow bed) to roll him over so I could get some sleep. Tonight he could snore all he wanted so long as he was all right.

'Let's get him into recovery position,' the guard said. It seemed he didn't need my help.

'Where was he hit?'

'Just as he'd got through the door, I'd say. Whoever it was scarpered when I came up.'

'I mean, was it his head or his neck or what?' I peered.

He slapped a pad on the back of Griff's neck and taped it in place. 'There. That should be all right.'

'If he's had a bang on the head, shouldn't I take him to Casualty?'

'I think you'll find it's A & E these days. I should let him sleep it off. See what he's like in the morning.'

A lot could go wrong between now and the morning. Maybe there was a chance of a second opinion. I took a deep breath. 'What about the police?'

'How many hours will it take them to get here? In any case, what'll they say? I mean, smell his breath.' He wafted away some whisky fumes. 'They'll say he came back drunk and fell and hit himself.'

'But if you saw someone running away—'

'Never saw anyone close enough to ID them. Look, I'd best be off. I've got the rest of my rounds to do.'

'You've been great — and I don't even know your name to thank you.'

'Anyone would have done the same.'

'No. Most people just walk away on the other side. Anyway, I know he'll want to thank you himself, er—?'

'Mal,' he said. 'I'll leave him in your safe hands then, eh?' He disappeared as quietly and quickly as he'd come.

I turned the key in the lock and returned to Griff. He was sitting up, and as I went in swung his legs over the edge of the bed. He was fingering the pad on the back of his neck.

'What the dickens is this?' He worried the edges of the tape.

'It's sticking plaster. Over your bump.' I sat beside him, smoothing it back into place.

'What bump?'

Concussion! That's what made people forget things. Should I call and ambulance or load him into the van and take him to A & E — thanks, Mal — myself?

He got to his feet, pushing gently past me. 'When I have used the miniature ablutions, dear heart, you can explain about this so-called bump and why, when you're clearly in your gladdest rags, you come to have such a wan little face. In the meantime, perhaps some cocoa might replace the roses in your cheeks?'

Which was his way of getting me to the far end of the caravan from the loo. He always preferred his private moments to be as private as possible.

* * *

While the doll's-house kettle boiled, I looked around the living area for signs of violence. There were none, not that I could see. Of course, having fixed furniture made my detecting more difficult. It would have taken more than the fall of a frail old man to wrench the bench seat from the wall, and the table that could have been tipped over in a scuffle was still folded neatly against the wall. My sleeping bag was still in its roll on the floor. No, it all looked exactly as when I'd left it.

Griff had changed into his dressing gown and slippers when he shuffled along to join me. Actually, to call it a dressing gown didn't do it justice, it was so fancy, with wonderful embroidery, gold and crimson silks on black satin. I'd tried to match the colours when I'd made him some slippers for his birthday. Yes, made: he'd got a pattern from a magazine from 1802 — it seemed that was one of the ways young ladies spent their time, when they weren't knotting fringes or knitting purses — and we'd thought it would be fun to see if we could reproduce it. I'd threatened him with a smoking cap in the same design for Christmas.

'Lina, my love, why are you boiling the kettle? And why is no milk bubbling gently on the hob? Dear me, fancy forgetting all your old Griff has taught you about cocoa making. You'd better let me—'

'You should be sitting down looking after yourself,' I retorted, switching off the kettle and reaching for the milk. 'You're sure I can't microwave this?'

He shook his head. Shook his head? Without wincing? 'Late as it is, we mustn't let our standards drop,' he said gently. 'A slow boil, with heat applied from underneath, not from somewhere inside. You'll find the whisk in the drawer, remember.'

I measured both cocoa and sugar to the last grain, and whisked vigorously. If he had been hit, Griff didn't sound very concussed. Not if concussed meant confused, fuzzy-sighted and with a shocking headache, like my first boyfriend after getting a boot in the head playing football.

I pulled down the little table, remembering to cover its Formica top with a Victorian linen cloth before placing Griff's mug in front of him. Mug? Yes, for cocoa. But it was a Royal Worcester china mug. As was mine.

Before I sat, I said, 'Let me have a look at that bruise, Griff. Anything to stop you pithering with that tape!'

He pulled away his fingers, looking like a guilty schoolboy.

'Brace yourself! I'll pull as quickly as I can.'

'Be careful, dear one: I haven't any hair to spare!'

The tape came off faster than you could say leg-wax. There was no sign of a bruise, not to my inexperienced eye. I touched — very gently — the place it was supposed to be. No, it didn't feel like a bruise, and Griff, the biggest baby in the world when it came to removing splinters or anything like that, didn't pull as much of a face as when I'd tried to make our cocoa with water. A much harder prod didn't have much more effect.

Giving up, I popped the dressing in the under-sink bin and sat beside him. I got up again quickly — I'd forgotten the biscuit barrel.

'What did you get up to this evening while I was on the razzle?' I asked as I passed it to him.

'A symposium, Lina. Another one for your mental vocabulary book. Did I ever tell you that when I was a lad at prep school they made us keep a vocabulary book, carefully indexed? Ah, so I did. Believe me, a mental one is much more sensible.' He patted my hand.

I didn't tell him I had a little book just like that myself. Actually I needed it less these days. Words tended to stick longer in my brain, not slipping away as if responding to some arcane law. 'A symposium?' I repeated. 'I thought that was to do with scientists or philosophers or something getting together to put the world right.'

'Good girl! Exactly so. These days, that is. The original use, however, was the one I have just employed. A symposium was a drinking party. And it was to a drinking party I hied myself this evening.'

'"Hied"?'

'Another archaism. But one which should be resuscitated.'

'Look, Griff, we didn't bring the dictionary with us. Either you'll have to use shorter words or you'll have to interpret as you go. And it's a bit late for an English lesson.'

'I stand — or rather, sit — corrected. I was on the juice, my love.'

'Do you remember who with?'

'Darling, it's one thing for an old man like me to ask his quasi-granddaughter about the company she keeps. It's quite another for her to interrogate such a senior citizen as I.'

'Senior you may be. Drunk you certainly were. And I found you in an unlocked caravan with someone sneaking away from the door.'

The cocoa might have been straight caffeine he looked so alert.

'Who?'

'No idea. Like I said, I found you on the bed. Next thing I found this security guard standing here—'

'*Which* guard and *where*?'

'The one you were fluttering your lashes at this morning. And he was standing in the doorway, with a little first aid kit.'

'Was he still wearing that gorgeous little bum-freezer jacket?'

'Griff! This isn't the time or place—'

'Exactly what I was thinking, Lina, my dear. If he was in uniform and thus, one supposes, on duty this morning, before ten, it seems an extraordinarily long working day, quite violating all those helpful European Directives, if that is, he's still in uniform, and thus on duty, at well after midnight. Unless my concussed brain means I can no longer tell the time?'

'He wasn't wearing his ID,' I mused.

'Really?'

'I had to ask him his name. Mal.'

'Mal. Mal.' Griff seemed to give the name far more thought than it warranted.

'He said he'd found you and had come to give you first aid. He found what he said was a bump on your head. Since you were out cold I didn't argue.'

'If I had indeed been out cold, perhaps I might have needed more than a sticking plaster. I might have needed medical attention best summoned by his radio or phone or whatever.'

'I didn't see him using either.'

'Did he say how he came to find me?'

'He said something about someone running past him — actually, someone ran past me, so that might have been true. He'd checked on the caravan door and — no, he didn't say where he'd found you. He reckoned you'd been hit just as you went in. He didn't say how you came to be on your bed. Do you know?'

'The usual way.' But he sounded uncertain. 'I walked in and lay down. But I'll swear I locked the door. Even though I might have been a touch befuddled.'

'The door was definitely locked? You had to use your keys?'

'Which I returned to my trousers pocket. Lina, be an angel—'

I was already on my feet. There were no keys in his pocket, as I established in ten seconds, nor any anywhere else, as it took me ten minutes to establish. Except mine, of course, safe in my bag.

'So how could he have got in if I had locked the door?'

'Griff — finish your cocoa, have another biscuit and be honest: are you sure everything happened as you said? Did you manage to find your way all the way back here in the dark? Even though you were a touch befuddled?'

I hated it when he hung his head. I'd rather he lied in his teeth than looked as if I'd caught him in a fib. He was so penitent he even swallowed down the disgusting skin he'd allowed to form over the cocoa.

'You know, I rather think someone might have lent me his arm.'

'And slipped the key into the lock?'

'I rather fear so. And then pocketed the key and — oh, Lina, I'm a stupid old soak, and I promise to sign the pledge and everything so long as you'll forgive me.'

'Nothing to forgive, Griff. I'll get a locksmith round first thing. So long as one of us stays put and bolts it when the other one goes out, we shall be all right.'

'We should be anyway, dear heart. There's nothing to steal in here after all, except *Sanditon* and *Northanger Abbey*, neither exactly irreplaceable.'

I nodded. Any dealer would know you don't keep anything of value in your caravan. Or in the van. And at a show like this, as at Detling, security would be very tight indeed.

I'd like to say I lay awake for hours puzzling it all out. But, as usual, as soon as my head touched the pillow, even on a board of a bed like this, I fell straight asleep and didn't wake till Griff brought me my morning tea. Except this time he didn't quite bring it. His head was still so foul and his shakes so bad he spilt it all over me.

CHAPTER TEN

Although I organised a locksmith, who grumbled about the weekend call-out but not about his extra fee, it was Griff who had to stay in for him. I put my foot down. There was no way he was fit to handle anything breakable, as he eventually had the grace to admit. So I went on the stall on my own. There was a steady trickle of customers from the first, and though there seemed to be less money changing hands than yesterday, people were soon touting little carriers and strange shapes in bubble-wrap. No one had yet bought anything from us, but people were hovering. I reminded myself that likely customers wanted to see a calm, positive face, not a sulky one. And I could have done sulky for England. The very day I wanted to take off and hunt for my ancestors Griff had to have the shakes and the mother and father of a headache. Headache spelt h-a-n-g-o-v-e-r.

Not wishing to scare off punters by looking — what was the word Griff used? — predatory, I sat down with a trade mag and tried to look cool and professional. It was difficult with damp hair. Griff had reminded me that once women had used tea to rinse their hair, but I knew it was chamomile, not English Breakfast, and I didn't think milk and sugar were involved either.

But someone was more than hovering. Someone was coming in to land.

I didn't pounce. Not when they were looking at eight hundred pounds' worth of hideous Royal Worcester. Let them feast their eyes on the twirls of gilt before I smiled and suggested they pick it up and have a closer look.

* * *

'Eight hundred and fifty pounds! You sold it for eight hundred and fifty pounds! I'd have been happy with six hundred. Hats off, gentlemen, a genius!' Griff crowed. Aside, he added, 'You may not recognise it as a quotation, dear heart, but that was how Schumann announced Brahms's arrival on the musical scene. Or was it Chopin's?' He stroked his chin. Yes, he'd managed to shave.

I smiled and nodded, even if I didn't see how the comment applied to me. I breathed a sigh of relief: Griff was more or less his usual self again. He'd sauntered up at about one, looking as if he'd managed to iron his skin as well as his clothes. The suggestion I'd picked up from a magazine — teabags on the eyes — had worked. Or maybe I was so chuffed by my success I didn't take off my rose-tinted specs.

'Time to celebrate!' he chortled, heading off again before I could stop him, the old codger. It wasn't that I minded being on my own — I'd quite enjoyed my morning, to be honest, practising charming the punters myself instead of watching Griff perform all the time — but I did need the loo. And I was very hungry.

But I was soon busy again. More smiles, more banter, more sales: that was the way to do it. I felt quite smug. Until I realised the next face I'd switched the smile on for was Larry Copeland. It might better to leave it in place, to see if it would bring a matching expression to his face.

It didn't.

'I hear the old soak got drunk again,' he observed.

It was one thing for me to call him that myself, but quite another for someone else to.

'I don't know—'

'Yes, you do. The whole site knows.'

'There was a bit of a problem,' I admitted.

'And an even bigger problem with the bloke that brought him back home — knocked him out and stole his keys. Did he take much?'

'Not much in a caravan to take, is there? It's all bolted down.'

'You don't keep anything in there?' He sounded quite concerned.

I shook my head. 'Just a kettle and so on.' His nod encouraged me to ask, in a tone meant to show I expected the answer to be no, 'Do you in yours?'

'Clean as a whistle.' He glanced over at his stall. 'But then, you've already given it the once over, haven't you?'

Was this a not very subtle attempt to keep me out? I grinned. 'I was just a visitor: I wasn't exactly looking for masterpieces under the bed.' He snorted. 'Come on, Copeland, we just had a meal and went to the disco: nothing wrong with that, is there? After all, you were out as well.'

His voice seemed friendlier. 'That's just it, Lina. I was out. Marcus was supposed to be in. All evening. Just in case.'

I wasn't at all sure how much to believe. So I just said, 'We weren't late back.'

'He shouldn't have gone out at all. That's part of our deal, Lina — he's out, I'm in. I'm out, he's in. See? But you come along flashing your boobs and he's off, leaving the place unguarded. Mind you, seeing what was on offer, I can't really blame him.'

Subject-changing time. 'But if there's nothing to guard?' I cast a mental eye round his caravan. If only I could trust my memory. No, no books or finished maps. Marcus' paint box and a jar with brushes drying upside down. A couple of dirty mugs. A laptop computer.

Now, if you just sold a computer like that down in the pub, you'd get a couple of hundred for it. True. But we were dealing all the time in things worth far more than that. All of us. And we dealt on trust. So what on earth could he have tucked under mattresses or slipped behind fold-down tables? Things like priceless maps or forged pages from books?

He looked at his stall again. 'You know yourself — if they find there's nothing to steal they'll trash the place. Anyway, if you two want to go on the razzle tonight, that's OK by me. Because I shall be staying in. And if anyone tries anything funny, they'll get more than they bargained for.'

'Especially dodgy security men,' I said, with another affable grin, as if we were mates seeing eye to eye after a silly tiff. 'So you want me to take Marcus over the hills and far away. OK. I'm sure I can manage that.'

But even as I smiled, I was trying to work out what on earth he was up to. I didn't believe a word. I didn't trust Copeland in general and in particular when he was apparently being nice and open.

We could have gone on fencing like this forever, I suppose, but there was another little rush of customers. A lot of them had gathered round Marcus. Copeland might have managed to say goodbye before he dived off, but I wouldn't have testified in a court of law.

At this point Griff bustled up, suspiciously as if he'd been waiting for Copeland to go. He produced with one hand a pair of plastic glasses pretending to be flutes, with the other a bottle of champagne. I had a cold feeling I'd never had before. After my sale, he could clearly afford to pay for even an extravagance like this — but could his liver? I'd never thought before about how much he drank.

'Oh, come on, dear heart. Smile! It's not poison!'

As usual, the bubbles got up my nose. But I wasn't going to let him swill the whole bottle. Especially when he pressed his hand to his stomach and went pale. Please God, not a heart attack.

Apparently not. He gave an enormous, echoing belch. 'Wind, you see. Nothing serious. It's just the tummy finds shampoo a mite acid.'

He turned his back so I wouldn't see him popping one of his indigestion tablets, but even if I hadn't seen, the smell of peppermint on his breath would have given it away. I took the bottle firmly and shoved it behind the stall's skirt. 'No more till you've had something to eat. I mean it, Griff. If you won't look after yourself someone else will have to. And I think that someone's me.'

So I dosed him on baguette and black coffee. Would that hurt his stomach? There was bound to be a second-hand home doctor encyclopaedia on one of the bookstalls: when he wasn't looking, I'd check. Meanwhile, the champagne wouldn't go to waste. I'd read somewhere that if you put a silver spoon down the bottle's neck it'd stay fizzy. Despite our dear-old-lady shoplifter, we weren't short of spoons. Marcus and I could check later that evening if the theory worked.

* * *

'Going out? Of course he's going out. He's got this friend in Knaresborough. Can't think why he came back last night: he doesn't usually.'

'He doesn't want us in the caravan, that's for sure,' I said, breaking off a bit of chocolate and passing it over.

He took it with painty fingers. 'I don't see why.'

'Marcus: invite me to the caravan this evening and I'll bet you fifty pence I can show you why.'

'What about food?'

What a weird question when I was almost offering myself to him on a plate. Only almost. It wasn't my knickers that would be got into, but, if I could manage it, Copeland's computer. I'd bet my teeth that he didn't want anyone to see what was in his database of customers and sources. That was why he'd pasted together such a weak story.

'Slip out and get something to bring back?'

'Harrogate's a bit respectable for your average Chinese takeaway.'

'In that case perhaps they'll run to an above-average Thai.'

* * *

In the end he started talking about an Indian, which surprised me, because there's no way you can get rid of curry smells from a caravan, and much as I love coriander chicken, I'm not sure I'd want to wake up in the morning to its perfume.

We stood outside the restaurant arguing.

'No worse than the smell of beer and fags my coz'll bring home with him on his clothes.'

'But he won't notice them: sure as God made little apples he'll smell curry.'

'We could eat at your place.'

'We could just walk in here and ask if there's a free table.'

He looked as shocked as if I'd suggested he streak down the main street. 'But you have to pay VAT if you eat in.'

It might have been my pocket the £850 was burning a hole in, not Griff's: I nearly offered to treat him. After all, curry wasn't one of Griff's favourite things, as it was mine, so we very rarely ate Indian and it would have been a real treat. But I kept my head screwed on. After all, the vase had been Griff's find. The fact that he kept thrusting crumpled fivers at me as commission was irrelevant as the more he thrust them the more I told him not to.

Eventually we bought fish and chips, to eat as we walked back to the caravan. It might be one thing to eat in the street in down-town London; it was quite another to munch in posh Harrogate. So it wasn't, as Griff might have put it, the best gastronomic experience in the world. And I deeply regretted my curry. I deeply regretted everything about the whole evening, actually. Perhaps Marcus had got so used to looking at his handsome face in the mirror every day he assumed he could simply get by on his looks. He certainly made no effort to talk to me, let alone entertain me in the way Griff's cronies did. OK, they were mostly older and it was clear that chatting was all we were ever going to do, given what Griff called their proclivities. But they had charm and it was a pleasure to walk down the street with them.

Why not simply thank him for his company and head back to Griff's caravan? One reason, to be honest, was that I really hate spending a Saturday night in. Saturday nights are meant to be loud and silly with too much to drink — though having seen Griff this morning I was having serious doubts about that, and had resolved never, ever, to binge again. Not that I had for some time. Saturdays were either working days or time to prepare for the next day's fair. Besides which, Bredeham didn't have a big, young population to go on the booze with. From time to time it was invaded by a whole lot of lads in bangers or on bikes, and there'd be a lot of curtain-twitching and talk of calling the police. Mostly the kids smashed a few bottles and had a couple of fights and then treated us to the sight of them throwing up or peeing against lampposts. So while a few local girls joined in, I voted with my feet. I might have felt about ninety-eight as I listened to the radio or read a book, but my halo was so bright I didn't need electric light.

As I drove us back to the caravan site, I was almost ready to call the whole thing off. But I knew I had to get hold of Copeland's laptop. Seducing Marcus was now so low down my list of priorities I decided simply to tell him the truth. Some of it. 'If Copeland wants us out tonight, and you're sure he was going to be out too, and he's suddenly pretending to be my best mate, I smell a rat, Marcus. Or if not a rat, something in the caravan he doesn't want me to see.'

Marcus spoke for the first time since I'd started the engine. 'There's nothing there, Lina. I know where he stashes things. I've actually cased the joint for you. Zilch.'

Perhaps a snog was on the cards after all.

* * *

Parking up in our slot, I sent Marcus on ahead just to double-check the coast was clear. I followed more slowly, first checking in at our caravan for mini-ablutions and a dab of lippie and to collect the champagne, the level of which had gone down so far it wasn't worth taking. At least Griff had been sober enough to double-lock the door; I did the same when I left. I was strolling along thinking of not very much, certainly not Marcus and a body I'd only recently stopped fancying like mad, when I heard shouts. Someone was running hell for leather towards me, carrying something. I merged into the shadow of another caravan and waited till the psychological moment to stick out a foot.

There was a satisfying thud as a figure in black jeans and hooded jacket went flying. So did something else. A laptop. I grabbed it. Other hands grabbed the figure, but were so incompetent that the hoodie came off in their hands and the thief — I think we'd all decided that was the term by then — sped off. I hung on to the laptop, and Marcus and several others, Titus but not Copeland amongst them, checked the jacket. A professional shoplifter would have been proud of it, it had so many secret pockets. But it wasn't supermarket loot they found, but jewellery, miniatures and pieces of silver, if not quite thirty. In other words, a lot of goodies dealers had thought too valuable to be left to the protection of the security staff guarding the showground.

One of whom now arrived. Not my acquaintance. This one, solid as an ex-policeman, came armed with a radio, which he used to summon assistance and to tell someone to shut the gates. My sort of guard.

To my surprise, he returned the stolen property with the minimum of fuss to the owners. Marcus declared the laptop was his cousin's. No one claimed anything that wasn't theirs, and identified other stuff as belonging to people not part of the posse. A couple of the older men, but not Titus, were chosen to accompany the guard as he went off to pop it into safe-keeping till it was retrieved. By now a little gaggle of guards had arrived to guard the burgled vans till the locksmith arrived, no doubt grumpier than ever but mentally trebling his prices before kindly offering bulk discount of five per cent.

Or had I been in the antiques trade too long?

'Tell you what,' I said casually, still holding the laptop to my chest, 'why don't we go and check this hasn't been damaged. It hit the ground with an awful bump.'

'OK,' he sighed. 'You win. So long as you tell me what I'm looking for.'

'Easy. Just the names and addresses of people he buys from. So I can work out who sold him that page.'

'Easy! Just about the most confidential material he has. The decaying aristocracy don't want folk knowing they're selling up their libraries so people like us can buy up old tomes and fillet saleable pages from them.'

'You always said you only handled books that were literally falling apart!' I hissed. 'Not destroying historical objects!' I thought of that wonderful volume in the Bodleian, and suddenly, instead of resenting Oxford's huge wealth, felt a rush of relief that there was at least one old library that wouldn't throw the odd book to hyenas like Larry Copeland.

Marcus flung up his hands. 'Do you want me to check or do you want to hang about in the dark talking ethics?'

* * *

'There!' we yelled. 'Bingo!'

Marcus had found Copeland's address book. Not email addresses — proper snail-mail ones. But I soon stopped chortling. It was long, and most addresses were incomplete, just a name and a postcode. Copeland hadn't brought his printer, of course, so it was going to be a long, tedious job copying them all by hand.

At this point my opinion of Marcus took a sharp upwards turn. He provided paper and pencil without asking.

Suddenly he stopped tapping, resting his hands either side of the computer. 'This could take forever. We have to use our brains here.'

'Yes,' I agreed cautiously, never having had much opinion of mine, at least. 'We ought to narrow the field a bit — is that what you mean?'

'Yep.'

'So we ought to look — say — where I was born.'

'Not many stately homes in London, Lina — well, there are, but stinking rich folk live in them and don't need to charge a fiver to get punters through the door.'

'OK, I lived in London, but I wasn't born there. According to my birth certificate I was born in Maidstone.' Before he'd done more than open his mouth, I added, 'Don't ask where I was conceived! But my mother was supposed to be a country girl.'

'Don't tell me — the classic rich man in his castle and the poor maiden at the gate. You're sure you don't know which bit of country?'

I shook my head. And there was nothing in my little box of treasures to help.

'I suppose we could check through all the parish registers for Townends,' he said, rubbing his hands. 'Everything's available on the Internet.'

'My mother's dead,' I said. 'And if all the social workers of Lewisham couldn't find any maternal family, I don't think it's worth trying. It's my father I'm after.'

'No family at all? Really?'

'Orphan Annie, that's me,' I said smiling. But it was through clenched teeth. He was wasting time we didn't have.

'That's terrible. Mind you, I always wondered how you landed up with an impossible old soak like Griff Tripp. Is there any time of day he's actually sober?'

'Griff is my friend, Marcus, thanks very much. My friend,' I repeated. No one but me criticised Griff. 'So does knowing my place of birth help?'

He nodded. 'Might do. I'll start looking for places in the South East, of course.

'Makes sense,' I said, mentally kicking myself. Why hadn't I thought of all this before? Before putting together my itinerary for the whole of Great Britain? Why was I so *stupid*? 'But how do you know which postcodes represent where?'

'Stints on the Christmas post,' he said, suddenly rubbing his finger on the touchpad and wiping everything.

'Hey, what are you doing now?'

'Setting up a game of FreeCell. So if Copeland turns up out of the blue, we can switch to this window and he won't know what you're up to. Those two aces out, and then . . .'

* * *

'What the hell are you two doing?' Copeland demanded ten minutes later. 'I thought you were going out.' His tone of voice said, *I thought I told you to go out.*

Marcus stood up, shielding me as I tucked my list up my knickers. 'We started off just checking it was all right after its fall, Coz. Then I discovered—'

'Fall? I told you not to touch the bloody thing!'

'It wasn't Marcus who dropped it.' I thought it was time to add my mite. 'It was Burglar Bill. That's why we're here. We were going to have a drink in Griff's caravan but there's been a spate of break-ins. Didn't you notice the damage to the lock?'

Evidently not. He dodged back to check. I hitched the list higher.

'We're still waiting for the locksmith,' Marcus said, quickly hopping back the database and killing it. 'And since the computer went flying when Lina tripped the thief, we thought we'd better check it. Like I said.'

'Which is how Marcus came to teach me FreeCell. We only meant to have one game, but we just got hooked. I suppose you couldn't get us out of this mess, could you?' I pointed to the screen.

'I think we should restart the game,' he said, elbowing Marcus aside and sitting between us.

CHAPTER ELEVEN

Copeland's advice about restarting the FreeCell game seemed to apply just as well to me and my parent hunt. Especially when taken with Marcus' theory that I should look local. So everything might be coming together. I thought I'd be too excited to sleep, but the sound of Griff snoring gently — he must be on his side, not his back — lulled me as it usually did. Plus the realisation, of course, that even if I stuck to Kent and Sussex, there were still a humungous number of stately homes to check out. The National Trust might have a good crop, but there were many others. If I was lucky I'd find they hadn't become hotels or whatever. Others were private homes, only opening their doors once or twice a year, if that. Yes, there was a long haul ahead — and a long day ahead, too. Enough of daydreams; it was time for the good old night sort.

Predictably, the following morning there was a lot of gossip amongst the dealers before the doors officially opened, and I found to my embarrassment that I was a bit of a heroine.

'Indeed, dear heart,' a mercifully unfuddled, headache-free Griff observed, 'if only the security folk had actually caught the miscreant you'd be in danger of sanctification. Even so, if you take up all those offers of a drink, you'll end up with an awful head. And yes, I do speak from experience, and no, I don't need nagging to mend my ways. Far more tonic than gin last night, I promise you.'

For once I didn't laugh. 'This isn't a nag, Griff, but you'll have to have more tonic than gin every time you go on the juice. It's much nicer,' I added, kissing him to show we were still mates, 'to have my morning cuppa still in the cup.'

You'd have thought that the third day of a fair would be quiet: if I were a serious collector, I'd want to beat everyone else to the bargains. But the good folk of Yorkshire weren't put off by the thought that all the best stuff must have gone. They swarmed in, aided and abetted by a wonderful sunny day, really hot for May — the sort of day I'd have wanted to be outside, starting my tan, if I'd had any choice. And they bought. We'd discounted some items, but I didn't buy the tight-fisted Yorkshireman theory: most were happy to pay up without a quibble, let alone a full-scale haggle.

After last night, we were all a bit anxious about our takings, not to mention the stuff left unsold. Many dealers, us included, had planned to stay overnight, rather than risk the long drive home after such a busy three days. But Griff was fidgeting to set off. I didn't mind driving, but wanted to wait till quite late to hit the road: we knew from experience that both the M1 and the A1(M) would be clogged up by people scurrying back to London.

'We'll be safer on the road, even if we're crawling,' he insisted. 'And I can assist with the driving.'

Even stone-cold sober he didn't have the best night vision, so I didn't exactly jump at the offer. Instead, I just repeated, 'Safer?'

'From all these burglarious types, of course.' He'd been getting more and more irritable during the day, despite our good sales.

It was on the tip of my tongue to point out that we were more vulnerable on the road. The combination of van and caravan made us an obvious target. Then I realised that by leaving early he was denying himself the post-fair booze-up he and his mates usually enjoyed. On impulse I gave him a hug. He looked bemused, as well he might, since he didn't know what had been going on in my head, but patted me kindly.

I could do with a bit of kindness, of course, since I was denying myself the chance of a last-minute snog with Marcus, who did no more than peck my cheek when I popped over to say goodbye. He and Copeland were going to stay over, heading to Bradford for a market on Tuesday, one that started at the unholy hour of seven in the morning, which meant that trade would be in at six. That certainly wasn't Griff's time of day, and in any case he didn't like to leave the shop, however capable Mrs Hatch's genteel hands might be, for too many days in a row. We'd had no phone call from either her or Tony Baker, so we assumed all was well and that there'd been no more incidents.

So I started to pack up, needing several plastic storage boxes fewer than when we'd set out. I was shoving the first into the back of the van when Titus Oates ambled past.

We were both clearly in two minds whether to speak, but we exchanged half-hearted grins and he walked on. I reckon we were about even now, since rumour had it that a packet of the stuff the thief had left behind in his hoodie was his, and not his usual stock-in-trade at all. At least, not the official one, and certainly not a legal one. Maybe next time our paths crossed I'd be able to ask him about my page.

* * *

'You were right about the traffic,' Griff conceded, as we pulled into the caravan's usual field just outside Bredeham. 'To misquote the poem, "A slow coming we had of it." My goodness, I'm so tired and stiff.'

I didn't know the poem, of course. It would have been easy to snarl at him that I'd warned him and that we should have stayed over or at least eaten before we set out. We didn't even eat a proper meal at one of the motorway service areas I'd made sure we stopped at regularly.

'Dear heart,' he'd quavered, 'not in one of those awful cafeterias!'

In fact he'd been so het up he'd insisted that one of us stay on guard while the other used the loo and bought a snack to eat in the car park. I'd never known him like this, and while I'd have liked to shake some sense into him, I wondered if his twitchiness might be to do with not getting his usual drink, like the bad temper I'd seen in mates denied their fags or spliffs. I wasn't holier than thou about either, but fortunately for me the very first time I'd smoked I had a really bad chesty cold, and been afraid I was going to cough my lungs up. It was a lot cheaper to go on abstaining. And more sensible, if that was what going without your fix did to you. Not to mention, of course, what smoking itself did to you.

Mind you, after the drive, I could have done with some sort of pick-me-up. Two hundred and fifty odd miles in heavy and often solid traffic, in the dusk and then the dark, was not my idea of an ideal Sunday evening's excursion. I'd had enough chocolate and burgers to guarantee mega-spots for a month and I still felt hungry.

It was the work of moments to park up, connect up to the electricity and uncouple the car. But Griff went back three times to make sure he'd locked up the caravan, even when I pointed out it was me who'd made the final turn of the key and clamped the wheels. I didn't argue about the extra checking at home, though, and was quite happy to go round with him to do it: gate, garage, van — four eyes were better than two.

He started his usual routine, opening his letters and putting them down while he wandered round. 'Just nurturing my babies, darling!'

I'd have thought the houseplants could have waited a few more hours for water, and would have preferred conversation in daylight too. And I'd certainly have preferred not to have to trail round after him picking up scraps of paper — he never could open envelopes in one piece and in any case we saved used stamps for some historic railway he'd once had a ride on.

If I wasn't careful I'd snap at him. So I headed for the kitchen to make some cocoa. Only to find he'd left the milk on the table. It was off. Very off indeed. No. Nothing in the fridge. Just this yucky cheese in the jug.

A couple of years back, I might have picked up the lot and slung it at him. I still felt like it, to be honest. Yes, jug and all. But it was a jug I liked, not because it was fine china but because of its shape, round and solid. It felt at home in your hands, as it had done in countless other hands for a century or so. And in any case, if I threw it at the wall, who'd have to get all the mess up?

Gagging because it smelt so foul, I couldn't pour it down the sink because I simply couldn't face podging the lumps until they got small enough to swill away. The loo? Occupied by Griff.

A drain.

The one in the yard was nearest, but that meant a whole fiddle with the alarm system. If I used one in the street, it'd be a fag carrying water to flush it away but there was only one section of the alarm system to isolate.

In broad daylight, after some sleep to put my brain back into gear, I'd have waited for Griff to complete his ablutions, even though he might have been removing not just each tooth and giving it a good polish before returning it to its socket, but brushing every strand of hair. As it was, maybe I should have passed the time soaking his breakfast prunes.

But all I was thinking of was getting rid of that smelly, slimy, lumpy mass. Like, now. Check: key in pocket to let myself in again; kettle full of water; stinking jug.

I stepped out into the dark, quiet street. Thin cloud was shifting to reveal a few stars, so bright you understood why folk wished on them and why our councillor hated the streetlights that obscured them. Across the street, a nightlight glowed in the new baby's room. Bending, I tipped the curds and whey carefully down the nearest drain. And fell over. Fell? Was bloody pushed!

An education like mine means you learn to bounce up before some bastard stamps on your fingers. So I was up and ready to run before whoever it was knew it. To run home, of course. Wrong. If Griff thought there was anything amiss, he'd have opened the door before you could say street crime, and whoever had toppled me would have shoved past him and into the house.

So — just like an athlete, feet ready for the starting pistol — I waited, tense and ready for action. Action as and when I could see who and where my assailant was. More flipping cloud. Yes, there was a figure already pushing hard at our front door. I almost thumbed my nose and jangled the key. No. No point in bravado. I stayed put, my right hand clasping the jug, as if it would comfort me like a teddy. At last the figure gave up, heading towards a car parked under one of the village's historic trees, much prized by our dratted councillor. Whenever pruning was mentioned, he spoke passionately of shade on hot sunny days. I muttered about providing cover on dark nights.

The car started, first time, and pulled into the street, headlights full up. I couldn't see the colour or make, but there was one thing I could see — it was heading straight for me. Olympic sprinters, eat your heart out: I was out of the non-existent blocks and over the nearest garden wall as if a gold medal depended on it.

So how would I be able to identify the car again? Without thinking, I hurled the jug at it, hard as I could. The windscreen didn't break. The jug did. And I sat on whoever's front doorstep and howled.

* * *

'It was my favourite, my absolute favourite,' I sobbed, as Griff gently but firmly took the shards from my hands and consigned them to the bin.

Tony, in the same fetching get-up as before, was swabbing the odd cut on my hand.

'It's just a jug, Lina, for goodness' sake,' Griff continued. 'We've sold hundreds better, and hundreds worse.'

'Shock,' Tony said, out of the corner of his mouth, as if I wasn't supposed to hear. 'Hot, sweet tea.'

'But that's the whole point,' I sobbed. 'I was throwing the milk away when this guy socked me and then he drove at me. And yes, I know I said his headlights were on main beam, but he must have turned them off as he went past — there were no tail-lights or lights on the number plate.'

'I've got plenty in the fridge back home,' Tony said. 'I'll be back in half a tick.'

'Here's the front door key. Don't leave the door ajar in case they come back.'

'They're miles away now,' he insisted, but took the key anyway.

'Brandy. You need a shot of brandy,' Griff announced, toddling off despite my insistence that I didn't. 'Well, I do!' he declared over his shoulder.

When Tony returned he declared it was better for me to stick to tea, or at least drinking chocolate, which he'd brought with him. He and Griff might see what parts the brandy reached. I didn't argue — I loathed the stuff.

'I reckon they were part of the Kitty Gang,' Tony said, swirling the brandy round in its balloon till even I could smell the fumes.

'Crikey! That's very reassuring! Being run over by idiots with a stupid nickname!'

'It should be reassuring. We've got extensive reports of old people being jumped when they let the cat out — or especially back in. Seems one of them makes a noise like a distressed moggie, the owner goes to look and — bingo! — he or she's smashed over the head and their house done over. The funny thing is, a couple of times someone's phoned for an ambulance: they can't be all bad.'

'Well, you've certainly put my mind completely at rest,' I observed. 'It could have been a thoroughly nasty person, the sort that drives their car at pedestrians lying in the road!'

'That is new,' he conceded. 'A very unwelcome development. I'll see the investigating officer hears about that tomorrow. Today.' He got up, yawning as he stretched. 'The best thing you can both do is get some sleep and tell the colleague I'll send round all about it. OK?'

'Hang on: how did Chummy know I was going to pour milk into a public drain?'

'I'm sure he didn't. He — or, of course, she — might have simply been waiting for any door to open. Or been just about to miaow outside a neighbour's — hasn't Mrs Hatch got a cat? You just provided a nice opportunity for a bit of opportunistic crime.'

The theory made sense. And I'd like to say I bought it.

Griff was still sober enough to shake his head. 'There are altogether too many coincidences for my taste. Surely you darling boys in blue should be as suspicious as I am, and start keeping a special eye on our humble abode?'

Tony muttered things about resources and priorities and beat a hasty retreat.

When I lay down to sleep, knackered as I was, my brains felt like a hamster on a wheel. The birds were already in mid-chorus by the time I fell asleep.

CHAPTER TWELVE

'Georgian. Definitely Georgian,' Griff declared, looking over my shoulder at the page I was pointing at. He'd got the idea that after the adventures during the night I must be an invalid and cosseted accordingly. We never opened the shop on Monday, so there was nothing to stop him pampering me.

I hadn't quite taken to the day bed in a decline, smelling salts at the ready, but Monday morning had brought thick, rain-filled cloud and it was too dark in the cottage to work without lights. So I agreed that a quiet morning reading, including some of those stately home guides, might be nice. Griff had found from somewhere a Victorian Paisley shawl in case I needed swathing. Then he'd found a couple of books on English vernacular architecture ("Everyday stuff, dear heart, not your posh palaces") and was playing a little game of spot the period, opening pages at random, covering the caption and saying which period the house had been built in. I hadn't the heart to tell him that all I really wanted was for him to push off to the bank and get rid of the money we'd picked up yesterday before Burglar Bill paid us another random visit. I knew a good proportion of our loot would never find its way into any official vault — that was why we discounted for cash. But he had to stash away enough to convince the taxman that everything was more or less above board.

'Listen,' I said firmly, getting up to follow him to the van, 'remember you're to take a different route to the bank from last week. Maybe a different branch altogether — why not Tenterden, rather than Ashford? You could pop in and have lunch with Aidan.'

'But that would mean leaving you on your own, dear heart.'

'And if you went to Tenterden you could pop into Waitrose.' That would get rid of some more cash. A lot. Griff loved a good spend on food when he was flush.

He beamed. I could never understand why but Griff had a passion for Waitrose that no other supermarket approached. 'Pass me the shopping bags, then.'

No, he wouldn't ever condescend to use checkout polythene carriers, and with the number you saw flapping in otherwise lovely hedgerows round here I suppose he was right. I nipped back inside for the heavy plasticised cloth ones we use, and a wicker basket that always gave him special pleasure.

I locked up the garage and the gate carefully behind him, and, as usual, locked myself into the house. There. Special treat day for me, too. Bother reading. I'd clean the bathroom. Griff always worried when I did housework. Hating it himself, he couldn't understand that anyone would find it satisfying to achieve gleaming enamel and beautifully buffed taps. We'd still got old-fashioned tiles on the floor, too, and restoring them to pristine black and white gave me another thrill. Thoroughly exhilarated, I turned my attention to the kitchen. Griff was a wonderful cook but not the best mopper-upper in the world, so the Aga wasn't looking its best.

After that, coffee made with some of the milk Tony had given us, it was time to open those books again.

And close them promptly. Thinking about Tony had reminded me of last night again. No, I wasn't upset. I was intrigued. True, the CCTV hadn't shown up much when we'd had the intruder, but what if it had seen anything that had happened in the street. We'd paid extra for one that wasn't fixed but would scan in response to movement. I'd moved enough. Would it have recorded anything that Tony's mates could use?

It was the work of seconds to fish the cassette out, replacing it immediately with a new one. It took a bit longer to locate the precise footage, but at last I had a grand view of my bum as I bent down to pour away the milk. The figure of my assailant was less clear. To the naked eye there was nothing that might give a clue as to its identity. No, his. It was a male, I'd swear to that. But that was all. I hadn't a clue about age or anything. Not after eight, maybe ten viewings. You'd need the sort of enhancement Tony had spoken about. And yet — and yet . . .

The more I told myself there might be something familiar about the figure, the less I knew what it was. In the end I did what I sometimes did when I was in what Griff called my divvy-mode. I walked away and concentrated on something else. In this case, those guidebooks.

Ruthlessly weeding out anything not in Kent or Sussex, for the time being at least, I looked at the National Trust properties first. And was ready to give up. Most properties were castles, and my memory certainly wasn't of great, thick walls and moats. A child would remember a moat and a drawbridge, surely? Far more than an old book? Lovely as Bodiam Castle and Ightham Mote might be, they were no use to me. What about houses? Bateman's? Chartwell? No, they'd been lived in by such famous people I'd surely have recognised a face. What about some others? Knole? No, according to the handbook it hadn't been altered since Elizabethan times. All the same, I marked it down for a visit, it looked so wonderful. After all, I'd stumped up for membership and there was no point in cutting off my nose to spite my face.

What about English Heritage properties? Griff had found me a 1990 handbook, assuming that not enough would have changed in the castle world to justify rooting out a new one. And castles there were — nothing but castles, apart from the odd chapel or fort. Didn't Kent have any eighteenth-century mansions, for goodness' sake?

I didn't know what to do. Or what to feel. What should I be feeling after raising my hopes so high, only to have them dashed? I wanted to cry, but it felt as if I was angry, not upset. Angry because someone had led me up the garden path — the Garden of England path, I added, furious, but smiling with grim amusement. Was that what Griff meant by a sardonic smile? I'd have to ask. I had no one to blame for my raised hopes but myself. But I was angry with Marcus for having suggested limiting myself to the immediate area. Like last night, I wanted to smash something. I was powerless in the face of all these grand buildings owned by old families and national institutions. First I hurled all the books across the room. Then I hit my temples with my clenched fists. There had to be an answer somewhere. I slapped my face to stop myself being so stupid. If only the pain in my face would numb out the pain in my head. I thumped again, like a boxer pummelling a hated opponent.

I found blood on a knuckle.

Mine.

Gosh, Griff! What would Griff think when he came back and saw me like this? I got to the kitchen so quickly I didn't remember moving. Cold water, plenty of it. Then I remembered the ice for Griff's gin. Ice'd be even better. In a tea towel. Two tea towels, one for each eye. There. And don't forget to refill the little plastic trays. He mustn't know. It'd upset him so much. I was angry with myself, furious. I slapped again. Left, right; left, right. Both together. At least it was slapping, not punching. But I must stop. I mustn't let him know I'd let him down.

Was that the only reason he mustn't know? Or was there another, that I was secretly ashamed? A woman my age shouldn't have temper tantrums, should she? Yes: foster-mother number three, or maybe number four, had been spot on — I was wrong in the head and ought to be put away for my own safety.

Forget that. And forget everything else she'd ever said. At the time it had only made me worse. But it wasn't going to now. I was a grown woman earning my own living and trying to dry out an old soak who was better than all the foster-parents in the world, even Iris. Griff would be proud of me one day. One day I'd be proud of me.

There. That was better. Back in the living room I peered at myself in one of the mirrors in the chiffonier. I looked as if I'd had a good cry — come to think of it, I had, too — but my cheek-bones and brows weren't too bad. Yet. The trickle of blood from my swollen nose was dwindling to a halt.

Picking up the books reminded me of my bleak joke about being led up the Garden of England path. Another idea formed, slowly, like when an icicle just starts to melt and you see a drop of water gathering on the tip, taking ages before it finally drops. The Internet. I'd bet all the takings from the Worcester vase — hadn't Griff been proud of me! — that there'd be something about Kent's stately homes on a website.

The trouble with truanting — not to mention being shunted to about eight different schools according to where my latest lot of foster-parents lived — was that I was missing great chunks of information that everyone else took for granted. IT had been a complete mystery, mobile phones excluded, until Griff took me in hand. Even now people thought it odd that a man of his age should be so much more at home on the Web than I was.

I no longer felt scared when I switched on his computer in case I blew something up, but this was the first time I'd ever searched for something myself. I know: it's embarrassing, isn't it? All the same, I was shaking, winding my legs round each other as

I squirmed round in the big executive leather chair I always teased Griff about.

I always teased him about his service provider, too.

'Don't tell me, dear heart. Such good fortune they're efficient and I've no desire to leave. You may think that Griffith.tripp@virgin.net is amusing. But imagine moving to AOL and having to tell everyone I'm no longer a Virgin.'

It didn't hurt too much to grin at the memory. When I'd checked out Kent I'd have another session with ice.

And there it was, the website of Kent, the Garden of England. It told me to explore, discover, experience and relax. Well, I couldn't have put it better myself. Scared, still, but with more and more confidence, I worked through what they had to offer.

The castles they offered first of all were agonisingly predictable. Leeds, Hever, Dover. So I couldn't hurt myself again, I sat on the fist that wasn't using the mouse and ploughed on. Would I like to organise my own tour? Yes, please. I typed in Stately Homes and got a list. Wow! Since when had Mount Ephraim Gardens and Sittingbourne Heritage Museum been stately homes? But I moved slowly down. Yes. Higham Hall. That was a genuine stately. But I'd been there a dozen times with Griff to the antiques fairs they held there. And I'd met the owners, manfully trying to rescue what had been an almost derelict house and transforming it into the most beautiful home. Except it wasn't manfully. It was womanfully. No unknown fathers there.

I scrolled down further. An A to Z of very nice piles indeed. All were still family-owned, and most had very restricted opening times compared with Trust or Heritage-owned places. Well, if you were actually living in your own house you'd want to make sure you'd cleaned the loos before Joe Public went poking round. With all this success, I dared print off a list. Yo, Lina!

* * *

I was so chuffed I finished the rest of the housework, doing the living room and bedrooms, which I never enjoyed as much. I don't know why, because in the normal run of things I love handling the china and glass that make the cottage such a pleasure to live in. Maybe it's because I like a good uninterrupted run at things. By lunchtime there was also a load chuntering in the washing machine: it'd dry on racks in the garage if the weather didn't improve. The only thing I couldn't do was have any lunch, because of course we'd run down our supplies of fresh stuff and Griff wasn't home yet.

Bredeham wasn't the prettiest of villages. True, there were some white-painted Kent boarded houses and cottages like ours, and a couple of black-and-white and thatched jobs, but generally speaking the houses were pretty undistinguished Victorian two-up-two-downs or some very ordinary 1930s semis. But the nice thing about it was that you couldn't walk down the street without seeing someone you ought to wave at if not actually stop and talk to. It could take Griff up to an hour to pick up his pension. I didn't know that many people yet, but there was still Mrs Bourne to flap a hand at, and her dog to fend off. The weird thing was that when I first came I was afraid. I felt it wasn't my street to walk down, that I needed permission. I had no right to be there. Trespassing, that's it. The first few times I found an excuse for Griff to come with me I was so scared. No, it wasn't anything to do with the villagers, because I've had the same feeling in other places. The first time I went into Canterbury Cathedral, for instance. Or the first theatre Griff took me to. Just like when I was in Oxford the other week, as if lowlife like me had no place on the pavement trodden by superior mortals.

Oxford! That was it. That was where I'd seen a man with a walk like the man's captured on video. Dan Freeman. The don who'd got me into the Bodleian. I clapped a hand to my cheek in disbelief that I could be so thick. The slap hurt. Oh, drat! My bruises!

Fortunately Bredeham was big enough to run not just to a pub and a village shop (even if it was a Londis) and post office, but also a butcher (he also sold Griff's favourite cheeses) a dentist (one day a week), a doctor (early afternoon everyday) and a chemist, which happened to double as a stationer and bookstore.

'Hello, Lina,' Mr Elworthy greeted me through the little dispensary hatch behind the counter. 'Won't be a second! How's Griff? Those tablets working?'

No, it wasn't the place I'd have gone to buy condoms or if I'd had to take the morning-after pill. Especially as within thirty seconds of his emerging from the dispensary he was round the counter peering at my face, first through his glasses, then with his specs in his hand.

'A drawer,' I said flatly. It felt strange to be resorting to downright lies again. OK, I used half-truths very, very occasionally in the trade, but nothing blatant like this. 'I thought I'd spruce up this chest of drawers while Griff was out. It had stuck — you know what old furniture's like — and I gave it all I'd got. And it came out like a shot. I've iced it, but you can't walk along the street with a dripping tea towel pressed to your nose!' I grinned.

'Drawer, eh?'

I nodded. 'Plus my fists.' I mimed putting my hands side by side on an imaginary handle.

'Lose consciousness?'

'Just a bit of blood from my nose. But I've got plenty to spare!'

'In that case you'll be pleased to hear there's a blood-donor session next week. On the village green.'

'I'll see you there,' I lied, loathing the very idea of all these Draculas and their victims.

'I'll make sure they save you some tea and biscuits,' he assured me. The creep: he knew I was lying. And I bet he knew I'd been lying about the chest, too.

Resisting the temptation to bluster, I ran a finger over my bruises. 'I suppose you haven't anything more user-friendly than ice?'

To my amazement he turned to the homoeopathic section of his counter. 'Safer to use round your eyes than the stuff I'd usually recommend,' he said, offering arnica cream. 'You can take these tablets, too. But my advice to you is to be careful round drawers. Black eyes aren't my idea of maidenly beauty.'

I paid up and shut up. And bought some sunglasses, too. But I needn't have bothered. Every single customer in Londis seemed to be peering at me — though on reflection perhaps they'd have stared at anyone wandering round with sun protection when the rain had come on extra heavy again.

* * *

It was like waiting for a thunderstorm to break. Even though Griff smiled and hugged me as usual, certainly not wincing at the sight of my face, and had nattered away about Aidan as he passed the bags of Waitrose goodies out of the van for me to take into the kitchen, I knew we were going to talk about my face. I stowed things in the freezer, refilled storage jars and put away the bags while he went upstairs and checked his emails. I made tea, reaching out pretty plates for the scones he'd bought from that home-made bakery in Tenterden, and little dishes for his homemade strawberry jam and some Waitrose Cornish cream. Still no sign of him — and, of course, still no mention of the bruises. Did he want me to confront him and confess? After all this time, I still couldn't. I tried praying to the Guy living in Canterbury Cathedral that Griff'd maybe say nothing and let me off. But I knew that he wouldn't, any more than I could go up to his study and confess.

At last he popped downstairs with an empty Unichem bag, which he threw into the recycling bin. He took my hand. 'Just remember, dear heart, that we lubricate all our drawers with candle wax. There's no need to tug them hard. Oh, Lina, my love, come here! As if I could be cross with you. As if old Griff ever raised his voice.'

'It'd be better if you did!' I burbled. 'But you're so kind and forgiving and I don't deserve it.'

'You didn't deserve a lot of things that have happened to you — well, none of us does, for good or for bad. But I did think you'd given that up. I didn't think you needed to do it any more. And I think it's all to do with this silly quest of yours, and I do wish you'd abandon it.'

'Tell you what,' I managed, through one of his immaculate linen handkerchiefs, 'I promise you I'll give one of them up, the self-abuse or the quest.'

He reached for the kettle. 'I think that calls for another little celebration. Calling self-abuse by its name, of course, silly. It's the first time you've ever done that.' He shook his head. 'I suppose asking you to give up both that and the quest is a bit too much.'

'Like asking you to give up both your booze and clotted cream on your scones,' I agreed, passing him the strawberry jam.

CHAPTER THIRTEEN

It wasn't until after supper, something wonderful and complicated with chicken, which Griff served with much pomp and ceremony and with a white wine from New Zealand I really rather liked and drank a lot of, that I remembered about the resemblance between my assailant's walk and Dan Freeman's. I wish I could say it was because I'd been too busy to give it another thought, but the truth was my outbursts had always left me feeling as though the Duracell bunny had nicked my battery and run off with it. As soon as I'd downed my share of that wonderful cream tea, I'd simply fallen asleep, my head on the kitchen table. And I remembered not because my sleep had left me refreshed and brimming with ideas, but because, after one of Griff's best ever meals, a policeman asked me.

Yes, one of Tony's colleagues, a pale young man in his thirties called DC Brent, had got round to paying us a visit.

'Fashionably late, I see, my dear sir,' Griff greeted him, showing him into the living room.

'Shifts,' Brent apologised, peering nervously through trendy, invisible-rim specs with gold sides. 'You get into a routine and then it all goes nohow. You know how it is.'

'We do indeed,' Griff cooed. 'Our life on the road simply ruins our social lives. And our sleep patterns. However do you manage to visit the land of nod during the day, dear boy?'

The dear boy edged away slightly. 'I'm here to brief you on our investigations to date,' he said stiffly. 'Firstly, we might just have an ID on the female shoplifter: if we pull her in, could you identify her?' He looked at me.

I blame the meal and all that white wine for my really unhelpful answer. 'I never saw her.'

'But aren't you the female who raised the alarm?' He consulted his file. 'A Mrs Hatch?'

'This,' said Griff, all camp erased from his voice, 'is my adoptive granddaughter, Ms Evelina Townend. Mrs Hatch is an associate of mine, a lady of mature years.'

The whole of DC Brent's body showed how sorry and embarrassed he was. 'Do you have an address, sir?'

Griff flashed me a glance: I could see the old imp was just about to two-finger police shorthand by giving the poor young man our address.

'Chapel Cottage,' I jumped in.

'Confusingly it's nowhere near the church, which is actually the other end of the village.'

'It's a converted chapel,' I explained. 'Just a couple of doors—'

'Indeed. Perhaps the villagers decided the original Baptists were simply too primitive for words. Now it's elegant in concept, but draughty in realisation. And such a dismal kitchen,' Griff sighed. 'May we offer you refreshment, Detective Constable? We were about to partake of a can ourselves. No, strictly non-alcoholic — I won't take no for an answer.' He pirouetted into the kitchen.

By this time poor DC Brent didn't look as if he knew his ears from his elbow. He looked even more confused when what arrived in a handleless cup turned out to be coffee.

Griff evidently decided it was time to be sensible. 'So there appears to be some success *vis-à-vis* the shoplifter. What about the attempted break-in, video footage of which I believe PC Baker passed to you for enhancement.'

'He did indeed, sir. And we apologise for the delay caused by lack of specialist staff: the officer who's the real whiz kid's just gone on maternity leave, and her replacement is still undergoing training. But he took it along to one of the training sessions,' he added, so triumphantly that we both assumed they'd got a good image.

'Well?' Griff prompted.

'And got zilch.' He gave a dry laugh at our expressions. 'Sorry, they did their best. But technology's only as good as the material it works on. Of course, if this were a high-profile murder, then we might be able to afford to send it to the US where they've got absolute cutting-edge equipment,' he added, as if trying to help.

'I have no intention of sacrificing either of us simply in the hope of that sort of response,' Griff announced. 'So is the case closed?'

'Not exactly. It wasn't ever a case at all to be honest, because nothing happened. But it might have helped solve other crimes.'

'Like the one which Lina was almost involved in last night. You were unaware of that? I'd have expected young Tony to tell you all about it.'

Trying to spare Tony a black mark, DC Brent muttered about briefings and shifts again, but flicked open his notepad. I gave a brief account of what had happened, Griff chipping in when he thought I was underplaying the danger I'd been in when the car accelerated towards me. 'Tony mentioned something called the Kitty Gang,' I concluded, embarrassed by the silly name.

'Did he indeed?' After a moment's blankness, he wrote vigorously. 'I suppose you didn't get any video footage of that incident?'

'As a matter of fact I did. And although it's probably not much help, the guy's walk does seem familiar,' I added slowly, doubtfully. 'No. Can't be.' I passed him the tape, but couldn't imagine they'd get any more from it than from the first one.

Brent's blond eyebrows would have merged with his hair, had it not receded so far. His glasses twitched up and down his nose. 'Who?'

'Someone I met in Oxford,' I said slowly, squeezing Griff's hand lightly to apologise for saying nothing earlier. 'A man called Dan Freeman. He's something to do with the University.'

'Tell me about him.'

'A librarian was rude to me; I got upset; he offered me a cup of coffee to cheer me up,' I said, receiving a reassuring squeeze from Griff.

'Do you have a phone number? An address?'

'Only Keble. Keble College. It wasn't that sort of cup of tea,' I added. 'In fact, it seems daft of me to say anything about him. What would a respected academic be doing moonlighting as one of the Kitty Gang? I know teachers are always complaining about being badly paid, but—'

'Any lead on the Kitty Gang would be useful,' Brent declared solemnly. Then the giggles that had been threatening all three of us bubbled up. 'If only it was called something else!' he choked.

'The Moggie Mob?' I suggested.

'The Feline Fraternity?' Griff capped me.

'Even plain Cat Burglars,' Brent concluded.

To celebrate the revelation that our guest was human, Griff produced more scones and the remains of the jam and cream. I waved the coffee pot but none of us seemed to want to risk more caffeine. Normally this would have had Griff into the chiffonier for the drinks. Either he decided that alcohol wouldn't go with the jam or he was trying to keep his promise. Either way, I heaved a sigh of relief and ladled on more cream.

'All the same,' Brent began, stopping for his tongue to chase a dab of jam.

I passed him what I called a paper serviette but Griff insisted was a napkin.

'All the same,' he continued, 'it sounds as if you could have been badly injured last night. However stupid the name we gave the gang, we should take the incident very seriously. I suppose you didn't get a glimpse of a registration plate?'

'The driver doused his lights as soon as he realised I'd escaped. And I'm sorry — I've tried and tried but I can't place the car.'

'With a bang on the head like that, I'm not surprised.' He leaned towards me, concerned.

I pulled back. I didn't want his attention and I didn't want his sympathy.

'That was done today, I'm afraid,' Griff put in. 'I came back from the supermarket to find the house like a new pin and Lina clutching ice to her forehead and looking as if she'd gone a couple of rounds with Lennox Lewis.'

'A drawer stuck — and then came unstuck,' I said, adding ruefully, 'I'd have thought the arnica should be working by now.'

'There's something I always use when I've had a rough game of rugby,' Brent said. 'Lasonil or Lanosil or something. Shall I drop some by? When I report back on this video?' he added, as quickly as if he needed some sort of excuse.

Before I could suggest I simply nipped along to Mr Elworthy's the next morning, Griff jumped in. 'That would be more than kind, er—?'

'Dave.' Brent produced what Griff would instantly accuse of being a winsome smile. I was never sure about men and winsome smiles. Especially when I didn't know whether they were directed at Griff or at me.

'The funny thing is, Dave, that Lina had already involved herself in a spot of heroism on Saturday evening. Not here, but up in Harrogate. A distinctly non-feline interloper had broken into a number of caravans and she managed to trip him as he tried to escape. I believe that ultimately he eluded the security staff, alas.'

'You wouldn't be suggesting that the two individuals are in fact just one — and an Oxford don, to boot?'

'Put that way my theory does indeed seem far-fetched. Now, are you sure I can't offer you a tiny drop more coffee?'

* * *

The following morning Griff summoned me to the computer to check the list of houses I'd found.

'If you double-click there,' he pointed, 'you get a description of the house. Some have photographs too — oh dear, how very amateurish. When will people learn that there's more to photography than merely pointing the camera and pressing the shutter? Now, click through the whole lot and tell me if anything rings any bells.'

'All I remember,' I said, sitting down and grasping the mouse, still warm from his hand, 'is a grey, marble fireplace and big windows, deep set, going almost from floor to ceiling.'

'So which of these could we eliminate without further thought?' he asked, peering over my shoulder.

One of Griff's little tests. I'd like to pass it. I peered at the first, a lovely black-and-white Elizabethan manor house overlooking a deep valley. 'That one — unless someone's made some alterations we can't see.'

'What you speak of would be a major alteration, structural, not just cosmetic. Is there a rear view?'

There was. It hadn't been altered. I tried the next. It was an early Victorian rectory. Click on photos: no, nothing.

'We could be at this all morning,' I said. 'Shall I press on while you phone Mrs Hatch and warn her about the police?'

'I fancy "inform" might be a better word, Lina. And if you think I'm going to leave you on your here so you can have even a smidgen of the temptation to hurt yourself the way you did yesterday, you can think again.'

I was hurt. 'I promised you I wouldn't.'

'Smokers promise never to touch another fag — but under pressure far less extreme than you might be enduring, they soon light up again.'

For *smokers* read *drinkers*. I said no more. I clicked away, sometimes bringing up a photo that sparked a response in him.

'Now you ought to wheedle your way in there. That belongs to that pop star who tried to save the world — I wonder if he still lives there? Such a darling young man he was. I was three-quarters in love with him. But he proved quite irredeemably straight, alas. And that one — no, you should go nowhere near there, not even on public open days. The owner's *nouveau riche* — well, I suppose very few owners are descended from the original family, but this one's got a reputation for being one of the East End's most successful criminals. Of course,' he continued, getting thoroughly into his stride, 'that's probably all too appropriate. The founding fathers of our so-called aristocratic families were Duke William's hitmen. They'd be tried these days for war crimes.'

'So the great and the good aren't great or good at all?'

'Mortals like the rest of us. *Noblesse oblige*, indeed. You wouldn't expect the descendants of the Kray brothers, if they had any, that is, to be rulers by divine right, would you?'

I'd never heard Griff quite as forthright in his criticism of the upper classes before. Was it just to put me off my search? What was the point in looking for my dad if he was no better than any other man? Was that his message?

'It won't work, Griff — I'd want to find my dad even if he were Hannibal Lecter. I might not stay to dinner, mind.'

'It's not a question of putting you off, child. It's a question of modifying your expectations.'

I looked him in the eye. 'Griff, any man who doesn't make any effort to see his daughter in nearly twenty years can't be all that much cop. But I just need to know.'

'So long as you pursue your inquiries in that spirit, I shall worry less. Proceed, dear heart.'

A couple more blanks and I said, 'You know your way around the county. You might have some idea of where it is!'

'Might. But don't. Lina, my child, have you any idea how many great old houses from whatever period are now used for something else? Posh hotels, head offices, schools — even chopped about to make retirement apartments. They wouldn't be open to the public, not even on the odd day that these admit hoi polloi.' He shook his head sadly, leaving me to absorb the implications.

I clicked the mouse again. Jacobean — unusual in this part of the world, I knew even without Griff telling me. But not the period I was looking for.

Late Victorian; Tudor; Georgian, like the illustration in Griff's architecture book, in other words. But it wasn't very big, not very grand. But the next one was very grand indeed. It was a Palladian mansion, and lovely.

'Early Palladian, I would say,' Griff said. 'Whereas this one—' he continued, as I clicked again, 'is quite late Palladian. Both are likely to have the sort of windows you want to see. Let's see if they have any rear views — tut, how very frustrating. But neither's very far away — in opposite directions, of course, one near Tunbridge Wells, the other near Canterbury. I'd certainly mark them down for a visit, dear heart.'

I already had. There were four other possibles, each of which went on my list. Griff shook his head gently. 'It will take an age to jot down all the details of opening hours and road access: allow me.'

Slowly but surely the details of each rolled out of the printer. Patting me on the head, he produced a large manila envelope. 'There. To be perused at your leisure. Meanwhile, in the words of the poet, "there's work to be done ere the setting sun". Did I say poet? Versifier at best . . .'

* * *

If I hadn't been working in silence on an especially tricky bit of gilding, I wouldn't have heard the scratch at the front door. There was only one person who announced his arrival like that, Joe Knight. Joe was half antiques dealer, half layabout, making a living I'd bet my new boots that the DSS knew nothing about. They'd see him as a sad case, barely able to read and write, and crippled with arthritis that would have made the heart bleed of even the hardest DSS doctor. We knew him as a lively old man, gnarled as a character in Griff's favourite Hardy, dependent on seasonal vegetable and fruit picking. This was always paid cash in hand — 'just to oblige a friend', if anyone asked. He used to oblige Griff, too, drifting to boot sales or village bring-and-buy sales, picking up stuff for pennies Griff would mostly pay him pounds for. Sometimes he'd bring his wife along, and I'd challenge myself to pick up more than one word in ten, her accent was so thick and her teeth so few and far between; others, like today, he'd be alone, touching the side of his nose when I took him through to Griff, still in the kitchen although he was due to open the shop in half an hour. This meant he'd rather talk to Griff on his own, if I didn't mind. Since he ponged even more than his wife, I didn't. I returned to my gilding.

Don't think I wasn't curious. I strained my ears for any stray conversation seeping up through the kitchen ceiling. Sometimes Griff told me what they'd been talking about and what he'd bought. Sometimes it wasn't things he brought, but gossip — when there'd be a good sale, and what the word on the street was about certain items tucked away with cheap tat. Other times Griff stayed mum, though I could tell he was embarrassed at not being able to tell me. Today I should imagine Griff would be after titbits of information about the outbreaks of thieving that seemed to be following us round the country. He might — and now my pulses quickened and I had to put down my scalpel in case it slipped and did expensive damage — even be asking about the *Natura Rerum* page.

Well, if Griff couldn't open the shop, I'd better. It always gave me a sense of power, fishing the keys and the float out of the safe and swaggering the two or three yards along the street to open up, checking always and certainly today that no one was lurking to jump me. Once in, I dived across to the control panel, hidden behind a picture, tapping the code swiftly into the alarm touch-pad. There. Peace and quiet. And then I went back to the door again. Like many rural antiques shops, ours was locked even when we were in it. Genuine customers understood, generally.

Mrs Hatch had left a note of what she'd sold, including a hideous brass planter from her own stock and three matching lustre jugs, ones with dancers on them. As a trio, they'd fetched more than three single items. I dusted round a bit, and settled down to study the contents of the manila envelope I'd brought with me. In a dusty corner were some old Ordnance Survey maps, no longer much use except to the most trusting motorist or walker. But if roads and footpaths moved, things like Tudor manors and Palladian mansions didn't. I could locate all the ones Griff and I had found interesting and plan approximate routes to them.

Griff had to tap on the bolted door to be let in. As I pulled back the bolts, he was already telling me to come back home quickly. Now. This minute!

What had happened? Had my dad—? Even as I told myself to get real, my fingers shook so much that I could hardly set the alarm, and then it took me valuable seconds to lock up. Griff didn't wait for me — he was already back in the kitchen when I let myself in. No middle-aged man. Just a very old lady, appearing from the newspaper in which she was wrapped.

'Look at this! Look at this!'

I took her from him: although the figurine was old, the woman herself, despite her wig, looked very young. She seemed to be reading some sort of list.

So what? I plonked down on a chair and stared into space.

'Isn't she lovely? And look — look under here. What can you see?'

It wasn't his fault, was it? And it wasn't often I heard him so excited. I looked. His swollen finger jigged around a blue letter L.

'Longton Hall. It's so rare I've only ever seen it in reference books. Goodness knows what it'll fetch. Oh, yes — I shall put it in a top-class auction. Or there's Archie at the BM who may want to buy it! My God, Lina, Longton Hall ware. We're talking high hundreds, maybe even thousands. Oh, certainly thousands.'

'What'll you tell Joe?'

'Nothing at all! Dear heart, that would give the darling man ideas quite above his station.'

'But Griff—'

'Enough, Lina. I know we don't see eye to eye on this matter, never have and probably never will. That's how Joe and I function. I never know how much or how little he's paid. He never knows how much or how little I make. Sometimes it's nothing, remember.'

'Not very often,' I grumbled.

'This concern for the underdog is entirely understandable and does you credit — as a person. But not as a businesswoman. Now, would you be kind enough to bathe this lady — I find I can't trust my hands at the moment. And I shall find the times of the afternoon trains to London.'

So I was to be stuck in the shop all afternoon, was I? Just when I wanted to be out and about, rubbernecking mansions. I snarled at the little lady. But she smiled hopefully back, and I hadn't the heart to be cross with her. With Griff — well, that was quite another thing.

* * *

I was even crosser when I got our first customer of the day. She emerged from a four-by-four big enough to have done service in the Iraq war, abandoned about a foot from the double yellow lines that were intended to keep traffic flowing down the village street. You might think I'd have welcomed her with open arms, since it was now well after three thirty, but it was the contents of her arms that worried me. A child of about four. There was also a child in one of these massive pushchairs, the sort that look as if they're going drag-racing any moment, but since that one was fastened in, it didn't present quite such a hazard — not if it was parked out of arm's reach of all the little things it was grabbing for. Its older sister — complete with a dripping ice cream — was the problem.

I was very slow opening up. The longer I dawdled, smiling apologetically through the glass door at my clumsiness, the more of that ice cream might find its way into the cupid's bow mouth than on to our *putti*. But at last I had to defeat the lock, and the little girl more or less fell on to me. The safest thing was to gather her up, looking as if I enjoyed being dabbed with sticky fingers.

'Aren't you lucky,' I cooed, 'having a lovely ice cream like that?'

The mother manoeuvred the monster-buggy inside. 'Victoria doesn't like strangers to pick her up,' she announced, in the sort of carrying voice Mrs Hatch used, only even more pukka. And not in the Jamie Oliver sense, either. Pukka sahib sort of pukka.

I ignored what she really meant: she didn't like Victoria to be picked up by strangers. 'She'll be all right with me, won't you, Victoria?' If I'd had a hand free, I'd have pointed to the discreet little notice forbidding food or drink in the shop. As soon as I could, I'd drop the cone into the bin, accidentally on purpose.

'Can I help or would you prefer to browse?' I asked politely, removing the cone from my ear.

'Just browsing. Look, you can see she doesn't like being held.'

I could feel. She was arching her body strongly against mine. At least to push she had to remove the cone from my ear. I helped. 'What a sticky girl you are,' I giggled, through set teeth. 'Has Mummy got a hankie to mop you with?'

Mummy managed to be deaf. Perhaps she was. Youngster Two was yelling fit to bust. It was reaching for a Venetian wineglass. In vain, I hoped — but you never knew with will power like that. I'd have moved it, only I was trying to reach the roll of kitchen towel I'd started to keep handy by the till. I'd started to keep something else handy, you see — but Victoria couldn't get her mitts on it till I'd got the worst off them. The little darling tried to bite me as I wiped.

'Now if you do that, I shan't show you something special,' I said. 'Come on, Victoria — let's get those hands clean.'

'Gosh, all this fuss!' I wasn't sure which one of us Mummy addressed

One of us had to win. Despite the screams it had to be me. It was. As a reward for her awful behaviour, I now had to show Victoria what should silence her for a few minutes at least, but then almost guarantee me a bit of profit. The junk box. Correction, my Plan A — the toy box. Then I could rescue the Venetian glass. Mummy had at last realised that Youngster Two was getting loud, so she returned to its buggy — I'd been right in both senses when I'd called it a monster-buggy — pushing it absentmindedly backwards and forwards while she scanned the shelves. In a supermarket the fingers would have grasped baby-height sweets. Here they were within millimetres of fragile glass. And if blood were shed I knew who'd get the blame.

Hooking out the toy box with my left foot, I managed to reach the wineglass just as the brat did. There. The top shelf for that. But now it was after a Baccarat millefiori paperweight, nothing special, but, in the way of glass things, heavy and breakable. Nearer and further, nearer and further, as Mummy pushed and pulled the buggy.

It wouldn't take much effort to smash a skull with it.

I resisted the temptation. Moved it into safety.

'Madam,' I said over the yells, 'this isn't really the best place to park.'

She turned, raising an eyebrow as if our grandmother clock had spoken.

'These things are very — dangerous,' I said, replacing *fragile* at the last moment. 'Look, he's after that poker now.'

Meanwhile, Victoria was dismembering a doll.

That was OK. They were meant to come apart. Part of my Plan A.

At last, the noise from the brat was so loud it penetrated even Mummy's cloth ears. With the speed of light I put part two of Plan A into practice, shoving a battered teddy into his hands. Blessed silence.

'Now, was there anything in particular?' I asked Mummy, smarmy enough to be Griff.

'I was thinking of something you don't seem to have,' she bellowed, dropping her voice as she realised the din had ceased. 'A present — something manly, you know?'

Manly? A year ago I'd have shown total ignorance. Now I could produce a hip-flask and a silver mounted riding crop, my face a perfect blank.

'I was thinking of a print. Or an old map. That sort of thing.'

My stomach clenched. 'Anything in particular?'

'Oh, something local. Hang on — a friend of mine's got the first page of some book or other, you know, coloured and framed. Such a scream.'

'You wouldn't know which one?'

She shrugged massively, as if not knowing just showed what an idiot I was.

'Could you tell me what it looks like?'

'Gosh! Well, it's got these funny little men on it, all dressed up in really weird clothes, holding spears and God knows what else. Theatre or something. Very pretty colours — amazingly bright for something hundreds of years old.'

I breathed out. Not my frontispiece. But possibly the frontispiece of an atlas I'd once seen Marcus working on. If she wasn't going to buy anything from here, she might as well buy from him and Copeland. I fished out his card, one of a collection we kept by the phone, and moved as if to hold the door for her. At this point, Plan A came into play again. Summoned by Mummy, Victoria came clutching a doll's torso. And there was no way she could separate the brat from the unfortunate bear.

'Drat,' she said, producing a credit card. 'Bloody pricey, teddies, these days, I suppose.'

'Collectors' items,' I agreed sadly. I gathered up the rest of the doll. 'But I'll throw in this as a little extra.'

As if getting a bargain, she reached as if on impulse for the crop. I wrapped it before she could blink. If my face had been blank before, it was impenetrable now. But as I locked up behind her, I could hardly stop myself bursting into song. Treat me as an unpaid childminder, would she? Well, she'd paid me now — and at a rate ten times the national minimum wage.

CHAPTER FOURTEEN

'So the Longton lady'll sleep with Archie tonight,' Griff said mistily. 'Safe and sound.'

'That'll be a first,' I said, 'Archie sleeping with a woman.' But actually, in view of all the recent hassle, I was pleased that she wasn't anywhere near us.

'Naughty, naughty.' He grinned, raising his glass of champagne in my direction. 'You know exactly what I mean. And the wonderful thing is that he'll find a buyer for us and preserve our anonymity — no small consideration after these last few days.'

I nodded, and wished I hadn't — movement joggled my bruises.

'Now, tell me about your afternoon.'

Full of champagne, plus some stuff he'd added to it to sweeten it called crème de cassis, rather like alcoholic Ribena, I gave him chapter and verse.

Cocking his head like a bird after an especially juicy worm, he asked, 'How did you feel about diddling all that lovely cash out of Lady Whatever Her Name Is?'

Yes, her credit card had revealed she was titled.

'Great!' But then I shook my head. I'd taken advantage of the woman, just as I'd accused Griff of taking advantage of Knight.

'No, not good. It felt brilliant at the time, but now it feels like — cheating.'

'*Caveat emptor*, dear heart. Business is business, as Arthur Miller ironically observes. While some things are certainly beyond the pale, some things are entirely legitimate.'

'As to business — well, it wasn't the wisest thing in the world to risk antagonising her. She won't be happy when she finds out that teddy bear's worth next to nothing.'

'I think your original feeling was better, dear heart. She used you. You used her. And she'll never admit having bought a duff toy. Look at the idiotic prices people were paying for the creatures at Detling. Absolute rubbish, no better than that specimen. Which reminds me, I bought a little present for you in London.' He hauled himself to his feet. 'You do realise you might have been talking to your sister, don't you?' He asked as he disappeared round the door.

My sister! Being related to a thick, arrogant cow like that?

'I know,' I said as he returned. 'That quip about my sister! It's all part of your campaign to show me that the aristocracy are nothing to write home about, isn't it? Like the castles and William the Bastard this morning. I looked him up after work,' I added.

'William the Bastard indeed. Wrong-side-of-the-blanket birth apart, he confessed on his deathbed that he was responsible for the murders — not deaths in battle, you'll notice — the murders of five hundred people. Are you sure you don't want to know what I found for you? Oh dear, Lina, you're not very enthusiastic about presents, are you? I wonder why that is. It's no doubt buried deep in your psyche.'

'I quite like presents,' I said, adding fairly, 'so long as they're not too useful.' All those useful knickers and tights and soaps and shampoos for birthdays or Christmas. I should have felt grateful. Perhaps I would have done if I hadn't been expected to.

'I think you'll find this far from utilitarian.' He produced a large bag from behind his back. 'I haven't ventured to wrap it — it objected too strongly.'

'It' was a teddy bear.

'He's a *he*, not an *it!*' He smiled invitingly and held out his paws. But it was Griff I hugged.

'Dear, dear — well, I suppose fizz always makes one weepy.' He mopped his eyes, then mine. 'I had a bear once not unlike this called Timothy. Gosh, he'd be worth thousands now.'

'But you wouldn't have sold him?'

'Who knows?' Griff shrugged. 'I think it might be that you inherited your mercenary streak from yours truly.'

'Well, I shan't sell this Timothy. Tim. Ever. Hey, what's this on his bow-tie?'

'A little something I also found on my travels. Strictly non-utilitarian again.'

This bear — about an inch and a half tall — was made of gold, clutching a ball made out of a coral bead. His eyes were diamond chips. Griff passed me his jeweller's eyepiece. 'Only yours if you can tell me the year and city of manufacture,' he said.

Knowing Griff he might just mean it. I peered closely. 'Birmingham. 1930?'

'1931. No matter. What's a year between friends?' Pointing at tiny loops between its ears and on its back, he added, 'It can be either a brooch or a pendant. I know such things aren't your actual fashionable gear these days, so I shan't expect to see you wearing him.'

'But you can expect to see him sitting around smiling. Is there room for him in that display case?'

Someone rang the doorbell.

'Tchh. Trust the outside world to interrupt our charming little sentimental idyll.'

I stayed where I was, sitting on the settee — whoops! — sofa, Tim snuggling up while I held the other bear in the palm of my hand.

'Lina, my dear — the police for you.'

Oh no! The fraudulent bear. If I grovelled enough, would that get me off? I promised the Guy in Canterbury Cathedral I'd never do anything like it again if he could get me out of this.

Dave Brent peered round the door, just like Griff earlier, producing a little bag.

* * *

'I was surprised he didn't offer to smooth that bruise cream on your cheeks with his own fair hands,' Griff said over breakfast the following morning. 'More black coffee?'

Dave's visit had been only partly official. He'd returned the videotape, confirming that at least we knew my assailant was male. His colleagues rather thought the car might be a Ford Focus. Which didn't, as he said, narrow it down all that much. Then, presenting the tube of ointment, the sort Mr Elworthy had rejected, he thought it might be nice to take me out for a drink when the case was over — he almost checked with Griff to ask him permission. Griff reminded him, rather too quickly, that the previous evening he'd said there wasn't a case, just some information that might help solve other cases. But that was the attempted burglary, I'd chimed in, not liking the fact that the discussion was taking place above my head. Trying to run me over had been a different matter, surely not connected with those damned cats. Which was presumably when we all fell about laughing and somehow Griff shoehorned me into my first date with Dave.

Next morning, Griff would have loved all the details — 'Nothing better than a good goss, dear heart.' I didn't exactly point out that I'd never asked for or expected a blow-by-blow account of his dealings with Aidan but he did accept that there were some things that I might not wish to discuss until the aspirins had worked.

And not then, either. I had a morning's restoration work ahead of me, while Griff looked after the shop. If business was slack, and you don't expect too much action midweek, then I'd take the van and leave him to it.

Today I was off on my first pilgrimage. Iffin Court. Oh, yes, I'd chosen it especially for the name, and because Griff and I could bury its importance to me under a mound of jokes about its name.

Like the one when he checked I'd got my mobile phone. 'Iffin difficulty, call me!'

He meant me to squirm so I did. 'Hang on. Is that what they call a pun? Some teacher told us about puns. Lowest form of wit, or something.'

'I think he might have mistaken puns for sarcasm. In fact, puns have a long and noble place in English letters. Shakespeare used them regularly with serious intent. As did the poet, Donne. "When you have done, you have not Donne, for I have more."'

'But Iffin a hurry, you've got no time for puns,' I reminded him. 'I've still got my gilding to finish.'

* * *

Iffin Court lay between the A28 and the B2068, not all that far from Canterbury. The A20 was nice and empty as usual, people preferring the M20. I'd much rather have driven up in an ordinary, anonymous car, not a van with the shop name plastered all over it. In fact, for general security, a car would be better, wouldn't it, a nice big estate job? Maybe this Longton Hall figurine would provide the cash. I knew more about cars than I'd ever let on, especially about starting them unofficially, you might say. I reckoned I could sort out something sound at an auction for under a thousand. But that meant confessing a bit more to Griff. On the other hand, I told myself, as I parked neatly and emerged, head high, he knew a lot worse things about me, or guessed, at least.

It was time to chase that memory. There was one pun we hadn't made. Iffin doubt, turn back.

Head still high, I walked towards the ticket office.

My mobile phone rang. Marcus?

'Hi. How's your search going?'

'I'm just going to the first place now. Iffin Court.'

'Iffin court, plead Not Guilty.'

I groaned.

'Why go there?' he asked, rather shirty. 'It's not on that list of postcodes.'

'I couldn't work them out,' I lied. I wasn't going to tell him I'd forgotten all about them. What with Kitties and teddy bears, I'd never got round to tidying out the caravan or even my bag. Maybe it wasn't entirely a lie, either — given the choice between having not just the full address of a place, plus photo, and just four letters framing two numbers, which would your brain forget to work on?

'What a good job I've had a chance to print off the whole list of Coz's names,' he said, sounding kind, to be fair, rather than patronising. 'What's your fax number at the shop?'

I rattled it off. 'Tell you what,' I added, 'I owe you an apology: I gave this poisonous woman your card yesterday. I hope her brats haven't dabbed their sticky mitts all over your handiwork.'

'*That's* how she got hold of us. She phoned last night.'

'So you haven't had the pleasure of her kids' company?'

'Strictly phone and registered post.'

'You got a sale, then?'

'She had her eye on a John Speed frontispiece: *The Theatre of the Empire of Great Britain*. Didn't have one in, of course. Then she started asking about other frontispieces. Just thought you might want to know.'

'You didn't tell her about mine?'

'Keep your hair on! Come on: we're in the same trade, Lina. You ought to know that customer confidentiality is paramount. Even when the customer's a mate.'

A mate, eh? Not *my woman* anymore. Who was using whom in this little relationship?

'Thanks,' I said. Even if I wasn't quite sure for what. 'Did you manage to sell her anything?'

'Why do you think I'm calling?'

To tell me about frontispieces?

'I only managed to flog her a Robert Morden map of Middlesex!' he crowed. 'And she wants us to locate a Saxton one, too. Retouching, framing: we're talking profit, here, Lina.'

I knew better than to ask how much profit. 'Great. Drinks are on you next time,' I said without thinking.

'Er—'

I could hear his writhe of embarrassment. I'd better spare him. 'Look, my battery's dying. I'll get back to you. OK?'

I stayed where I was, thinking. Was that why my so-called date with Dave Brent hadn't exactly set the Thames on fire, apart from the fact I was tired out and already semi-sloshed when we set out? Because I still had the hots for Marcus? No, I didn't think I had. I was pretty sure he didn't have them for me, and if life had taught me anything it was not to give love until you were sure of receiving it. But that didn't mean I didn't like him. Yes, as a mate.

So what now? Should I give up, and nip into Canterbury to scour the charity shops for anything worth selling on? And if I spotted anything they'd really underpriced I'd have told them. Or put a donation in their jar. Whatever.

Or, since I was here and it was quite a nice day, clean-smelling after all the rain, should I hand over my fiver and snoop round Iffin Court? The grounds themselves were worth a visit. From where I stood there was the sort of view they put on postcards, rolling fields, old churches, even a cricket ground over to my left. Behind me stood Iffin Court. I turned to face a gentleman's country residence probably built between 1760 and 1800. My period, whatever Marcus had said.

Iffin doubt, do it.

CHAPTER FIFTEEN

'So you had a pleasant afternoon?' Griff asked, but not as if he wanted to know. He eyed the plant I needed both arms to hold, but didn't comment.

'Oh, yes! Iffin Court's lovely. No help to me at all: the owners are a couple who need to waste some of what they make in the City. But it was useful, all the same. I thought this would look nice in that planter we can't shift,' I said, depositing my burden on the kitchen table, 'the Crown Devon with the crazed base.'

'The jardinière,' he corrected me, without smiling kindly as he usually did when he had to correct me. 'Perhaps you're right.'

'The whole of the enterprise,' I continued, more and more alarmed, 'is geared to making money. But they do it so prettily you feel grateful they're letting you buy. Tubs and hanging baskets everywhere — they'll be a picture in a month's time. We've still got time to plant some up. And that jam you always make and we never get round to eating — we could have a corner for produce like that in the shop. You know, like the toy basket. So that even if people come in just to get out of the rain, they're likely to buy something. And once they've opened their purses, they might as well buy something else.' I was gabbling. Because there was something wrong, really wrong, and I didn't know what it was.

Griff took his glasses off and laid them beside the plant on the table. My stomach clenched. Even with quite a stern telling off he'd peer over them. Any moment he'd rub his face and begin. If I'd been the crying sort I'd have sobbed: he was going to take away the lovely memories of my time at Iffin and replace them with horrible ones. 'You're clearly a born entrepreneur,' he began. 'But I never thought your enthusiasm would permit you to steal other people's trade secrets.' He picked up the sheets of fax paper. 'This is industrial espionage, Evelina. Unethical. There is only one thing to do with this and that's to burn it. Can't you imagine the harm it will do us in the trade if it gets about that you've got hold of Copeland's list of contacts?' His eyes blazed. I'd never seen him like this.

'I didn't "get hold of it". Marcus sent it to me so—'

'What a foolish boy. I presume it was in response to your blandishments.'

'He's a mate. I asked him to find out where Copeland had got that frontispiece from. That's all.'

'This is very far from "that's all."' He counted out the pages, his hands shaking. 'Eleven A4 pages of addresses. Single space.'

'He promised it'd be just the ones down here.'

'Is Northumbria "down here"? I think not.' In one swift movement he balled them and opened the Aga door.

'No!' I made a dive but got no more than a burnt wrist for my pains. That wasn't the pain that brought tears to my eyes as I watched the paper burn.

He slammed the door shut, standing in front of it. Did he think I was going to plunge my whole hand in? Well, I suppose I might have done.

'That was the way to my father and you've destroyed it. Griff, you bastard — I hate you! I HATE YOU!'

* * *

I screamed a lot more than that before I finished. I told him a lot about his sex life he already knew. I said he did dreadful things I knew he didn't. I shouted. I raged till my throat was sore. I must have done things I never remembered afterwards because I ended up with earth under my fingernails.

And now I was cowering in the caravan, huddled under my sleeping bag, still crying. OK, as a dramatic gesture, the caravan was a cop-out. But what else could I do? I'd slammed out of the house. The rain had come on again, all the heavier after the sun, and I'd got soaked to the skin just running down the village street. A village isn't like a town. The evening bus had come and gone. The railway station was nearly two miles from the centre. Thumbing a lift? Even my pounding head knew that at this time of night it was too risky: I'd get some fatherly type who'd drop me at a police station or another fatherly type who'd want to comfort me with a quick shag. No to both, thanks very much.

It was quite by chance I'd turned in the direction of the farm and the caravan field. But the idea of using Griff's own place as a refuge struck me as brilliant revenge. He'd spend the night worrying about me — even in my blind anger I knew that — and all the time he'd be providing the shelter that meant I didn't need to go back home. Next morning I'd trash it, just to let him know.

I couldn't go back home. Ever. Not after all the things I'd said. Maybe things I'd done. Half of me wanted to remember; the other half made sure I couldn't. My memory for detail simply shut down. It hadn't for months, not with all those little exercises Griff used so patiently to set.

What if I'd hurt him? Good grief, what if I'd hit him the way I hit myself? I could have injured him. I was strong for my size, just as he was frail for his. I might even have killed him and not known. The things I'd said had been enough to give him a heart attack. One or two bubbled up in my memory: it was all I could do not to slap them down by punching my forehead.

I couldn't go back. I couldn't go back and find him lying dead because of what I'd done.

I couldn't go back full stop.

Ever.

But I had to know he was all right. I stood in the rain trying to make my feet turn back to the village but they wouldn't work. I didn't realise what I was doing till the rain dripped off my nose.

I'd set out with nothing except my bag. No Tim, of course. I could have done with Tim.

No, I couldn't. I might have put a knife through him and torn him apart.

What had I done to Griff?

My mobile. I had my mobile. Reception wasn't good round here. But it was worth a try. The caravan itself was in a black spot. Out in the lane, in the rain again, I stared at the phone. Who was I going to contact? Griff'd never speak to me again, not after the things I'd said. He'd never speak to me again if he was dead, would he? If I'd killed him.

I closed the phone. There was no way I could phone Griff himself. No way. I couldn't bear to hear his voice; I couldn't bear not to hear his voice.

I scrolled through the numbers in the memory. Marcus? No, he'd started all this, him and his enthusiasm and incompetence. Mrs Hatch? No, she disapproved of me far too much, though she never let on. Dave? Tony? Tony. He was the one. Him and his skimpy towelling robe.

'Have you any idea what time it is?' he asked.

'None at all. But you've got to go and see that Griff's all right.' I cut the call.

Back to the caravan. I had enough sense to peel off my soaking clothes before huddling in the sleeping bag. There were the towels we'd used in Harrogate: I'd not got round to washing them, of course. Nor to emptying the fridge. There was even a little water left. And there was the first aid kit for my poor burnt hand.

My phone rang. Tony. Stark naked I had to go out into the field to hear what he said.

'He says to come home.'

'He's all right?'

'OK,' he said in the sort of voice you use when you're not sure. 'But he says—'

I cut the call. No. I couldn't. Switching off the phone, I dived into the sleeping bag again.

* * *

Thank goodness for the emergency dressing gowns we kept in the caravan. In my panic the previous night, I'd forgotten that our pitch was nearest the farmhouse, which overlooked it. Griff had chosen it for security. Now I had the insecurity of seeing all my clothes scattered about, and the knowledge that as they cleaned their teeth the farmer and his sons would be able to peer down at me.

The clothes were still sodden, of course. Horrible. But I put them on anyway. Very quickly. Now I could check my resources. The rations we always topped up at the end of each journey were very low. But there was enough milk for a splash in my coffee and enough to dampen some breakfast cereal. There was only a tenner in my own purse, but in the one I use for business, over a hundred quid in cash, most of it profit from the Harrogate sale I'd not got round to sorting into our accounts. Then there was the credit card Griff made me carry just in case there was a real emergency. Somehow I didn't think running away from him was the right reason to use it. I could get some clean, dry clothes from a charity shop, but the shoes'd be a problem. I hated other people's trainers with a vengeance. And then what? I'd made myself voluntarily homeless and unemployed. Nothing from the DSS for six weeks, then. Seasonal work? There were enough asylum seekers, poor guys, working for virtually nothing, to pick every vegetable in Kent, not to mention doing equally illegal hotel and café work. Begging or selling the Big Issue? Didn't fancy either. Couldn't busk to save my life. Belt-tightening was in order.

At this point the caffeine might have kicked in. I could get Marcus to let me know the best postcodes for my hunt. Who knows, by the end of the week I might be living in luxury?

* * *

If you live in a decent-sized city you take certain things for granted. Cheap and regular public transport is one of them. Living in the country, you have to plan all the time if you want to get from an A that isn't on a railway line to a B that isn't on a regular bus route. Journeys that would take less than half an hour by car become epic voyages. Especially when you don't have timetables to hand, and you've no idea where to start from in the first place.

At least I had a rough idea about buses to Ashford, so it was there I headed first, making sure I sat hunched, hood up and staring out of the window at the familiar countryside. It was a waste of time, I dare say — in a village like ours someone would probably have recognised me if I'd dressed in a complete gorilla outfit. At least there were plenty of charity and ordinary, cheap shops in Ashford. I'd have loved to get undies from the specialist lingerie shop in what used to be the marketplace, or even, more realistically, from M & S. But it'd be bottom of the market stuff for me. I could just afford a new waterproof top and new, if cheap, trainers: I knew from experience that folk only gave away anoraks and raincoats when they'd lost their weatherproofing. And I simply couldn't bear the smell of other feet. Really, truly couldn't. Then I did a circuit of the charity shops, picking a T-shirt here, jumper there. And a couple of bits of jewellery I could sell on for four times what I paid. I'd pop the profit in one of their boxes when I had enough to survive on. I kept the receipts to remind me and also to prove to a potential buyer I hadn't knocked them off somewhere. Local maps from W H Smith, nothing like as good as the old ones back home at Griff's.

I mustn't think of it as home anymore.

Bus station and railway station got me travel info. And I put a call through to Marcus.

'You're joking!' he gasped. 'But you're like father and daughter. Well, a lot better than most girls and their dads: they have rows.'

'Griff and I had a row. Actually it was over the fax you sent. He thought I was being unethical, doing industrial espionage, blah, blah, blah.'

There was a long pause, so long I was glad I'd asked him to call me back. 'I suppose in the wrong hands . . . Shit! I never thought. Sorry.'

'So will you find me just the ones very close to Ashford or Bredeham? And Marcus — hang on — I want you to do something else, too, before you call back.'

* * *

I think it was because he was feeling guilty that Marcus did exactly what he was told fairly quickly, calling me back while I was in a loo changing. I stowed the still damp stuff into one of the now empty carriers — it'd be a pain to ferry it everywhere, but that was life. I couldn't afford to ditch it. I'd go and have a coffee while I mulled everything over. There was a coffee shop in the marketplace, with a few tables in what might at any moment be feeble sunshine.

There. Now I could scan Marcus' summary of very local posh piles and their opening times this month. He'd bring a list of those further away or with irregular opening times to the next fair. How I was to be there, I'd no idea, but it was the only safe way I knew of making a living. Unless I went to college and got a qualification for my restoration work — and who knew how I'd afford that — I could only get work for friends or by word of mouth. In a world without Griff's protection you needed more than that.

The coffee I was drinking nearly came back at the thought of him. Why hadn't he been in touch? He knew my number. I'd have expected some message — after all, I'd checked he was all right last night.

If I thought about him, I'd cry. And Lina didn't cry. Well, not very often. I wouldn't hit myself, either. Calmly as I could, I looked at the information I'd written down in a notebook that wasn't quite bottom of the range, because I didn't want any tacky, girly designs on the cover. Griff had always told me to behave professionally, and fishing out My Little Pony to record a price or whatever was going to impress no one. Plus I didn't like any of the girly designs.

Yes! There were two places open this very afternoon. Two! One was near Tonbridge; the other was near Canterbury, not all that far from Iffin Court. I knew it was easy enough to get from Ashford to Canterbury by train. There must be a bus from Canterbury to Hythe, which was, like Bossingham Hall, due south of Canterbury. I checked. If I legged it, I might just get the Canterbury train now. Sorry — no tip. The waiter had a regular wage. I no longer did.

Legs were going to become my most valued form of transport. It was quite a step from the railway station, Canterbury West, to the bus station, but nothing motivates you more than the knowledge you'll have to wait another two hours if you miss the next bus. But I was in luck. The bus in question actually left Stone

Street, the main road south I thought it would follow, and took to the village roads to the east, yes, actually to my goal, a hamlet called Bossingham. Yes! But it was clear that Lord Elham's pad lay a good long way from any nasty, vulgar thing like a public highway. The driver seemed to stop anywhere passengers asked, and happily pulled up in the lay-by by impressive wrought-iron gates.

'Mind you, it don't open for another hour,' he said. 'Why don't you go on as far as the village? There's a nice little pub called the Hop Pocket — you could get some lunch there.'

Largely because he closed the doors before I could get out and pulled away, I agreed. But I didn't want a sandwich or drink. I was sure I'd seen those gates before. Sure.

I'd seen thousands of gates before. Well, hundreds. In those books Griff liked me to study. One pair must look very like another.

OK, then. Bossingham itself and the Hop Pocket. The village was dead ordinary, or at least this part — mostly bungalows, though with a cluster of older houses where the road took a sharp bend. A sign said there was a twelfth-century church a mile away. I needed food more than exercise. The Hop Pocket was little more than a double-fronted cottage, with a porch tacked on in front. Inside it was the sort of pub you dream about, not smart at all, wooden floors there because they've been there for ages, not self-consciously twee because they make a cool ambience. OK, there were a few hops scattered about, and a hop shovel, but no one had run riot with a mishmash of old artefacts simply because a designer who wouldn't know his arse from an ear of corn had told him to. I found a corner table and a local newspaper and checked the blackboard menu. I read, you might say, from right to left, going for price, not what Griff would call gastronomic appeal. All the same, the sandwich I bought was full to overflowing, and after buying my first drink I took courage and asked for a glass of tap water. The lad behind the bar was only my age, and, finger to lips, handed one over.

'D'you know anything about Bossingham Hall?' I asked, toasting him silently.

He pulled a face. 'His Lordship — that's Lord Elham, though of course Elham village is a few miles away — he doesn't come in here. Everyone else in the village does; not him.'

I gestured: was he snooty?

The barman shook his head. 'By all accounts he's just weird. Even the people working at the Hall say that. You know, the volunteer guides and so on.'

'Weird in what way?'

But at this point a party of walkers stomped in, reorganising tables and shouting contradictory orders. Weird? Well, I'd have to find out for myself.

CHAPTER SIXTEEN

Through those gates, then. Into an avenue of chestnut trees and oaks, on to a road rough with potholes. Where the trees might have met, on the horizon, was Bossingham Hall. Imagine making the journey in a luxurious coach, to be greeted by a candlelit house. You'd already be planning which clothes your servant would lay out, which jewels she'd clasp round your neck and wrists.

No upholstered chaise for me. No, nor posh car. In fact motorists were sent on a diversion, so at least as a pedestrian I had a journey more in keeping with history. The house dominated the long walk. And it was long — a mile or more, I'd say. *If* this were the house, *if* my mother had brought me here, had she made me walk? Had she had the luxury of a buggy? Or had the poor woman been forced to carry me? A toddler can weigh heavy. Had I been quiet, or struggled, like Victoria, the child in the shop? Had I had a terrible tantrum, the sort to make her curl with embarrassment or simply bend and slap me, as I'd come to slap myself?

As I got closer I could see that the hall was a typical Palladian mansion, on a fairly large scale. It might even have had a facelift to transform it from an ordinary old house into something the neighbours would talk about. And they would have talked about it. It had a lovely symmetrical frontage, with a central portico like a Greek temple, four columns topped by a pediment. They might have said that the new wings were a bit on the large side. Should I have thought so? If only Griff had been with me to guide my eye.

He'd have been incensed that present-day visitors weren't admitted via the great front door, reached by a wide and impressive flight of steps. We were sent to the side, where a couple of blue-rinsed ladies intercepted us. I paid my money and took up what felt more like an order than a kind invitation to leave my heavy bags with them. Flexing numbed fingers, I cast financial sense to the winds and bought the glossy guidebook too. I could call it research. Then I followed the signs, which took me via a corridor full of Lely-lookalike ladies, all long noses and pursed mouths a-simper, to the entrance hall, which didn't look at all impressive. Why not? I walked to the front doors and turned back to face it, as if I'd been a visitor arriving properly, not just a customer. It was only then that I got the full impact of the symmetrical stairs, starting either side of the hall and meeting in the middle as they rose. If only I'd known all the proper terms. But I didn't, and I had to be content with a long and uneducated gawp. Mustn't it have been wonderful to live in a place like this in its heyday? Probably, though, I'd have been no more than a tweeny, and would have spent more time dusting the statues and banister rails than admiring them. The son of the house would probably have got me pregnant, and I'd have been turned off without a shilling or a reference.

Was that what had happened to my mother? Had she been a servant here?

I bit my lip, and took a deep breath. I was moving too fast. Sure this place felt familiar, but I might simply have seen others like it in Griff's books — no architect worth his salt wouldn't have wanted to put similar staircases in similar halls, once he'd got all the head-scratching out of the way and knew how to make cantilevers work. There! A word had come back. Was that an omen?

I worked my way through the house, loving the proportions of each room, even if I felt some of the later Victorian colour schemes really vulgar, not to mention the fact that they clashed with the fireplaces. No, not a greyish-white one in sight. Their marble was more yellowish than the one in my memory. One in the morning room was rust-coloured, and whoever had chosen crimson wallpaper should have been ashamed, especially when it was supposed to be an informal room. The library was my favourite room, not just full of books, as you'd expect, but with two very nice cabinets full of china to die for — Meissen, Sevres, Derby. The dining room was a bit of a letdown. The furniture wasn't much better than Ralph Harper's stuff, out of proportion and full of mismatched veneers. There was part of a Worcester dinner service on the table, and what looked like Stourbridge glass, but I wouldn't have thought any of it top of the range. The drawing room must have been very pretty in its heyday, with a yellow satin wall-covering and chairs with toning upholstery. It was a pity someone hadn't taken a needle to it years ago: now it would need a full restoration. Visitors were allowed to see only two bedrooms. They both had hidden doors: I'd have given my teeth to nip over the elegant cord keeping us at bay and sneak a look at what lay behind. Ever since Griff showed me my first stately house, that's what I'd wanted to do. Forget the public rooms — up to a point at least — and show me where real life was lived, the servants' rooms and their bedrooms. We were allowed a peep into a bathroom, presumably once a dressing room, with a two-seater loo and more mirrors than I'd have thought Victorian ladies would have considered decent. Perhaps they still had hipbaths in their rooms, and left this sort of thing to peacocking gentlemen. And that was it. I'd seen no more than about a tenth of the house, but my tour was over and I was being courteously directed to the gift shop and tearoom, which was situated in the original kitchen.

Forget the gifts. But a Coke wouldn't come amiss, and I had a plan. I could read the guidebook while I drank it and maybe talk my way in for another poke round.

For *maybe* read *definitely*. The guidebook was a mine of information about the owners, the Duke of Elham, which they kindly told us was pronounced Ealham, even giving a family tree on the back cover. They traced their ancestry back to the Conquest, would you believe? Yes, the original castle was built with the hush money William the Bastard doled out to his cronies, even if the book didn't put it quite that way. Anyway, once the family had got a toehold in the country, they'd spread all over it, like a patchy rash. They had estates here, there and everywhere at one point, though some had been sacrificed to pay debts — they must have been a spendthrift lot. Then they came into money in the eighteenth century, though trade, the book said, and decided to go to town on Bossingham Hall, which was nice and convenient for London, where they spent most of their time. There were some lovely portraits from this period, including a spectacular Reynolds of the then Lady Elham, and a Gainsborough of her sister-in-law. Clearly whatever the trade had been it was what Griff called lucrative: I realised with a shudder that at that period it might well have involved human cargo. Yes, I'd been at one school long enough to go on a trip to the maritime museum in Liverpool, with its slavery exhibition. There were even worse things to be than skivvies at a great house, or homeless antiques dealers.

The Victorian period had seen the family solemnly respectable, encouraging Nonconformism in the area. But one of their sons had been a mate of Edward, Prince of Wales, Victoria's eldest son. He'd got involved, the book said coyly, in some of the prince's sexual peccadilloes. I'd never seen the word before but I had a shrewd idea what it meant. The family fortunes rose during the first world war, dipped in the thirties, and never really picked up again. Perhaps that was when they flogged the decent dining furniture, popping in cheap replacements.

This was the only major estate still in the hands of the family, who now held it in trust. The present Lord Elham, who did not enjoy good health, lived very privately. There was no mention of where he lived, of course. But my divvy's instinct told me I'd find someone interesting on the far side of some of the green baize doors I'd seen, marked, in large letters, PRIVATE. So I'd have to get through them, one way or another, wouldn't I?

* * *

'There's so much I never registered,' I told Blue Rinse One, whose face this time had no welcome in it. 'There are hardly any other people around now, so I could get a proper look at the Bow figures in the blue corridor, instead of a baby in a rucksack and a Japanese girl with a camcorder.'

'Video? That's highly irregular!'

'Especially close to such valuable stuff,' I agreed, shaking my head at the wickedness of people ignoring all the NO PHOTOGRAPHY signs. 'She moved on to another cabinet — can't remember what the room was called, though. Sorry.'

'Can you show me where she was?'

'Of course.' Right. I was in. OK, it was a ploy, but I'd have challenged even Griff to object to it. It was worrying, of course, that she should be so easily taken in: maybe I'd point this out when I'd finished. Anyone could have invented the same story, leaving security very weak at the front entrance.

She set off briskly, leaving Blue Rinse Two to guard the fort. I bobbed along behind her, feeling like a little tug in the wake of a liner.

'Just where was this room?'

In my imagination, of course. 'At the far end of one of the corridors upstairs.' It was true that there were cabinets there, with a mixed bag of items, some of which should have been given more public airings. 'Along here, I think.'

'There's no sign of her now.'

Nor had there ever been. 'I'm sorry. But maybe one of the room guides stopped her?'

She nodded, but clearly wasn't happy about leaving me for my second bite of the cherry. However, I avoided her eye, peering hard at the display. Rockingham; Minton; Chelsea — if only I could have reached them out and handled them. Even when she'd gone, I lingered. However, what I was supposed to be doing was something else I wasn't supposed to be doing at all — searching for and opening one of those 'Private' doors.

Whatever I did, I mustn't arouse anyone else's suspicions. Blue Rinse had a shrewd idea I'd conned her. She might even warn the room guides — or guards — as she returned to base. So I set off again at what I hoped was a typical tourist pace, dawdling here and there, but always making my way purposefully to one of my goals.

Only to find the unmistakable signs of an alarm system. It didn't look as sophisticated as ours, but I'd bet Griff's treasured figurine to a Ty Beanie that it'd make more noise than I'd like. The other one was protected too. And I'd bet that there was no chance of nipping through one of those hidden bedroom doors — they'd be bolted the far side.

I was just about to droop with despair when I found that if I ignored a one-way sign I could get back to the library. The china in there would have been worth a visit in itself. So I stood and stared, once again itching to hold some of it in my hands.

'You seem very keen?'

I jumped. A lady, elderly but definitely not blue rinse, had materialised.

'I just love the stuff,' I said simply. 'That Meissen group. Look at the delicacy of the modelling. And the colours are—' I searched for a Griff-ish word '—simply exquisite.'

'You're an expert?' It didn't sound like an accusation.

'Not yet. But I'm studying hard.' Half of my brain was inventing a CV that would pass muster; the other simply wanted to respond to her smile. 'Are you part of the family?' Crikey, was I after a grandmother now, as well as a father?

'Just a volunteer. If I didn't come here as a guide, I might even come as a visitor, I love the china so much. What's your interest?'

'Restoration.' The truth just popped out. Part of it. 'Still learning.'

'I'm afraid some of this could do with your attentions. Look at that poor sweetmeat dish. You wouldn't mend a crack like that, would you?'

I gave her a two-minute rundown on how it should be rescued.

'And how much would it cost?'

I thought of a figure and doubled it. Then I was more honest. 'And I really couldn't do it for less. When I'm fully qualified, I'd have to charge what I said first.'

'I doubt if the trustees would pay even the more modest sum.'

'But it'd be worth it!'

'You and I both know that. But there's been some sort of dispute, and economy is the order of the day.'

'A family row! In a place this size! Why don't they just go to opposite end of the house and cool off?'

'If only they could. One wing's closed up altogether. It's used to store items awaiting the ministrations of someone like you, or items marked for sale when the market picks up.'

'What about the other?'

'Oh, that's as good as closed up. Lord Elham lives there. And though it was he who organised the trust, he's not speaking to any of the trustees.'

'Why on earth not?'

'Because left to himself he'd have sold the whole house, contents and all.'

I gasped.

'Quite. So when they threatened legal action, his heirs, that is, all distant cousins, he made a pre-emptive strike, and said he'd spare them death duties provided he was allowed to live on rent-free. He owns nothing now. But they don't own anything either, not as individuals. And if they start bickering, it goes to the National Trust instead.'

'Canny old bugger!' Whoops. Old ladies didn't like swearing.

She didn't so much as blink. 'Canny bugger indeed. But not so old.'

My heart sank. I needed old. Mature, at least.

'About fifty, I suppose. Sixty at most.'

That'd do.

'He's a complete eccentric, and—' Her pager beeped. 'Ah! That's my signal to tell you that the house is closing and that you should make your way to the exit, where the shop and tea-rooms will be open for a further hour.' She smiled. 'But I have to check each room on my patch as I go, so if you want to come with me and have one last look you'd be very welcome.'

* * *

In the end she introduced herself as Mrs Walker and, while I collected my bags from Blue Rinse Two, bought me a cup of tea and a slice of cake, chattering away about her life and how she came to work at the Hall. It seemed she'd spent her life as a history teacher, retiring to the village with her husband, who'd contracted some rare cancer years after working in the petrochemical industry and died within six weeks of its being diagnosed.

'So why didn't you go back home,' I asked, aghast, 'now you're on your own?'

'Do you know Streatham? Then you'll know it's not the prettiest or cleanest of places . . .'

More of her life. More and more. Well, teachers spend their lives talking, so I suppose they miss it when they give up. I can't say I was excited, but she'd bought me a huge slice of gateau and given me a bit of information I could go on, so I tried not to fidget or yawn, even if I was concentrating more on how to get back to Bredeham than on what she was saying. But she'd mentioned Lord Elham again.

'*In all the papers?*' I repeated.

'Well, not the better ones. But the tabloids. They say he's reformed now. But in all my years in the classroom, I've never known a leopard change its spots.'

So what colour were mine? I had a nasty idea that if she'd known what my background was she'd have run a mile. Or maybe not. Maybe she'd have taken me in hand, the way Griff had. I had an idea she wouldn't have given up on me, like my other teachers had. The Mrs Walkers of this world didn't. Not even when Blue Rinse One stood over our table, looking far from happy.

'I never found that Japanese woman,' she said, without bothering to greet Mrs Walker.

'Japanese woman?'

'This young lady says she saw one with a camcorder.'

'I haven't seen—' Mrs Walker looked at me and changed gear, beautifully smoothly '—her since about three thirty. I told her not to use it. I even made her wipe what she'd shot already.'

'Thank goodness for that,' I said sincerely. 'Most items stolen from places like this are stolen on demand. A dodgy buyer wants X, a thief takes pictures to confirm that they're talking about the same X, and then an accomplice goes back and steals it. Or maybe they're simply checking the security. Which reminds me,' I said, going into Griff mode, 'I was terribly grateful to you for letting me back in, but doesn't having just one person on duty leave the Hall rather vulnerable?' I was very glad that Griff had made me pronounce the 'l' in the middle of the word. It would have mattered if I hadn't.

'Evelina is an antiques restorer,' Mrs Walker said quickly. 'An expert in her field. She was very concerned too about the state of some of our china.'

Before Blue Rinse could ask why I'd fiddled my way back in, as opposed to simply paying again, I stood, flipping one of Griff's business cards at her. I gave Mrs Walker a second. 'My boss would be delighted to assist in any way he can,' I assured her. I'd better tell him that he would over supper.

Except I wouldn't be seeing him for supper, would I?

CHAPTER SEVENTEEN

Every moment of the journey home I wondered what to say to Griff. I had plenty of time to think. From Bossingham to Bredeham's about half an hour — forty minutes at most — by car. It should have been about the same from Canterbury to Bredeham by train. First I had to get to Canterbury, of course, and I was two hundred yards from the end of that wonderful avenue when the bus sailed past. A two-hour wait or risk hitching? I got a brilliant lift from an anxious young clergyman with bright yellow, curly hair and blue eyes, who might have been a cherub except he was tall and rangy with the most joggly Adam's apple I'd ever seen. He insisted on driving me all the way to the station.

'No, honestly. Just drop me where you're going. I shall be fine.'

'I'm sure you would. But I'll take you to the station all the same.'

I dug into my memory. 'Acting on instructions from the Boss, I suppose?' I grinned, pointing upwards in case he didn't twig. 'Going the extra mile!'

I was rewarded by a guffaw. 'Right. I'm Robin, by the way.'

'Lina.'

His effort was wasted by an hour's wait at the station while they sorted out a signal failure. When the train actually arrived, it was so slow I wanted to get out and push. Then of course it would be a couple of miles' walk from Bredeham station to the actual village. But I'd got to get there first, and there we were, stuck at another signal.

So what did I say to Griff? None of the words I tried was right. I went over them all. OK, 'sorry' for a start — but 'sorry' didn't begin to cover what I felt or what he deserved. At last, I did what I should have done hours ago: I phoned to tell him to save me some supper.

Or I would have done, if I'd got through. The phone rang and rang. The answerphone didn't cut in. Had I — or rather, the phone — dialled the wrong number? I tried manually, digit by careful digit. Same response.

At last we inched towards Bredeham. Bother all the instructions about not opening carriage doors until the train's stationary — down in the South East, we'd still got carriages that took Noah and his animals to the Ark, so there were no automatic safety systems. I was out and halfway down the platform before I realised I'd forgotten my carrier bags. I'd grabbed them and was on my way again before the train had officially stopped.

It's a good job I couldn't see what awaited me outside Griff's cottage or I wouldn't have bothered. Aidan's Merc. All that hot sweaty journey, all my efforts to reach him and he wouldn't even pick up the phone because he was too busy entertaining Aidan. In bed with Aidan. I just kept on walking. I hardly noticed the deep cuts the carrier bags were making in my fingers, hardly noticed the blisters my new trainers had rubbed up, hardly noticed anything except the huge pain in my chest that made me want to howl out loud. No, not that sort of pain, not the sort I worried about if Griff rubbed his chest before popping an antacid. The sort of pain Griff's poets wrote about.

I hardly noticed this car coming up alongside me either. It slowed almost to a stop, and then accelerated away. Nothing special. A metallic-blue Focus. I hardly registered it except to hope someone didn't want long, complicated directions. I registered it a bit more when it turned and came back towards me, and a very great deal more when it repeated the process, stopping thirty yards behind me. I wasn't supposed to notice that, but I was using the pharmacy window as a mirror. There was no real food in the caravan, so I'd have to stop at Eddie Ho's for a takeaway, or get something in Londis I could heat in the microwave. Food apart, and I mustn't forget the small matter of breakfast, I needed to lurk somewhere for some time, long enough to get some idea of whether the Focus driver was really hanging about on my account or simply waiting for his girlfriend. If only I'd taken a closer look when I'd had the chance. There was no way I could check him out now.

But I did do something Tony or Dave, the policemen, would have approved. I could write down the registration. Mirror image it might be, but I could sort that out later. A something or other recollected in tranquillity. I could also do something even brighter — amazing how ideas came when you least expected them. What was Dave's phone number?

I should have called him anyway, to thank him for the evening out. That's what Griff had dinned into me. He always wrote personal thank you messages in elegant cards, but had conceded that my generation might prefer to text. On the other hand, maybe Dave should have phoned me — in Griff's book of etiquette, that would have been the advice. Actually I suspect the reason that neither of us had called the other was that the evening had not been a success, and that both of us preferred to bury our mistakes. So instead of Dave, I phoned Tony.

Who was on duty, of course, and not taking calls. I left him the Focus's number anyway, and told him I'd be in the caravan later — but not to tell Griff. Dave? He wasn't taking calls either.

Now I felt more alone than I had before — especially as the Focus was still parked with no sign of activity.

OK: which first, Londis or Eddie's? I could get more for less at Londis, I reckoned — Eddie would have been horrified if I'd only wanted rice or noodles or chips, and there was no way I could explain my sudden meanness. Iris had insisted I shop for end-dated products, and a root around the Reduced basket found a couple of ready meals, some fruit juice and a loaf of bread. Add some long-life milk and an apple and I wouldn't starve. I wouldn't die of carrier bags cutting into my fingers, either, even though I now had another to manage.

'That'll tear,' the girl on the till said, pointing at the handle. 'Here — if you repack everything, you might get away with these two. Got far to go?' she added, weighing them in her hands.

I told her.

'We can drop you off if you like. 'Cos these here are bloody heavy and my dad'll be picking me up as soon as the boss takes over,' she said. 'He's over there. See? That red Honda. You can go and tell him Shaz sent you if you like.'

'I'll hang on for you,' I said. 'You're sure he won't mind?'

'Got to go past the farm anyway, I told you.' She peered. No sign of her boss yet. 'Cow. Always does this. Pays by the hour, works you by the hour and a quarter.'

* * *

Safe and sound in the caravan. Or was I? Safe, yes, thanks to Shaz and her dad and Saturday's new lock on the door. But I wasn't very sound, because what I'd really hoped to see was a note from Griff. He must have worked out where I'd be. And he'd have known what contact from him would have meant to me. But he was too busy with Aidan and his bloody Merc. I banged everything down on what'd soon be my bed. Better to thump something that wasn't my own face. At least no one had stared at me today: a combination of ointments and tablets and heavy make-up had got me through. All I had to worry about now was what I should do the following day.

* * *

The librarians in Ashford were very patient with me, as I wrestled with what I'd described as research. They probably thought that a college project on Bossingham Hall was legitimate, especially as I could rattle off loads of information about the place, but might have wondered why I wanted so much information about Lord Elham. I'd have tried to come up with some silly explanation if Griff hadn't drummed it into me that you should never tell anyone more than you had to.

Griff wouldn't have approved of the newspapers I found myself scanning. He insisted on papers with news, not gossip. But it was gossip I needed. I found plenty of it, too. If Lord Elham had come from any sort of family but an aristocratic one, my bet was that what the columnists kindly referred to as his high spirits would have landed him in young offenders' centres such as Feltham. With his taste in drugs and booze, he'd have probably had to steal to feed his habit, ending up spending more time in jail than at home — or, more likely, on the streets. As it was, he might be stuck in only one wing of his home — but hey, what a wing, what a home. And he'd had good fun getting there, by all accounts. This party, that match. Henley, Lords, Wimbledon: but I don't think he was there as a brilliant sportsman, or even to watch: in each photo there was either a glass or a young woman flaunting her tits. OK: sour grapes. The tits were usually bigger than mine, and always in much nicer dresses than I could dream of. Usually I stopped myself getting bitter by reminding myself how happy I was with Griff. Today even my scribbling of notes was furious.

And then depressed. My mother certainly hadn't been the sort of woman you'd find at any of the places he'd been photographed. Not front of house, as it were. Backstage, yes. The woman passing the drinks or the canapés. That'd be my mum. Or even a washer-up. So how on earth could I link this man with her?

I worked on and on. I must have got every reference to Lord Elham ever printed. He loved the press, didn't he? If I'd been up to half as many jinks as he had, I'd have retired to a nunnery, or whatever girls like me did these days. Unless I'd been a Kylie or Lady Victoria or anyone else who seemed to grab publicity with both hands.

I packed up my things and headed out, thanking the women who'd been so helpful.

'No problem. Let us have a copy of the book when it's published!'

'Book?' I repeated blankly.

'Or dissertation or whatever: there's more than just a project there, surely! Or you could write yet another piece on him. Sell it to *Hello!*'

We both knew she was joking, but as I worked out where I could get the cheapest cup of drinkable coffee I was beginning to get the glimmer of an idea.

* * *

By the time I'd got my caffeine-fix and a burst of sugar into the blood, via a doughnut that really wasn't very nice, I knew what I was going to do. The first thing was to nip off to a phone box and dial a 118 number for a number — cheaper than calling from the mobile. Amazingly the guy wasn't ex-directory. I put on a Mrs Hatch sort of voice and announced I was from Day Trip Films — yes, I know it sounded mad, but look at the names of real-life film companies getting stuff on TV. And somewhere deep down, I wanted some association with Griff, though whether for luck or revenge I didn't know. As for me, I wouldn't be Evelina, though I suspected that might be just the name for a girl from Day Trip Films: I introduced myself as Lena, as in Horne. After all, he might just have memories of an Evelina, and fear a trap.

He didn't sound suspicious, not at all. I might have been the long-lost cousin whose call he'd longed for for years. He took the lure of a biopic without question, and agreed he'd love to talk to me. Talk? Drawl, more like. Was it his education or too much booze?

'Oh, yes — any time. Diary's not very full these days. Only one condition. Have to be pretty, eh? Oh, and bring a bottle of champers. Decent stuff — don't want to upset the old tum with Chateau Rot Gut. Tell you what — nothing on the box this afternoon. Why not toddle along after lunch?'

There was no way I could toddle anywhere as I was. I might be clean and decent, but what I needed was the sort of clothes Lena as in Horne might wear: the suit and boots I'd bought at the Outlet. The suit and boots I'd left at Griff's. Drat. But forget gear — what would a Lena as in Horne say?

'Oh gosh. Golly, that'd be great.' I mustn't admit I was stuck with public transport. I'd get there somehow. 'About four?'

'I don't know what time you have your meals, my dear,' he brayed, 'but four will be fine. You know how to get here?'

Perhaps it would sound better if I pretended I needed directions.

He gave them and rang off.

I should have been over the moon. But when I tried to work out what my emotions were, there was a good deal of panic. I couldn't go and interview a lord like this. I couldn't go and interview my possible father like this. I couldn't go and interview anyone like this. The Outlet was just within striding distance, but if I had to shell out for champagne, which would have to be good, that must take priority. I braced my shoulders and looked round. As I'd proved the other day, Ashford had its share of charity shops: Lena as in Horne would have to be into retro-chic and, given the walking she'd have to do, whatever she chose would have to work with trainers. Her budget had better run to some sticking plasters too, to protect yesterday's blisters. As I headed for the shops — sorry, no tip today, either — I made myself a big and solemn promise. If I ever had the chance to get a lot of money, no matter what it involved, I'd grab it with both hands.

CHAPTER EIGHTEEN

It was a good job I'd pretended to be ignorant: Lord Elham's directions took me not up the long avenue but past the Hop Pocket pub, and down a lane that stared as a gentle slope and ended as a steep hill. I took the unmarked track to the left he'd suggested, warning me that it wouldn't be good for a low-slung car and urging a slow walking pace. At last I was rewarded by a glimpse of chimneys. The track was so bad it helped me get my story ready. My car was in dock, and I was so eager to get my interview I'd come by cab, the driver refusing to risk his suspension for the last stage. Hence my arrival on foot, rather later than just after lunch. Just after three, in fact.

This morning I'd buried my emotions in the search for decent gear. Now I could worry about where to put my feet — it'd be easy to twist an ankle in one of the ruts. But sometime I'd have to unearth and face them. Meanwhile, I'd know all too soon how it felt to see a man who might be my father, face to face.

But it was me I saw first. His front door, tucked away at the back of the east wing, was panelled with bevelled glass. As I rang the doorbell I saw what he'd see: a small woman in something like combat gear, baseball cap at a rakish angle. The surprisingly painful trainers had gone: I sported baseball boots instead. Not second foot, as you might say. Still couldn't face that. But dead cheap from the market. The clothes I'd set out in were in a stylish rucksack I'd picked up from Oxfam for fifty pence. Yes, Lena as in Horne looked good.

Lord Elham didn't.

Despite Griff's propaganda against the upper classes, I rather hoped that Lord Elham would be a handsome hero. Whenever Iris had overdone things, she'd retire to bed with hot chocolate and a Regency romance by Georgette Heyer. She swore she knew them all by heart, but that didn't stop her having a wallow in escapism. She persuaded me to try a couple. After six I had to admit I was hooked. I never dared tell Griff, but when I was rifling through old books I'd look for copies for myself.

This lord wasn't a heroic dashing six foot, greying lightly at the temples and generally sleek and elegant like some of the money-splashers we saw at shows. He was about five foot six, and, while he wasn't really fat, wore his trousers under the bulge of his belly. His hair was in dire need of conditioner, and his skin looked pasty and unhealthy like that of ex-cons during their first week out of jail, even the young ones I'd come across who'd only had short sentences. I tried not to look at his teeth as he gave a welcoming smile. It was harder to keep my eyes off a fork that emerged prongs upright from his shirt pocket.

I had to ignore the welcoming pong as he opened the door. The place smelt like a dossers' den. No, there wasn't any piss in the general stink, but I picked up food, dust of ages, unwashed male and booze, all in one quick breath. Plus there was something else, I wasn't sure what, but I could have done without it.

We shook hands. I made my shake the sort Griff insisted on, firm but not an unpleasant grip. His was barely more of a brush. I suppose the half bow with which he invited me in might have been courtly. But it was no better than Griff's. He ushered me past a room full of Wellington boots and waterproofs — that was the smell I hadn't identified. Old rubber, with old sweat inside. At least he didn't seem to have any dogs, something I wasn't really looking forward to. I found myself in a nondescript room, sixteen by sixteen, maybe, though it was hard to tell with all the clutter in it. Once, perhaps, it had been the estate office, since the butler's and housekeeper's accommodation would presumably have been near the kitchen and this looked as if it had never been grand enough to be on show. The wainscoting was grained brown, and the curtains were brownish, heavily textured stuff, which gave the place a forties or fifties feel. The furniture was a funny mixture of what I was fairly sure was a Hepplewhite sofa, one of those clever library chairs concealing a couple of steps, a brass-inlaid nineteenth-century chiffonier Griff would have given his teeth for, and a set of 1960s G-Plan dining-chairs and a matching table which was blotched with tomato ketchup and other things I didn't want to touch. In one corner was a huge wide-screen TV, the sort that had a music system built in. Home cinema: that was it. Even that was smeared.

Lord Elham cleared a couple of *Readers' Digests* from a dining-chair and pushed it forward for me. I didn't see any good reason not to park my rucksack on the table, apart from manners and a desire to keep fifty pence worth of investment clean. I put it at my feet, retrieving the bottle of champagne, the best that Oddbins near Canterbury station could provide. Within reason.

He shuffled off in his Scholl sandals, stowing it in something I'd not noticed since it was tucked behind the door — a fridge, on which stood an electric jug-kettle. It seemed to house nothing but bottles. A couple of still sealed cardboard boxes had Pot Noodles stamped on them. At the far end of the table was a pyramid of upside-down Pot Noodle pots. They didn't seem to have been washed before they were made into sculpture. Beside them was a smaller pyramid of whisky glasses, all engraved with some sort of scene I couldn't work out without standing on my head. From this distance they looked like lead crystal.

What on earth had I let myself in for? I mustn't start thinking; I must start acting. In both senses. Time for my reporter's notepad and a couple of pencils. The duke reached out a bottle similar to the one I'd brought, parking it on the fridge, and, bending with a grunt, hunted for something else. OK, what sort of glasses would he find? Nineteenth-century goblets? Plastic picnic cups? Habitat champagne flutes? He came up slowly, clutching his back with one hand. He put his trophies on the fridge while he removed the cork gently — just a quiet pop and no waste at all — and poured.

'There. Cheerio my deario!' He passed me my glass, holding his to be clinked.

I clinked very carefully indeed. I was drinking from an eighteenth-century wineglass, with a double opaque air-twist stem. Dropping it would set me back — or his insurance company, with luck — by at least four hundred pounds. The bonus was that the bowl was so small it'd take many refills to get me even remotely tiddly. Except I hadn't had any lunch. I'd better factor that in.

'Not a bad tipple,' he declared. 'Not vintage. The Vultures won't pay for vintage. Nor will the Scrooges.'

'Better than an alcopop, anyway,' I agreed.

'Alcopops — what are they?'

I explained.

'Here, write a down a few names on that pad of yours. Must try those. Now, this film — tell me who'd be playing me. Or is it all a bit nebulous at the moment? Would I get power of veto? Don't want the wrong sort of person playing me — couldn't stand that Depp person. Have to be pretty short, of course — but then, a lot of them are. Look at Paul Newman. That pretty boy Capriatti or whatever. He'd be all right for me as a youngster, I suppose, but I don't see him handling a cricket bat.'

Was he serious or was he taking the mickey? I was saved the trouble of answering as he made for the fridge again.

'Always have a little something at this time of the afternoon. Care to join me? Ah!' Clapping his hand to his head he wandered out of the room.

I was ready to panic. What was I doing, alone in this weird room with a madman — except he'd just gone out, of course. Was he coming back? And what with? I'd been a total fool, putting myself in a position where no one knew where I was, and, probably, no one cared. He didn't know that, of course. He thought I came with my boss's backing, that if I disappeared someone would come looking. I'd better make sure he continued to think that. Just in case, I flicked on my mobile. If there were any signal round here I could always dial 999.

All the same, something was missing, and I was pleased it had gone missing. My normal sense that I didn't belong, the one that had bugged my early weeks in Bredeham, my visits to Oxford — where was it? I looked around again. Perhaps I felt a tip like this was my rightful place in life. But how could I possibly feel that if my natural instinct was to clean it all up?

'Here we are,' he declared, coming back clutching a fork. 'What flavour? I can recommend the Bombay Bad Boy Beef. Or the Hot Chicken's very acceptable too.'

I plumped for the beef. At the very least it'd provide blotting paper for the fizz. Funny, I'd had a vague hankering for a Pot Noodle ever since I'd come to live with Griff, but I knew that he'd see it as an expression of his failure to educate me properly, so I'd kept my secret to myself. I'd tried to cut down on crisps and other snacks, too.

'There's quite a cult following for these,' he said, boiling the kettle. 'There's a website, and you have to have a password to get in. Bloody childish, I suppose, but a harmless bit of fun, don't you think?'

I nodded. Was he on something? Or was his fuddled head the result of being on other things, and a lot of them too, according to my research, when he was younger? We'd always sneered at drugs education at school; maybe if he'd given the talks we'd have taken more notice. No. You never think that you'll end up in a shirt and trousers with Pot Noodle stains down the front.

I'd have liked to scald the fork before using it, only managing a quick wipe with a tissue when I thought he wouldn't notice. There must be a kitchen, somewhere, surely — that was where people usually kept their forks. And washed up. There must bc a bathroom and bedroom. There must be far more rooms in this wing alone than in your average family home — so why were things like a fridge and a kettle kept here? Griff and I had once had a horrendous week of picnicking when we had a drain problem and we couldn't use the kitchen. But this chaos had a more permanent air. It wasn't just a week's mess. Look at those pictures: the frames hadn't seen a duster in months. And the windows: you could have written your name in the grime.

'Thank you very much,' I said. 'I've never had champagne with Pot Noodles before.'

'Champagne really is the only stuff to drink,' he said earnestly, sitting at the table at right angles to me. 'Doesn't give you a hangover.'

I smiled and flicked open my pad. 'As you can see,' I said, 'I've already done a certain amount of research for this project. But we wanted to talk to you informally before involving lawyers to talk about contracts and—'

'I don't like lawyers. What's your phone number?'

I reeled it off. 'Easier to get me on my mobile.'

'Office?'

'Usually we leave the answerphone switched on.' I wrinkled my nose as if in disgust, trusting he didn't like the things, either, writing the mobile number down, tearing off the sheet and handing it to him.

'Who'll play the leading ladies?'

'We haven't got as far as casting yet,' I said trying to sound firm.

'Ah. Yes, so you said. Have to be a lot of leading ladies, of course,' he sighed.

'We were thinking of focussing on just one relationship. Which would you suggest?'

'One! This'd be what they call a low-budget movie, eh?'

'More an in-depth portrait of one period of your life. Your glory days.' Goodness knows where that sprang from but it pressed the right button.

He smiled happily, staring at the TV screen as if watching a replay. Perhaps he was.

'Was there any special woman then?' I prompted.

'My dear child, they were all special.'

I jumped. No, he was only using a term older people often use to younger ones. That was all. What I should be paying attention to was the simple word, *all*. I repeated it. 'All?'

He chased a bit of noodle round, waving it on the end of his fork. 'Yes, all.' As if there were nothing more to say.

'Could you elaborate?' I asked.

'Thought you were supposed to have done your research, my girl. What was your name again? Oh, yes, Lena. As in Horne.'

'I did find your name romantically linked with a number of women,' I said, 'but thought that was because gossip columnists always exaggerate.' Perhaps his teeth hadn't always been that bad. These days I couldn't imagine *one* woman wanting to be kissed by a mouth like that, let alone enough to warrant *all*.

'Yes, indeed.'

'Would you have time to tell me about your life in your own words? That might clarify things for us.'

He peered at the TV. 'Rather late for that. I always watch *Countdown* at this time. But if you came a bit earlier tomorrow I could go through it. I could show you round a bit, too.'

'I'd love to see the place,' I said. 'I always get so frustrated on those National Trust tours when all you get to see is the public rooms, not the real ones. Don't you?'

He laughed. 'Why should I want to go traipsing over other families' houses? There's enough here to look at. See that — over there, by the fireplace? Any idea who painted that?'

'Stubbs,' I said promptly.

'Not a bad guess. But it's more likely a contemporary of Stubbs — the horse's legs aren't very good. See?'

I picked my way over. The carpet might have been very good once; I suspected it had been made for a much larger room, and was now folded over to fit this.

'Real Stubbs on the West corridor. You ought to take a look. Costs a fiver though, doesn't it? Tell you what, come again. Yes, come again tomorrow. A bit earlier. I'll give you a bit of lunch. Or you could bring something. I'm always partial to a bit of smoked salmon.'

It wasn't one of my favourites, but might have the edge on Pot Noodles. Griff would tell me what to take with it. Except I wouldn't be going home to Griff.

He got to his feet, too. I was being ushered to the door. For a moment I stood my ground. 'It'd be really helpful for casting if you could look out a few photos — of your ladies.'

'What?' He sounded flabbergasted. 'All of them? Tell you what, if we can find it, I'll show you the list.'

CHAPTER NINETEEN

What the hell did Griff think he was up to? He'd only let himself into the caravan and rooted through my things! No note, no nothing. Except a carrier bag with an empty shoe-box inside it dumped by the sink. I'd kill him. I'd bloody kill him.

I strode into the village to ask what on earth he thought he was doing. OK, he had a perfect right to be in the caravan. It was his, after all. He had a key. But to go in and not leave me a note! And to pick up my clothes and drop them on the floor — Griff, a man who demanded such meticulous tidiness! What was happening in that skull of his? Any moment he'd turn into another Lord Elham and then where would we be?

Lord Elham. Was he mad or was he bad? How much of this present lifestyle was real? That was the easier question. All that dirt and mess would have taken time to accumulate. They were genuine. But was he? Was he putting on airs of innocence to hide something? If so, what? None of my research showed anything to hide. But—

No, I mustn't think about Elham, or I'd lose my head of steam. I had to be furious with Griff, or I'd throw myself into his arms and howl that the man I'd hoped was my dad was a dopehead, and weird with it, but that I had to go and see him tomorrow in case he was simply a very clever man.

As I turned the bend into the village, I could see some activity ahead. Outside our cottage. A man in a hoodie talking to Griff. I speeded up, even more when I saw a Ford Focus parked about twenty yards further down the street. But hoodie man was still talking and Griff was pointing, as if giving directions — no, there was nothing to worry about. Someone was simply lost and Griff, the gates open and the van half inside, was helping.

If I sprinted before, I hurtled now. It wasn't help the man wanted, it was the van. Hoodie stepped towards Griff, grabbing his shirtfront. Griff was struggling. He wouldn't stand a chance: he was too frail. The other bloke must have thought he was quids in.

Not with me to reckon with, he wasn't. I'd learned to fight years ago, but never with any rules. Head down, I went for the man's midriff. But not before Griff staggered back too. I heard him stumble — couldn't see, because I was in mid head-butt. Hoodie dropped the keys. My fingers just missed them. The Focus roared into action. Hoodie was up now on all fours retching. That didn't stop him fumbling after the keys. But I got there first, flinging them out of his reach. And not just that — hard as I could, I threw them at Tony's front window. I knew what to expect. Hoodie didn't. Suddenly the quiet street winced at the sound of Tony's alarm. That, and the scream of the Focus' tyres.

'Sweeter than the *Hallelujah Chorus*,' Griff declared, and went out cold at my feet.

* * *

'Sweeter than the *Hallelujah Chorus*,' Griff said every few minutes, as we waited for the ambulance.

'Just a spot of concussion,' Tony said, trying to sound reassuring. Reassuring nothing: wasn't concussion serious? 'When his head hit the pavement. And yes, I'm sure you're right — that wrist looks broken to me. Bones break easily when you're his age.'

'I thought it was women who had osteo-whatever,' I objected.

'Oh, men too.'

'Sweeter than the *Hallelujah Chorus.*'

'Absolutely,' I agreed, smoothing his hair back with one hand, the other holding his good hand. What I wanted was an even sweeter sound — a nice two-tone ambulance horn. Even a wail if they felt like it. I'd heard about old people and shock, all right, and I was scared.

'Did Tony get those thugs?' Griff asked suddenly, returning my grip.

'He got the number. So his mates will.'

Tony had found a blanket and tucked it gently up to Griff's chin. 'Was it the number I left on your answerphone?' I asked him.

'Yes. But that's not a lot of consolation. It's a cloned number. In real life it belongs to a church organist in Warwickshire. Sorry.'

'And they're probably changing it even as we speak for another cloned number?'

'Probably. Plenty of lanes round here to provide cover — there's a lot to be said for cities and CCTV.'

'You'll get something from our security camera,' I said.

'Probably no more use than before. Unless it caught him full on his face. Ah! Sounds like help at last.'

The paramedics treated Griff as he hated to be treated, a slightly deaf old bat. Chattering inanely, they popped a support round his neck and another on his wrist. Then they stowed him in the ambulance. I wanted to go too, but Tony laid a hand on my arm.

'They'll almost certainly want to keep him in overnight. If you follow in the van, then at least you'll be able to get home.'

I hated the idea, but he was right. The garage and house needed to be secured, and I couldn't leave that to him, not when he had his own window to worry about.

* * *

By the time I arrived at the hospital — and I certainly didn't hang around admiring the view — Griff had already been registered and was being seen by the medics. I hung around, feeling useless and miserable — after all, I'd only gone into the village to give him a right rollicking — and guilty. If I hadn't walked out, I'd have been there to prevent him doing anything as silly as talking to anyone with the van as vulnerable as that. Wrong. The villains hadn't been after the van. If they'd wanted the van, Focus man could have been in the driver's seat before you could say Kitty Gang. After all, the engine had still been running when I'd arrived. Why hadn't I clocked that at the time?

They'd been after the house keys. Perhaps they were Kitty Gang members after all. I'd have to make sure that next time they came, Griff wasn't on his own. It'd be the work of five minutes to move back home again. It'd be the work of slightly longer to make sure that Griff wasn't there at all. Yes, I had to get him out of the house into a place of safety.

A coffee told me the answer. What about farming him out to Tenterden and Aidan? OK, I'd never liked the man any more than, to be honest, he'd liked me. But he and Griff were friends, if not lovers — and if they were lovers, what business was it of mine? Slipping outside, into what was now a thin drizzle, promising more later, I dialled Aidan's number. I couldn't do much in the way of breaking the news — a fall is a fall.

'And yes, he was pushed,' I added. 'There's a gang preying on older people in the area at the moment. The police know all about them.'

'So why don't they *do* something?' He sounded pettish.

'The thing is, I think he'd be safer out of the way for a bit. This is the second time they've marked us out for attack, and this time they may have broken his wrist.'

'Can I speak to him?'

'I haven't even seen him myself yet. The doctors are still with him.'

'You're at William Harvey? I'm on my way.'

'Wouldn't you rather—'

But he'd cut the line. I awarded him a whole row of brownie points.

They were just looking for me when I went back in. The dear old NHS had X-rayed him, plastered his arm and even found a bed for him so they could keep an eye on his head injury.

'A bed? You mean, he won't have to spend the night on a trolley? Promise?'

The doctor, who didn't look much older than me, eyed me coldly. 'There's no need for sarcasm.'

'I wasn't being sarcastic, just grateful. Can I see him — just for a minute — before he goes up to the ward?'

'He's already gone up.' She scribbled the number. 'But I dare say they'll give you a minute with him. No more. I've given him something to help with the pain. And not the brandy he thought would help.'

'That's my Griff,' I grinned. 'Thanks, doctor. Look, when you discharge him, you'd better give me all the instructions about physio and such — I'll make sure he carries them out.'

'I'll make a note, Ms Tripp.' She managed a smile, which I appreciated all the more since she looked as if she'd been on her feet for the last twenty-four hours. 'Wonderful old man, your grandfather, considering.'

'Considering what?'

'Well, the probable state of his liver.'

'It wasn't booze that made him fall,' I assured her blithely. 'He was pushed.' And then I asked the question I didn't really want the answer to. 'He's an alcoholic, isn't he?'

'You'd know the answer to that better than me. Even if he isn't, he's certainly drinking to excess far too often.'

Her bleeper chirruped. 'Talk to your GP,' she added, over her shoulder.

Chew on that, Lina.

Having done the decent thing and called Aidan, the least I could do was leave a message for him with the reception staff. Then, following their directions, I went to find Griff.

* * *

I didn't recognise him at first. He took such care never to let me see him without his dentures or in any way unkempt. And there he was, this frail old man, dressed in a hospital gown that showed his poor scrawny neck, lying on his back, mouth slack and toothless. Thank goodness I'd brought his toilet bag with his clothes for tomorrow. If he consented to go and stay with Aidan, he'd want to be spruce before he was picked up.

I took his hand again, and leaned across to kiss him.

He whispered something. I bent closer to hear. But whatever it was, it slurred into a snore.

There must be a tissue somewhere in one of my pockets. No? I tiptoed out, rubbing my nose fiercely with my cuff.

* * *

'My goodness! He's—' Aidan leapt up and strode across, gripping my shoulders.

'He's just asleep, Aidan,' I insisted through my sniffs. 'He'll be fine. You'll be able to see him first thing. I tried to stop you coming, but—'

'My dear child, I had to come. I'm in BUPA. I can get him proper treatment, private ambulance, everything.'

'I don't think he'll need anything like that. What I do think he'll need is a haven for a couple of weeks. Until the police have sorted everything out.'

'You mean stay with me? An invalid? Bedpans and everything?' His voice rose with each question. 'No wonder you want to palm him off on me!' Zip went the brownie points.

'Especially bedpans. And probably blanket baths. Oh, don't be ridiculous, Aidan,' I exploded at last. 'The only reason I don't want him to stay in the cottage is his safety. Or I'd nurse him happily. And no,' I added, really quite worked up now, 'you can rest assured I won't steal all his property and sell it to the Kitty Gang. I shall look after it as if it were my own. Griff's my friend too, you know. I love him.' There. And the three simple words — which I'd rather have said to Griff himself, if only the old codger had been halfway conscious — reduced me from snivels to full-flown tears. I'd have liked Aidan a lot more if he'd produced a hanky, not just watched in horror as my nose dripped.

* * *

There was a note Blu-tacked to the front door:

> *IF THERE'S A LIGHT ON, I'M STILL AWAKE. SOUP ON OFFER. TONY.*

So that was why I was so weepy. I was hungry. Nothing since His Lordship's Pot Noodles. Bombay Bad Boy, indeed. How old did he think he was?

The light in Tony's window was still on. I was very tempted. What was there to hold me back? Thinking of Iris and her pigs, I rang Tony's doorbell.

He was wearing that snazzy bathrobe again. And, as before, nothing else that was visible. Oh, apart from a big grin.

'I'd almost given you up,' he said, almost scooping me in. 'Food or drink first? Come on in and tell me all about Griff.'

* * *

I sometimes wondered, not very hard and not very often, why I never fancied going to bed with Tony. He was attractive enough, after all, with his long, muscled limbs and friendly smile. He was bright enough to appreciate Griff. He was in a respectable job — unlike some of the mates I'd mixed with when I was young, I didn't object to the police as such, or as Griff would have put it, *per* something or other. His hobby, classic motorbikes, didn't seem to occupy too much of his time. So why, with a stomach pleasantly full of soup, garlic bread and rosé wine, didn't I want to round off an interesting day in his bed? It would have been less effort than nipping home, with all the keys, bolts and burglar alarms that that involved. He'd probably have given me quite a pleasant time. He'd almost certainly have had handy the condoms it had made Griff so embarrassed to talk about. Three or four years ago I certainly would have done. I'd actually bonked blokes I didn't like much at all. You do all sorts of things when you're young and lonely and — yes, stupid. I wasn't exactly in my dotage and the cottage would feel horribly empty, but — no, unless I felt a real spark, I'd sleep in my own bed. With Tim the Teddy Bear for company if needs be.

Tony did his best to persuade me. He was good at kissing, no doubt about that, and not bad at all at several other things, but a tiny corner of my head told me that he'd never shown much interest in me when Griff was around, apart from making sure I noticed his legs. Was he simply chancing his arm at an opportunity that might not present itself again?

'Look, Tony, I'm really sorry, but I just don't feel like it tonight. It's been a bit of a day, what with one thing and another. At least now that Griff and I are friends again I shall be able to use the van to get around. Buses, trains! They're awful.'

His expression was hard to read, but despite now-steady rain he insisted on walking me the few yards home, looking carefully up and down the street for cars or hoodies. 'Are you sure that that van's the best means of transport?'

I looked at him for a second, ready to tell him just how long it took to get from A to B without your own wheels. But that might involve mentioning that B stood in my case for Bossingham. Until I'd sussed Lord Elham to my own satisfaction, I wasn't going to share him with anyone. Slowly I took in the implications of what he was saying. 'Are you saying it might just be sensible to take it in for its thirty-thousand-mile service and borrow a courtesy car? Preferably one that doesn't announce to the world it belongs to Ashford Ford or whatever?'

'I'm saying just that. I'm not happy about your living on your own, either: you haven't got someone — else — you could stay with?'

Why hadn't he smiled like that when he was trying to get me into bed?

'Tell you what,' I said as casually as I could, 'how about I cook supper tomorrow — well, it's today, now, isn't it? At least I'll have some police protection for the evening.'

CHAPTER TWENTY

Griff had had a good night, the nurse I phoned said, but she couldn't say officially when he'd be allowed out. I could try again at ten thirty. No, there was no point simply turning up hoping he'd been discharged.

Ten thirty — and it was now only seven! No, despite being as knackered as I ever remember, I hadn't slept well, and had given up when two wood pigeons had stomped around on the roof with their stupid *c'coo-coo*-ing. Why couldn't they manage a decent song? *C'coo-coo, c'coo-coo!* Only six o'clock! Anyway, I had a lot to do. A really nice hot shower started me off: then, with a bit of luck, I was ready for anything. Griff wasn't very efficient about opening the post or checking calls on the answerphone. I'd better sort everything out so I could report to him later. He'd need a bag packed, too, with enough of his favourite clothes for a week, but only those he could slip on over that wrist of his. And food — Aidan wasn't much of a cook, as if the kitchen was the place for the lower orders. Griff might have objected to Aidan's tone, but he was happy to be let loose in Aidan's designer kitchen. Usually.

So now I had the mixing bowl out. Scones first. Griff loved scones. Mine might not be as good as his, or even as those from the Tenterden baker, but they'd be mine. Bread was already proving in the airing cupboard.

I don't know whether it was the smells or the stickiness that made me feel better. There's nothing more gluey than scone mixture and few things more satisfying than taming it with a well-floured rolling pin. This one had belonged, so Griff said, to his grandmother, made for her by a prisoner of war. Which war he didn't say and my history wasn't good enough to work it out. But using something as old and well-worn as that, I felt calm and happy — until the ideas started popping into my head.

What if it had been someone else in the caravan? Griff would have tidied it up, not trashed it. And it wasn't in his nature not to have left a note. Even knocked silly by that fall — just how many times had he mentioned the *Hallelujah Chorus*? — he would have said something about his visit. That box in the carrier bag. What on earth was that doing there? Griff loathed carrier bags, refusing point blank to use them himself. It had taken me weeks of nagging to persuade him that at least at fairs we should have a supply of the standard ones advertising future fairs. As for the shop, I used any supermarket ones coming our way, usually via Mrs Hatch, who couldn't or wouldn't understand his reservations, and in any case pointed out that what we were doing was true recycling.

And an empty box? Why take an empty box all that way? If he'd taken along a few essentials to replace our supplies, he'd have needed a bigger box.

Despite the warmth from the Aga and the efforts of my arms, I felt cold. What if it hadn't been Griff and whoever it was had got in not through the door but through a window? I'd never checked they were secure. As soon as I'd sucked and scrubbed my hands clean, I got on to the phone. Farmers kept early hours, and Mr Hardy wouldn't mind checking for me — and if he did, tough: it was part of his contract.

'I did hear some banging, like, in the night. Hang on — I'll have a quick shufti.'

Hang on? It would have made more sense to ring back in ten minutes. Mr Hardy had two speeds, snail and giant sloth. I had to risk leaving the phone to get out the first tray of scones. Even as I slid them on to the wire tray, I could his deep voice, made tinny by the phone.

'Hi, Mr Hardy. Sorry about that — something in the oven.' Not a joke about buns, please! No, I was all right.

'You're an early riser, Lina, and no mistake. There's folks missing the best part of the day—'

Any minute the next tray of scones would be ready. But it was useless to urge him. At long last he declared, 'So maybe you'd better get up here when you've next a minute. Flapping in the breeze it is. That was the knocking I heard in the night, see — that window the far side from me.'

'I'll be up as soon as my bread's ready for the oven,' I said. Now I had wheels, life could speed up again. I could check the caravan and be back in time to retrieve my loaves.

* * *

Blu Tack! Whoever had broken in had Blu-tacked the seal back in place so nothing had seemed wrong. It was wrong enough now. The overnight wind and rain had loosened it, and now I had a soaked carpet to deal with. I stamped the towels on to it, and reported back to Mr Hardy.

'And with Griff being in hospital I don't know when I can get it repaired,' I concluded, handing over a few scones as a bribe.

'You leave it to me,' he said kindly. 'Break-ins in my park? Never heard the like.'

* * *

Aidan didn't need to pull rank on me, when we turned up together to collect Griff: the van or his Merc? Not a lot of competition. So

I tailed the car, making sure that no one tailed us. He had gates like ours, which opened sweetly as he pressed a button somewhere. They twitched a bit when they saw the van was to be admitted too, but eventually I was in and parked on the side drive of his lovely Georgian house. Even as I lusted after the fanlight over the front door, Griff, terribly pale and clutching my arm very tightly for support, conceded with a thread of a voice that retiring to the sofa with a decent cup of tea might be the most sensible thing he could do.

At first Aidan assumed I would make it, but either because he didn't trust me in his pride and joy or because he felt guilty at letting me get on with the work (less likely) or simply because Griff had fallen asleep, he eventually joined me. I was unpacking my baskets on his kitchen table.

'Bread? Scones? Banana bread?' His voice rose with each goodie I produced. 'But that's what shops are for.' He shook his head in disbelief.

'There's some of his jam, too, and his favourite chutney. You know so much more about wine that I thought I'd leave that to you. But he mustn't drink too much, not with his painkillers. In fact, he ought to cut down on alcohol anyway, Aidan. His liver.'

'Oh, that must be like leather by now! I wouldn't worry about that.'

'I do worry. And so should you, if you care for him.'

'Don't start telling me what I should and shouldn't do, young lady.' He drew himself up to his full six foot and looked down his nose. No, Duke of Wellington he wasn't. He hadn't enough chin for a start.

'Shhh. He'll hear you. Now, there's one more thing I want you to do. That van of ours. It's become a liability. You've got a nice big garage. Can I pop it in there?'

'A van!' Not for the first time I wondered why of all his lovely gay friends Griff should have latched on to this particular man.

'It's got our name all over it. If the Kitty Gang are targeting Griff, then if his van disappears off the face of the earth, they'll have to find another victim.'

'And I suppose you'll be doing athletic things on a bicycle.'

'I shall hire a car. It'll cost an arm and a leg, so I don't want Griff to know. He'll worry.' He'd worry about me if he knew about the caravan break-in, which was a very good reason for not telling him. We still weren't quite back to our old selves. Neither of us had had the courage to talk about our quarrel, even to mention my temporary absence. So I hadn't had to talk to him about Lord Elham. I'd have loved to. Fey and camp Griff might be, but he knew his people, Aidan apart, that is, and if I could have brought the two men together, he'd have sussed out the situation in minutes. Even after his concussion, he was fly enough to accept without blink or question the folder I'd brought with me and slid into his hand. And I'd bet all the china in Bossingham Hall he'd find somewhere to hide it without letting on even to Aidan what it was.

* * *

After the big, heavy van, it felt quite weird to drive the little Ka I'd hired in Ashford. It was so light and sounded so different — no heavy diesel engine throbbing away, I suppose, though the sound insulation wasn't quite as good as I'd have expected. As for paying for it, I wasn't robbing Griff. I was using money from what he insisted was our investment account. Investment? Well, keeping your skin intact might just qualify. I wasn't so sure about using the van to nip across to Bossingham, though. That seemed a bit dodgy, morally speaking.

But it turned out to be a business trip — of sorts — after all.

Lord Elham greeted me like one of his long-lost cousins, if not his daughter. 'Come in, come in. How's the car?'

'I had to hire one. I left it at the end of your track.'

'Come and have a drink. Have you eaten? Something more traditional? Beef and tomato? Chicken and mushroom?'

'Is that really all you eat? Pot Noodles?' Drat, I'd only forgotten the salmon and stuff, hadn't I? Perhaps his memory was too dodgy to have remembered, too.

I seemed to be in luck. 'Highly nutritious! Meat for protein, vegetables for vitamins, noodles for carbohydrate. Plenty of variety. No need to cook. Bingo. Spot on.'

I wasn't sure that Griff or Iris for that matter would agree. 'Don't you have a kitchen, then?'

'Oh, I've got a kitchen, all right! Bit of a tip. Quite interesting in its own way, but a bit of a tip.' He kept us hovering in the entrance hall.

I might as well risk it. 'I suppose I couldn't see it? Background, you know.'

Shrugging, he said, 'Walk this way.' Oh, the old joke — a weird set of John Cleese funny walks.

I followed more sedately, keeping my eyes peeled. All the closed doors I passed made me feel like that woman who married Bluebeard and made the fatal mistake of asking him to open them. No wonder he didn't want to ferry his meals this far.

Or — good grief — cook them in this kitchen!

This wasn't the *Country Life* high-ceilinged, copper-saucepanned affair I'd taken afternoon tea in. This was a much more ordinary room, with a lower ceiling and furniture and fittings straight from the nineteen forties or fifties: Griff would have known. And it was filthy. I don't mean someone had forgotten to wipe it down after cooking — the table, stove, draining board and so on. I mean the stove was encrusted. The sink was stacked high with saucepans. Not a single surface was clear either of crockery or of decayed food.

Trying not to gag, I said mildly, 'I can see why you wouldn't want to cook in here. Unless it was cleaned up a bit? I mean, as a room it's pretty interesting.'

'Don't let on, for heaven's sake!'

'Who to?'

'Those English Heritage chappies of course. And chappesses — they were far worse. You know what the miserable bitches insisted? That I open the house to the public! My home. Swarmed over by the world and his wife.'

Thank goodness I'd kept quiet about my visit. 'Why did they want that?'

'Want? Demanded! Said I wouldn't get the money if I didn't. For the roof, of course,' he explained, just as irritated as my maths teachers used to be when equations did my head in.

'You mean they paid for it?' No wonder they wanted something in return.

'Only half of it! I had to fork out for the rest myself! Bloody trustees,' he added mysteriously. 'So now I have to have Joe and Josephine Public here all hours of the night and day.'

My recollection was that he admitted them something like four hours a day and not many days of the year. I was about to point this out when I saw a lovely little blue-and-white egg cup, standing forlorn amongst all the rubbish. I pounced, cradling it in my hand. 'Isn't it lovely?'

He peered at it, then at me, as if I'd expressed delight at a dog turd.

I turned it over, pointing. 'See the mark? Spode.'

'Filthy.'

'Easy to clean it up and make it presentable.' I wasn't quite sure how, but it was printed with the bird section from the border of the Indian Sporting series, and would more than pay for the day's hire car.

'Have it.'

'I couldn't possibly. It's worth too much.'

'Nothing's worth anything if you don't want it and don't know how to get rid of it. I told you, have it. It's yours. No argument.' As I tucked it in my rucksack, he produced a charming smile. 'There, that didn't hurt much, did it?'

'No, but—' I swallowed the rest of what I meant to say. I'd make it up to him by getting him a little microwave and introduce him to the slightly more nutritious concept of TV meals for one. 'You know, you ought to clean this up a bit. Rats. Plus you'd make a few more bob on other stuff you might find.'

'I could do with a few bob. The DSS don't give me much.'

'*DSS!*'

'That's right. How else am I to live? I don't own any of this now, you know. Now I've put everything right, the trustees have taken it on. Bloody kites. Darned hyenas. I just live in this corner, grace and favour, they say. Don't own anything anymore. So it'd be nice to diddle them, wouldn't it? How, that's the question?'

'I might have the odd contact,' I admitted cautiously. And truthfully. Kitchen stuff wasn't really our line. But there were specialists who'd dribble at the sight of that enamel bread bin. And the wooden plate racks. They didn't do anything for me, but who knew what I'd find if I mined underneath all that mouldy rubbish. Black Death, maybe. It'd be a job for gloves and a facemask. Lots of bin liners. Boiling water. I might. I just might. It'd be more satisfying, after all, than cleaning up Griff's genteel spills.

'OK. Spot of lunch,' he announced.

Just being in here and touching the egg cup were enough to put me off food, even Pot Noodles, until I'd washed my hands. 'Is there a bathroom I could use?'

'Of course there's a bathroom! This is a civilised country, my girl. Don't use thunder boxes here, for heaven's sake. Out in the yard. No! Hang on. No Joe Public sniffing around today? Right.

You might as well use one of the state latrines. No, not one of the old two-seaters — the ones they keep for visitors. Follow me.'

Not arguing — I didn't fancy using his loo if it was in the same state as the kitchen — I followed him along the corridor leading to the main body of the house. He tapped in the simplest security code, as if he'd had to humour his trustees by having one but cocked a snook by choosing a doddle any burglar would suss out. Well, 1234 didn't sound like rocket science, even to me.

So here we were, the other side of the green baize door, but not in a corridor I recognised. Not that I'd have let on if I had seen something familiar, of course. Here the pictures seemed pretty ordinary; the display cabinets were full of stuff I'd have loved to pick over, just crammed in, willy-nilly. The lighting was so poor I'd have been hard put to identify anything. But I wasn't here to peer and covet. I was here to see if anything rang any bells — and yes, to use a loo.

'You know what I've always wanted to do?' I heard myself saying. 'Those "hidden" doors in posh bedrooms. I've always wanted to go through one to find what's the other side.'

'Would you get bigger or smaller?'

'Why should I do either?'

He sighed. 'Alice, of course.'

'Alice?'

'You've never read *Alice in Wonderland*? Or *Through the Looking Glass*? My dear girl, where were you educated?' He sounded like an uncanny echo of Griff, talking about tea, the day this whole thing started.

I wasn't about to tell him about Iris and the rest of my upbringing — in any case, up-dragging would be a better way to describe it. 'I'll put it on my list,' I said.

'There must be a copy somewhere — I'll look it out for you before you leave. As for the doors, let's find a bedroom and you can see for yourself.'

Yes! But instead I asked, 'Do you have many books?'

'Hundreds of the darned things. Oh, those with the best bindings are in the library of course. Tooled leather bindings, that sort of thing. Some are fake, of course — just fronts glued together on a shelf that's really a door. You could have a look at that if you wanted. Step through it. So long as you promise not to get any smaller.'

CHAPTER TWENTY-ONE

'You've been in that huge, rambling, isolated place with a strange man, all by yourself, without telling anyone where you were! You must have been off your head, Lina — mustn't she?' Marcus was almost squeaking in disbelief.

It was nothing to my squeak when he'd turned up on the doorstep, at exactly the same time as Tony. So much for a sexy evening. They got on so well they could have managed without me, except that I was cooking supper, which they were now waiting for, drinking Beck's from bottles while I toiled. Griff would have danced round producing, with a twiddle here and a tweak there, a pretty and a tasty meal. I was relying on the recipes he'd dictated to me as he cooked them: spelling had never been my strongest point, and I sometimes I couldn't tell whether I needed a teaspoon or a tablespoonful of something. And with ginger or chilli I reckoned it mattered.

'It's certainly not the safest thing to do. Especially if Bossingham's a mobile black spot. And without telling anyone — you really were putting yourself at risk. Look, I've got some leaflets back at the station about how to take care of yourself — the Suzy Lamplugh Trust—'

'It's all right. Lord Elham's no problem. He's a noble, for heaven's sake.' And, though I certainly wasn't letting on to Tony, maybe my dad. 'I told you all about him,' I hissed at Marcus, who at last seemed to get the message and shut up.

'*Noblesse* doesn't always *oblige*, Lina.'

'But he's lent me a book—'

'Just to get you to go back again.'

'Oh, I'm going back all right. There's two-thirds of the house to explore yet. He's asked me back for lunch tomorrow.' More Pot Noodles. Nostalgia was one thing, but if they'd been lampreys, I'd definitely have been surfeited. Or was that music? My bloody memory!

Either for my benefit or Tony's, Marcus heaved an obvious sigh of relief. 'Well, you won't be able to go, will you? You'll be otherwise engaged, Lina.'

I sat up very straight. 'I don't do lies. Not unless I have to,' I conceded.

'This has what Griff would call the virtue of being the truth,' Marcus crowed. 'Folkestone, Lina — have you forgotten Folkestone?'

'You'd have to forgive her — it's not all that memorable,' Tony laughed.

'It is if you've got a gig there. The Grand Hotel. Doors open to the public at nine thirty, remember. That's why I came round. To offer to help you set up.'

I didn't slap my face. But I plonked my hands on it hard enough to remind me of the last time I got cross with myself. 'No van,' I said. 'I've put it in what you might call a place of safety.' I smiled across at Tony.

'Ah. Hence that nice silver Ka I saw earlier. Where is it now? Triple-locked in the garage? So how will you manage?'

'Pack carefully. Oh Marcus, I might really have messed up. How on earth could I forget a fair?'

Marcus said kindly, 'Easy enough when you were worried about Griff.'

I stared. 'How did you know about Griff?'

'The grapevine. The girl in the village shop, actually, where I got those.' He pointed to some tulips, which already looked as if they'd got bad headaches, adding quickly, 'According to her, you should have pierced them with a pin, just below the flower. And then put a teaspoon of sugar in the water.'

Bother flower arranging. The girl on the checkout. That'd be Shaz, the one who'd made her dad give me a lift to the farm. Had someone found out from her where I was staying? She wasn't the sort of girl who'd even heard of Griff's theory that the least you said about anything to anyone at any time the better. If the person asking for me had been clutching a convincing-looking bag, she'd only have got her dad to give him a lift too, wouldn't she? I'd better talk to her. Now. Londis would be open till ten. I stared at the vegetables lying chopped, all ready for their stir-fry. Could I think of an excuse to nip out? If only I smoked. But there was no way either of these lads would let me walk even that far unaccompanied. I wouldn't mind an escort, come to think of it, though it wasn't anything like dark yet. But I just didn't want them in the shop with me. What would curl them up to see me buy? I nipped up to the bathroom, returning looking as flustered and embarrassed as I could.

* * *

'Trust me, you don't want to know,' I insisted as we set out. 'Just tell yourself you're going for a nice stroll on a pleasant summer evening. Or it might still be spring. You could even pop into the Rose and Crown and set up a round. We might do better to eat there, come to think of it. I'm no Delia, remember. Not even Jamie's Jools.'

'No way. Not after we've psyched ourselves up for whatever it is. Come on, Lina, even you can't ruin a stir-fry.'

'What do you mean, "even you", Tony Baker? Griff insists I'm a woman of parts.'

'Some of them very nice too,' he said, but without much enthusiasm. He'd taken the arrival of Marcus with no fuss at all, not at all the reaction, I'd have thought, of a young man with his mind on one particular part, the one he'd been after last night. He'd not shown any more sign of locking horns with Marcus than Marcus had with him. It was fine by me. Last night's sleeplessness was catching up with me. Passion? I could think of absolutely nothing nicer than an early night tucked up with Tim the teddy.

The first words Shaz spoke were to ask me if my friends had managed to find me. 'They'd been so worried, they said, you leaving your new shoes in their car. They wanted to know which cottage you lived at, but I sent them off to your caravan. I didn't say anything about your row with Mr Tripp. Everything all right between you now? And how is he? Fancy me forgetting to ask that! Oh, I am sorry.'

No point in asking how she knew about that. The whole village was probably wringing its collective hands at Griff's injuries, not to mention sucking its collective teeth at my goings on. 'Fine. Oh, bad enough for the hospital to keep him in a bit.' That wasn't quite a lie. 'So I've got a friend staying over.' Neither was that.

'Not that gorgeous looker that popped in for some flowers? Scrummy. Let me know when you've finished with him!'

'Promise.' For some reason I had to put in, 'And it was only a bit of a tiff, Griff and me, not a real a row. You know what families are like.' I was just about to leave, when I added, 'I had a couple of lifts that day: I suppose you wouldn't remember what sort of car it was?'

She was shrewder than I'd thought. 'They weren't real friends then? I'm ever so sorry. I wouldn't have told them. In fact, I offered to look after your shoes for you — save them the trouble. But they really insisted.'

'Don't worry, Shaz. You did your best. But the car — any ideas?'

She turned to look down the street. 'Look — that one there!'

'Ah. A Ford Focus!' Surprise, surprise.

'No. I mean yes. That Ford Focus. The one that's just parking now.'

'You're sure?'

'Well, it looks like it. Mind you, I suppose they all look the same now. Hang on — there's a passenger getting out. That bloke—'

I peered, but unless, like Shaz, I pressed my nose against the window, I could see nothing but my own reflection.

'Were there two men last time?'

'No. Just the one. Before you ask, he was just ordinary. Dead ordinary.'

I risked shoving my head round the door. In the dusk, all the colours and distances flattened, this man looked dead ordinary too. Suddenly it all seemed a waste of time. All I'd done was confirm what I already knew: that someone had found where I lived by asking Shaz. I was no nearer to knowing who. At least the van and the frontispiece were as safe as I could make them. More importantly, Griff was out of reach, too. I grabbed the tampons and marched towards the pub. More or less. Pretending to be completely preoccupied stowing the tampons, I drifted along. My eyes were peeled, of course, and my ears straining. But to a vicious driver I was positively inviting a hit and run. I didn't mind pretending to be bait.

Especially as absolutely nothing happened.

* * *

While the men washed up, I nipped into the living room to phone to check that Griff was still all right.

'My dear Evelina, of course he is. There's hardly been time since your last phone call for him to have had a relapse.'

'Can I speak to him, please?'

'He's preparing for bed.'

'I've seen him in his dressing gown before now.' As I was sure Aidan had.

He gave a brief snort, presumably at my lack of logic, but I heard the clatter of the handset being out down. There was a long silence: Aidan wouldn't do anything as vulgar as yell.

'Lina, dear heart, isn't it your bedtime too?' Griff grumbled gently.

'As soon as I've got rid of my two male chaperons,' I said.

'*Two!*'

'Tony Baker and Marcus Copeland. They both thought I needed looking after.'

'I wonder why. Tony, yes, but young Marcus? How could he have known?'

I was just about to tell him about Shaz when I stopped. Yes, what had brought Marcus to the village in the first place?

'It's a good job he did — I'd have forgotten about Folkestone. The Grand. Tomorrow. Any instructions?'

'Good quality. Nothing too heavy.'

'Yes, we're talking about genteel retired people on good pensions — right?'

'Absolutely right. Good girl. Now, rid of those swains of yours and hie you to your bedchamber — you have to make an early start tomorrow. Good night, my child.'

'And you, Griff. Sweet dreams.'

I pushed the kitchen door slightly ajar.

While Tony washed up, Marcus was drying the dishes. What had really brought him to Bredeham? Why had he supplied me with all the information about his cousin's contacts? Was it really because he was my mate? Or — I stared down a tunnel of doubt that was all too familiar — was he yet another person I'd trusted only to find them betraying me at the first opportunity? Hell, I'd been so naïve! *So* naïve! It'd make sense for him to want to get hold of *Natura Rerum*, just as it would any dealer. Find that and he'd be able to cut loose from his cousin and build up his own business.

Did that mean I thought Marcus was capable of stealing it?

Stealing was what people did, wasn't it? In my old world at least. But in Griff's you didn't even steal information. Which world was Marcus in? Somewhere in between?

'What's the latest?' Tony asked, over his shoulder.

'Fine. He says thank you both of you for looking after me,' I invented.

'I'll look after you tomorrow, too,' Marcus declared, dumping the damp tea towel on the table.

I shook it and hung it on the rail. 'I shall be fine.'

Tony chimed in. 'It'd make sense. He could go with you to Bossingham Hall and—'

'I shan't be going to Bossingham Hall tomorrow, shall I? Not if I'm working. I'll phone Lord Elham and cancel.'

'Why not suggest you go later in the day? It's not very far out of your way if you went via—'

'I'm not taking a car full of china up his drive, and I certainly wouldn't risk parking it where I couldn't keep an eye on it. So it'll be another day—'

'—another dollar,' Tony concluded.

'OK, what I'll do is sleep over here tomorrow night. Then I can go with you on Monday.'

'Marcus, I am seeing Lord Elham on my own. There's no earthly reason for you to turn up — a total stranger — as my muscle, thanks very much.'

'But—'

'Leave it, Tony. Listen, both of you: I'm quite happy to let someone know when I'm going and when I expect to be home. Griff, for instance. Coffee?'

As I made it — instant, since I was pissed off with both of them — I tried to work out how much alcohol Marcus had had. Failing, I asked point blank.

'About twice the legal limit, I should say,' Tony replied for him. 'Better let Lina look after that shiny motor of yours, mate.'

'Gee, thanks.'

'So how will you get home?' I demanded, determined to make one thing clear without having to spell it out. 'The last train ran ten minutes ago, if I know railways.'

'Come on, Lina — you've plenty of room here.'

I shook my head. 'Griff's house, not mine. And you can imagine what the village would make of it: Griff's away, so Lina'll play. And it'll grow. By tomorrow lunchtime it'll be, Lina was snogging her bloke while Griff was having emergency open heart surgery.'

Tony at least nodded that he understood. 'Looks like there's only one thing for it, mate — my sofa. So now we've fixed that, how about some of that nice Scotch you always offer me, Lina?'

Another shake of my head. 'Griff's whisky, not mine. And since I've got to be up at six tomorrow to sort out the Folkestone stock, I'd better be turning in.' I stood up, the technique my social workers had always used to say the interview was over.

Tony grabbed me as I staggered — well, I would, the way my knees buckled. He looked at me anxiously. I wasn't going to tell him how scared I used to be.

Come on, Lina. Talk your way out of it. What about the tampon excuse? Yes, that'd do. 'I always feel a bit wobbly at this time of the month. All I need is a hot water bottle and a good night's sleep and I shall be fine.'

CHAPTER TWENTY-TWO

There was no way Marcus was going to come with me to the Grand. Hoping that after all the booze he'd put away it would take a great deal more to wake him than my travel alarm, I set it for five and put it on the pillow right next to Tim Bear. Griff had trusted me with setting up before: I wouldn't let him down this time. I selected stock carefully — a quite different range from the stuff we'd taken to Oxford, for instance. The grey generation were much more silver in my book: they were happy to spend well on good-quality items. Just to make sure I checked Griff's database for regular customers building interesting collections. As a result, I added a couple of Mason's ironware jugs, and a pretty Rockingham cup and saucer. Pity the jugs were a little larger than I'd have liked, the Ka's space being limited, but I got them in the foot-space behind the passenger seat.

The house, garage and gate all locked and checked at least twice, I set off down the motorway to Folkestone. No, there was no sign that I might be followed. I'd hired the basic model, perhaps a bit underpowered, but even so compared with the van it was driving heaven.

I was so early there was plenty of parking. Since the Grand's on a cliff-top area known as the Leas, where there's a good breeze even on a quiet day like this, I made several journeys to and from the car, not risking balancing boxes of fragile goods one on top of another. Setting up was a doddle, with good power access for the lights. I was beginning to enjoy myself.

'What, no Griff?' It was Josie, nose almost on a level with the tables making up the stall.

We'd agreed a story yesterday. 'He had a bit of a fall. He's a bit shaken so I'm flying solo today.'

'The booze, I suppose?'

Heart sinking, I still shook my head firmly. 'He's cutting down. No, some idiot jostled him on a pavement. But he's fine.'

'That's a relief. Now, any more nice little restorations for me today?'

I produced some of the stuff I'd rescued from the house sale.

'Very nice. Anyone but you'd try to pass them off as mint condition. And anyone but me, that is. That Majolica plate you wouldn't sell me — I see that guy from Devon's marked it very high for a restoration job. Yes — over in that corner. Opposite me.'

'Arthur something — with a twee trading name.'

'That's him. He was asking about you. A lot of questions. Was I sure that Griff was your grandfather, that sort of thing.'

'Why should he think he was? I've never—'

'No, but some people think you must be — there was talk of father and daughter, but they did the maths.'

'They might consider Griff's preferences too,' I laughed. 'But why was he asking after me, this Twee Cottage man?'

She shook her head. 'Darned paedophile, maybe.'

'But he's old! And I'm twenty!'

'You may be twenty, but you only look about fourteen. There are a lot of nasty men around, Lina. Any trouble, you talk to old Josie. Right?'

'Right. I mean, thanks. Josie — if you hear of him asking any more questions, you'll try and find out why, won't you?'

This was weird stuff. I'd thought he was a bit flirtatious when we'd done the deal involving a Staffordshire figure I hadn't brought with me today. I hadn't known he'd be here, of course — didn't he say that he'd be at Stafford? — but I felt I'd been somehow unprofessional.

A pair of hands squeezed me round the waist. 'Hallo, young Lina — how's things?'

I suppose it was better than being goosed. In any case, I needed the bloody man's expertise, didn't I? 'Titus! I didn't know you'd be here today! Not your usual sort of venue.'

He touched the side of his nose. 'More buying than selling. Some of these older folk have champagne tastes and beer incomes. So they like to sell the odd autograph or letter. It's all very discreet, of course.'

I nodded. There'd be lots of Mrs Hatches around in retirement towns like this, as well as the well-heeled punters I hoped to attract. 'Tell you what, Titus, could you do me a favour? I need some information.'

Titus didn't do favours: that was what his face said, quite clearly. But then he muttered, 'I suppose back in Yorkshire you saved me from a pretty tricky situation. OK, what do you want?'

I glanced around. Paranoia or what? Everyone in the room seemed to be looking at us. 'Why don't I buy you a coffee?'

'Make it breakfast — full English, mind — and I'll throw the information in free.'

* * *

'A page from *Natura Rerum*!'

'Shh. Look, it's almost certainly a fake, isn't it? Because anyone in the trade'd know the book was worth more in one piece. But I reckon someone with — with your experience — would know if it was genuine. And if it isn't, who'd done it.'

'Not me, I can tell you that, here and now.'

'Shh. No, I'm sure you wouldn't,' I lied. 'But would you recognise anyone else's handiwork?'

'I might. Of course, you'd need to run proper tests — that'd take time and money.' He almost rubbed his hands together in glee.

'I know they would. That's why I'm asking someone who . . . who knows more than most official experts to have a look.'

'Where is it then?' He stuck his hand out.

'In a safe place. If I'd known you'd be here, I'd have brought it along.' I shrugged. 'So I'll need to get it to you somehow.'

'You won't be trusting it to the post.' It sounded like an order.

''Course not. I know you don't have a shop: where do you work from?'

'That's for me to know and you to find out — not.'

If he wanted me to beg and cajole, he'd be disappointed. 'We'll have to meet up somewhere. Not at our shop. It's not there.'

'Why not?'

'Just in case it's the real McCoy, of course.'

'So someone else knows you've got it?'

'A spate of burglaries in the village,' I said casually.

'I thought your place was supposed to be like Fort Knox.'

Now how would he know that? Unless Griff had blabbed while he was drunk. 'Even so.' I shrugged.

'So where is it?'

'Same sort of place as your base.' But we were going to have to trust each other sooner or later.

'You're a bit young to be learning to play with your cards so close to your chest.'

I pulled my most streetwise, cynical face.

'What does Griff think?'

'He suggested you.' Perhaps that'd loosen some of the tension.

The waitress brought our breakfasts.

'You're sure this is on you?'

'That's what we agreed.'

'OK, Lina — how far are you from Tunbridge Wells?'

'Very little, if only we could rely on crows. By car—' I made a snaking gesture with my hand.

'Yeah: rolling English drunkard roads.' He sloshed ketchup all over his bacon. 'What about Tenterden? Is that too far? You can buy me lunch.'

I'd better not bounce with glee. 'Your turn to treat me, I'd have thought!'

He snorted. 'All right on your own side, aren't you? OK. We go Dutch. Tomorrow suit you? Plenty of good pubs. How about the White Lion?'

'Sounds good to me. Twelve thirty?'

* * *

Some of the first punters through the door were those for whom I'd brought along the Mason's jugs, but they made their way to our stand by way of all the others.

'No Griff?' Mrs Barker asked, checking the rim with her fingertip for chips.

'Not today.'

Mr Barker inspected the other jug. 'This is perfect, as far as I can tell. You didn't give it a helping hand, did you?'

I shook my head firmly. 'We always say if it's restored, you know that.'

'Not like that guy back there. Trying to pass a Majolica plate as perfect.'

'Cracked right across,' his wife added.

'And cunningly repaired by me,' I said ruefully. 'I sold it to him as restored, too.' Curiosity got the better of me. 'What was he asking?'

'Three times what it was worth,' he said. 'What's your best on these?'

I told him. 'If you want the pair, you could take off another ten.'

'Twenty!'

'Fifteen,' I grinned. We always played this game. But I nearly dropped one when she asked, 'Is that man — could he be your father?'

I gaped. 'The Devon Cottage guy? Why?'

'He looks very like you.'

'Me! No! Absolutely not!'

'He isn't, then,' Mr Barker concluded, counting notes from his wallet.

I managed a grin. 'He might be. I never had a father. I remember my mum. But she was killed,' I added flatly. Why on earth was I beginning to get emotional?

'You poor child,' Mrs Barker said, pressing my hand. Her husband made sympathetic but embarrassed sounding noises. 'So did Griff adopt you?'

'I wish he could. But I think I'm too old, legally, I mean.' I swallowed. 'My last foster-mother and he are great mates. That's how we ended up together. He's my friend. My very best friend.' And I'd nearly lost him. 'Sorry! He's not very well,' I managed.

She burrowed in her bag for a tissue for me.

As much for something to say as anything, I suspect, Mr Barker said, 'So that cracked plate guy *could* be your father.'

I squared my shoulders. 'No way I'm having a parent who tries to palm shoddy goods off on his customers!' Did that mean I'd rather have a tipsy lord? When they laughed, I added, 'Sorry about — all that. Griff had a bit of an accident the other day — I've been so worried about him.' She looked so concerned I could have told her everything.

But he was plainly embarrassed. 'You'll have to tell him to take more water in it, won't you? Oh, only joking, Lina!'

'No, you're right. He does drink too much. But I shall stop him.'

'If anyone can, you can,' Mrs Barker said, patting my hand kindly. 'Now, is there anything else we should look at? One of Griff's specials?'

* * *

You know how you can feel eyes on you? And you look up suddenly and all you can see is people looking any way but at you? That's how I felt for the rest of the morning. I didn't have time to check: there was a constant stream through the doors, with whole families milling round touching. At least the hotel had asked people not to bring ice creams in, and the two men selling admission tickets were enforcing the ban. But I'd have been a lot happier if the kids had been down on the beach, shingle and all, and I dare say they would have been too. Thank goodness I'd pigged out at breakfast-time — there was no way anyone could sneak out for a lunchtime bite.

Lunchtime! And I hadn't phoned Lord Elham! At least the food wouldn't spoil. But I couldn't just not turn up.

I didn't want to use the mobile in here, with all the racket around me. It'd sound as if I was in a pub: I didn't want to give the impression I'd stood him up for a quick half with my mates.

At these gigs you often had to ask a neighbour to cover for you, but I didn't know the ones either side and those opposite were invisible in the crush. Josie? She'd do it if she could ask her neighbour. Who happened, of course, to be Twee Cottage.

Tough. Now I came to think of it, I needed a loo. I could make the call from there.

'Come tomorrow!' Lord Elham said. 'Same place, same time.'

Same lunch!

'Sorry. I'm tied up for lunch. And I shall be pretty busy the rest of the day.' I'd need time to get today's sales records straight. Not to mention spending some time with Griff. 'Would Tuesday suit?'

This time he sounded huffy. 'I suppose—'

'I have to work on other projects too, you see,' I found myself whining. 'You know how it is.'

'Good heavens, no! Never worked in my life. Leave that sort of thing for the lower orders.'

Of which I was one.

'Come a bit earlier. See the rest of the place: no invaders on Tuesdays.'

Or most other days.

'Tuesday at — let me see—' I thumbed through an imaginary diary. 'Would noon suit you? I'd have to be away by about two, though.' I couldn't expect Mrs Hatch to hold the fort all the time. A flash of inspiration: 'Could I bring a camera?'

'One of those paparazzi bastards? Not likely!'

'Not a cameraman. Just my own camera.'

'Hmm. No objection to the odd box Brownie. Tuesday it is, then. Don't forget the bubbly, will you — running low.'

* * *

If Lord Elham wasn't very satisfactory father-material, I certainly didn't want to be related to Arthur Habgood. He was sitting reading, while two or three people were hovering with intent by Josie's stall. I dived in as if I owned the place, taking money from folk who didn't even ask for 'my best'. When I pressed the cash into Josie's hand I reported, 'Not a single haggle. A couple of pretty plates, as seen, and a willow-pattern plate, origin unknown.'

'For the asking price?'

'Not a penny less. And someone was asking about some Rockingham you promised to get hold of. Look — over there. I'll send him back to you.'

* * *

Humming to myself, I felt my bum-bag. Yes, pleasantly full. A good day's pay for a good day's work. Now it was just a matter of packing everything up. Bubble-wrap time, not just for me, but for all the dealers. No matter how tired you were — and people like Josie looked absolutely knackered — you still had to be careful of course, because the more careless you got, the more fragile the china became. So the last thing you wanted was some idiot making you jump.

'Need a hand?'

It was Marcus.

CHAPTER TWENTY-THREE

We drove home in convoy. At least, Marcus thought that's what we were doing. But if I hadn't still had a load of china and glass in a rented car, I'd have tried to shake him off. I was still fuming at the thought of being looked after — 'the little woman needs help to lift heavy boxes', indeed! Worse, while I was yelling at him, I'd missed the departure from the Grand of Mr Habgood, whom I'd meant to pin to the wall. If people wanted to know about me, they knew who to ask. Not my colleagues and friends: me.

'I only wanted to help,' Marcus bleated, as we finally pulled up in Bredeham.

'I know.' My temper had subsided a bit. 'But there's helping and helping. Now, a big help would be to make sure no one tries to grab me while I'm putting this car away. OK?'

'Would another help be to make a cup of tea?' he asked, once we and the boxes were safely inside.

'Yes. Or better still, coffee. Then I suppose you'd like a meal before you head back to Copeland's place.'

He looked dead shifty.

'Or—' I prompted.

'Actually, we've had a bit of a — well, we're not seeing eye to eye at the moment. I couldn't tell you all about it in front of Tony, but I — well, perhaps we both need a bit of a breather. So I was thinking: I need a roof over my head. You could do with a bit of protection.'

What about my fear that he was after *Natura Rerum* too? 'Let me have a think.'

The thinking was done for me. The answerphone was flashing impatiently. The first message was from Griff, saying he'd be slipping out to some friends of Aidan's for supper, so not to worry about phoning. He was sure I'd done wonderfully at the fair, and he'd love to see me when I had time. It sounded as if he didn't think I would. I phoned back with a message of my own — I'd see him about eleven next day. Next came Mrs Hatch, her consonants furred with what sounded like a stinking cold. OK: flu. She didn't see how she could possibly come to the shop until possibly Thursday — and she couldn't guarantee even that. I phoned to tell her machine not to worry — I had a friend staying who could help out. For *could*, read *would*. Yes, Marcus'd definitely be singing for his supper. There was still the problem with village gossip, but that could be dealt with as and when I knew how.

* * *

'No problem,' Marcus said. 'So long as I can work while I mind the shop. All my things are in the car. It's parked at the back of Tony's,' he added.

'You'll still be doing work for Copeland even though—' I squeaked.

He shook his head glumly. 'I suppose we need each other.'

I dug a word from the back of my head. 'Symbiosis,' I said.

'Eh?'

'It's like me and Griff. We've both got strong points, both got weaknesses. You and Copeland — you're strong where he's weak.'

He nodded. 'Coz needs my talents; I need his money. Symbiosis.'

'OK.' It seemed like the principle Iris had worked on when she'd introduced us. 'And your staying here with me is a symbiotic arrangement.'

'Yes. I suppose it is.'

I nodded, so pleased with myself I could hardly get my head through the door.

* * *

To my surprise, I got back from unpacking the china in the shop to find that Tony had dropped in. He was sitting at the kitchen table nursing a Beck's. Marcus passed me one.

'I've got some frozen curries if you don't fancy cooking,' Tony said. 'And naan and rice and everything.'

'Can't refuse that sort of offer,' I said cheerfully. I hadn't been looking forward to an evening with Marcus, not if he wanted to tell me all about his tiff with Copeland. *Tête-à-tête*: that was the term, wasn't it? That and symbiosis too! Yo, Lina!

* * *

'Staying with Tony every night,' Griff repeated slowly, putting down his coffee cup the following morning. Aidan didn't go in for antique china, but at least this was Wedgwood. Aidan was humming loudly in the kitchen, so I'd know what a sacrifice he was making leaving the living room to Griff and me. 'Well, it should stop any village gossip about you, dear heart.' Was it my imagination or did he stress 'you' very slightly? 'Now, are you quite sure about showing Titus this page of yours? You may be in for something of a disappointment.'

'It's got to be a fake, hasn't it? Actually, I hope it is. Yes, honestly. It'd be horrible to think that someone had torn a page out of a book as old and rare as that. No, what I hope is that Titus will be able to identify the forger. That still might get me back to the owner.'

'You don't think after all that it is Lord Elham?' He peered over his glasses.

'I hope not. He's not the sort of father I'd want, not one bit.'

He stared, forgetting his coffee, while I told him why not.

'Does that mean you'll stop going to Bossingham Hall?' He sounded anxious.

Wrinkling my nose, I confessed, 'Not really. The whole place just fascinates me. You can see why. I'm seeing things your paying visitors never see. Corridors behind bedrooms. Attics. It's magic, Griff. It really is.'

'I'm inclined to agree with those young men: you shouldn't go on your own. Not without telling someone, at very least,' he added, with what sounded like a note of pleading, 'what time you're going and what time you expect to be back. I know you've been safe so far. But he may simply be getting your trust — grooming, it's called.'

'I thought that was what paedophiles did,' I objected.

'I know you're a grown woman, my love, but you — you don't look your age, let's say.'

It was easy enough to translate that: short and thin with a chest nearly as flat as a board. I nodded. 'I will take care. I promise.'

'And you'll take care with Titus?' He looked at his watch. 'It's a good ten minutes' walk and you don't want to turn up puffed. He might mistake it for being flustered or anxious.'

In other words, push off and get it over and done with: yes, Griff was as nervous as I was.

* * *

'Cheers!' Titus toasted me with bitter.

I raised my glass of shandy. But I didn't know what to do next. What I'd really have liked was to show him the page and then beat it, fast. We'd agreed to lunch, however. Dutch treat. Flustered or anxious? I was super scared. If only Griff had been with me — even Marcus.

'Have you ordered?'

I shook my head. 'Only just arrived. Don't you want to look at the page?'

'I always think better on a full stomach. There.' He passed one of the sheets I'd noticed hanging by the bar. 'Look like giant bog paper, don't they? Funny idea, disposable menus. Anyway, beef for me. What about you?'

I barely glanced at it. 'Ploughman's, please. Cheese.'

He got up to order, returning with a numbered wooden spoon. I slid a fiver towards him, which he pocketed without a word or, come to think of it, any change. 'So why was that guy so interested in you yesterday?'

'No idea. He could have asked me if he was really interested.'

'Perhaps he thought you'd done such a good job on that plate he'd offer you some work.'

'I'd rather not have done such a good job if he was trying to pass it off as perfect,' I said. 'Sorry.' Actually, apologising only made it worse, didn't it? Blushing, I stared at the big fireplace, empty now, but in winter, home to a lovely roaring fire. I'd often thawed out here while waiting for Griff to finish his visit to Aidan.

'You stick to your trade and I'll stick to mine.' Titus jabbed with a surprisingly elegant finger. 'OK? Now, that paper. If anyone gets nosy, slide it under these menus.'

I didn't point out he'd wanted to eat first. Putting the folder on my lap, I slipped out the frontispiece and laid it on the table.

He did what I'd done: smelt it, felt it. He ran a finger down the cut edge. The he got out a little magnifying glass and peered. Then he held it at arm's length: so much for discretion and hiding it. At last, he put it down on top of a menu and supped from his glass. 'It's good. I'll say that. It's very good. I'd even say the paper was genuine. Yes, cut from another old book.'

Ready to die with embarrassment, I touched the cut edge. 'Stupid cow: it's the wrong side, isn't it? Why didn't I notice till now?'

'Because you were seeing what you wanted to see. And if Larry Copeland had got round to framing it, no one'd have been any the wiser.'

'So he'd known it was a fake. You don't suppose that he and Marcus — did it themselves?' The waitress was bringing food across. Automatically, I slipped the page under a menu.

He roared so loudly that the waitress took a step back. 'Get out of it! No, not you, sweetheart. Hey, that looks good. Got any horseradish? You're an angel!'

The ploughman's might have been paste and sawdust for all I could taste. For all I'd said out loud that I knew it was a forgery, part of me had wanted it not to be. But if there was one person in this world I wasn't going to cry in front of it was Titus. I swallowed some bread with the aid of a gulp of shandy. 'Why not?'

'Young Marcus looks very pretty with a paintbrush in his hand, but this is quality printing, Lina. It takes years of practice to make woodcuts as good as these.' He shoved the menus aside. 'Look at those curves.'

'Do you recognise the handiwork?' Yes, that was more important. Much more important.

His face told me I was in for another disappointment. 'I wish I did. I'd give him a job tomorrow! If I indulged in that sort of thing, of course, which you know I wouldn't dream of.'

'Of course not. It's good, is it?'

'If he'd used the right ink, excellent. Provided he's got a large supply of old books he doesn't mind cutting about, he could make a real living. Now, that's much more sinful, in my humble opinion, than anything I might be doing. No, you have to draw the line somewhere.'

Warming to this subject, he leaned his arms on the table, stabbing the air with his fork to ram home the point. 'Here, did you read about that bloke who's been slicing maps out of old atlases — absolutely ruining them. The police in four countries are after him. Seems he . . .'

* * *

'So the various attacks may be nothing at all to do with your sad little page, dear heart?'

I shook my head firmly. 'That pre — pre—'

'Presupposes?'

'Right. Presupposes that the people who attacked you and tried to burgle us didn't—'

'They attacked you too, remember. With a car. Twice.'

'Yeah. Well. They missed. It presupposes that they didn't know the page wasn't genuine. And they're after the rest of the book.'

'Which, even minus the frontispiece, would be enormously valuable, if not intrinsically, in terms of scholarship. If the frontispiece could be restored to it, then, well—' He gestured: the sky was the limit. 'Lina, I wish there were somewhere for you to go into hiding, too. Until this whole business has subsided.'

I shook my head. 'Collectors have long memories, Griff. That Ruskin woman down in Devon, or the spectacle case one: neither of them would forget a good specimen.'

'They wouldn't attack and maim to get hold of even the best *sang de boeuf* ware.'

'Others just might.' I got up, leaning over to kiss his forehead. 'I'm glad you're here, safe with Aidan.'

Griff took my hand. 'He says you've been terribly fierce about my alcohol allowance. My dear child, in my dotage I may be, but I can read the instructions for the painkillers. Avoid alcoholic drink.'

'So you're on the wagon?' I was ready to jump up and down.

The old fox smiled slyly. 'I'm avoiding the tablets.'

CHAPTER TWENTY-FOUR

Lord Elham showed no sign of reining in his boozing either. He was halfway through a bottle when I arrived at about eleven fifteen on Tuesday morning. Did he open it when he got up, when you or I would have a cup of tea, or mix it with his orange juice or cornflakes? Silly me! He didn't eat cornflakes, did he?

I'd spent the rest of Monday trying not to be upset at not possessing a clue to a fortune or a father, and finding that the best way to occupy my time was to complete as neatly as I could the paper records of Sunday's sales. Try how I might, though, my handwritten entries never looked anything like as neat as Griff's. Funny, when you think how deftly they can repair fine china. When it came to the computer record, my hands sweated so much I had to give up. It was either that or hit myself again. No, I mustn't do that. I must leave the task to Griff: that was one job he would be able to manage one-handed. A calming hour's restoration work was called for. How about working on Lord Elham's egg cup? I'd never known anything take so long to clean, but underneath the dried egg of ages it was a perfect specimen.

'That's not mine? Really?' he demanded, holding it up to the light that struggled through his filthy living room windows. 'I'd never have believed it.' He was only going to go back on our deal, wasn't he? Yes, down it went on that yucky table. 'What's that lot?'

'Our little job for today. Could we go to the kitchen, please?' I'd brought with me a roll of black sacks, rubber gloves and, on impulse, the facemask I sometimes wear. I thought I'd be glad of the facemask. The camera was in the bottom of the rucksack, but I thought I'd start what promised to be a really satisfying job first.

'I told you,' I said firmly, as, arms akimbo, I surveyed it, 'this kitchen's a health hazard. I bet if the English Heritage people saw it—'

'Not the Gestapo! Spare me!'

'What we'll do is this. We'll decide when we're going to stop. And we'll work flat out till then. But then we do stop. Full stop. Let's just see how much we can get done. Bottles in this sack, so they can go to the bottle bank—'

'How on earth does that work?' he asked, with a delighted grin.

He wasn't so keen when he heard the explanation.

'We'll clear this table altogether, shall we, so if we unearth any china, and it's worth repairing, I can sort it out. The rest we put in this sack. Paper rubbish in that. Food — yuck — in that.'

He nodded. 'What time shall we finish? Noon? Oh, all right. Twelve thirty. Then what?'

'I suppose we stop for lunch.'

* * *

We'd both earned the champagne by the time we'd finished. No, stopped. It'd take another three or four long sessions to get the whole kitchen anything like clean. Then it'd need decorators. After a Chow Mein Pot Noodle, I looked at my watch.

'You don't have to go yet! You haven't had your free trip round the house yet. You only saw a bit of it the other day. Come on — cock the old snook at the Gestapo.'

'These people may be fierce,' I said, not joking at all, 'but they're trying to save beautiful and important things. The

Gestapo were bad through and through.' Half one of my unfinished GCSE projects said so. 'So you should find another nickname for them.'

'Goody Two-Shoes, eh? All right. Let's look at some of the naughty bits. See if they'll shock you. No fainting, now — my back isn't up to carrying damsels downstairs. Mind you,' he continued, 'I was always more interested in carrying damsels upstairs. Now, the library first. Do you know, they won't even let me have keys to the bookcases? Good job I'd already taken some of my favourites. Not that I have much time for reading, these days.'

'What would you read if you did?' I managed to ask. Naughty bits? Damsels? My palms were sweating.

'These?' He looked about him. 'Well, I don't know that I would — most of this stuff's in Latin or Greek, you know. And it's too heavy to take to the bog with you. Or the bath. Imagine taking great tomes like that when you took your ablutions.' He roared with laughter.

I peered at the leather-bound volumes. There wasn't much to get excited about, from my point of view, histories of Rome jostling with estate rolls. But there were some old-looking, possibly first edition Fieldings, *Tom Jones* and *Joseph Andrews*: what a pity he hadn't retrieved those! Yes, and a row of Fanny Burneys, *Evelina* included. It was on the tip of my tongue to tell him the truth about my name, but I remembered Griff's dictum.

Lord Elham was restless. 'You can pay a fiver to see this any day of the week. Let me show you my nursery. And the schoolroom. It's right over my present quarters. Heaven knows why they wouldn't let me have that floor too.'

Perhaps they thought he had enough as it was.

'Come on. Let's sneak up a servants' staircase. I know you'll enjoy that.'

I did.

The nursery hadn't been prettied up with Victorian toys like those you see in National Trust properties. It was a gloomy little room, with some empty bookshelves, a cupboard and little else. No artistically placed dolls' houses and ancient prams. Compared with the child's bedrooms I'd occupied, the wallpaper was dreary, and I'd bet the paintwork oozed nice toxic lead. Still, Lord Elham wasn't exactly a young man: perhaps children's wallpaper wasn't available when he was growing up. And with no children—

'Didn't you ever feel like doing this up for your own children?' I heard myself asking.

'Good heavens, no!' His laugh was as explosive as Titus' yesterday. 'I–I say, look at all this stuff in here,' he interrupted himself, squatting by the cupboard. 'You seem to know about these things — must be worth a mint, eh?' He fished out jigsaws, board games, a child's loom — goodness, it still had some moth-eaten wool on it. 'Meant to make a scarf with that. See — I was trying to weave a gun in there. The Gunners, see. Arsenal. No team down here to support, you see.'

A normal little boy. 'Did you ever get to see them?

'One of my godparents was a director. Best seats — met the players.' He reeled off a list of names than meant nothing to me.

I was on my knees beside him. Chess and draughts. Guns. A modelling kit. A John Bull printing set. Ah! A Stieff teddy bear, still with his button in his ear.

I held him out. 'He's a real collector's item.'

'Good gracious. Old Edward. Good job the Gestapo didn't get hold of him. He's coming down with me. Come on, time for some more champers. What are you doing?'

'Putting all this stuff away.'

'Oh, leave it for the bloody Gestapo. No, it all belongs to the Vultures, doesn't it? The bloody trust,' he explained. 'But Edward — he belongs to me!'

I stayed where I was, putting everything away as neatly as I could, until I heard him calling, 'Lena, where are you? Champers time!'

'Can't I see the schoolroom first?'

'Why not? Here you are. This is where my nanny and then the governess slept.'

'That sounds really Victorian!' So was the room. You wouldn't have needed to remind its occupant that she was one of the lower orders. The room screamed it.

'Suppose it was. Anyway, normal enough after that. Prep school. Eton. Cambridge. For a bit,' he added with an impish smile. 'Soon as I'd got my hands on the old man's dosh, Cambridge went hang. Pity, I suppose. Still, it wouldn't have done to become a desiccated old academic. Ever met any of the old farts?'

Tell him about the Oxford scholar I'd met? No, keep schtum.

'Talk about narrow-minded.' His voice changing, he added, 'Single-minded, too, I suppose. Sometimes I wish I'd had something to focus on.' He looked around the room. 'Not much of a place, is it? No wonder none of the governesses stayed very long.'

The schoolroom was more interesting. Someone had taken the trouble to frame photographs and sketches. The curtains were what caught my eye, not just because they looked newer than everything else in the room. I'd never seen a design anything like it, strong shapes that looked like Japanese letters printed in a deep orange on a lemony ground. I took a corner and held it out.

'My goodness! Look at the time. We'll miss *Neighbours!*'

'These curtains—'

'Another time, another time.' He was out of the door by now.

I sprinted after him. 'But what are the naughty bits you talked about?'

'Look, I'm worried about Harold—'

* * *

I'd never got used to Griff's habit of an after-lunch nap, but I'd come to expect it. After all, he wasn't a young man. But to see Lord Elham dozing off irritated me. He was only in his fifties, and hadn't exactly exerted himself in our kitchen-cleaning activities. Perhaps it was the booze. I'd had one glass only — well, I was driving — and he'd had the rest of the bottle. Half of me was tempted to grab the egg cup again and go. He probably wouldn't miss it. But whatever else Griff had taught me over the last couple of years, he'd dinned into me the importance of good manners. And I knew that sneaking off without saying thank you was not good manners at all. Especially with an egg cup worth three or four hundred.

I mooched back to the kitchen, putting my gloves on. I might as well make myself useful. I took them off again. Lord Elham didn't want a clean kitchen, and wouldn't thank me for my efforts. All this was simply a response to some button in me that the sight of so much dirt was pressing. If only I could remember what it was.

I wandered over to the pile of china I'd thought worth salvaging. By some miracle most of it was simply dirty. Well, what were sinks for? I turned the hot tap, holding a hand out hopefully. Nothing. OK, there was a trickle from the cold tap, but that was useless, especially without Fairy Liquid or whatever. Useless. So I loaded as much as I thought safe to carry into a filthy washing-up bowl, and set off for the official part of the house and the ladies' loos I'd used the other day. Plenty of hot water, some of the Vultures' fine toilet soap, and three sinks side by side: soaking, washing, rinsing. Perfect.

* * *

'Who the devil told you you could wander round my house?' Lord Elham's pale, flabby cheeks were puce, and quivering with rage.

'You did,' I said.

'I did?'

'Just before your nap. You told me to amuse myself. So I did. By rescuing some of your china. There's a couple of dessert dishes here I reckon are two hundred years old. Probably more.'

Iris had a cat who used to fix you when you had fish scraps. Lord Elham looked so much like Araminta I nearly laughed.

'Really? Worth a bob or two?'

'Probably. And this game pie dish — look at those gorgeous colours.'

'And all you were doing was washing up?'

'No hot water in the kitchen. Nor any soap. So I used the ladies' loo. Anyway, now you're awake, maybe we could talk a bit more about your past. That's what I'm here for, after all.'

He looked at his watch. 'Not until after *Countdown*.'

'In that case, I'd best be off,' I said firmly. 'Now, I shall be busy tomorrow and Thursday — but maybe we could meet again on Friday?'

'So today's Tuesday, is it? Well, well.' He set off towards his wing, ushering me and my bowlful of goodies along the corridors and through the security door. 'How did you know the code?'

'You showed me the other day.' True.

He looked a bit puzzled, sheepish, even. 'Sometimes do things I shouldn't when I've had a drop. You won't tell anyone, will you? Promise?'

'Cross my heart and hope to die,' I said promptly. 'Now where shall I put these? It's a shame to put nice clean stuff back in that filthy kitchen.' While he bit his lip, considering, I added, 'If you do any more sorting out in there, you will remember the system, won't you? A different sort of rubbish in each sack.'

'Me? Oh, yes. Yes. Different sort of rubbish in each sack. But that's not rubbish.' He pointed at the washing-up bowl.

'No, not rubbish at all. Where shall I put it?'

'But you're to take it with you. And that egg cup thing: that's yours. I gave it to you. Everything else — you're going to flog it, Lena — flog the lot. And bring along some more bubbly, remember.'

'That lot'll buy you a lot of bubbly. But you'll have to wait. It takes time to sell things. Sometimes months. Tell you what, give me some paper and I'll make a list of everything I've taken. Each time I see you I'll tell you what I've sold and how much I've — how much it sold for.'

'For free?' He was sharper than I'd expected.

'Would you want me to take some commission? Ten per cent's usual—'

He looked at his watch again. 'Ten — fifteen — twenty. Take what you like. So long as you remember my bubbly.'

* * *

'A different colour?' The car hire clerk looked at me as if in all his fifty-something years he'd never heard anyone talking so much gibberish.

'That's right. I need a different colour car. Any colour except silver. Red? Green? Black? Come on, you must have Kas in different colours. Kas as in Ka,' I explained, before he could embark on a long discussion involving Nissans and Skodas and what have you. What I didn't explain was that I thought I'd been tailed from Bossingham by a metallic-blue Ford Focus. Knowing the roads round Ashford quite well, I'd managed to shake it off in Stanhope, the sort of council estate I knew all too well. There had to be some advantage in driving bottom of the range rental cars, and changing them when you felt like it had to be one of them.

'We have a black one. Green Nissans, if you'd rather have green.'

'A green Nissan would be fine.'

I signed a new set of paperwork and took the keys. 'I'd better empty the car first. The Ka, that is.' Bloody Ford — they must have known the name'd cause this sort of confusion.

The guy sighed. Shaking his head, he followed me into the car park. If he'd thought me touched before, the sight of me tenderly ferrying an old enamel washing-up bowl apparently full of scraps of lined foolscap paper from one vehicle to another must have had him reaching for the phone to summon the men in white coats. As for his expression when I pulled a ginger wig over my thatch, goodness knows. I was too busy checking that no one else was interested in my activities.

* * *

'It's all a bit cloak and dagger,' Marcus said, serving dollops of rather runny lasagne. 'A bit paranoid.'

'I think Lina's being sensible,' Tony objected.

'If you'd had people drive at you in an attempt to burgle your house, you might be a bit paranoid,' I added, deciding not to mention the tail. Perhaps I was being paranoid. 'Which reminds me, how was the shop? Any problems?'

'Apart from dropping asleep with boredom? It's about time you and Griff started to sell on the Internet, Lina — that's the future.'

'Did you sell anything?'

'A set of sherry glasses — for the marked price. And I persuaded them to take the decanter, too. There wasn't a price on that, so I invented one. A hundred and ten.'

I nearly choked. 'The price was for the whole lot,' I said. 'And rather steep, as I recall. Earning your keep and cooking the supper — Marcus, you're an angel.'

He flushed deeply and shuffled in his seat. What on earth had I said?

CHAPTER TWENTY-FIVE

Battle and Wye. Griff always used to say it sounded like a philosophical question. In fact, they're two villages hosting fairs that we've always done because they're in our area. Battle's where William the Bastard won his battle — get it? Wye's just a pretty village with some lovely old houses just down the road from Bredeham. I did the first on Tuesday, selling not a lot but enough to cover our expenses, and Wye on Wednesday, selling some high-quality glass and one or two restored items, pointing out to the punters exactly what work I'd done. One woman pounced on the egg cup, practically drooling, but blenched at the price, hardly surprising since five hundred and fifty pounds would have bought twice over the stuff on one or two other stalls. OK, I was being optimistic, but that was the price in the latest trade mag.

'What's its provenance?' she asked.

Not that was something I hadn't thought about. I could hardly tell her the truth, in case Lord Elham's Vultures got to hear about his selling off not the family silver but the family blue-and-white ware. I rattled off the technical stuff, hoping she wouldn't notice.

'In other words, you don't know,' she said, putting it down and patting it a tender farewell.

The pat settled it. She loved it. 'In other words,' I corrected her gently, 'I do know, but the person selling it's asked for confidentiality. I'm just selling it on commission,' I lied. He'd said it was mine and mine it was. What was the term Griff used? 'Gentlefolk fallen on hard times.'

You could almost see the picture forming in her brain: Darby and Joan beside a cold and empty hearth selling off their inheritance. She picked it up again.

'There's one identical in the Miller's Guide,' I said. 'Guide price six hundred. Mind you,' I added fairly, 'I think that was at auction. That always bumps the price up a bit.'

'So what would your best be?'

'*Their* best would be five hundred. Look, I'll throw in a silver spoon to eat your egg with.' And so the deal was done. I'd have to ask Griff's advice about the paperwork later, because she was fishing out her chequebook. Just in time I got her to make out her cheque to me, not the business. I wasn't at all sure where that would leave me taxwise, probably no better off. But at least I could claim the champagne as a legitimate expense, now. What a good job I'd kept all the receipts.

* * *

'A microwave? What on earth do I want with a microwave?' Lord Elham peered with something like distaste at it, still nestling in its box.

I'd kept my word to myself, popping into Comet for one that was small and foolproof. It was now almost lunchtime on Friday, and I was about to test it.

'You can heat up ready meals in it.' I showed him the haul I'd picked up from Sainsbury's. 'I won't say they're the most nutritious food available, but if you never eat anything except Pot Noodles, you'll end up with scurvy or beriberi or something.' Iris had been big on vitamins but vague as to the consequences of ignoring them.

'But that means going out all the time: I can get Pot Noodles by the box.'

'You've got a freezer under your fridge. You could pack a lot of ready meals in there. And places like Tesco and Sainsbury's actually deliver these days.' But I could see he wasn't convinced.

On the other hand, he enjoyed the chicken tikka masala I heated up. He was casting covetous eyes at my Goan prawn curry, but I polished it off briskly. After all, it might not be good for him to tackle too much meat after such a low everything diet. As for the mineral water I'd also bought, it was clear from the revolted glances he threw at it that only one person was going to drink it.

* * *

I made another assault on the kitchen while he watched *Neighbours*. This time it wasn't Harold he was worried about but Lou. My worries were more to do with the buildup of black sacks: he could do with his own private bottle bank and a special refuse collection. Meanwhile, I stowed everything in an outhouse, full of rusted farm implements, a bonanza for a specialist, or even a country life museum. Now the floor was relatively clear, I thought he might be tempted to have a go himself: it wasn't nearly as daunting as when we'd started.

He seemed impressed, but not enthusiastic when I showed him. 'Not a lot of point in looking at the house today,' he grumbled. 'Full of day-tripping council tenants.'

Biting back the remarks yelling to be uttered, I said quietly, 'There are other rooms in your section. What do you keep in there?'

'Same as in here, of course. Place just sort of silts up. Well, you know how it is.'

'So as soon as one room gets dirty, you—'

'Never bother with a bit of dirt. Supposed to eat a peck of dirt before you die, or some such thing.'

'There's dirt and dirt.'

He looked sheepish. 'Well, if you want to cast your eyes over some of my dirt, we'd better have another little drink. That bottle you brought — should be chilled now. Mind you, young lady,' he added, 'I need more than one bottle a day. Sold any of that stuff yet?'

'Not yet. It's going to take time. I told you, I did sell the egg cup you gave me, which is how I was able to afford your microwave and your ready meals.'

'Ah. A bit of quid pro quo. Awfully decent of you, Lena, to think of an old buffer like me. A present, too,' he said, ambiguously.

'As for your stuff, properly preparing items like that takes more than a quick dunk in lavender-scented soap.' It was as if he was young, I an old, wise teacher. 'Now, the most useful thing for me would be to see the first room you used. Then we can sort of work up.'

'Suppose that'd be my old bedroom.'

I'd meant down in this wing, of course, but I'd take in what I could, when I could. I nodded.

'Means braving the lumpen proletariat.'

If I wasn't careful I'd tell him what I thought of his snobbery. But I didn't think film researchers were supposed to yell at their subjects. 'Do visitors see it, then?' As if I didn't know the answer already.

'Good heavens, no! Only the state bedrooms: Queen Elizabeth slept here, that sort of thing. She didn't, of course. Wrong period. No evidence that Victoria did, either. But Edward did, while he was Prince of Wales. Him and Mrs Keppel. And, before you ask, Joe Public doesn't see their room. The Vultures talk about light levels and damage to the hangings. Mean sticklers! Just want to spoil other people's innocent pleasures. What are you waiting for — we'll go through the passage Edward's valet would have used.'

The house was so big and sprawling that we didn't see anyone, not even a guide. But then, as he said, we went through servants' territory, emerging through one of those hidden doors.

'There.' He pulled the curtains.

For one used to gods and goddesses disporting themselves, or heroic scenes of military triumph immortalised in tapestries, these hangings did come as a bit of a shock. I knew that giggling was the wrong response — far too immature. But what else could you do, when confronted with men quite so keen, and women equally eager? In the company of a man not just old enough to be my father, but possibly just that?

'Many's the good session I've had in this bed,' Lord Elham said. This was the first room I ever had sex in. I don't know which tickled the girl most, the sight of all those cocks up there or the real thing in front of her. Thirty-two bedrooms in the place.' He sank on to the bed, putting his hands behind his head. 'Shagged in all of them. Shagged in each one, then started again here.'

'Thirty-two women! That's terrible.'

He pulled himself on to one elbow. 'No such thing. It was positively expected.' By now he was sitting upright. 'You know about old things. Where's your sense of history? Seventies — Flower Power. Drugs and sex. Bonk all you like. Especially a man in my position. Maybe it's different these days, with AIDS and goodness knows what else.'

'But—'

'I treated them well. Fresh bed linen for every woman, dinner and decent wine. Breakfast.' He nodded as if he'd proved his point. 'Got round again, another thirty-two.'

My voice sounded hollow even to me. 'Didn't you ever sleep with the same woman twice?'

'Oh, yes. Managed twenty a night with one woman.'

'I meant, didn't you have long-term relationships?'

'Oh, I get you. Oh, one or two. But I'd always roger her in the same room — I had to maintain my standards, you see.'

'What about marrying?'

'Having too good a time for that, my goodness!' He threw his head back and laughed. Then his face slid into sadness. 'Always thought I'd find a decent woman when I was in my forties and have an heir. Didn't work out. So all these Vultures will get a little bit of the place. Bastards.'

I tried to sound journalistic. 'When you say it didn't work out — was there someone special and she wouldn't have you?' I swallowed painfully. Could that be my mother?

'Never found anyone special enough to ask. Tried to go round the thirty-two rooms again, but things were different in the eighties. More materialistic, that sort of thing.'

It was better to keep up with the conversation than to have a pick at my feelings. 'Materialistic?'

'Girls started making all sorts of demands.'

'Wanting commitment before they—'

'Pretty nearly. Said I had to use a johnny — imagine that? Putting a bloody Wellington boot on the old man. Not having any of that, and so I told them. Nude bathing or nothing.'

My swallow hurt. 'All this nude bathing. What about — the consequences?'

'Clap, you mean? Pox? Oh, a couple of times.'

'I meant — babies.'

'God bless my soul, I suppose there must have been. Forgotten all about them. Hey, somewhere downstairs is that little book I told you about — we'll go and find it, shall we?'

* * *

Putting my feelings into words had always been beyond me. There were a lot of feelings going wordless here. My knuckles were white from being crushed against each other. They wanted to smash or punch or — I didn't know what. My face, because I came back again and again, just like one of his favourite bedfellows? His lovely china and glass because he didn't deserve them? The man himself? It'd be so easy to grab one of those heavy cut-glass candlesticks and smash it through the skull under the wispy hair. One blow. Finish him for good and all. No one knew I was here. I could just do it. No one'd notice for weeks. I could rid the world of a bastard, cram the car with loot and be in France before midnight. Or just go home, actually. No one had catalogued his goodies. I could just sell them bit by bit. And be surprised at the news when it came. I grasped the candlestick more tightly.

The man was a dopehead. Everything about him said so. Could I blame him for being so immoral, any more than I could blame that kid at school with Asperger's for swearing? There was another word: Griff had tried to explain the difference when he was talking about Lord Byron. Not *immoral*, but *amoral*. Perhaps that was the word for this noble lord, too. And yes, thanks to Griff I knew words like *irony* and *sarcasm*, and that was what I meant when I called him noble.

Delicately, I replaced the candlestick, giving it a little polish for good luck.

By the time I'd caught up with him, he had got back to his wing and flung open the doors to a couple of his other rooms. Aladdin's Cave, that was what I'd got in front of me. Aladdin's Cave times two. If the kitchen could have kept me in funds for six months or more, what about these? Following him, I scanned the first and the second. He'd obviously moved furniture down here before the Vultures got a look in: I didn't know enough to identify makers, but quality leapt out at me.

'No,' he said, 'not in here. Let's try this. You see,' he said, gesturing at a table laden with china and crystal, 'I thought if I had this it would spare me washing up.'

Selling it would have spared me working for five years.

'No. Not in here. Let's try this one.' He opened another door.

There was the grey, marble fireplace, the deep windows — and all my memories. I reeled. 'Lord Elham,' I managed to croak, 'I think you might be my father.'

'Do you?' he asked, as flat and unexcited as if I'd told him my watch was running slow. 'I suppose we could always find out. It'll be in that book.'

CHAPTER TWENTY-SIX

Whatever I'd expected, this wasn't it. It was all so flat and ordinary. I've known blokes watch the football results with less emotion than this guy presented with a possible daughter. Maybe the heir he'd wanted.

'It'll be in the book. And that'll be somewhere in here,' was all he'd say.

I scooped a pile of sheet music — music? I'd not seen any anywhere else — off the big sofa and sat down hard. It was the room all right. Fireplace, desk — completely covered, these days, with heaps of paper — and the lovely windows. You could push them up and step straight out on to what must have been a lovely terrace. Now it was green as far as I could see, with balustrades cracked down to their iron cores. Urns overflowed with what looked like weeds: I might be living in the country these days but I hadn't caught up with things like that yet. When my legs could work again, I'd make it to the windows themselves to see if the Vultures had cleaned up the bit the public could see.

But my legs might have been made of water for all the good they were doing me. Off in yet another room I could hear Lord Elham bustling round, muttering under his breath. More loudly, in my head I could hear raised voices, Lord Elham's and my mother's. And instead of this ancestral mess, all I could see was the book on my lap. What had it got me into?

'Lena? It's time for *Countdown!*'

Eventually — I've no idea how long it took — I must have dragged myself into his living room. Sticking my hand out for the champagne glass he was offering me, I sank it as if it were water. He might have been taken aback: he topped me up with no more than half an inch, before scuttling back to his seat and staring at the screen. If I sat down and let myself compare the champagne drinking I'd fantasised about and this, I might cry. Or smash that tower of glasses. He might notice that.

As it was, it was easier to lick my lips, dry despite the drink, and ask, 'What sort of book am I looking for, Lord Elham?' Clearly not the one I had been looking for originally. But *Natura Rerum* was pretty low in my priorities now.

'Oh, a little thing,' he said, over his shoulder. 'Smaller than an exercise book. Greyish green. Probably marked French Vocab. In there somewhere.' He waved a vague hand.

Griff said he used to have a vocab. book. He'd suggested I have one. And now my — and now Lord Elham turned out to have one too. All this interest in words. If only I could find some that would describe what I was feeling. Halfway describe — I didn't need any fine tuning.

Taking my glass with me, I peered into the room he'd been rooting about in. *The* room. Where on earth to start? It was like the kitchen all over again, even to the mouldy plates and glasses. This must have been his pre-Pot Noodle period, when he'd still used china. In this case, ironstone — a Mason's dinner service, not the most expensive in the world and some pieces badly chipped. Perhaps it had been servants' hall ware. I'd heard of people wringing their hands, and this was what I found I was doing, kneading my palms and thumb pads, grinding the bones against each other. Where should I start looking? In this topsy-turvy world, the bureau was much too obvious. My nose wrinkled at the thought of opening drawers, sifting through pigeonholes. And my head told me that a bureau was a place for precious things and that Lord Elham hadn't considered this book precious.

Lord Elham. Possibly Dad. I'd not used his name, apart from the first time we'd met, all the hours we'd spent together. Maybe I'd expected him to tell me to do the usual casual thing first-name thing. But he hadn't. Ever. And the first time I get a really good clue that he was who I always thought he was, I call him, formal as you like, Lord Elham. He hadn't, even then, said, 'If you think we're related, you'd better call me Rupert.' He just went on watching daytime TV. Was this a father I wanted?

But I couldn't leave it alone. If only I were a true divvy, and could dowse my way to it. If I sat and emptied my mind, as I sometimes did at sales for Griff, maybe, just maybe, I'd come up with something.

* * *

'Ah, there you are,' Lord Elham greeted me. 'Found it yet? Missed a jolly good programme.'

'I've no idea where to start.' My spread hands said it all. 'But I've an idea — I get them sometimes — that it might be not in this room but in the one to this one's left as you go out.'

The look he shot me suggested that there were still one or two grey cells functioning in that dopey brain. What on earth had I said?

'No. It's in here. Have you tried the bureau? Why on earth not?'

'I thought it might be private.'

'Private?' He shook his head. 'Or you might not have tried the bureau because you didn't have the key. That might be the real reason, mightn't it?' I could have smacked his cunning face.

'If I'd wanted to open it, I could have used one of these,' I said, jiggling a little set on a ring.

'What are they?'

'If you go to an auction, you want to be able to look inside wardrobes and so on. Very few have keys.'

'Let's see. And these can get you into anything?'

'Most things. In the eighteenth and nineteenth centuries they didn't have all that many different types of locks, not for everyday furniture: well, they weren't expecting burglars and if a servant had been caught red-handed—' I gestured a cut throat.

'Well I'm blowed. Let's see if they work on this, shall we? Which do I try first?' He poked and twisted. At last the lock yielded. He pulled down the fall-front — to reveal more lottery tickets than I could ever imagine. 'Never won. Well, I might have done. Never got round to checking. I don't suppose there's a list of past winning numbers anywhere, do you?'

'You could try Ceefax? It'd be like matching needles in haystacks, though.' And I was more interested in that book.

Suddenly, leaving tickets drifting down like pink snowflakes, he half closed the bureau and left the room. Equally abruptly he returned. 'Here it is. It was there all the time.' I never did learn where *there* was. He slung it to me, for all the world as if it was the evening paper. I caught it: I suppose it was about seven inches by four, with the greenish-grey cover he'd described and, yes, the words *French Vocab* on the cover.

'This is confidential.' How about that for a stupid response?

'Suppose you're right. Right, what name am I after?'

'Townend. Helen Townend.'

He pulled a face. 'Hmm. Doesn't ring any bells. I'd have remembered a Helen. All those jokes about a thousand ships.' He ran a finger down the first page. 'See, I've got quite a system. Columns. Surname; Christian name; when and where and how. Offspring if any. Diseases if any. Payments if any. Gosh, shocking writing. You'd have thought a decent school would have knocked a decent fist into me.'

I had to look. 'Are you left or right-handed?'

'Ah, that's something they *did* knock into me. I wanted to be left-handed, but they thought it was too *sinister*. *Sinister* — get it?' He roared with laughter, I've no idea why.

'Did you spell badly?'

'Well, you can see.'

One of my mates who'd been just like Lord Elham had been diagnosed as dyslexic. No, not just like him. A good deal brighter. They'd given him special tuition and he'd got an A Level in Maths.

My eyes travelled down the lines. Words like *pox* and *clap* peppered the pages. And here and there the letter M or F.

'These are babies?' I prompted. So I was reduced to being a mere F.

'Yup. An A means we had to get rid of it. Privately, of course. No queuing in line for an NHS quack.'

'How very decent of you,' I muttered.

He didn't notice the irony. Or was it sarcasm? 'Well, *noblesse oblige*, you know. Flowers, champers, a private room.'

'What about the Ms and Fs? Did you keep in touch with them and their mothers?'

'What? All thirty of them?'

'Thirty?' I hoped my voice sounded steadier than my legs felt.

'Give or take a couple.' He ran a grimy fingernail down the Offspring column, muttering as he did so. 'Thirty-one, actually. Assuming they're all alive.' He peered at me. 'And you think you're one of these Fs? Are you like your mother? You don't favour our side.'

Thank goodness for that. 'My mother died when I was very young. But she brought me here once. I remember sitting looking at a book while you talked.'

'Extraordinary. Fancy your remembering that when I haven't a blind clue. This room?'

'The fireplace — it's a different colour from most of the others, isn't it? And those windows. Imagine what it was like for a toddler, being able to step through windows into the sun!'

As if to check for himself, he walked over to them, dodging piles of books. 'Hmph. Like Alice.' He opened one, stepping out and then back in.

I nodded. 'Wonderland. I'm sorry — I forgot to bring the books back.' It was just a matter of honour: they weren't first editions, not even good editions, so I wasn't robbing him of a fortune.

He waved an airy hand. 'Plenty of books — you can see that. Come over here. Let's have a proper look at you.' As I feared, he gripped my chin, turning my head this way and that. 'Are you sure your name's Townend?'

'It's the one on my birth certificate. I was born on Bastille Day, 1984.'

He dropped his hand sharply and made a hex. 'You're not going to send me to the guillotine, I hope? Or get Big Brother to watch me? Let's check by dates, then. You don't look twenty, I must say.' He opened the book again, muttering the names he read: 'Carter, Lane, Greenaway — Good Lord, she had the most wonderful — er, body.' He had the grace to look embarrassed. 'Ah! Tunnell. Does that say Tunnell? But it could be Townend. Possibly. You're sure she was a Helen, your mater?'

I nodded.

'Seems you may be right. Well I'm blowed. How do you do?' He only wanted to shake my hand!

And I only let him.

'Good job I didn't try to bonk you, eh? Mind you, got a touch of the old brewer's droop these days — wouldn't have managed much anyway. Well, fancy my having a daughter. Quite a taking little thing. Not so keen on your name, mind. Not a singer's name. She should have done better than that.'

The old snob. 'She did. I'm actually Evelina. After the novel.'

He snorted. 'And a name running throughout the family, one each generation. Clever girl. Then your mater died?'

'Bus crash.'

'And it's taken you till now to find me!'

'She didn't put your name on the birth certificate,' I said dryly.

'Well, there you are. Decent woman, by the sound of it.'

'Tell me about her,' I said, finding a chair and sinking on to it.

He shook his head as if I'd asked him to sing in Chinese. 'I was hoping you'd do that. Nice to know who you've had a child with. These days these women'd send the government after you for maintenance. Helen didn't.'

'What if she had?'

That cunning look again. 'No DNA in those days. But now you're here, you'd better stay. Have a meal. You could move in. You'd be very useful, sorting out this, selling that. Come on, what do you say?'

I shook my head. 'I've got a job, thanks.'

'Ah, those film people. What a coincidence, eh? You making a film about a chappie who turns out to be your father.'

I shook my head. One of us had better stick to reality. 'That was a ruse. I was trying to track down that memory I told you about. The room with the fireplace and the book.' And, yes, my father. And just look what I found!

'Book? What book?'

'The book you gave me to look at when you were talking to Mum. Look, I'd better start at the beginning—'

He glanced at his watch. 'Another day. Another day. The news is just about to start. Yes, come back another day. And don't forget, make us some money. And bring plenty of champagne. I need a drink after all this.'

* * *

I don't remember the walk down to the car, getting into it or driving several hundred yards in it. But I must have done, because next thing I do remember was seeing this guy peering hopelessly under his car's bonnet. I'd whizzed by when I realised it was the nice young clergyman who'd insisted on giving me a lift all the way to the station. It was miles to a public phone, across a great sweep of road without even hedges between it and the huge fields it crossed. Not much fun being there when it was dark, with nothing but some scattered reflector posts for company. Giving him a hand or a lift was the least I could do. Especially as I knew more about starting cars than most. I wasn't sure he would approve of my methods, though. Pity I couldn't greet him by his name, but it had drifted away, buried underneath all this afternoon's crap, no doubt.

He looked up, startled. Well, reversing smartly had always been one of my party pieces. I'd had to give it up because it scared Griff so much.

'Lina!' He looked really chuffed to see me. But then he'd have been glad to see anyone halfway human with a set of wheels. 'It's wonderful to see you,' he said. 'There's not much traffic along here at this time of night, and what little there is doesn't stop — see what I mean?'

We were practically swept off our feet by the disappearing Focus' turbulence.

'Late home after work,' he said. 'Must be new round here. I usually recognise the villagers' cars.'

'And you don't know who that belongs to?'

He shook his head. 'Not yet. Mind you, come to think of it I have seen it around these last few days. Perhaps people down for their holiday. Though people on holiday usually respect the speed limit.'

I nodded, thinking more about the car. And glad, to be honest, to have something other than my problems to concentrate on.

The trouble with modern cars is that so much of the engine is sealed and everything's computer checked at service. There was nothing obviously wrong.

I scratched my face. 'You've called the AA or whatever? Ah, it's a mobile black spot round here, isn't it?' I'd try just one more thing. Weren't clergymen and professors supposed to be absent-minded? What if he'd simply run out of fuel? I sat in the driver's seat and checked the gauge. No, he'd got half a tank. So why did it sound so empty when I tried the ignition?

* * *

'It's very kind of you,' he said, stowing his brand-new, green petrol can between his feet.

'You went out of your way to take me to the station,' I said, 'so I'm just returning the favour. And don't thank me till we're sure it is just a faulty gauge. It might be something more serious. In which case I shall take you somewhere you can phone from. I hope you're not in a hurry? Because if you are, I could always drop you wherever and you could get a lift back.'

'It was a meeting at the Cathedral. I don't suppose they'll miss me. What are you doing round these parts?' he said, with the ease of someone used to making conversation with strangers: all those weddings and funerals, I suppose.

'Looking up family,' I said, wishing I hadn't. Hadn't said it or hadn't done it? Either.

'Always difficult, meeting people who might be related to you but are really complete strangers,' he said.

'You're telling me.' Heavy rain clouds had brought dusk down early, and the road was dark enough now for me to have to concentrate on driving. He'd think that was why I wasn't explaining. Maybe. But my head kept rerunning the day's events, every word, every action, going past in slow motion. Even Lord Elham stepping through the big window and talking about Alice.

He'd shut it but not locked it.

I pulled over. 'I'm sorry. I have to make a phone call — it won't take a second.'

Nor would it have done, if I could have got a signal. Predictably swearing and predictably apologising, I pulled back on to the road again, wondering what to do next. Even as I told myself not to bother, that I didn't owe the man anything, I remembered all the little incidents that had put my life at risk and that had landed Griff in hospital. They hadn't wanted to hurt a foolish old man or a silly woman. They wanted to find what I'd wanted to find. The owner of *Natura Rerum*. And as sure as that Guy in Canterbury Cathedral had made little apples, I'd probably led them to him. And he'd left a window open. I smacked my face hard enough for the clergyman to look hard at me.

* * *

Pushing the reluctant Micra up this track was terrifying. It leapt from rut to rut, threatening to ground its sump on every third tussock. A four-wheel drive with several litres under the bonnet — that was what I needed.

After all that there was no sign of a Focus. But they could have stowed it in one of the out-buildings. As the rain slashed down, I decided not to bother looking but to check that open window, scrabbling over a wall just too high for me to vault, though.

It was still open. But that didn't mean anything.

Now what? Tiptoe round like a cat burglar and risk giving the old guy heart failure, or call out like you would to your dad? "Hey, I'm home!" — that sort of thing?'

I might manage a neutral *cooee*. No reply. Nor, which was worrying, the sound of the TV. Yelling as convincingly as I could,

'Police! Armed police!' I ran along the corridor, pushing open the living room door.

Lord Elham's vocabulary book, his catalogue of sexual activity, lay on the table, blotched with blood.

The front door slammed. There was the sound of feet, then a revving car. No, it didn't sound like the Nissan — they must have hidden theirs somewhere. And what was the betting it was a Focus?

So did they take Lord Elham or leave him?

I was already out of the door, checking all the rooms along the corridor. They appeared untouched, though they'd already been in such a mess I might have been mistaken. The locked door remained locked.

They'd taken him.

No, not necessarily. He might have made it to the rest of the house, through the security door. Yes. Blood smeared on the carpet led straight to it. It seemed to have done its job: marks all round it suggested they'd tried to jemmy it and failed.

I tapped in the code. The door opened a crack, a dead weight pressing against it. I was through the gap before you could say Lord.

* * *

'I do not want an ambulance. I do not need an ambulance. You will not summon an ambulance.' He sat on a bathroom stool, peering at himself in a huge, gilt-framed mirror. 'I do not want the police. I do not need the police. And I forbid you to summon the police.'

We were in the main house still, using the ladies' loo I'd sought out earlier in the week. There was far more blood on the paper towels than I liked. 'You've had a nasty bang on the head. You need proper attention.'

'In that case you can drive me to Casualty. I've always wondered what it was really like.'

'And the police? Wouldn't you like to see what the Old Bill's really like? You've been broken into. People have tried to steal from you.'

'They've taken nothing, as far as I know.'

'You want to do a spot check now?' I asked sarcastically. 'Or shall we get that head looked at?'

'My head, if you insist,' he groaned. Never a good colour, he was greyish-yellow now. 'The hospital, if you'd be so kind. But first you must secure the window. You'll find that the shutters lock.'

'OK. I'll do that as soon as I've phoned home. They'll be worried sick about me. Where's the nearest extension? Back in your wing? Come on: I'll give you a hand.'

* * *

'What is this family of which you were talking?' he demanded as the car hiccupped and slipped down the track. 'I thought your mother was dead. Is it her relatives?'

'She didn't have any. I was farmed out to kind strangers.'

He appeared to ponder on that. I'd meant him to. 'What sort of people took you in?'

'A succession of people. I was sent to foster-parents. Some good, some bad.'

'Foster-parents? So where would they live?'

'Some in nice middle-class roads, some in terraced houses. Some even on council estates.' Let him chew on that.

'And who paid them?'

Not you! 'The local authority. I don't remember my mother — anything about her. I'd really like to know — anything.' We were almost by the Hop Pocket. The map showed a lane that would get us straight on to the B2068, but it didn't say how steep and winding it was, trees appearing from nowhere in the headlights. Perhaps he was concentrating on it, too, or perhaps his head was hurting more than he admitted.

At long last we emerged. Although it was further, I thought it might be quicker to take the motorway back to Ashford. I'd learned from the same programme as he had that the sooner head injuries were treated the better. And I also had an idea that you weren't supposed to let the patient lose consciousness, that you had to talk to them and make them talk. So I tried again. 'Do you remember how old my mother was? Or how she earned a living? Anything? Please try.'

'She was just a girl, Lina. You know, a girl.'

'Something must have made you want to sleep with her.'

'What all the women had, or I wouldn't touch them. Nice tits, nice legs and a nice fanny.'

And a nice thing to say to her daughter. Swallowing, I tried again. 'What about her personality? Her character?'

'Good grief, I wasn't thinking of marrying her! She must have been a nice girl, Lina — I only bedded nice girls. I mean, one has to draw the line somewhere. I have an idea she'd had a fiancé — a student, or something. He'd given her this tiny little ring—'

Yes, the ring with the pitiful little stone. 'So what happened? Did he find out about me and drop her?'

'I don't think he was on the scene anymore. She might have had me on the rebound, you might say. I don't know. Lina, what's it matter, old thing?'

It was far too hard to explain, especially to a concussed old idiot and on a road which from being as straight as a die now twisted into an awkward series of bends, just the place to meet the removal van lumbering towards us. 'What if those burglars cased the joint and are going back with that van to empty your place?'

'They'll find a burglar alarm connected to the police station. The Vultures fixed that. They only got in because of that window being open. Won't get into the main house — that security lock.'

'Does the alarm apply to your wing, or just the main house?'

'Might be mine — no, I think it's just the main house. In any case, what's a load of old furniture and stuff? Junk.'

Apart from being my livelihood. 'Family treasures? Heirlooms?'

'All in the public part. You've seen.'

I gambled. 'Apart from the Hepplewhite bureau and all that Adam stuff? Not to mention *Natura Rerum!*'

'No one'll find that,' he said confidently. 'Lina, would you stop this infernal machine a moment? I believe I'm going to cast up my accounts.'

Which meant he was going to be sick. I knew about that from *Casualty*, too. As soon as he was ready, I bundled him back in the car and drove faster than I ought. If I was stopped by the speed cops, so much the better. They could provide another thing I was sure he'd always wanted — a police escort.

* * *

'Lady Elham? Lady Elham?' The receptionist was peering round the waiting area, shielding her eyes with her hand, as if she were about to discover America. At last her gaze settled on me. 'Your father's asking for you, your ladyship.'

As I hurried to the desk, she added plaintively, 'I've been calling and calling, but you didn't respond.' I'll swear she almost curtseyed. But it went against the grain, I could see that. And I couldn't blame her. I was dirty, bloodstained and probably spotted with vomit from when I'd held the old buffer's head while he was throwing up — there was certainly a whiff of it about me. The sooner I could stow all my clothes in the washing machine and me in the shower, the better.

My smile was meant to be apologetic, not condescending. 'I don't use the family name,' I said. 'If you check on the next of kin form you'll see. I'm Lina Townend. There. Now, how is . . . my father?'

'He's insisting on discharging himself. We're very reluctant. He should be kept under observation. But he said you'd do it.'

I asked, very carefully, 'You're sure it would be in his best interests to stay overnight?'

'Absolutely.'

'Well, tell him I've already gone home, but I'll be back first thing tomorrow to pick him up if he's well enough.' Even as I turned on my heel, she was telling her colleague how heartless I was — wouldn't even see the poor old dear. The comment I cherished was the one that came back, 'That's the aristocracy for you: selfish to the bone.'

CHAPTER TWENTY-SEVEN

'Marcus? Marcus?' No, there was no sign of him when at last I let myself into the cottage, not so much as a cooking smell. Perhaps he'd gone back to Copeland; maybe he was just out with Tony. So long as there was some food in the fridge and plenty of hot water in the tank, he could have gone to Timbuktu as far as I was concerned. There was one phone call to make before I did anything, however: I had to tell Griff that I was home safe and sound. First time round Aidan's number was engaged, so I had my shower and started on something like supper, dialling as I munched. Yes!

I gave him a very short account of my doings. I thought he'd notice it wasn't very full, but he was more concerned with a single fact.

'You left an old man in hospital when he wanted to go home?' Griff was outraged, squeaking down the phone. 'Lord Elham? Your father?' His voice went up a few notes with each question.

I reached across to pop more bread in the toaster. 'Why not? He'd have done the same for me. And after his goings on, the hire car's such a mess they're going to sting me for the valeting deposit if I don't spend an hour trying to spruce it up.'

'But your own father! We all have duties, my dear—'

'I'll tell you my father's ideas of duty when I see you, Griff. Tomorrow I've got to get some clean clothes to the hospital for him — got to buy them first. D'you suppose he's a Marks and

Sparks man? Then I'll take him back to Bossingham Hall, but he'll have to whistle for me this weekend, because it's the Ramada Fair, unless I can find Marcus and get him—'

'Marcus? But he's gone back to Copeland, dear heart.'

Despite the fleecy dressing gown, I shivered. 'How do you know?'

'He phoned to tell me. About half an hour ago. I thought you weren't going to tell anyone where I was,' he added reproachfully.

Nor was I. Nor did I. Blast and bother!

'He must have pressed the redial button,' I said as lightly as possible. Since all Griff's personal files were still in his office, it'd be the work of moments for Marcus to have checked the phone number amongst those in his address book and come up with Aidan's place. I stopped pretending. 'Griff: are you and Aidan still up and dressed?'

'Of course we are — we're not love's young dream, darling!'

'Well, go and check into a hotel. Set every burglar alarm he's got and scarper. Now. Don't argue, Griff, just do it! And take the page with you.'

Cramming dry toast in my mouth, I took the stairs two at a time. If I couldn't trust Marcus, did that mean I couldn't trust Tony Baker? What about Dave? He and I might not exactly have clicked, but there had to be someone out there halfway honest. Dave's number. Where the hell was Dave's number? Biting my lips to stop the panic, I tipped everything out of my bag.

* * *

'Why didn't this lord fellow call us? Burglary and assault at a stately home — he'd have had a team round before you could say House of Lords.' Dave was driving along the slow winding road to Tenterden as if he'd got radar fitted to those neat spectacles of his. It was his own car, so we didn't have the benefit of sirens or flashing lights — just his skill. Which I had to admit was considerable. 'What is he, anyway? An earl? A duke?'

'I've no idea — it's not the sort of thing you ask someone, is it?' But I should have remembered: I'd done all that research after all. 'Hang on — is there something called a marquess?'

'Of course there is.'

'Well, I think he's one of them. As for his behaviour, let's just call him eccentric.'

'Are you sure it's just that? Some perfectly sane people pretend to be mad so they can get away with things. Does he have something to hide?'

Of course he had something to hide. That John Bull printing press. The lino-cut printed curtains. The woodcuts on the schoolroom walls. My revered father couldn't have revived some of his old talents, could he? He had plenty of old tomes to cannibalise for blank pages. He had time on his hands. He had champagne tastes, which he deeply indulged, on a beer income. He'd admitted he had *Natura Rerum*. And he was dead cagey about that one room when he'd been happy for me to see the whole of the rest, his bedroom apart, that is. Perhaps he'd been saving that for a day when he hadn't had brewer's droop. I swallowed bile.

Dave was waiting for an answer. Remember Griff's maxim that the less you said the better: 'Just plain weird.'

'In what way?'

Maybe he'd lose interest if I fended him off. 'I'll tell you all about him when you don't need to concentrate on the road, Dave, if you don't mind.'

How had Lord Elham described it? Casting up your accounts? I wasn't given to car-sickness, but if I didn't keep my eyes straight ahead, I'd be doing the same.

'So you've been attacked by the Kitty Gang — possibly. Griff's been attacked by the Kitty Gang — possibly. And now this Lord

Elham's been attacked by the Kitty Gang — possibly. A lot of possiblys, there, Lina.'

And some he didn't even know about: where did the Oxford guy fit in? The old lady and her spoons? The thief from Harrogate? 'And a lot of real attacks, don't forget. I don't care who or what these people are called, so long as we stop them attacking Griff or his friend.'

'What d'you think they'll do if they find no one at home? Trash the place? Torch it?'

I gulped. Not with car-sickness, either. 'Aidan's got the same sort of burglar-proofing system as we have, with bells on. But I suppose a petrol bomb . . .' Straight through that exquisite fan-light? 'No,' I said firmly, 'because what I think they're after would be destroyed, wouldn't it?'

'Another antiques dealer, is he, this Aidan?'

'Griff's lover,' I said firmly. They said some gay men were more promiscuous than their straight counterparts. I hoped Griff hadn't been like Lord Elham. Or at least if he had, I hoped he'd left his partners with more kindness in his memory. So long as these days he was my dear old Griff, I'd simply have to draw a line under his past. Maybe one day I'd manage to do the same with Lord Elham; somehow I doubted it.

'So what are they after that would burn?'

'A piece of paper they think was torn from a valuable book and is worth hundreds. I know it's a forgery, and more to the point I've found where the book is. More or less. And it's worth thousands. Perhaps hundreds of thousands. It's not my area, so I don't really know.'

'You mean you haven't found out?' he gasped.

'Why should I? Not my book, after all. But,' I added, 'if people are prepared to do so much just for a page, the whole tome must be worth—'

'Killing for? So how did this duke get away from his assailants?'

'Oh, the Devil looks after his own. They knocked him out. When he came to he had the sense not to bother telling them, so he crawled through to the main house, which is separated from his quarters by a serious door. There's a trail of blood: I think he was telling the truth. And jemmy marks — they obviously tried to follow him but they gave up. Maybe because I arrived.'

'Why didn't they wallop you?'

'I didn't exactly tell them I was unarmed and on my own. Dave, that lorry was pretty close!'

'Close your eyes if you don't like it. And don't scream again — it puts me off.'

'Sorry. But won't your Tenterden pals be able to do everything?'

'Your expectations of a rural force are a tad higher than mine. In any case, you said you wanted to come along,' he added accusingly.

'Only to make sure Griff's all right. Not to try a spot of citizen's arrest!'

'Bloody right. If there's any action you stay in the car. OK? I don't want to be worrying about looking after you when my mind should be on the job.' He killed his speed abruptly. Already we were in the outskirts of Tenterden.

I navigated him to Aidan's house, not that it took much doing once we'd turned into the right road. Dave's pessimism was ill-founded: there must have been five police vehicles littered about the street, with a dozen men and women in uniform milling around looking ghostly in the blue flashing lights. That was something that had always puzzled me: why didn't they switch them off when they'd arrived? I turned to ask Dave. But he'd already got out of the car, and was running towards his colleagues. There didn't seem to be anything I'd describe as action, so I got out too, peering over the car. Several of Aidan's neighbours were doing the same:

ultra-respectable people pretending to disapprove but probably as excited by stuff straight off the TV as my birth father would have been. Birth father. Biological father. Whatever. Maybe I could try living with those terms for a few days. He certainly didn't feel like a father sort of father.

One of the neighbours peeled away from the others and started to walk towards me. If it was OK for him to be on the move, no doubt it was OK for me, too. What about the car, though? Dave had left his key in the ignition. Talk about leading folk into temptation. I fished it out, locked the car and pocketed it.

And then I bunched my hand round it, so the key, a cylindrical affair, not the old-fashioned flat sort, protruded between my first and second fingers, like a mini knuckleduster. After all, I'd had enough to make me think twice about anyone, even a neighbour in such a respectable place as Tenterden, who was wearing a black hoodie.

For a moment I wondered if it might be Marcus under that hood. After all, there hadn't been any more attacks while he'd been staying with us. Was it possible that he'd been the person I'd tripped in Harrogate? Security had never caught anyone, and the thief had had a lot of things a quiet person like him might just have known about. But he'd been with me too soon, surely — he simply wouldn't have had time to shake off his pursuers and return to me. No, the theory didn't hold water.

Casually I crossed to the other side of the road, still clutching the key. I felt a lot less casual when Hoodie crossed too. What next? The police were still far too occupied doing whatever police officers do in a minor crisis to notice people walking along the pavement, whichever side of the road they chose. Actually, I might just choose the other side again.

Mistake? When he followed me he would come from behind. But while I'd never won any school sports-day prizes, I could run faster than most on the streets. And for screaming I might have got an Olympic medal. But what I was best at was digging the elbow into an attacker from the rear, and yelling at the same time. It was a good job, really, because that was what I had to do.

I was good enough to bring him down, but must have been out of practice, because he stumbled half upright and tried to scuttle off. I lunged and floored him again, pushing his hood back. I stared straight into the eyes of someone I'd met. The friendly Harrogate security guard who'd been so kind to Griff. Mal.

My stomach's turn to sink. What if he was one of Griff's boy-friends now?

I didn't get the chance to ask, of course. Not with all those interested policemen gathering round.

* * *

'Where could be safer than London, dear heart? You insist that Aidan and I keep out of the way, he has his flat there, complete with key-code entry, and now you're not happy. You tell me you are, but I can see you're not.' Over the silver and linen that Aidan's sort of hotel runs to even for breakfast tables, Griff cocked his head sideways. 'Come, Lina: eat those scrambled eggs before they lose their fluffy perfection, then tell me what's troubling you.'

So hungry it was hard not to wolf everything in sight, I had no trouble obeying the first instruction. The second was harder. Swallowing hard, I tried several times before managing, 'I — just wish — I don't know.' *I just wish you could be there to go home to and make everything as it was before that darned page turned up.*

'Are you afraid of being in the cottage on your own? I could ask Mrs Hatch—'

I shook my head. I didn't want Mrs Hatch. I wanted my Griff. But if he caught on, he'd throw up the chance of safety in the Smoke and come back to Bredeham and put himself at risk. 'I shall be fine,' I lied firmly. 'I've got a lot to do, after all. Looking after Lord Elham, for one thing, and there's the Ramada fair — we usually put in a presence there.'

'There you are, then,' Aidan announced, plonking down his serviette — no, his napkin — as if no one need worry about anything. 'I'll settle up, shall I, while you have your little chinwag about price-fixing. Take care, Evelina, my dear.'

His dear. Maybe I'd have liked him more if he hadn't had that upper-crust accent that can make its owner sound as if he's patronising you even when he's not. But he was at least trying to be tactful, leaving Griff and me alone.

'I notice,' Griff started, reaching for the butter, catching my eye and toying with the low-fat spread instead. At last he abandoned both for margarine, not paint-pot orange in a plastic tub but deep and treacle-gold in a proper bowl, just like we had at home. 'I notice that you always refer to your birth father as if he's a complete stranger. Have you not discussed a more intimate nomenclature?'

Shaking my head wasn't enough. I owed him more than that. 'He's never asked me to. And he's not the sort of man you can ask — ask anything that you want. It's like—' I was floundering '—like trying to reason with a toddler. He sort of throws his toys out of the pram.'

'Violence!'

'No. He retires to his favourite TV programme. Griff, I'm afraid he's not a very nice man. I can't tell you all about everything now, but — Oh, the police!'

Every head in the room turned, of course, but I don't think anyone else got to their feet ready to run.

'Panic not, fair one. I know old habits die hard, but aim for a little decorum!' He put his tongue into his cheek to remind me he was teasing. 'He probably wants to talk to us about that security guard. I'm afraid the delay will irritate poor Aidan.' Suddenly he took my hand. 'Are you sure you don't want to come too? Or want me to come home?'

It was a good job the arrival of the policeman stopped me replying. We exchanged polite good mornings as he briefly flipped his ID, and a rabbit-eyed waitress offered more coffee as he sat down, parking his cap on the chair Aidan had left vacant. I'd hoped for more than a uniformed constable. I wanted something more like in *Morse* — a heavy-weight, plain-clothes chief inspector and his sergeant.

'We don't have those resources,' PC Brown said. 'But that's not to say CID aren't involved with the Kitty Gang. And maybe with this, if we can prove a link.'

'Couldn't it be its own little gang? An antiques gang? After something only valuable to a dealer or collector?' I asked.

'Such as what?'

'Such as something CID know all about.' I crossed my fingers on the lie. At least they would when I'd talked to Dave, who seemed the best prospect, all things considered. 'But what did the security guard say? The guy I floored,' I added with a helpful smile.

'I wouldn't say that too loudly. Criminals these days like to sue for assault.'

'But he grabbed me from behind. If I hadn't had Dave's car key in my hand, he could have overpowered me. When he put his arms round me, I didn't think it was a friendly hug. After that, all I did was try to hold him down till someone came to my assistance. And in the struggle I recognised him as someone who said he was a security guard at a big antiques fair in Yorkshire.'

'Delectable in a green uniform with a battle-dress top, as I recall.' Though it had been his bum Griff was more interested in. 'He appeared, officer, to have been extremely solicitous about my health, claiming he'd found me unconscious in the open door of the caravan. But he could equally have hit me on the head in order to sift the contents of our home from home. When we go to far flung corners of the country, we take our own accommodation,' he explained.

'"We?" Are you related?'

I heard my voice come out loud and clear. 'I wish we were. Griff's much better than my real father at taking care of me.' There, I'd nearly said it. I'd nearly told him how much I loved him. Nearly. One day I would.

As it was, he took and squeezed my hand. 'What do you think brings the young man down here? He certainly wasn't invited.'

'Ah, that's something we need to find out. It wasn't to visit you, sir?'

'When I was staying at the home of my long-term partner? Absolutely not. In fact, I was down here very much to keep out of harm's way.' He patted the plaster on his wrist. 'My last little encounter with Kitty or whatever. I'm sure my partner Aidan won't have told people I was there, apart from those we met for supper the other night — he'll furnish you with their name and address. And the only other person apart from Lina here to know my whereabouts is a young charmer called Marcus, who for some reason phoned to tell me he was abandoning Lina, who he was supposed to be assisting in running our business, to return to his cousin and lover, a print and map dealer called Laurence Copeland.' He reached for my hand. 'I did hope, my dear, that you'd have realised without my spelling it out, that he dances at both ends of the ballroom.'

PC Brown wasn't as quick on the uptake as I, nor as thrown by the news. Why hadn't Griff told me before? It would have explained so much! My face must have said something of what I felt.

'Ballroom dancing? Why shouldn't he? Oh. Er . . .'

Griff squeezed my hand a little tighter: 'Experiential learning, I think they call it, dear heart. I hope you're not too upset.'

'Not so much by that as by the thought that he might be in cahoots with Peachy Bum from Harrogate.' I sank back into my chair. 'And,' I added, 'by the thought that it may be him who roughed up Lord Elham last night. I wish I could sort the whole thing out!'

Aidan reappeared. 'I wish you could too, my dear, and quickly too. Griff, your carriage awaits you. The sooner we slip into the anonymity of London, the better.' He helped Griff to his feet. 'Meanwhile, Evelina, disregard that last comment. Do nothing, absolutely nothing, because every minute he can't keep on eye on you our old friend here is in agonies of worry. Now the professionals are involved, for goodness' sake regard your safety as a priority.' He patted my hand. 'Promise?'

I managed to smile back. Perhaps he wasn't as bad as I'd thought. 'If I have anything to do with it, my skin will stay in one piece.'

Griff shot me a look: he knew that was no sort of a promise. But he submitted to being led quietly away. Not until he'd had the hugest hug either of us could manage, though. He nodded in the direction of his chair — he'd left a nicely anonymous envelope containing that page.

As he left, in walked Dave Trent, looking as unpolicemanly as it was possible to look. The two officers eyed each other. Dave flashed his ID. 'DC Dave Trent. And who the hell are you?'

CHAPTER TWENTY-EIGHT

It'd be nice to claim that I'd done the same neat job of flooring the man in uniform as I had that hoodie. Or that Dave had been as deft with his footwork as with last night's driving. But we were both frustrated by an old, old lady, bent as Josie, with a Zimmer frame. Maybe she thought that Dave was a villain, the other man a cop in trouble. No one could have blamed her, after all. Or maybe she hadn't a clue what was going on, and was simply jammed in the doorway with her frame at a funny angle because she still needed L-plates.

Dave spat into his mobile phone, before turning his attention to me. 'How come you couldn't tell the guy was a fake? You must have seen IDs before!'

'No need to drag up my past.'

He blushed, putting up a hand in apology. 'I meant with all these burglaries and assaults. Honest. Sorry. But—'

'Because he did what most policemen do: he gave it a quick flash and put it away.'

'What did he find out? When he was questioning you?'

'That Griff and Aidan have gone off to London, leaving both Aidan's house and our cottage unprotected. That I recognised the man who jumped me last night. Not a lot else. I'm not as green,' I told his disbelieving face, 'as I am cabbage-looking. When he didn't seem to be up to speed, I said I'd told CID everything. Which I suppose I better had. But not,' I added, 'till I've phoned the William Harvey and told them to tell Lord Elham I shall be a bit late and to look after his headache a bit longer.'

In the end I agreed that Dave counted as CID and that I'd bring him up to speed as he drove, more slowly, this time. But then it seemed we were heading not for Bredeham and the hire car, but Maidstone, and Kent Police headquarters.

'No thanks.'

'What do you mean, no thanks?'

'I don't do police stations. Not when I can avoid it.'

He accelerated. 'Looks like this time you can't avoid it.'

'Just stop the car, Dave. Unless I'm under arrest?'

He slowed, but only a little. 'You're not under arrest. The guy you clocked is. Well, he's being held for questioning. But they need a proper statement from you, Lina, or they have to let him go. It won't take long. Just a matter of telling an officer exactly how you met him before, and why you floored him this time. Otherwise, he'll be free to hound you some more.'

'He will be anyway. They won't hold him just because he may have walloped Griff. I told you, I don't do copshops, not unless I have to. Just pull over and I'll hitch back.'

He swerved into a lay-by. 'I can't make you do this, Lina, but I shall think a lot less of you if you don't. You've got guts. OK, you may have had bad experiences in the past, but you won't this time.'

'Want a bet?' I sneered.

'Why did you have a bad time last time?'

I heaved an exaggerated sigh. 'Why don't you just check my record?'

'You haven't got one. Some of your mates might have. But you must only ever have had warnings. So you can't play that card. In any case, there's something radically different about this time. You're the real victim, not the possible perpetrator. So,' he continued in an aunt-y sort of voice, 'people will be nice to you, and show you pretty mug shots and bring you nice cups of tea.'

I responded in my best imitation of Aidan Morley: 'How very charming of them. OK. But you'll have to get me back pronto to pick up His Nibs.'

'Promise. Mustn't keep your father waiting, must we?'

I shook my head. 'You know something: I might have sprung from his loins, as Griff would put it, but he's not my father. Never will be. If I'm not careful, he may become my child.' I meant to think it, not say it aloud, but perhaps that didn't matter. In any case he said nothing; he just looked at me sideways and put the car into gear.

It wasn't the promise of cups of tea that finally swung it. It was the thought that I might spot a mug they weren't expecting me to identify — Dan Freeman's. I'd had the idea that he might be a pedestrian that our security camera had picked up, after all. I wouldn't mention at the outset his connection with Oxford: I had an idea police officers might feel the same sort of fear-tinged respect I'd had for brainy academics.

* * *

Dave didn't seem to have said anything about my grubby past. No one sneered at me, or uttered thinly-veiled threats if I didn't cooperate. In fact they were so polite, I wondered if Dave had mentioned that I was the daughter of a Title. A WPC the same age as me kept me company, worrying a rapidly growing zit on her chin when she thought I wouldn't notice. What I did drag out of her as she showed me the photos was that Hoodie couldn't offer any reasonable explanation why he'd come to Kent, or why he'd grabbed me from behind. Reluctantly I mentioned Marcus; but I kept quiet about Tony. I had no more than suspicions about him, after all, and I had an idea that suspicions wouldn't do his police career any good, if they proved to be empty. She got more interested when I mentioned what I referred to as our other night visitors, and positively lavished photos and tea on me.

After an hour of looking at faces, I flung up my hands in despair. 'It's all these fixed expressions,' I moaned. 'In real life people's faces move all the time. And they put on glasses, they change the colour of their hair—'

She abandoned the spot to point at the screen. 'Computers can take off glasses, change hairstyles.' *Remove spots?* 'Forget the inessentials. I always think concentrating on the eyes is best. You can't change those.'

'Coloured contact lenses? Sorry. I didn't mean to be flip. Look, could you really make a few of these guys bald? Because Dan Freeman had so little hair it hardly counts. Very tired skin — I wanted to slop moisturiser all over it. And his eyes — they seemed to cry out for their spectacles. You know, as if he'd taken them off — no, he couldn't have done, because there weren't any little marks on his nose. I'd have remembered those.'

Another ten minutes convinced me I was wasting everyone's time. Dan Freeman was not on their books. Perhaps, after all, the original Dan had been a decent, honest man, simply helping a person in need, and I'd simply been confused when I thought the Bredeham lookalike resembled him.

They'd follow up the Marcus connection with Hoodie, they said. While I waited for Dave I dithered. Should I phone Marcus and warn him? He'd given me all the information that had enabled me to run Bossingham Hall to ground, so I owed him for that. And for the decanter sale, of course. But somehow he must have had a hand in getting Hoodie to Tenterden — him or someone he'd let into the house. Probably. Possibly. Now I knew why people smoked. To occupy their hands and mouths while their brains did something else.

* * *

'First stop Bredeham to pick up the hire car,' I told Dave.

'Sure thing, Miss Daisy,' he replied, tugging his forelock, or where his forelock would have been if he'd had one. He added in his normal voice, 'And then?'

'Then I thank you kindly and go on to Ashford to pick up Lord Elham.'

He digested that. 'Aren't you afraid of Marcus using your spare house keys to get back in and rob you?'

'I was last night. But then I changed the burglar alarm code, so even if he did get in, he'd waken the dead.'

'Including Tony, living conveniently opposite.'

'Including Tony.' I couldn't help sighing. But it wasn't for lost love, it was for lost trust. Whose side was he on? Whose side had he been on from the start?

'Fancied him, did you?' He spurted past a Euro-lorry.

I didn't want to split emotional hairs. 'For about ten minutes. But now Griff's given me a teddy bear.'

His laugh was surprisingly gentle. 'You'd rather take a teddy bear to bed, is that what you're saying?'

'You know where you are with a teddy bear.'

'But not with human beings?'

'Not the ones I've come across, Griff apart. And he can still surprise me.'

'His relationship with Aidan Morley, for instance? You don't seem to like him very much.'

'Griff says I have this tendency to inverted snobbery. But Aidan and me are from different worlds: him and his public-school accent and his posh house and his wonderful Merc and—'

'And Griff,' he concluded for me. 'It's all right not to like someone — to be jealous of them.'

'I didn't say I was jealous of Aidan. I said I didn't like him. He's not a very nice man. Lots of people don't like Griff, which is a shame, because he is a nice man. Much nicer than Lord Elham.' Yes, I'd change the subject to him — see how it felt to finger my bruises, you might say. 'I wonder how he dealt with his NHS breakfast. Now, he's supposed to be a noble, in fact he used to sit in the House of Lords and rule the country, when he could be bothered, but — he's a shit, Dave.'

'So why are you being so nice to him?'

'Because even shits need looking after. And we seem to have a sin — a symb — oh, that relationship where you both need each other. Symbiosis, that's it. He needs me to stop him dying of food poisoning or something, and I quite like the way he passes antiques my way.'

'You're not setting yourself up for an accusation of obtaining goods by false pretences, are you?' He sounded like one of my social workers. Not the nicest, either.

'Nothing false, no pretences,' I snapped. 'And I keep a record of all our transactions. All signed and sealed.' I looked out of the passenger window, but had to give up. No point in losing a perfectly good breakfast.

His voice was much kinder when, a few minutes later, he broke the silence. 'Would you like me to come along with you? Pack him up and take him home? After all, there may be a reception committee waiting for him. And you, of course.'

It was tempting. Very tempting. But I wasn't sure if he'd be there as my friend, or as a policeman having a good sniff round and finding all sorts of things he shouldn't. And, yes, I had a bit of unfinished business with Lord Elham, in the shape of the forged page.

* * *

'How dare you ask such a thing? Me, a forger!' Despite his bandages, despite being crammed into a bright-red Ka's passenger seat (the rental people were beginning to hex me when I went in), Lord Elham did his best to get on his high horse.

'My colleague was really impressed — said it was the highest quality forgery. It'd have taken real skill to produce anything that good. You could make a good living, he said.'

'I already have.' He preened himself. 'No reason why I shouldn't carry on.'

I pulled the car over. 'There's every reason. No. Sit still and listen. *Natura Rerum* is priceless. As soon as I got hold of what people thought was a genuine page, people have been after me or Griff, my partner. Sometimes they've tried to throw sand in our eyes by making it seem like a general outbreak of theft.'

'Are you sure it's not?' So he was listening, after all.

'After last night? Look, Lord Elham, however I try to tell myself there's been a whole series of coincidences, I don't believe it anymore. Someone's been after me, after Griff and now after you. And I'm very much afraid it's not just one someone. And I'm even more afraid that it's not just criminals who'll be taking an interest. The police don't like forgery, no matter how good it is.'

'I never claimed it was the real thing. *Caveat emptor*, and all that. Or didn't you learn Latin at that state school you went to?'

Why was he bothering to be nasty now? Or perhaps he wasn't. Perhaps he simply didn't understand. 'State *schools*,' I said. 'Maybe if you'd forked out for me to go to a posh public school—'

'Thirty times — no, thirty-one times seven years at—' He shook his head, then held it still, wincing. 'Could I have afforded it, Lina?'

'You've no idea what happened to your other children?' I started the car again, checking carefully for other cars behind me. 'Never the least bit interested?'

'Nappies! All that crying and puking. Maybe when they got older. I mean, you're quite interesting, aren't you? Tell you what, you should come and live with me. All those bedrooms — no one'd know.'

So he didn't want me in his own private section. Good job, really. It'd have taken a week to make a room habitable.

'The thing is, Lina, you've made me quite nervous. All these people after me. And now the police, too.'

And there I'd thought he might actually want my company for its own sake. 'Tell whoever you've been supplying that you're giving up,' I said. 'The antiques trade being what it is, everyone'll get the message pretty quickly. Get rid of your printing equipment fast — I know someone who'll probably give you a decent price. And — most of all — get rid of that damned book. It shouldn't be shut away in one man's house. It should be there for everyone to see.' Like the one in the Bodleian, where you practically had to give a sample of your DNA before you could see it? 'You know, the British Museum or something. But make it part of the deal that the public can have a look.'

'The deal?'

'When you give it to them.'

'*Give!* I thought you said it was priceless. How much would they give me for it?'

I swallowed what I wanted to say. 'Is it yours to sell?'

'It's not the Vultures'. No, they own the house and contents, but not the stuff in my wing. That was the agreement. And *Natura Rerum*'s always been in my wing. Ever since the deal was mooted, anyway.'

'Where is it?'

'Why do you ask?'

'For God's sake, so I can put it somewhere safe before we both get killed for it!' I put the car into gear. The Ka. Whatever. 'Tell you what, take me back a different route from usual.'

'How should I know which way?' He spread his hands helplessly as if I'd asked him to explain one of those Greek things in geometry without a diagram.

'You live round here. You were brought up round here. You must have gone on walks or pony rides with your governess.'

'Can't bear gee-gees. Never could. Big hulking things. And yet chaps breed them and race them and bet on them. Seem to enjoy riding them, too.'

I didn't argue. Come to think of it, I'd seen more horses round here than I'd ever seen, munching their way through fields. There must be a reason for them. 'What about walking or drives in the car? I only want you to guide me through the back lanes, for goodness' sake, so no one tails us.'

'No, they're very narrow. You stick to Stone Street.'

I gave up, and concentrated on the road ahead. And, of course, behind. Perhaps he was right: it was better to be on a nice straight stretch like most of the B2068 — Stone Street — where you could see a mile behind as well as ahead.

'Wheelbarrow Town,' he said suddenly.

'I'm sorry?'

'There's a road through Wheelbarrow Town. Head for Lyminge. There you are! That garage!' He flung his arm across my chest. 'Right!'

I barely had time to signal, which must have pleased the guy coming up behind me at well past the sixty limit. Lord Elham directed me through increasingly narrow lanes. Then we reached another comparatively straight road, across heathland.

'The Minnis. Never been enclosed,' he informed me.

'Where's this town, then?'

'A couple of miles back.'

'Eh?'

'Just a few cottages. But I always liked the name. Nice names round here. Ever had piles? No? Too young, I suppose. Anyway, if your name was Lin, and you'd got piles, I'd take you to Linsore Bottom.'

He expected a laugh, so he got one. Suddenly I was in a familiar cluster of houses, the Hop Pocket to my left. I took the right, and then started up the track to Bossingham Hall. The Ka's suspension didn't like it one scrap. Neither did Lord Elham's head. So I stopped, reversing to the lane, intending to go back up it and into the grounds through those wonderful front gates. Until, that is, I saw a blue Focus nosing its way towards me. Bother the poor suspension. How on earth could I have possibly chosen a red car, this of all days?

But there must be a lot of Focuses on the road, and I must be getting neurotic. At any rate, this one, carried on the way it was going, to Linsore Bottom for all I knew. Griff'd love that name, especially as a woman friend of his was always banging on about her haemorrhoids. But for the moment, what I had to think about was getting up to the house safe and sound, hiding the car, and making sure we locked ourselves away from the police and other intruders.

CHAPTER TWENTY-NINE

'There's that play,' Lord Elham reflected, staring into his champagne glass, 'where this chappie gives up conjuring and makes a speech about it. Lina ought to know, but she went to these rotten schools, you see. You got any idea, old boy?'

Titus looked desperately to me for help. I wasn't surprised. It wasn't every day you got invited to a stately home to clear out some illicit loot you could use in your own illegal sideline, and then, black sacks stowed in your white van, quaff champagne in a crystal glass. This had no doubt been his idea of dying and going to heaven — until, that is, the loony lord started talking Shakespeare.

'*The Tempest*,' I said, having seen it — and been totally confused by it — with Griff, who'd blamed himself for my puzzlement and read it through with me two very wet winter evenings in the caravan. 'Something about charms being overthrown.' I'd tried to learn the whole speech to please Griff, but what little had stuck had slipped away now.

I hadn't had an easy time persuading Lord Elham to do maybe not the honest, but at least the sensible thing. The moment we'd reached the Hall, he'd wanted to glue himself to the television: apparently even an afternoon of watching a women's cricket match in Durham was better than confronting unwelcome truths.

'Look,' I'd persisted, 'I wasn't exaggerating this morning when I said you — we — were in danger.'

'You will stay then?' He'd been as eager as a puppy.

'On a few conditions. One of which is that we get rid of evidence that'd send you down if the police decided to pay you a visit. I can take the lot to the tip. Or I can contact my mate Titus Oates.'

'Is that really his name?'

'Of course not. But no one ever uses his real one. He'd dispose of it for you, no questions asked.'

'Do you think he'd let me do some work for him? I get so bored.'

'You'll have to ask him, won't you? He's told me your work's good.' Carrot, then a bit of stick. 'You might get quite bored in jail, of course. And there'd be no champagne there.'

'Hmm. That writer chappie — not a real lord, was he? — he didn't think much of it, did he?'

'Not one bit.' On the other hand, a prison diet, while not the sort of thing Griff would let me eat, might be healthier than eternal Pot Noodles — even than eternal frozen meals for one, two of which I'd reheated for our lunch. 'The other thing we have to do — and fast — is get *Natura Rerum* into safe-keeping.'

'They'll never find it,' he said, reaching for the remote again.

'They tried to run me over; they attacked a frail old man; they socked you. Would they stop at a touch of torture, d'you suppose?' Preferably him, not me, but you never knew. And what I did know was that I'd blab at the first opportunity. I'd hate the idea of the book falling into bad hands, but it hadn't brought me much luck so far, and I didn't feel I owed it anything. At least, that was what I told myself. But I wasn't sure.

'My goodness! Torture?'

'We're miles from anywhere: no one'd hear us scream. And if they decided to kill us, who'd find out? They could be away from here and living off the proceeds in Spain before they found our bodies.' I didn't tell him that I'd known the same temptation to violence. Now, though I could have wrung his neck, I couldn't have done him real harm.

'But — Lina, you're joking.'

Arms akimbo, I demanded, 'Do I look as if I'm joking?'

'That's what Nanny Lyons used to say. She used to frighten me, Lina.'

There was nothing in the rules to say I couldn't play the scary nanny too. 'Lord Elham, if you want to die a lingering death, you can do it on your own. Or we can get rid of all your forgery equipment and ask the police to come and guard us. As for the book, we need a place of safety for it. With someone we can trust to give nothing away.' OTT or what? It was hard not to laugh at the poor man's rabbit eyes, or even more at my own attempts at being a dominatrix. But underneath I was deadly serious. And scared. 'Well, shall I phone my contact?'

* * *

Standing at the side door, we waved Titus off. No, I'd seen nothing of my father's workroom or its contents, much as I'd have liked to. If the police did get involved, I didn't want to know what had been hidden in there so I didn't have to lie. He and Lord Elham had dealt with everything, while I made further inroads into the kitchen — I didn't find anything special, but at least I couldn't overhear them making plans for Lord Elham's future employment. There'd been a load of rubbish sacks to drag into the yards, but to my irritation the lock on the kitchen door hadn't yielded. It was amazing what a dab of rancid lard could achieve, though, and by the time I'd finished it turned as easily as on the day it had been made. And it locked as easily after my last trip out. I wasn't taking any risks.

Herding Lord Elham back in, I turned the front door key just as firmly. 'Now,' I said with the same nanny-tone that had been so useful before, '*Natura Rerum*. We have to get rid of it. Now. You give it to me, I drive off and put it somewhere safe, and then I come back and I'll watch TV with you. How about that?'

Like a lamb he toddled off, returning with something in a Tesco carrier. Perhaps that was his attempt at camouflage. The living-room table was still too filthy to put anything important on, but the kitchen one was clean enough, thanks to my efforts. I headed back there, laying my burden gently onto the newly scrubbed wood. Yes. There was the twin of the volume I'd handled so tenderly in Oxford. This time I didn't have any cotton gloves, so I confined myself to just the one page — the one it fell open to. Lord Elham's sideline hadn't done the binding any good. Yes, there it was: my childhood, in my hands. And what good had it done me? Why didn't I simply bag it up again and drop it on the lap of the old soak who was already hooked on some stupid teatime quiz game?

Because of that breaking glass, that's why. No, not a champagne glass — crystal makes quite a different sound from a window. And there was a yell from Lord Elham.

I didn't hesitate. I grabbed the book, shoving it back into the carrier, and let myself silently out of the kitchen door. The yard was almost blocked by a Focus and a couple of large white vans — they'd come mob-handed, then. But there was room for the Ka to squeeze through. Just. Which would make less noise, a bolt down that pathway or a slow roll? What on earth could I do once I'd made the lane? I had to make sure the book was safe before I went back to the Hall — no, I wasn't about to leave Lord Elham to his fate, however tempted I was. After all, he'd kept his side of the bargain. 999? Yes, if we hadn't been in a mobile blackspot. What about the people at the pub? I couldn't ask them to fight for an old book if threatened with violence.

In any case, the Hop Pocket was closed — wouldn't open till seven. Where next? Someone was having the first barbecue of the summer. A hundred yards distant, a woman was leading two horses away from me. And then I spotted a familiar car: Robin, the clergyman's. Diving out of the Ka, I waved him down.

'Has your church got a safe?' I yelled.

No wonder he gaped though his open window.

'This is a matter of life and death,' I added, thrusting the carrier at him. 'Get it into a safe—'

'I'm just on my way into Canterbury—'

'Will the Cathedral still be open?'

'Yes. There's a concert there. That's where I'm—'

'Go and enjoy yourself,' I said. 'But make sure you put this in the safe first. One more thing. As soon as you can, use your mobile call the police. Bossingham Hall. No, don't ask any questions. Just call the police. Some men have broken in — they're threatening Lord Elham with violence.'

'Where are you going?'

I was too busy scooting back to the Ka to answer. In any case, I didn't want him coming over all chivalrous and trying to tackle Lord Elham's visitors. So afraid I was swallowing bile, I tried to work out a plan. It'd take several minutes before he could make that call. Why shouldn't I simply knock on one of these nicely painted front doors and ask to use the phone? I didn't look threatening, did I? But they were all tight shut. If only there were someone walking along the road, putting out rubbish — anything. I started to panic — Lord Elham was as stupidly stubborn as they came: he could be badly hurt by now.

At last! A middle-aged couple emerged from their home — a bungalow with the best-trimmed lawn I'd ever seen — with their dog. Which didn't like my rapid approach, and showed its teeth.

'Accident!' I yelled, over its snarls. 'At Bossingham Hall! The private wing. Lord Elham — Could you call the police? And ambulance?' There was little doubt that'd be needed. And not necessarily for Lord Elham — as soon as the man, nodding helpfully, went back into the house, I turned back to the car.

'Are you all right? Do you need a cup of tea?' the woman asked kindly.

The dog didn't second her invitation.

'No time. Got to see what I can do!' I was in the car before I could change my mind.

* * *

There were plenty of weapons in the outhouses. The trouble is, if you use something hard and heavy and maybe sharp on someone, you have to use it right, or they can grab it and use it on you. A pitchfork looked impressive, and this one fitted my hand nicely, but it'd be no use against a gun. And it might get tangled up with things — a short cudgel would be better. A broken spade handle was just the job.

There was no sound from the house as I approached, keeping low on the far side of the vehicles. But then came the slam of wood against wood. I risked a look. Two men, neither familiar, were carrying out that lovely bureau, and had banged it on the doorframe. Murder in my heart, I gripped the shaft more tightly. With a hard enough whack I could lay one of the bastards out cold, and maybe get the second too. Tying them up and locking them in the removal van would improve the odds no end.

The first went down with the tiniest grunt, the bureau completing the job as it fell on him. At least he was soft and would cushion it, reducing the chance of damage. The second man was so busy cursing his mate, it was easy to take him out too. It didn't take long to drag him into the nearest van, and truss him with the long tapes meant for the rest of Lord Elham's furniture — damn it, they'd already stowed his desk.

The man under the bookshelves didn't look too good. Gently easing the bookcase upright — thanks, Griff, for teaching me lifting techniques — I peered more closely. Maybe I shouldn't move him, but leave him for the paramedics. But I wouldn't take any risks. I tied his wrist and ankles.

Now for the house. I clutched the spade handle with more fear than I liked to admit. But I had to do it, however much I wanted to cower outside the door, waiting for the Fifth Cavalry. Now? Now!

But even as I braced myself, luck tapped me on the shoulder. A third man came out, carrying a couple of Hepplewhite chairs. 'Andy? Mick? Where are you?'

He'd know when he came to, tied back-to-back with the guy in the van.

How many more? I daren't assume that was the lot. Much as I wanted to stop to set the chairs upright and dust them down for damage, I had to go and find out. Where on earth were the police? That vicar couldn't have let me down, could he? And if he had, what about the villagers?

No. They couldn't all be corrupt. Even if by some terrible mischance the clergyman was a fake — he'd been in the right place each time, hadn't he? — the bungalow couple wouldn't be in league. So why were there no blue flashing lights?

Answer — and a cold sweat to go with it — probably because they'd all go to the main gates and find them locked. And think everything was a hoax and go back to base. OK. So I was on my own again, at least until I could get on to the landline phone inside. On my own with however many thugs and a lord with at least one head injury and a dope habit worth two. Whatever. Come on, Lina. Do your stuff.

I did.

The dust of ages filled my nostrils as I tiptoed inside. Trying not to sneeze, I headed for the living room. No TV. The phone ripped from its socket. Bad signs. But no groans either. And no sign of Lord Elham, though it was clear that this was where they'd broken in. Of course, all the other rooms would be shuttered and locked. As much to stop the whooshing sound in my ears as anything, I tried to get my brain into gear. How could I possibly work out where they'd taken him?

Stubborn he might be, but he'd not been keen on the idea of pain. And he was as cunning as he was stubborn. What if he'd taken them to the obvious place to keep a book, the library? Then he could have a good fumble round searching for keys.

It was a long shot. But it was so quiet in this wing, it might be the right one. As I hesitated, I caught a glimpse of something glistening in the passage carpet. Flakes of glass. Dabbing in the code, I clutched my shaft and pushed through the door.

But I didn't go directly to the library. Instead I dashed to the area where on quieter days they admitted Joe Public. Somewhere there would be the front gates' control mechanism. Not to mention the front door key. And a working land line.

* * *

Of course I ignored the police advice to stay put and do nothing. I had to find out if my theory about the library was correct, after all. And to see how Lord Elham was shaping up. The answer was not at all well. I could hear groans from the top of the staircase, answering the sound of something hard on soft flesh. I could see the splatters of blood on the carpet when I put my eye to the crack between the double doors.

The next whack provoked a scream. Scary or what? I muscled in. And hit Tony Baker as hard as I could. Lord Elham was barely conscious, and his pulse was feeble and irregular. If only I knew some first aid. But even as I bent over him, he grasped my hand. 'The others,' he groaned.

'What others?'

The only reply was a rasping groan. Where on earth were the paramedics? And why wasn't there a phone in here? If I did the wrong thing I could make bad worse. At least I could cover him with my jacket. I started to slip it off.

Mistake. The bastard coming up behind me turned it into a straitjacket and I was well and truly trapped.

CHAPTER THIRTY

So here I was, in one of the vans, still parked at Bossingham Hall. I was trussed far more viciously than I'd tied the men I'd socked. I seemed to be on my own. I'd tried to talk to my captor but he not only didn't reply, he also taped my mouth. At least I'd left my mark — I'd bitten his thumb as hard as I could. OK, that had earned me a stunning slap, but at least if the police ever did turn up there'd be something for their forensic mates to work on. He also taped my eyes, which I took as a good sign. Some criminals got sniffy about being seen and disposed of their victims if they were.

Hang on: I was not about to be a victim.

I was going to think my way through this.

I would do when I'd got my breath back after being shoved flat on the floor with nothing to cushion my fall.

Tony Baker. How had he got involved with all this? And why? He'd seemed to go out of his way to be helpful, though not very efficient. Did that mean that, as I feared, Marcus was caught up in it too? Nothing Copeland did would really surprise me, of course. But what about Hoodie? And Dave? Where did they fit in? Not to mention Dan Freeman? And also, now I had nothing particular to do except think about people whose paths and mine had crossed, the guy at Folkestone asking whose granddaughter I was? The helpful clergyman: was he the decent man he ought to be?

But my thinking time was over. Except for thinking on my feet. To which I was hauled with no more warning than the sound of trainer-clad feet on the van's tailgate.

He yanked off the tape brutally. But believe me, when brutal hair removal equals swift, I'd chose brutal every time. 'The book. Where's the book?'

I tried to roll with the smack that came with the question. And with the return blow. 'I honestly don't know,' I said, trying to sound frank and reasonable. 'What does Lord Elham say?'

'I asked *you*.' The voice didn't sound naturally rough, more like a fifties black-and-white film actor trying to sound rough — you know, the sort of thing you get on TV on a wet Sunday afternoon, Laurence Harvey pretending to be a working-class lad despite the socking great plum in his mouth. I'd no idea who it might be.

'I've told you I don't know. Why should I?'

'You've been here often enough. Selling things for the old soak. Right?'

Remind him you're a person with feelings: that was what they told people confronted by criminals. 'Right. But only one egg cup so far. It's a matter of digging stuff out of the rubbish and cleaning it up. Did you ever see such a place?'

The result of all my friendly attempts was another slap. How would I convince Griff I hadn't done this myself?

'The book!'

'The one with the page I bought? A copy, anyway. I told you, I've no idea. I'd hand it over if I had — the old guy's nothing to me.'

'He's your father, isn't he?'

'Nope.' Well, he still didn't feel like a father — never would, probably. 'I think it's probably a guy from Devon. Another antiques dealer. Devon Cottage or some such. But I hope you haven't hurt Lord Elham. He's a dopehead — hardly knows one day of the week from the next.'

'The bloody book.' He took another swing at me.

Swallowing blood from inside my cheek, I mumbled. 'Told you. No idea.' My tongue told me that at least two teeth moved with very little encouragement. Good job my dentist still took National Health patients like me.

'Better come up with something better than that. Or the old guy gets it.'

'How do I know he hasn't got it already? He looked pretty ropey when I saw him.' *Someone come soon — please.*

'Let's talk properly,' the voice said.

Suddenly my hands were freed. 'Yes, please!'

But my enthusiasm didn't last long, not when my right arm was yanked up behind me, the joint screaming, and not when sharp, long nails dug into the thumb. Or it might not be fingernails at all. 'You do pretty delicate work, don't you? Restoring china. You must need all your fingers for that. What's the minimum you need to work with? Come on, Lina — that book.'

I took a deep breath. It should be safe by now, provided the clergyman hadn't run out of fuel again. And provided he really was on the side of the angels. But I still gambled for extra time, even by the second. 'OK, OK. I might be able to take you to it. Roughly. I told you the truth, honestly. I don't know exactly where it is.'

'You'd better find out pretty soon. And tell us.'

'You won't get it without me. I'm the only ID it's got. It's in Canterbury.' It would be by now. Always assuming the clergyman was pukka.

While he and another man — Tony, I rather thought — had a whispered conversation, I fantasised about making a grand entrance to the Cathedral, propelled by a bent policeman and his mate, demanding the keys to the safe. What if I made a bolt for it, claiming asylum on the altar steps? Would the old guy who lived there strike these two dead if they touched me? It hadn't quite worked out that way for St Thomas, had it? And I wasn't sure about the ins and outs of being a martyr and a saint in the twenty-first century. So I rather hoped it wouldn't come to that. In any case, if there was a concert taking place, there'd be stewards to grab me and a whole orchestra to get tangled up with.

And to put at risk. With several million pounds at stake, these blokes could get really nasty.

And did. All of a sudden, my hands were yanked up again, but not taped. 'Who the hell are *you*?' There was a sound of bone on bone, and my captor sagged, letting me slip.

So help had arrived. And to my everlasting shame and regret, to celebrate I passed clean out.

* * *

'I'm all right. Perfectly all right, I tell you.' It wasn't the paramedics' fault I was growling. It was my own. I'd come to quick enough as soon as the blood got back to my head. But in turkey-mode, eyes blacked out, there'd been nothing I could do except lie still and think — no, not of England, but of what might or might not be going on around me. There were armed police: their warning shouts would have awakened the dead. Then some medics arrived, to be despatched inside. At last the noise subsided and someone picked me up quite gently and propped me in a sitting position, not at all comfortable with my hands behind my back. Whoever did the next bit ought to have trained on leg-waxes: so slowly were my gag and blindfold removed I almost wished my vicious captor were back. But there was no sign of him. When my hands were free I had a feel round my face: some eyelashes still there, not a lot of eyebrow, and an upper lip as clean as a whistle. But I didn't linger anywhere long. My cheekbones and cheeks felt as bad as in the old days, screaming for arnica or whatever. But if I wanted answers, they and the jiggly teeth would have to form words. 'How's Lord Elham?' I asked the middle-aged paramedic who'd plucked me. 'He was in the house — in the library.' Not a nice word to say with bruises like these. Could they actually have broken something? 'In his fifties. Beaten up.'

'Was that His Lordship? Wow. I've never treated a Lord before.'

'Why didn't you go with him to A & E — isn't that the usual system?'

'Because he wouldn't go until he knew if you were OK. You could share an ambulance, he said.'

'If I admit I'm ill enough to go with him he'll worry.' *It'd be a first if he did.* 'Tell him I'm fine — don't need any treatment.' I closed my eyes to avoid further argument.

'I'm afraid you might, you know,' a vaguely familiar voice said. 'We've met before. Robin Levitt.'

I raised a lid with care. The clergyman. 'Why are your knuckles bleeding?'

'I had to hit someone.'

'In the Cathedral? *Natura Rerum!*' I was scrabbling to my feet before I noticed he was holding out his undamaged hand to lever me upright. There.

'It's fine. In the Cathedral safe, as you asked — er — Lina. Are you sure you're all right? Here.' He passed me a folded tissue.

'It's just so rare,' I sobbed, 'to meet someone who is what he says he is and does what he promises.'

He patted my shoulder very cautiously. 'Is there anywhere in this madhouse we could find a cup of tea?'

'Not sure about tea,' I admitted. 'But if you get rid of the medics, I can tell you where there's plenty of chilled champagne.'

It was great to hear the wail of the ambulance taking Lord Elham away. They wouldn't need the siren to cut through swathes of traffic, not out here, but maybe to warn other hapless drivers on the narrow lanes to find a gateway and pull into it. Fast. Maybe police drivers. There was no end of coming and going, with incident tape looped all over and people in white suits and photographers dotting purposefully round like ants. I felt quite sorry for Lord Elham — he'd already had his experience of real-life *Casualty*, and I'm sure he'd have swapped a real-life *Bill* for it, now the incriminating evidence had safely been removed, at least. Before I could fight my way into the living room and that welcoming fridge, I was intercepted three times, each time by a different policeman who was inclined to bluster but gave way at the sight of Robin's dog collar.

The fridge almost within reach, yet another hand grabbed my arm.

'Scene of crime, Miss, if you don't mind.'

'She needs somewhere to sit down, officer. One of the victims,' Robin said.

What if he wasn't a decent man? What if he'd stolen *Natura Rerum* and was about to dispose of me?

'I ought to be making a statement,' I said with as much authority as I could muster.

'Better get her to Maidstone,' someone muttered.

'I'm staying here.'

Robin lost his nerve. 'You'll only be in the way here — you can see there's so much going on. If you like, I'll accompany you — if that's all right, Sergeant?'

'You a witness too? In that case, thanks but no thanks. Two separate cars.'

'I'm staying here.'

'The reverend's right — you're in the way.'

'In the way? When there are a hundred rooms in the house? I think not.' *Think Mrs Hatch — and square those shoulders.* 'In my father's absence, I'm responsible for the place. Find me a couple of bottles of champagne from the fridge in there and I'll wait for the investigating officer in the Yellow Drawing Room.'

* * *

Robin clearly didn't know whether to be amused or embarrassed by my show of authority. Neither did I, to be honest. He was openly terrified when I produced my keys from my back pocket and proceeded to open a display cabinet.

'We've got to drink the stuff out of something,' I said. 'And though I'd say this wasn't top-quality glass, at least eighteenth-century air-twist stemmed flutes are not to be sneezed at. I'm sorry you're missing your concert, Robin — please sit down — but I'm very grateful for your company. Just who did you hit, by the way?' *Please don't let his knuckles fit my bruises.*

'The man who'd slapped you. The first time I saw you you'd got bruises all over your face: had he done it before?'

I reached for an unopened bottle, pillowing my cheek against it. There's something quite stylish about soothing bruises with bottles of ice-cold, vintage champagne. Oh, yes: Lord Elham might have given me fizz to drink, but it had always been ordinary stuff, if anything costing more than twenty quid a time could be called ordinary. The stuff the police had found for me was truly, frighteningly excellent: it killed pain as well as any aspirin, and perked me up no end after my humiliating failure.

'I used to self-abuse,' I said, sitting down hard on sofa, its satin upholstery worn to ribbons, 'if I got stressed. And I've had quite a bit of stress recently.'

'You might be in for a bit more,' Robin warned, as the door opened to admit two more men, one in the very well-cut suit of a senior officer, the other less well dressed but vaguely familiar.

It was to the second I turned, rising. 'I think you owe me an explanation,' I said, 'Mr Dan Freeman.'

'*Detective Sergeant* Dan Freeman. Attached to Scotland Yard's Fine Art and Antiques Squad. How do you do, Ms Townend?' He held out his hand, which I shook. He was taller than I remembered, and with that disgusting long lank hair close cropped all over he looked much younger. Even his skin looked different, as if he'd found some decent moisturiser. 'Or is it Lady Elham?'

As I shook my head with irritation — and wished I hadn't — the uniformed officer chipped in, 'According to His Lordship you're his daughter. I presume you only get the title when he dies—'

'He's as ill as that! I must—'

'No, no. Not well, but stable.'

'What's this about a title? Because I'm not—'

'When that clergyman turned up he was convinced he was dying.' He turned to Robin for confirmation. 'He yelled out, "I'm not proud of much I've done, but I'm damned proud of that daughter of mine. Pity she didn't get much education — she'd have made a good heir."'

'Talk about damning with faint praise,' I said, sitting down again.

'Or,' Robin put in, 'praising with faint damns.'

The other men worked that out, Freeman more quickly than the other, and grinned as if they'd thought of it themselves.

'So are you here to arrest me, Sergeant Freeman? Or will your colleague be doing the honours?' I played Griff with a dash of Mrs Hatch. That seemed about right for a nearly ladyship.

'Neither of us will be. This is Detective Superintendent Close, by the way.' We exchanged gracious nods. 'Nor any of our colleagues. We just thought you'd like to make a statement about this afternoon's events. And any others, of course. And we'll update you as far as we can.'

There was a tap at the door. What I presume was another detective, a young woman in a denim trouser suit I coveted, murmured to the superintendent, who smiled at Robin. 'Seems your car's parked a bit awkwardly, sir. And we can't start it. Do you have the knack?'

Robin and I exchanged a grin.

'I suppose you forgot to check your petrol gauge.'

'Or to fill it up again,' he grimaced. 'I'd better come and have a look. Though I must say Lina seems to know more about these things than I do.'

'Looking after Griff's van,' I said briskly, not wanting to discuss hot-wiring. 'When you do get it started, I couldn't bum a lift, could I? To the Cathedral? Or, if it won't, and they'll let me use that Ka, I could drive you.'

Close looked at his watch. 'You may have to leave it till tomorrow, your — miss. It'll be all locked up now.'

'With your evidence, officer, in the safe. It's my busy day tomorrow, I'm afraid, Lina, starting with early Communion, so I'll push off home now. It's not all that far to walk.'

'Someone'll give you a lift if you ask,' Close said, offhand.

I hauled myself up. I ought to say something, but I wasn't sure what. Too much booze, maybe — I was coming over tearful again. And here we were, shaking hands, as if I really were a ladyship. If only he — anyone — could give me a good, solid hug and tell me everything would be all right.

Robin squeezed my hand gently, and bent to kiss my cheek. 'I promise you the book'll be safe until you care to collect it. Will someone make sure Lina gets home safely?'

'Of course, Padre.' Close almost saluted. Hmm: I suppose that meant he had a military background.

A tiny voice in my head insisted that I was home. Home at Bossingham Hall. I opened my mouth to say it. Then I thought of our cottage and Tim Bear, and shut it again. Robin flapped a hand and left, closing the door.

'Let's begin at the beginning,' Freeman said, sitting in the chair Robin had vacated.

'*Under Milk Wood*,' I cut in, surprising myself as much as him. 'Griff read it to me,' I explained. 'Griffith Tripp. Actor and Antiques Dealer. The one I'd like to be my father but isn't.'

'Unlike the man who is your father, but isn't likeable,' Close said; if I was surprised before, I was amazed now. 'How do you feel about not being Elham's heir?'

So was this to be me making a statement or them making accusations? I braced myself, wishing Robin had stayed.

I tried shaking my head emphatically, but settled for gently. 'I can't be his heir. He can't adopt me. I'm too old. Plus there are another thirty of us with equal claims. In any case, Griff's the person anyone with any sense would want for a parent. I owe everything to him. He tried to put me off this hunt of mine. He always swore it would end in tears. That's the beginning, you see: my hunt for my father. It led me to do all sorts of silly things. Hang on. It led all sorts of other people to do silly things. Nasty things, come to think of it.' My head was beginning to hurt inside as well as out — was it the champagne or all those blows? 'I suppose I couldn't have an aspirin or two? And one of Lord Elham's TV dinners to help them down?'

Freeman said, 'I think all this can wait till the morning, sir, don't you? Which is your bedroom, miss? We'll get a WPC to bring you a sandwich or something.'

'I want to go home,' I said, wishing I didn't sound so plaintive.

'But Lord Elham said you were in charge here—'

My head swum. 'Will your people be here all night? Well then, I can't see you needing me to stand guard.' Yes, forget what I'd said earlier. No one needed me here. 'My home's back in Bredeham, as I'm sure you know. Just opposite Tony Baker's house. Do I take it he won't be there to keep an eye on me as he always promised Griff when he was going to be away?'

'You take it right, miss,' Close said grimly. 'I fancy there'll be a For Sale sign going up there soon.'

Dan Freeman drove the Ka for me, Close following in a police car.

'You'd better talk to keep me awake,' I said. 'About Oxford, first and foremost. Why did you go to all that trouble for me at the Bodleian? Lie for me? Forge a letter? And then go and talk to the librarian afterwards? No, you didn't know I'd seen you, did you? I thought you were a criminal.'

Laughing, he shook his head. 'Yours wasn't the only copy of the *Natura Rerum* frontispiece in circulation, of course. We'd been approached by two separate dealers who were afraid someone had damaged a priceless book. It's not unknown. Libraries both here and in Scandinavia have been robbed — violated — by a man who cuts pages from volumes of maps. I'd been sent to discuss additional security for the Bodleian's *Natura Rerum*. I'd been working undercover before that, and hadn't had time to change my appearance.'

'I was a suspect, was I?'

'Yes. By coincidence you turn up and start asking to see it. It's a good job you didn't try to smuggle in a razor or we'd have had you under arrest before you could say metal detector.'

'Quite right too. Even—' I shut up. I'd only been going to say that even old reprobates like Titus drew the line at such wanton destruction. The less said about Titus the better, especially considering what his van had carried recently. What would he do with all the stuff? No, I didn't want to know. 'Where did Tony Baker fit in? And Dave Trent? And all that stuff they talked about the Kitty Gang?'

'Actually, they were only lying a bit. The Kent police did have an Operation Kitty to deal with outbreaks of crime against vulnerable pensioners. Whether Kitty refers to felines or small amounts of cash, you'll have to ask them, not me. Baker seems to have targeted you and Mr Tripp from the start. Police officers are trained to pick up clues from people's behaviour, remember, and he knew you were excited about something. When your shop was robbed, he thought other people were on to whatever it was too.'

'Was that enough — pure supposition?'

'He knew various unsavoury people, Lina. Including an old lady with a penchant for teaspoons who was actually doing two things — casing the joint, as it were, and hoping that when you told Tony about her you'd say something along the lines of, "at least she didn't get X."'

'X being whatever it was I'd got hold of.'

'Quite. But that didn't work, so under the pretext of advising some of your colleagues about security, he learned you'd got hold of what everyone wanted to be a valuable piece of paper but most suspected was a forgery. So Baker brought in a few reinforcements.'

'The security guard at Harrogate? Marcus?'

'Marcus is what is technically known as a prat. He really did come down to seek solace when he had a bust-up with that cousin of his. At least, that's what he said in his statement. No, he wasn't one of those walloping you, Lina. But he didn't do Lord Elham a lot of good.'

'Where did Dave Trent fit in?'

'First of all as an entirely legitimate police officer. He suspected Tony was up to something, however, and taxed him with it. Tony offered to cut him in on the deal. He accepted. We are talking millions here, Lina.'

'I just hope that curate guy's straight,' I said.

'He stowed something in the Cathedral safe,' he said. 'We checked. And he did phone us. And he was concerned enough about you to come haring back. He even hit someone — yes, the guy who hurt your face. A good right hook for a clergyman.'

'So, just for once, someone has been telling the truth. That's something, I suppose.' I said it coolly. But as before, I rather felt like doing a handspring, as if I'd found a particularly rare pearl. 'So who was the guy he socked?'

'His name's Malcolm Hamilton. He was a security guard. He claims you hit him very hard last night.'

'I thought your people were going to keep him in custody.'

'We couldn't tie him in with any crime. No reason to.'

'You will tonight, won't you?'

He must have heard the panic in my voice. 'Would you like me to arrange a police guard? Or fix a hotel room?'

'I'd rather go home.' And I could phone Griff, whatever time of night it was, and if I knew him he'd be back for lunch tomorrow. And if I didn't hope for it too hard, he might even be home to cook my breakfast. 'Yes, please. Take me home.'

EPILOGUE

'All these young men fluttering round the place.' Griff smiled happily, helping himself to a last sautéed potato. 'I might have died and gone to heaven. That golden-haired cherub's just the sort I'd like to meet me at the Pearly Gate. And that crop-haired detective's polished up quite nicely.'

'On the limited evidence I have so far,' I said, my face still sore enough for me to be cautious how I smiled, 'they're straight. In both senses. As are most of the other young flutterers.'

'But fluttering they indubitably are. Around you, dear heart.'

'And don't put on that face, because Dan's too old, and Robin's as poor as a church mouse.'

'What about the auctioneer? You don't feel he might be just a smidgen—?'

'Married. Two kids. In any case, once the book's safely sold, you won't see him again.'

'It's a good deal of responsibility that Lord Elham's placed on your young shoulders.'

'Whose shoulders would you place it on? All that rough treatment seems to have shaken up the few grey cells he'd got left.'

I topped up Griff's glass. We'd agreed that he'd stay on the wagon every day till suppertime (he was working on a wonderful non-alcoholic, tomato-juice cocktail which even I liked) and then drink only the best — which was good, since Lord Elham had told me to help myself from his cellar. We were drinking a red Rioja a lot older than I was with one of Griff's wonderful meals.

'Whose idea was it to give his old college time to raise the money?'

'His. Yes, honestly. He really seemed to regret not having made the best of his chances. Getting thrown out of Cambridge — that's quite an achievement, isn't it? But it was me who said—'

'"It was I", darling.'

'—who said it should stay in this country if Cambridge can't raise the dosh. Because I should like to see it again, and I won't be able to if it goes abroad.'

'You've no regrets about not accepting it, as he wanted? You're sure?'

I speared a mushroom. 'It wasn't his to give, any more than it was mine to accept. There'd only have been a huge lawsuit if his trustees had thought I was doing anything for my own pe-peculiarly?—'

'Pecuniary advantage. I suppose so. And they'd have been totally churlish if they'd tried to stop him selling one of the nation's treasures. Especially as he's putting it into yet another trust for all you children. But it was terribly puritan of you to ask for that clause about no one touching it till they'd reached thirty years of age, my love. Quixotic, even.'

I pulled a face. 'It'll allow the lawyers time to trace a few more of us. And I don't want a load of money, not yet. But it'll be nice to think that if I do ever get any paper qualifications and want to go to Uni, that I won't have a bloody great student loan, won't it? And any of my half-brothers and sisters who've already got one will be able to pay it off. I mean, imagine having a job like Robin's that pays chicken feed and having that — that albatross hanging round your neck.'

He nodded, saying, so terribly casually I knew he was fishing, 'It was nice of him to go with you to the Cathedral with you.'

'Who else could have gone? The authorities there knew him. And I wanted to see where they'd stashed it.' That was one disappointment: it had been in an ordinary office-type safe, not some great vault filled with gilt church plate. And I wasn't just being coy about Robin. It seemed to me anyone having a relationship with a man whose main relationship was with Someone Else might be taking on rather more than she could chew. And until all my teeth were fixed, and the wire had come out of my wretched sore jaws, I wasn't reckoning on biting anything tough.

I cleared the table, so knackered I'd have loved to stack all the china, but knowing Griff'd turn to and do it if I left it. His bombing around the countryside had tired him more than I liked, and he'd been further drained by the knowledge that he'd not judged people as clearly as he liked.

He was still staring into the dregs of his glass when I came back. You could see how much effort it took not to top it up. It would have been so easy to indulge him but I hardened my heart.

'You weren't,' he said, his usual firm delivery something horribly like a quaver, 'thinking of taking up your father's offer of an apartment in his wing? Now you've cleaned it all up, you deserve a reward.'

I pulled up a chair and sat beside him, holding both his hands and looking into his eyes. 'I've got china to sell on commission it'll take me years to restore. I've got all that wonderful furniture to learn about. What more reward do I want?'

'Some people might think it's your duty to go and look after your father.'

'Some people might think he deserves to be stuck in a grotty old folks' home. Council run, for preference, the old snob. OK, I'll keep an eye on him — after all, I shall need to deliver his profits from time to time. And I ought to get him to eat a bit better. But I don't have to live with him to do that. And if I did, I still wouldn't.'

'And what about that man from Devon who was checking up on you? Didn't he say he was your grandfather? Though I must say that Habgood's not very close to Townend.'

'According to him, my mother changed her surname to her stepfather's.'

Griff stared at me. 'You do look very alike. Will you have the DNA test he wants?'

'I might. Just to put his mind at rest. His, not mine.'

'But to turn down the chance of a family—'

'I've an embarrassing amount of family! One has,' I said in Lord Elham's drawl, 'to draw the line somewhere! No, you're all the family I need. The thing is, I ought to have said this ages ago, but I've never quite managed it, have I? You're better than father or mother and a couple of grandparents all rolled into one.' Finger on lips, I looked round guiltily before pouring an extra half-inch into both our glasses. 'It's you I love.' There, I'd managed it. 'Griff, my dearest of friends, I love you.'

THE END

ABOUT THE AUTHOR

Judith Cutler's very first short story, written in her teens, won a national prize. Since then she has continued to write short stories, many of which have appeared in anthologies. Judith is best known, however, for her novels — which now total fifty. She is delighted that Joffe Books are now giving some of her favourites a new lease of life.

THE JOFFE BOOKS STORY

We began in 2014 when Jasper agreed to publish his mum's much-rejected romance novel and it became a bestseller.

Since then we've grown into the largest independent publisher in the UK. We're extremely proud to publish some of the very best writers in the world, including Joy Ellis, Faith Martin, Caro Ramsay, Helen Forrester, Simon Brett and Robert Goddard. Everyone at Joffe Books loves reading and we never forget that it all begins with the magic of an author telling a story.

We are proud to publish talented first-time authors, as well as established writers whose books we love introducing to a new generation of readers.

We won Trade Publisher of the Year at the Independent Publishing Awards in 2023 and Best Publisher Award in 2024 at the People's Book Prize. We have been shortlisted for Independent Publisher of the Year at the British Book Awards for the last five years, and were shortlisted for the Diversity and Inclusivity Award at the 2022 Independent Publishing Awards. In 2023 we were shortlisted for Publisher of the Year at the RNA Industry Awards, and in 2024 we were shortlisted at the CWA Daggers for the Best Crime and Mystery Publisher.

We built this company with your help, and we love to hear from you, so please email us about absolutely anything bookish at feedback@joffebooks.com.

If you want to receive free books every Friday and hear about all our new releases, join our mailing list here: www.joffebooks.com/freebooks.

And when you tell your friends about us, just remember: it's pronounced Joffe as in coffee or toffee!

Printed in Dunstable, United Kingdom

73536525R00180